# girl
## at the
# grave

# girl
## at the
# grave

Teri Bailey Black

**TOR
TEEN**

A TOM DOHERTY ASSOCIATES BOOK

NEW YORK

GIRL AT THE GRAVE

Copyright © 2018 by Teri Bailey Black

A Tor Teen Book
Published by Tom Doherty Associates
175 Fifth Avenue
New York, NY 10010

www.tor-forge.com

Tor® is a registered trademark of Macmillan Publishing Group, LLC.

The Library of Congress Cataloging-in-Publication Data is available upon request.

ISBN 978-0-7653-9948-9 (hardcover)
ISBN 978-0-7653-9950-2 (ebook)

Our books may be purchased in bulk for promotional, educational, or business use. Please contact your local bookseller or the Macmillan Corporate and Premium Sales Department at 1-800-221-7945, extension 5442, or by email at MacmillanSpecialMarkets@macmillan.com.

First Edition: August 2018

Printed in the United States of America

0 9 8 7 6 5 4 3 2 1

# For Mom and Dad,

*who filled my childhood with books and free time.*

# 1

*Feavers Crossing, Connecticut*
*1849*

"The whole head is sick," the Reverend Mr. Oliver read with gravity. "And the whole heart faint."

A tuft of his soft gray hair stuck up at the back of his head, wobbling like a feather, and I wished I could smooth it for him. The rector was an awkward, dreamy-eyed man, a widower with no children. But I liked his gentle, rolling voice, which filled the dining hall with beautiful phrases I barely understood, let alone believed.

But I wanted to believe. I wanted to believe there was some hope for the hopeless. Some worth behind the worthless. Some forgiveness for the unforgivable.

My classmates liked Friday devotionals for another reason. Boys and girls were kept separate at Drake Academy, taught in different buildings, even eating at different hours, but apparently the board of trustees approved of coeducational worship, for we were brought together for the rector's weekly visits. The dining tables were pushed back and the chairs lined up in tidy rows with an aisle down the center. Not unlike church, the trustees must have imagined. They didn't see the way Lucy Meriwether sat on the far side of her chair so her hips touched

Rowan Blackshaw's. Or the way she whispered in his ear, her lips nearly touching his skin. He tilted his head toward hers, mesmerized.

But I saw everything from my seat in the back corner.

Today, I felt like a wet cat brought indoors—and smelled like one with my damp wool dress. The boots I'd polished last week were now caked in mud; my hemline wet and heavy; my long curls soaked, sending drips down my neck. I squeezed my chest, holding in the shivers.

After three and a half years of trying to fit in at Drake Academy, all it took was a little rain to remind me that I never would.

No one else looked wet. Most of the eighty or so students boarded on campus—the boys in the new dormitory building and the girls in the founder's old home. A few local students walked like me, and Rowan Blackshaw rode his horse when the weather was fine. But on mornings like this, the other locals arrived in carriages. I was the only one who walked every day, regardless of weather.

Beside me, rain splattered and dripped on the window. It should be snowing in December, not raining.

"From the sole of the foot, even unto the head," Mr. Oliver read from his Bible, hardly aware of us. "There is no soundness in it, but wounds and bruises and putrefying sores."

"*Putrefying sores,*" Jack Utley whispered to his friend, and their shoulders shook with suppressed laughter. They would repeat the phrase for days.

"Man in his natural state," the rector droned on, "unassisted by the grace of God."

Rowan Blackshaw looked over his shoulder and found me in my back corner. I met his stare with feigned indifference, but my chest tightened as it always did. He looked annoyingly dry and well-tailored, wearing a dark blue jacket, soft neckcloth, and well-polished boots. Only his dark hair looked slightly damp and tousled, the only untamed thing about him. Except his eyes, which smoldered with . . .

*What?*

Contempt. Rowan Blackshaw had reason to hate me. But sometimes it almost looked like something else.

I forced my attention back to the rector, determined to listen.

But it was impossible to be in the same space as Rowan Blackshaw and not feel his presence. And he seemed to feel the same way, his eyes finding me whenever our paths crossed. More than once, I'd imagined his burning stare on the back of my neck, only to turn and see that I hadn't imagined it.

*Contempt . . . or something else?*

The sermon ended, and the girls' sewing teacher, Miss Dibble, stepped onto the dais to lead us in a closing hymn. Our voices rose in solemn, faltering unison, overshadowed by Simon Greene's exceptional piano playing, then the Reverend Mr. Oliver offered the benediction.

"Amen," we finally murmured, lifting our heads.

But we weren't finished. The headmaster, Mr. Foley, always gave closing remarks. He stepped up to the low dais, slim and severe in his black suit, and the room fell silent, students straightening in their chairs.

"Only one week remains before your Christmas holiday," he intoned, studying the assembly with his usual fierce attention—all except my back corner, which he carefully avoided. "Today, I have the pleasure of announcing the honor students for the term, who will be invited to the Honor Tea next Friday, along with their parents. Come forward when your name is announced."

Whispers rose like bees, even though the same students were honored every term. But the freshmen had yet to learn the names of their favored few, and Mr. Foley began with them—three boys and three girls, aged thirteen or fourteen, who looked startled and wandered forward with uncertainty. Then the sophomores were announced, who strode forward with more confidence, showing the freshmen how to line up beside Mr. Foley. Then the juniors.

And finally, my senior class sat at attention.

"Rowan Blackshaw!" Mr. Foley announced with pleasure, which didn't surprise anyone—least of all Rowan, whose grandmother was on the board of trustees and surely knew in advance. He rose and walked to the front, accompanied by a flutter of whispered congratulations, for he was well liked—worshiped even, which I'd never understood. He wasn't part of them. Not really. He was richer than anyone else, for one thing—an extraordinary feat, since most of the students at Drake came from affluent families. And he always seemed slightly overdressed, as if a servant had buttoned his jacket that morning and brushed lint off his shoulders.

But it was more than that.

Rowan pretended to care about their teasing banter—laughed at their jokes, slapped shoulders, returned the girls' doe-eyed flirtations—but some quiet part of him remained aloof. He barely paid attention to his friends' raucous stories, his focus drifting to some far-off point. And he was constantly scribbling in the leather notebook he carried everywhere, slamming it shut whenever someone walked near.

"Jacob Macauley," Mr. Foley continued, which was also expected. But then, "Simon Greene," which generated a murmur of surprise, since Simon had never been honored before. He looked startled as he rose from the piano.

Mr. Foley lifted his chin above his starched collar. "And now, I am pleased to announce the top girls in the senior class." But he didn't look pleased, and everyone knew that he didn't approve of girls attending Drake. The founder's widow, Martha Drake, had been an abolitionist and women's rights advocate, and she'd refused to donate another penny after her husband's death until girls were admitted, even turning her own home into their dormitory. Two years ago, she'd died, but her fellow activist, Josephine Blackshaw, now sat on the board of trustees, ensuring girls remained.

"Lucille Meriwether," Mr. Foley announced with solemnity.

Lucy did her best to appear surprised as she rose and walked forward, wearing her favorite color, lavender, while her best friend, Philly Henny, looked ready to burst with pride.

"Jane Stiles." Jane's little yelp of relief carried across the room. Her father was the governor of Connecticut, which placed her firmly at the top of Drake Academy's social structure, but she never relaxed. Never stopped reaching for more.

"And lastly—" Mr. Foley paused to clear his throat, but everyone knew it would be Meg Miller, the tallest girl in our class. It was always Tall Meg. "Valentine Deluca."

The air seemed to leave the room. Whispers ceased, Lucy froze halfway up the two steps to the dais, and Rowan's gaze quickly shifted to my back corner. Other than the heavy beating of my own heart and the pattering of the rain on the window, the room fell silent.

"Come forward, Miss Deluca," Mr. Foley said with an edge.

Slowly, everyone turned to look at me. I felt rigid beneath their stares, hardly able to breathe, but I somehow managed to rise and walk— aware of my muddy boots and wet hair and the murky stench of wet wool wafting off me. I stumbled up the two steps to the dais and walked toward Jane Stiles, who shifted closer to Lucy.

"Congratulations, honor students of Drake Academy. Letters will be mailed to your parents, informing them of your achievement and inviting them to the Honor Tea." Mr. Foley's gaze flickered to me, and I knew my father wouldn't be receiving an invitation. Which didn't matter; he wouldn't have attended. "You are dismissed. Proceed to your first class."

Everyone's attention immediately shifted elsewhere, bodies rising, chairs scraping. Next to me, the other honor students turned to congratulate one another, their relief already sliding into smug confidence. I stood uncertainly behind Jane for a moment, feeling out of place, then turned and slipped away, down the two steps to the dining hall floor.

"Valentine," a feathery voice called, and I turned to see my sewing teacher, Miss Dibble, approaching—a blond, easily flustered woman of about thirty-five years. She was something of a joke among the students; she had a tendency to whisper to herself as she sewed and had an obvious infatuation with the history teacher, Mr. Albright, who avoided her. "How surprising!" she declared in her whispery voice. "How very unexpected and surprising!"

"Is it?" I asked, stiffening. I knew I deserved the award; sitting next to the same girls in class, year after year, some things became obvious.

"Oh, not that you aren't an excellent student, of course, only that Mr. Foley—" Miss Dibble glanced over her shoulder to make sure the headmaster was a safe distance away. "Well, he's never acknowledged it before, has he? Do you think someone forced his hand—someone of *particular influence?*" Her eyebrows lifted above blue eyes.

Miss Dibble could never resist an intrigue, and my being honored was the most intriguing thing to happen in weeks, but she was fooling herself if she thought someone of influence had spoken up on my behalf. "I can't think who."

"But, your benefactor, surely," she said with hushed eagerness. "The person who has paid your tuition all these years. Don't you see? They must have learned that your achievements were being overlooked and insisted you be recognized."

She'd managed to pique my interest. "My benefactor? Do you know who he is?" All these years, I'd wondered.

Miss Dibble's expression faltered. "Well, no, but surely you do?"

She'd come to learn my benefactor's identity, not reveal it. "Foley refuses to tell me. It's part of the arrangement."

Her eyes widened. "But, you must have some idea?"

"Who cares enough about Valentine Deluca to pay for her education? I cannot guess." I glanced at the arched opening in the back corner of the dining hall. My friend Sam was probably waiting.

"Well, in any event, I hope you have something appropriate."

I forced my attention back to Miss Dibble. "Appropriate?"

"To wear! You can't wear any old thing. It'll be evening attire." Her gaze flickered down my plain wool dress.

The Honor Tea. A flutter of nerves ran through me. Tea and cake with the headmaster and trustees—not to mention Jane's father, Governor Stiles. I used to dream about going but never believed it would happen.

Miss Dibble patted my arm. "I'm sure we can find something. I've saved all my dresses from when I was your age. I'll go through them tonight."

Her generosity touched me. She'd been best friends with my mother growing up—something she'd only told me in confidence, hoping others had forgotten. "Thank you, Miss Dibble. That's very kind."

"Now, I must hurry to class. I have the freshmen first hour, and they're completely hopeless." She flashed a vague smile as she hurried away.

I glanced at the dais. The other top students still lingered, enjoying their moment, which meant I had a few minutes for Sam. I made my way to the back corner and entered the narrow room between the dining hall and the kitchen, where food was served.

My best friend, Sam Frye, leaned against a long buffet table, his arms crossed, his apron soiled by something dark and greasy. Breakfast had been cleared, and I could hear the clatter of lunch being prepared through the far door. He grinned when he saw me. "What were you doing up on the stand? You looked like you might faint."

"I almost did," I admitted. "I'm a top student."

"You won a prize?"

I flashed a wry smile. "Not exactly, but Foley's finally admitted I attend this school." In the distance, a pot clattered to the floor, followed by a woman's harsh scolding. "You'd better get back before you're fired." Sam worked in the kitchen, hauling heavy bags of flour and crates of potatoes and enormous, steaming pots of stew. He wasn't allowed to interact with the students.

But he only shrugged a broad shoulder. "Right now, I'm unloading fish in the yard, can't you tell?"

"Curious; you don't smell like fish." He smelled like freshly turned soil and split-rail fences and a log cabin with smoke curling from its chimney, like always. His hair was the color of summer straw, his face tanned and handsome, his lips quick to smile. His eyes were an unearthly shade of green. Sam was seventeen, but I still saw a freckled ten-year-old when I looked at him—the ten-year-old who'd taught me how to fish and chop wood and kill a chicken. The friend who'd helped me survive after my mother died.

"I need a fancy dress for the Honor Tea," I told him. "Miss Dibble says she'll help me."

"Honor Tea? Is that as exciting as it sounds?"

We heard voices approaching from the dining hall, and I pulled Sam into the alcove where dishes were kept, stacked on shelves. I yanked the curtain across the opening just in time.

"There'd better be bacon," a boy's voice said. Jack Utley. His parents owned the general store in Feavers Crossing.

I peeked around the edge of the curtain and saw two boys and two girls—the other seniors who lived locally, including Rowan Blackshaw. The four of them made their way to the end of the long room, where extra food was left out for growing boys who couldn't wait until the next meal.

"No bacon," Jack complained. He was shorter than the others, and his jacket was too tight, tugging at his waistline. "There was lots at breakfast. Thieving kitchen staff is taking it home."

Sam released an indignant breath near my ear.

Their backs were turned, so I dared to keep watching. Rowan uncovered a platter and slid it toward Jack. "Here it is."

"Did you see Valentine's shoes?" Philly Henny asked. She lived across the road from me. We used to play together, a lifetime ago. "She left mud on the dais."

"It should have been Tall Meg up there," Lucy stated. Her blond hair was pinned up today, intertwined with a lavender ribbon in an intricate manner, letting everyone know her family kept a lady's maid. "Valentine cheats, everyone knows that."

"Does she?" Jack sounded envious. He'd been a lazy student back in grammar school and only attended Drake because his rich uncle paid for it. He slid more bacon into his mouth and spoke around it. "Why doesn't Foley expel her?"

"Because Foley's a toad," Lucy said. "She's cast some sort of spell over him—over all the teachers."

"Maybe she's a witch," Jack said.

Which was all Lucy needed. "Of course she's a witch. Haven't you seen her in the graveyard? She says a magic spell and the graves open up. She sleeps in a coffin."

Jack struggled to not laugh, his mouth full.

Sam shifted behind me, and I pressed my back against his chest, holding him in place. There was a gap at the edge of the curtain, but if they didn't look this way, they wouldn't notice us.

"That's where she gets her dresses," Lucy went on. I could hear the smile in her voice. "She takes them off the dead. Then she eats their rotting flesh. She doesn't eat normal food, just decaying bodies. And rats and toads."

"Rats and toads," Jack chortled. "You hear that, Rowan? Valentine digs up graves."

"Shut up, Jack." But Rowan said it lightly. It took more than Jack Utley to rattle him.

"But didn't you hear? What if she digs up your—"

"I said shut up."

Jack's laughter faded.

"Come on, we're late," Lucy said. "There'd better be some umbrellas at the door." The girls' classes were held across the grounds in the old, original schoolhouse. Lucy left the way they'd entered, and the others followed.

All except Rowan, who paused in the doorway, turning to look back. His gaze settled on the curtained alcove, letting me know he'd known I was there all along, then he disappeared through the opening.

*Contempt?*

It had almost looked like guilt.

Sam yanked the curtain open and started after them, then stopped and came back, frustrated. Because it wasn't worth losing his job. And it wasn't anything that hadn't happened before. Or wouldn't happen again.

"It doesn't matter," I told him.

"How can you stand it?"

"It's just Lucy. No one takes her seriously. She'll say anything for attention. Now, go get that fish before you're fired. I've got Latin." I stepped away.

But Sam reached out and took my hand, holding me back. He waited for me to look up and meet his green eyes. "Four more months, Valentine, then you'll graduate and be free of this place."

I forced a weak smile.

What Sam didn't understand was that Drake Academy was the only place where I did feel free, where I managed to escape the truth for a few glorious hours, lost in the Napoleonic Wars and the proper stitch to use when attaching lace and the conjugation of French verbs. I squeezed his hand and released it. "Bye, Sam."

The dining hall was nearly deserted, only a few stragglers remaining. I hurried across it, then made my way across the main foyer to the row of wall pegs where my cloak hung alone. I pulled it on and opened the front door.

Outside, heavy sheets of cold rain fell. I glanced at the umbrella stands and found them empty, so I lifted my skirt and ran.

# 2

"Tomorrow, that man will be gone," Mama whispers as she puts me to bed, her eyes sparkling in the dance of candlelight.

I am six years old. "What man?" I ask, but she blows out the candle without answering.

Before the night is over, Mr. Blackshaw is dead.

And three days after that, Mama is dead as well, hanged at the gallows.

# 3

---

Drake Academy sat at the end of a quiet road, surrounded by dark woods, a short walk from Feavers Crossing.

Rochester Hall dominated the grounds—four stories of evenly laid bricks and gleaming windows, with the dining hall and library on the ground floor and the boys' classrooms upstairs. Pathways connected it to the rest of the buildings: the boys' dormitory; the old schoolhouse where the girls had classes; Drake House, where the girls lived; and a stable and caretaker's cottage.

By lunchtime, the rain had stopped, and by the end of the school day, the sun was breaking through.

I stayed late in sewing class to help Miss Dibble find her scissors and was one of the last to emerge. Most of the students had already returned to the dormitories, but a few locals remained, climbing into carriages in front of Rochester Hall. Lucy and Philly left in the Meriwethers' carriage, and a couple of younger girls were picked up by a buggy, one sitting on the other's lap. When the Blackshaws' carriage arrived, Rowan offered rides to Simon Greene and Jack Utley.

I would walk, as usual, but wasn't sure which way to go. I usually took the shortcut through the woods, but part of the trail always flooded after heavy rain, so I begrudgingly decided to take the longer road through town.

As soon as I'd passed through the stone pillars that marked the entrance to Drake Academy, the well-tended grounds fell behind and the woods crowded back, the air thickening with the smell of damp dirt and bark. I tightened my cloak. I'd sewn it a few months ago in an attempt to be fashionable, but the fabric wasn't as warm as I'd hoped. Still, I refused to return to my old green coat.

Behind me, I heard the stealthy crunch of footsteps. I took a few more steps, then glanced over my shoulder to see a scrawny woman of about thirty years a short distance behind, wearing a strange coat made of animal hides. I smiled. "I heard you, Birdy."

She flashed a grin. "I almost got you that time."

"You almost got me," I agreed. Once in a while, I pretended to not hear so she could sneak up and tag my shoulder. "Here, I brought you something." I dug into my coat pocket and pulled out a napkin tied in a loose knot.

"Is it bread?" she asked, opening it.

"Apple cake, saved from my lunch. They don't serve that every day."

"Cake!" She took an enormous bite.

I liked watching Birdy eat. No delicate manners, just genuine hunger and appreciation. I would have brought more, but I'd been lectured by Mr. Foley about the unseemliness of sneaking food into my pockets. *This isn't some barbaric orphanage; it's the finest school in Connecticut.*

Birdy ate as we walked. "I like cake," she said around a mouthful.

According to stories, she'd been found on the riverbank as a child, soaking wet and unconscious, with no family or possessions. Whether she'd been simpleminded before the near drowning or only after, no one could say. She'd been young enough, back then, to stir compassion; an elderly woman had taken her in. But now, she was a grown woman who lived in an old trapper's shack and stole to survive, and people were less sympathetic.

"You like cake, Valtine?" she asked. The middle part of my name always eluded her.

"I think everyone likes cake, Birdy." She'd been nicknamed Little Bird by the woman who'd taken her in, which had evolved into Birdy. And some people called her Birdbrain. Once, I'd tried to explain to her why she shouldn't respond to that name, but she hadn't understood why it mattered, accepting her status in this town.

Something I refused to do.

She finished the cake and stuffed the napkin into her pocket. She must have collected a hundred by now. "My blanket is wet. I don't like the rain."

"I'll ask Sam to patch your roof."

"Rain makes me wet. It makes me wet and drown."

"You can't drown in the rain, Birdy," I assured her, not for the first time. "Stay away from the river and you'll be fine." I cast her a sideways glance. "It wouldn't hurt you to take a bath, you know. You can do it at my house." She never washed, as far as I could tell. Her hair was a greasy brown, about six inches long. Every summer, she cut it close to her head to keep cool, then it grew out until the next summer's cutting. Like a sheep getting shorn. And today, she did look a bit like a sheep, with her gaunt face and long neck; her boxy coat made of patchwork hides; and her skirt too short, exposing boots like dark hooves.

"I don't want to drown like the raccoon. You remember the raccoon, Valtine?"

"I remember the raccoon, but you're not going to drown, Birdy. Here, let's do the alphabet," I said to distract her.

"I'm not sure I can do that anymore."

"Sure you can. What comes after *A*?"

Birdy grinned, unable to resist. "*A, B, C, D*." Which was as far as she ever got. She could be clever about some things—like stealing eggs and trapping animals—but had a hard time holding on to letters.

"What's next?" I prompted, touching the sides of my head. "Sounds like—"

"Ears!" she cried, triumphant. "And *OPQ!*"

I laughed. "That's right."

She called out her favorite letters until a dog barked around the next curve of the road, then her eyes widened in alarm and she darted into the woods. Birdy never went near the Fryes' farm, for good reason.

I sighed and continued alone, trying to ignore my own unease as the trees opened up to reveal a lumpy field full of dead winter stalks, outlined by a split-rail fence. My eyes darted as I neared a sagging barn, looking for trouble. But the barnyard was deserted today, even the animals put away.

It wasn't until I rounded the next bend that I saw Sam's mother, Mrs. Frye, sitting on a stool in front of the log cabin, plucking a chicken with her strong, bony hands. I hugged the far side of the road, hoping to pass unnoticed, but the dogs barked and jumped against their ropes, and she looked up.

"Sam ain't here, so keep walking!" Mrs. Frye called out. She was a gray wisp of a woman, worn down by too many years with a mean husband and six wild sons.

"Maybe she's looking for me, Ma," a boy's voice called out, and I noticed Sam's older brother Jep walking toward me on the road, carrying an ax. He waited until I was closer before saying in a low tone, "You wanna visit the hayloft, Rat Hair? Make sure the roof ain't leaking?" He'd invented the nickname back in grammar school, before I'd figured out how to tame my curls, telling everyone I kept a pet rat in it.

I walked wide to go around him, my heart racing.

The Frye boys had been the worst of my tormentors when I was younger, chasing me in the school yard, then following me home through the woods. They'd tied me to trees and stolen my mittens.

They'd all looked the same with their straw-colored hair and devilish grins; only their heights distinguished them. But over time, I'd noticed differences. Like Jep being the ringleader, even though he wasn't the oldest. And Sam never participating in his brothers' torments, only watching uncomfortably.

When I was about ten, I'd found Sam alone near the creek, hunched and crying, trying to wash a bloody cut on his forehead while cradling a bruised wrist. Everyone knew that his father was a brute. Or maybe one of his brothers had done it. Without a word, I'd dipped my skirt in the creek and dabbed his forehead, then I'd told him to come home with me so I could bandage his wrist. And from that day on, we'd been best friends.

Much to his mother's dismay. Sam was her favorite son, and she had high hopes for him. "My Sam is a good boy!" she called after me. "You leave him alone, you hear?"

I hurried on without responding, knowing she didn't see the truth— that her sons were considered even lower than I was for the trouble they caused.

As soon as I'd left the Fryes' property behind, Birdy materialized. "She don't like you 'cause you're pretty."

"She *doesn't* like me because my mother was a murderer," I corrected. I drew a weary breath, and when Birdy continued with the alphabet, I remained quiet.

Not far from the Fryes' land, we entered the main part of Feavers Crossing—which bustled today, now that the rain had stopped. We wove our way around muddy hems and rolling carts, knowing every rut in the road. The town flourished because of the bridge, which was the only way to cross the river for many miles. Some of the buildings were small and simple, built by the earliest settlers. But others were broad and stately—like the new inn, built for all the parents who arrived twice a year to drop off and pick up their students at Drake Academy.

Birdy looked longingly at the Beasleys' old stone house as we passed. "Can we stop and see the baby, Valtine?"

"No, Birdy. You stay away from that baby."

"I like babies."

"I know you do, but you can't touch them. They don't belong to you."

A few years ago, Betty Cooper had entered her kitchen to find Birdy standing over the bassinet. Everyone had been in an uproar, insisting she be driven out of town. Sheriff Crane had locked her up for a few days until things settled down, mostly for her own protection.

"You stay away from the Beasleys, Birdy. You promise?"

"Promise," she said, but we both knew it was a meaningless vow.

As we neared the yarn shop, her steps slowed again, her eyes darting down the alley. "Miss Jane started a new sweater. You wanna watch, Valtine?" The alley window gave a good view of Miss Jane behind the counter.

"You can't go looking through people's windows, Birdy. I've told you. It isn't decent."

My gaze drifted across the street to the bank owned by Rowan's family—an imposing building with dark, fancy windows and a golden doorknob. Rowan's father had run Blackshaw Bank before my mother killed him. Now, his grandmother ran it. And soon, Rowan would take over.

We passed more shops, then entered an older, quieter part of town, centered around the Reverend Mr. Oliver's church. There were newer churches in Feavers Crossing—white buildings with tall steeples—but I liked Mr. Oliver's best, with its arched windows and mossy stones.

Beyond the stone church, we came to the graveyard Birdy and I both knew so well. The shortcut I took to Drake Academy entered the woods at the back of the graveyard, so I had reason to cross it daily. But I tended to linger. Even today, with chores waiting, I followed Birdy under a low-hanging branch and entered the uneven rows of headstones and crosses.

Some of the graves were new and well-tended, but others looked ancient, their markers blackened by age. The ground sagged and headstones tilted. At the back of the graveyard, the woods continually encroached, limbs reaching, vines creeping.

"John Slack!" Birdy cried as she wove her way around the graves. "Nellie Mortimer!"

Years ago, I'd tried teaching her to read with the headstones. It hadn't worked, but she still remembered a few names. And I remembered them all, without meaning to. I touched the crumbling pillar of George of Surrey as I passed. Died 1727. Aged 43 years.

Today, the graveyard looked even more forlorn than usual after the rain, the headstones weeping, the shadows deep and damp. A large crow cawed from the top of an old stone cross, then took off in a rush of black wings.

My gaze slid to a small, neglected plot of land in the distance, on the other side of a stone wall—unhallowed ground, where they'd buried thieves and savages when the settlement was new. Now, the town buried criminals near the jailhouse, but Mr. Oliver had suggested my mother be buried here, closer to our house.

Father and I never went near it.

The headstone of Isabella Barron Deluca stood out among its humble neighbors, chiseled of fine white marble, refusing to show its neglect. I'd once asked Father how he'd afforded such a fine headstone, but he'd only shaken his head.

I followed Birdy to the grave of the old woman who'd taken her in as a child: Ida Howe, 1775–1842. The storm had knocked a large branch across the headstone, and the two of us dragged it away, soaking ourselves in the process.

"Damp day!" a cheerful voice called, and I turned to see the Reverend Mr. Oliver approaching, his gray hair fluttering in the breeze.

"Congratulations on your award, Valentine! Quite an accomplishment!"

Beside me, Birdy tittered. She had a schoolgirl infatuation with the rector, which he was too absentminded to notice. I reached for her hand.

"Don't run," I urged softly. But she pulled free and darted toward the woods, disappearing down the trail.

Mr. Oliver's kind eyes followed her. "It's good of you to help her, Valentine. She bolts whenever I come near. Is she in need of anything?"

"Her roof leaks, but I'll get Sam to fix it."

A clattering noise drew our attention to the road, and I saw Sam's father, Mr. Frye, scowling and muttering as he cleaned up a dropped box of tools.

"He's repairing a window," Mr. Oliver said in an apologetic tone. "I just scolded him for snooping in my art studio, so he's in a bit of a temper."

Mr. Frye worked odd jobs in the winter, when his farm was frozen. "It's good of you to give him work," I said. Many wouldn't; things tended to go missing. Sam had the steadiest job in the family, working at Drake Academy.

"I was quite touched by your award this morning, Valentine. You've accomplished quite a bit with . . . well, little assistance from your father, to be honest. It speaks well of your character."

"Thank you."

Mr. Oliver seemed to hesitate, then shifted closer, his voice dropping to a somber low. "I have something to tell you, Valentine. I've debated whether I should or not. Some truths are best kept hidden. But after seeing you on the stand this morning, I've decided you deserve to know." He drew a breath for courage. "I've been told, quite recently, that your mother was wrongly convicted. That she was . . . well . . . innocent."

I stood perfectly still, confused, my heart beating faster.

"A dreadful mistake," he said gently.

I shook my head, knowing he was wrong. No one knew better than I that my mother was guilty. "What did you hear?" I asked.

"Not much. They wouldn't tell me who fired the gun, but they insisted it wasn't your mother."

"Who? Who told you?"

"Ah." His eyes wrinkled, apologetic. "I can't say, I'm afraid. But they were there that night and saw everything."

I felt faint with surprise. "My father?"

"No, no, not your father—"

"Then they lied. Because no one else was there."

"This person wouldn't lie, Valentine. They spoke to me in a moment of genuine distress. They've been haunted by that night for more than a decade. An innocent woman hanged! Nothing can bring your mother back, of course, but if she was innocent—if she did not do that heinous thing—I think you deserve to know."

"My mother was guilty, Mr. Oliver. She confessed."

"But if that confession—"

"I saw her do it." My heart thundered in my chest. "I saw her shoot Nigel Blackshaw."

The rector's eyes widened, startled. "Is that true, Valentine? I've never heard that before."

"Because no one knows. Because no one ever asked." I stepped back, already wishing I hadn't told him. I'd spent eleven years trying to forget that night. "Please, don't tell anyone."

"No, of course not. Goodness." His expression softened. "You were very young. Perhaps you misunderstood what you saw—or have forgotten—"

"My mother fired the gun. I don't know what you heard, or from whom, but they were mistaken." It felt wrong to insist upon my own mother's guilt, but I'd accepted it long ago. I took another step back, my throat tightening with emotions I didn't want to feel. "I have to go."

"Yes, forgive me. I can see that I've upset you, and that wasn't my intent. I only hoped to reassure you. To help you reconcile your feelings toward your own mother."

I gave a weak laugh as I turned, wishing more fervently than he knew that such a thing were possible. Out of the corner of my eye, I saw her marble headstone.

"Valentine!" Mr. Oliver called after me. "Can we discuss this further?"

But I didn't turn back.

And that was the mistake that started everything.

# 4

---

I hurried along the road, past my neighbors' well-kept houses, frustration crawling inside me. My hands clenched and unclenched.

For eleven years, I'd tried to heal the wound, and with just a few words, Mr. Oliver had ripped it back open.

Who'd told him my mother was innocent? She wasn't. And why dredge it up now, after all these years? Would people never forget? Could I never move past it?

I smelled something savory cooking as I passed the O'Donnells' tidy brick house. Inside, I heard Mrs. O'Donnell call to someone, then an answering shout from upstairs. The house wasn't big enough for the six of them, but they didn't seem to mind.

The Carlisles' goat bleated as I passed their fence.

Part of me couldn't help but hope Mr. Oliver was right—that my mother had somehow been innocent.

*Don't.*

I used to think that way when I was younger. I'd been young and naive—only six, unable to accept that the loving Mama I remembered deserved to be hanged. But I was no longer six, and I'd heard enough stories since to understand what I'd seen that night.

My mother was a murderer. She'd pointed a gun at Nigel Blackshaw and fired.

Rowan's father.

Ahead, darkness appeared at the side of the road—a large house set off by itself, half-hidden behind a rusted gate and overgrown trees. Paint peeled, and shutters hung at an angle. One window was boarded up, another cracked, and all of it shrouded beneath a cloud of sorrow.

It had been a fine house once, when my mother was my age. She'd grown up here with a wealthy father and twin brother. Maids and nannies. She'd had her own white horse in the pasture behind the house.

Then tragedy had struck. It wasn't visible from the road, but the back corner of the house had been damaged by fire, starting on the second floor, growing up to the attic. The flames had been put out before they destroyed more than a few rooms, but those rooms remained blackened and scarred, boarded up to keep the weather out, but never repaired. A sad reminder.

"Valentine," a soft voice called, and I turned to see Mrs. Henny across the road, tidying her garden, holding a basket of wet twigs and leaves. The Hennys' house had once been our caretaker's cottage, before my grandfather fell on hard times and sold it, along with most of his land.

"You shouldn't be outside in the damp," I told her, approaching. Mrs. Henny had nearly died of influenza a few weeks ago.

"Oh, I just had to see how my garden survived the storm. I'm feeling quite robust today." But she didn't look robust; she looked gaunt and pale. Her hair had once been a lovely strawberry blond, like Philly's, but was now mousy gray. "Philomena tells me congratulations are in order."

I was surprised Philly had mentioned it. An awkwardness flowed between the two of us, pretending we'd never been friends. Pretending we'd never sat on each other's beds, playing with dolls. After my mother's hanging, Philly had been too busy to play—or napping—or away visiting relatives—until I'd finally stopped knocking.

"A top student," Mrs. Henny said, smiling kindly. "Quite the honor. Your father will be proud." Her smile twitched at the lie. Living across the road, Mrs. Henny knew better than anyone how little my father would care.

I turned toward my own house, avoiding the path that led to the front door and going around to the back, along the old carriage drive. Which I knew was foolish; it was just an innocent patch of gravel walkway, Mr. Blackshaw's blood long since seeped into the ground. But I hadn't gone near the front path in eleven years.

I worked harder to keep the backyard in order, but it still looked ramshackle: the woodshed leaning, the wheelbarrow broken, the garden full of dead stalks from last summer. The chickens clustered at the coop door, hoping for release, but I ignored them and went inside to the kitchen.

My thoughts stirred as I went about my usual evening chores. I stoked the fire into life, then filled the wood bin and fetched water from the pump behind the house. I'd left a pot of beans to soak all day and now hung it over the fire to boil. Then I chopped some salted pork and added it.

Father had sold the stove years ago, when he'd been out of work, saying his mother had cooked over an open fire and so could I. Sam's old log cabin didn't have a stove either, so he'd helped me figure it out. Hooks dangled from a rod for hanging pots, and Sam had set up an iron shelf for baking over coals.

With the beans cooking, I had a moment to spare and went to my cloak hanging on the wall to retrieve the magazine article I'd stashed in the pocket. I always had to wait for the new edition to arrive in the school library, so no one would notice a page missing in the old edition.

I brought the article to the table and eagerly read it again.

Alvina Lunt had completed her investigation of all the asylums and almshouses in Pennsylvania and found the same deplorable conditions she'd discovered in other states—people of unsound mind confined in cages and stalls; chained and naked; starved and beaten into submission. She called on the legislature to provide funding for a new hospital for this "class of unfortunates."

She'd done the same thing in four other states, with considerable success.

I retrieved the large keepsake box I kept on the shelf and added this latest article to the dozens I'd already collected. One of them even had a sketch of Alvina Lunt: a brunette woman of about forty years. She lived in New York City—only two days away. Someday, I hoped to meet her. Maybe even help her.

Her story had struck a chord in me when I'd first read it, a year ago. When she was my age, her drunken father had broken both her legs, but it was during her long stay in a hospital that she'd become aware of the cruelty happening in the basement where the lunatics were kept. Since then, she'd devoted her life to helping them.

Alvina Lunt didn't come from money or an important family. She walked with a cane and never married. But she was doing something powerful with her life.

I ate and cleaned up, then sat by the fire to darn socks, listening for the door, hoping Father would come home tonight. He drove a delivery wagon for a glass manufactory, which took him out of town for days at a time. I was used to being alone in the house, but tonight, I needed to talk to him about what Mr. Oliver had said about my mother being innocent. Father and I were the only people still alive who'd been there when Nigel Blackshaw died, so if anyone knew the truth about that night, it was Father.

But the night deepened, and I finally gave up and left the warm kitchen.

I passed dark rooms on either side of a grand foyer: my grandfather's office with an enormous desk and empty bookshelves, everything cloaked in dust; a dining room without its table and chairs, only an elegant chandelier that was never lit; a large drawing room with furniture draped in sheets and bald spots on the walls where paintings used to hang.

I heard a floorboard creak in the drawing room and paused in the opening, my heart beating faster. I lifted my candle and tried to see past the flickering light, into the dark corners. No one was there, like always. The air smelled damp and stale, like a tomb. Father had promised to fix the leaky window but wasn't home enough to remember or care. The fireplace was cold and full of cobwebs; the portraits removed; the family who'd once laughed and talked and served tea in this room, all dead.

I was the last of the Barrons.

My mother had grown up in this house during its days of grandeur. She'd moved to New York City at my age, then returned after my grandfather's financial ruin and death, bringing Father and me. I remembered her polishing candlesticks and beating heavy drapes, trying to restore the house to its former glory.

But I'd given up trying to maintain the large house alone; I only cleaned the rooms I used, leaving the rest to the ghosts.

I climbed the grand staircase, following the circle of light cast by my candle. Upstairs, we only used two rooms: one for me and one for Father. The rest of the second floor remained hidden behind a curtain that hung across the hall, concealing the burned part of the house. My mother used to wander past the curtain, saying the charred rooms reminded her of those who'd passed on.

And, for the same reason, I never went back there; they reminded me of her.

I was in my room, preparing for bed, when I heard Father enter through the front door downstairs. I quickly tied my nightgown and descended the staircase, pausing halfway down to watch as he lit the hall lantern, then took off his coat and hung it on a hook by the door. The lantern distorted his shadow, making him look larger than he was. In truth, Joseph Deluca wasn't a tall man, but he had an intimidating appearance, with dark hair and brooding good looks.

Disappointment clung to him like a shadow.

After my mother had died, he'd awkwardly tried to care for me, then seemed relieved when I'd learned to manage on my own. Sometimes he brought me a small gift from one of his trips or helped me fix up the house. But mostly, he was distant and moody, and we lived separate lives.

He moved toward the kitchen, and I hurried down the last few steps. "Father."

His eyes looked tired as he turned. "Valentine. The roads are bad, so I am delay." He'd emigrated from Italy when he was twenty-two, and an accent still blanketed every word.

"Are you hungry? I made beans."

"No, I eat enough. I just warm by the fire." He hesitated, his dark eyes shifting. "You work hard, Valentine. I wonder, sometimes, if you like a woman to help you."

"A woman?" I frowned. We couldn't afford a servant. "No, I don't mind the work. But I wanted to ask you—" I tucked my arms against my waist, unsure how to begin. In eleven years, we'd never talked about the night that had changed both our lives.

"You need money for the food?"

"No, there's enough in the jar."

"Tomorrow—" He coughed into his elbow. He'd been sick and the cough lingered, echoing through the house at night. "Tomorrow, I leave for long delivery."

Which meant I wouldn't get another chance for a while, so I summoned my courage. "Someone told the Reverend Mr. Oliver that Mama didn't kill Mr. Blackshaw. That someone else fired the gun."

Father's eyes widened in alarm. "Who tells him this thing?"

"He wouldn't say. But they told him they were there when it happened. So, I thought . . . I thought it might have been you."

"No. Never. I say nothing, never." His eyes darted, then returned to me. He spoke carefully. "You remember that night?"

My heart beat heavily. "Of course I remember. How could I forget?"

A slow breath of regret slid through his lips. "All these years, I wonder. You are very young, so I think you forget. I hope you forget."

"No, I remember." We stood in the shadowed light of the hall lantern, facing it together for the first time. *The explosive roar of the gun. Mr. Blackshaw's wide, startled eyes as he fell. Mama being led away in the dark.*

"What did you tell him, the priest?"

"The truth. That she was guilty. That I saw her fire the gun myself."

Father cocked his head, his eyes sharpening on me. "And he believes you?"

"I don't know. But why would someone tell him she was innocent? Was someone else really there?"

Father didn't move, his face half-lost in shadow—and with a start, I realized he was hiding something. That there was something I'd forgotten. Or something I'd never known.

"Who was there?" I asked. "What are you not telling me?"

"It is not good, thinking these things."

"Please," I begged, my heart hammering in my chest. "Just tell me what happened."

"You were there," he said heavily.

Questions clawed. "But I was too young. I've forgotten. And I never understood why she did it. No one ever talks about that—not the real story, just lies and gossip. And now someone says she was innocent." I drew a steadying breath. "Please, just tell me what happened."

He shook his head. "It is not good, talking these things. It is long time ago. You go to the big school now. People forget your mama."

"But they don't forget! That's the problem! I live with it every day—see it in every face. I try to improve myself—try to prove that I'm decent and good—that I'm not like her. But I'll never get past it. Never be anything but the daughter of a killer. And I don't even know why! I've never understood—" My voice choked to a stop.

"Ah, Valentine," he breathed, coming toward me. For a moment, I thought he would embrace me, but his hands took my shoulders instead. "I fix this," he said quietly. "You say nothing to the priest. You understand? You say nothing, and I fix this."

I stared into his brown eyes, sensing more behind the order than I understood. "Fix what?" I asked hoarsely. "Say nothing about *what*? *Why* does someone think she's innocent?"

He gave my shoulders a final squeeze and released them. "You forget that night. You say nothing, and I fix this." He turned and made his way to the kitchen at the back of the grand foyer.

I started to follow, but stopped, knowing it was pointless. Joseph Deluca was a man of few words, and he'd just given me all he intended to give. For now, at least.

I climbed the staircase and put myself to bed, my mind turning. When he returned from his delivery trip, I would ask him more questions. I wouldn't stop asking until he'd told me everything.

But my heart thumped with uncertainty. There'd been something in his eyes, just now, that filled me with foreboding—something dark and secretive, lurking at the bottom of it all. Something I didn't know. And I wasn't sure I wanted to know.

I blew out the candle and lay alone in the dark. Or as alone as I ever felt in this house, with its creaking floors and whispers in the shadows.

Downstairs, I heard the front door open and close, and Father's footsteps on the gravel walkway below my window. I sat up, surprised. Father never went out again after coming home.

I pushed back the quilt, tempted to follow him. But I was in my nightgown, and he would be gone before I could change and pull on shoes, so I lay back down and listened and waited, rehearsing what I would say when he returned.

But I fell asleep.

And dreamed of the night Mr. Blackshaw died.

# 5

---

*I am asleep within sleep, lying on the same mattress within the same room, small and curled . . .*

*When Mama's voice startles me awake, distant and angry. I sit up, confused. She'd been happy when she put me to bed. "Tomorrow, that man will be gone," she'd promised, her eyes sparkling in the dance of candlelight.*

*But now her voice is full of distress. I push back my quilt and step down to cool floorboards. Then I creep down the staircase, shivering in my nightdress.*

*As I descend, her voice fades and is replaced by a man's voice—but not Father's. Father's voice halts and skips, thick with accent, while this voice rolls smoothly, vaguely familiar. I follow it out the door and see three shadowy figures in front of the house, illuminated by silver moonlight. Mama stands on one side of the walkway, with Father behind her. And a man in a dark cloak stands before them.*

*Mr. Blackshaw.*

*I don't like Mr. Blackshaw, with his thin smiles and watchful eyes, but he is Mama's friend. She spoke to him in the woods yesterday, hushed and anxious, then grabbed my hand and pulled me up the trail, back to our house.*

*"Tomorrow, Isabella!" Mr. Blackshaw had called after her. "That is my promise!" Which made Mama smile.*

But she isn't smiling now. Tears glisten on her pale cheeks, and she holds a black pistol with both hands, pointing it at Mr. Blackshaw's chest. But not Father's pistol. This gun is bigger and has a golden bird on the side.

"You deceived me!" Mr. Blackshaw growls.

"Yes. And now I will kill you and not shed a tear of remorse." Mama's voice sounds hard and sure, but the gun trembles.

Mr. Blackshaw stands still, breathing hard, then reaches a cautious hand toward her. "Give me the gun, Isabella, and we'll forget this ever happened. You'll think more clearly in the morning."

"Clearly? I have never thought more clearly! Never seen more clearly!"

Father steps forward and whispers in her ear, placing his hand over hers on the gun. Gently, he tries to take it, but she resists.

The dream darkens, my attention stolen by a polecat shuffling along the edge of the yard, its stripe glowing silver. Is the polecat really there, or has my mind placed it there to bury a less welcome memory? Even in my dream, I wonder. Mrs. Henny says polecats portend bad luck, in which case, this one must be real.

Their voices draw me back, no longer shouting, but low with despair. "Isabella, please," Mr. Blackshaw begs, his cheeks damp in the moonlight. He steps toward her.

"Stay back!" she shrieks.

Frightened or angry? I want her to be frightened, but I am never sure. I am sure of only one thing.

He takes another step.

The explosive roar comes from nowhere, and yet from everywhere, jolting my bones and filling my nostrils with the burning stench of gunpowder. I cough and blink—and see Mr. Blackshaw sway on his feet, looking startled, then topple slowly backward, landing hard on the walkway, his arms sprawled. I watch, fascinated, as one of his legs twitches.

Then lies still.

Father notices me, then, and lifts me into his arms, into the house and up the staircase. The strength of his arms feels unfamiliar and I want to resist but feel frozen by the deafening ring of gunfire in my ears.

And Mama's shrieking wail.

*Father sets me on my bed, hastily pulls up the quilt, and leaves me alone. But I immediately leave the bed and climb up to the deep windowsill—and see Mr. Blackshaw far below, illuminated by shifting moonlight, his cloak spread like the wings of a great black bird.*

*Father's voice rises like acrid smoke, thick and angry. And then Mama's voice, broken and full of tears. Their shadowy figures pace and argue and finally wander away, leaving Mr. Blackshaw to lie alone, staring up at the dark sky.*

*Silence falls, as if the night holds its breath. I rest my head against cold glass . . .*

*And awake to the crunching wheels of a carriage. And then a wagon. I watch as two men carry Mr. Blackshaw to the wagon and spread a blanket over his face, then they return to the house and escort Mama to the carriage. As she walks, she turns and looks up at my window, and for a moment our eyes meet across the distance.*

*The last time I will ever see her alive, although I don't know that at the time.*

*But she knows.*

# 6

---

When I awoke the next morning, I felt a moment's warm contentment, knowing Mama was downstairs in the kitchen, kneading dough at the table like Mrs. Henny had taught her. I listened for her gentle movements and the hum of her voice.

Then cold truth fell.

It was always this way after the dream. Throbbing silence where Mama used to live.

I forced myself from the warm bed and changed into a simple dress for weekend chores. A sheen of ice coated the window; winter had finally arrived. I pulled on my wool petticoat and wrapped myself in my thickest shawl—a shawl I'd knitted myself with yarn Sam had given me for my birthday. I washed up, then attempted to brush out my long mane of honey-brown curls.

In the mirror, I saw my mother's face—more from rumor than memory. "Spitting image," Mrs. Utley murmured to her husband when I shopped at Utley General Goods. Not the playful prettiness of Lucy Meriwether or the delicate loveliness of Philly Henny, but the sort of beauty that sparked rumors and made other women distrust you. Full lips that Lucy whispered were tinted. Long curls that unleashed themselves in the slightest breeze. I watched the other girls at school and tried to behave like them. Sit and walk like them. I longed for their poised, respectable prettiness.

But even in this, I couldn't escape Isabella Barron Deluca.

My sewing teacher, Miss Dibble, said my eyes were softer than hers, my personality more thoughtful. She said my mother had been popular and full of fun at my age. No one had ever accused me of that.

The house was so quiet, I knew Father was gone. I crossed the hall and peered into his room, hoping to see some indication of where he'd gone the night before, but of course there was nothing. And no reminders of my mother either, though I couldn't help searching. No silver hairbrush on the dressing table. No scent of her powder. Just Father's razor, a bottle of hair oil, and the smell of leather boots.

Where did Father go last night? To fix things, he'd said. Maybe he'd gone to see Mr. Oliver. Or the person who'd said my mother was innocent. He'd been surprised that they'd spoken up after all these years, but not that they existed. He knew their identity.

And he hadn't seemed surprised by their claim that my mother was innocent.

I descended to the kitchen, my head swollen with thoughts. Today, I didn't even have school to distract me; seniors didn't have classes on Saturdays. I stoked the fire into a roaring blaze, and the room slowly warmed. I made porridge.

The fire had terrified me when I was six, with its snapping heat. But I'd had no choice but to learn its fickle moods and hungers, and within a year of my mother's death, I'd been stoking and feeding and tending its flames with a confidence beyond my years.

Step by step, I'd learned to survive without a mother.

I forced myself to eat, then I washed up and swept the kitchen floor.

The bristles scraped across the wooden floorboards, past the same old stains.

And my thoughts scraped with them.

*You say nothing to the priest. You say nothing, and I fix this.*

Father wanted me to keep quiet and forget that night.

Because I'd seen something I wasn't supposed to see. Because I knew something I wasn't supposed to know.

*What did I see? What did I know?*

My arms swung in steady rhythm.

If my mother was innocent, it must have been Father who fired the gun. I'd seen him trying to take it from her. But I found it impossible to believe Father would kill a man, then say nothing as Mama hanged for his crime.

*Except to save his own neck.*

But then, why did she confess?

Because she felt responsible. Because the argument had been hers, not Father's. Nigel Blackshaw was her childhood friend, not his.

My heart beat faster and the broom swept harder, dirt and crumbs flying ahead of the bristles.

Mr. Oliver said he didn't know who'd fired the gun; he wasn't told.

My arms stopped, and the broom halted.

But Mr. Oliver knew this secret witness who claimed to have been there. I would convince him to give me their name, then I would talk to this person and learn the truth.

My chest rose and fell. Suddenly, it all made sense. Mama, who'd held me on her lap and kissed my forehead: innocent. Father, who scowled more than he smiled: guilty.

*You say nothing, and I fix this.*

Father wanted me to remain ignorant and quiet, so no one would know what he'd done. But I would talk to Mr. Oliver and find this secret witness. I would learn the truth.

Today.

This morning.

Now.

Morning fog cloaked the road, hiding my neighbors' houses. All I could hear were my own crunching footsteps and cold breaths. I tightened my knitted shawl, burying my hands in it, trying to not think, trying to not doubt.

What would I do if I learned Father was the one who had fired the gun and said nothing as his wife hanged for his crime? Would I tell Sheriff Crane? If I did, Father might be arrested and tried for murder—maybe hanged. Was that what I wanted? Was that what he deserved?

I would be fully orphaned, haunted by a second hanging.

But it would clear my mother's name.

*Mama, innocent.*

Clearing her name wouldn't bring her back, but it would free my memories and allow me to love her.

In truth, I barely remembered her. I'd been too young when she died and had heard too many stories since, memory blurring with rumor.

"I grew up with Isabella Barron," Mrs. Utley told her customers at Utley General Goods. "And she was very spoiled. Very flirtatious."

Mrs. Duncan blamed it on my grandfather. "His wife died, and he let those twins run wild. Too much freedom. Not enough work."

But Miss Dibble spoke glowingly of all the Barrons—especially my mother's twin brother, Daniel. According to Miss Dibble, Daniel had been quieter than my mother, but smart and adventurous—and attractive. Her eyes misted whenever she spoke of him. But Daniel had died in the fire when he was seventeen. They'd found his body on his bedroom floor, overcome as he tried to get out.

After that, everything had changed.

My mother went to New York City to escape the grief. And my grandfather, left alone, fell into despair. The workmen who came to repair the burned rooms were told to go away. Servants complained of not being paid. Silas Barron invested foolishly, and by the time he died of lung fever a few years later, most of the money was gone.

"We were all surprised when Isabella returned to Feavers Crossing," Miss Jane told her knitting club, her needles clicking. "Nothing for her here except that big, empty house. But she moved into it with that foreign husband and the baby." I was the baby. "None of us knew what to think when we saw her again, so visibly unhappy. So poorly dressed. Not the same girl at all."

*The evil turning of Isabella Barron*, as Mrs. Utley called it, not long after my birth.

My mother didn't go to church after returning to Feavers Crossing (according to Mrs. Duncan); neglected her appearance (murmured by Lucy's mother, Mrs. Meriwether); rejected attempts at friendship (sniffed by Miss Dibble); and then murdered her childhood friend Nigel Blackshaw.

Only, she might not have murdered anyone.

I passed the graveyard, shrouded in mist, and approached the old stone church. I wasn't sure if the door would be locked on a Saturday morning, but it opened easily, and I walked inside to the frigid foyer, then farther inside to the echoing chapel. But no one was there.

I left and walked across the road to the two-story rectory where Mr. Oliver lived. The door hung ajar, which meant he must be about. My heart beat faster, knowing I might soon know the truth. "Mr. Oliver?" I called.

I heard movement inside, followed by a crashing sound—dishes breaking.

I stepped into the small parlor, alarmed. "Mr. Oliver?" The room was deserted, so I moved deeper, peering through the kitchen door on the right.

The rector lay on his side near the table, a chair toppled behind him. I cried out and hurried forward, dropping to the floor, rolling him onto his back. Blood streamed from a gash on his forehead, and I saw blood on the tile floor; he'd hit his head when he'd fallen.

He released a strangled sound at the sight of me, his eyes widening. But the rest of him appeared unable to move. White spittle clung to the corner of his mouth.

Panic rose. "Oh, Mr. Oliver, I'll . . . I'll go for help." But when I started to rise, he gave a feeble moan of protest, and I sank back to his side, knowing I couldn't leave him this way.

I saw a broken teacup and saucer behind him. He'd been having his morning tea when he collapsed. A heart attack. Or stroke.

His eyes held mine, begging for assistance. Whatever the cause, his condition seemed dire. Fear crawled up my throat. "What can I do for you?" His face was pale, his lips purplish. His breathing seemed labored. "I . . . I don't know what to do," I admitted. Beads of sweat dotted his forehead, so I grabbed a tea towel off the table and wiped his brow, then cleaned the spittle from his mouth.

It should be Mrs. Henny here, with her nursing skills, not me. "Is . . . is it your heart? Is there medicine I can get for you?"

I heard movement and looked up to see Birdy in the back corner, cowering in the doorway to Mr. Oliver's art studio, half-hidden by the doorframe.

Relief poured through me. "Birdy! Run for help!"

But she didn't move, her eyes riveted on Mr. Oliver. "I didn't mean to. I didn't mean to hurt him. I just touched him."

My heart dropped. "What happened, Birdy?"

She didn't reply, tugging at the green knitted cap on her head, pulling it lower.

"Run for Dr. Wellington!" I ordered. But she didn't move, and I saw that she was useless. "All right, I'll go. You stay with Mr. Oliver." But when I started to rise, the rector moaned, and I sank back to the floor.

"Paaa . . . ," he breathed, and I saw that he was trying to tell me something. Blood flowed from the gash on his forehead.

I leaned closer, my heart drumming in my chest. "Do you need medicine? Tell me—" His eyelids fluttered closed, and panic filled me. "Mr. Oliver!" I shook his shoulders, then whimpered in relief when his eyes snapped open, unfocused at first, then widening with dread.

He knew he was dying.

A helpless sob filled my throat. I could do nothing.

Except comfort him, I realized, the way he'd comforted so many in their final hours. "I'm here," I told him, forcing my voice into a calm low. I placed my hands on either side of his face, wanting him to feel my touch. "I won't leave you, Mr. Oliver. I won't leave you." His skin felt clammy. *I should pray*, I thought, a tear sliding down my cheek. "Our Father who art in heaven," I whispered. "Please, God. Please help Mr. Oliver."

"Paaa," the rector breathed, his watery eyes clinging to mine, begging me to understand.

"What?" I whispered. I held his cold cheeks and felt his life sliding away beneath my hands, his face sagging, his body relaxing.

But he rallied long enough to tell me what he needed to say. "Paa . . . son," he sighed with his final breath.

*Poison*, I realized with a start.

And his spirit left him.

# 7

I held Mr. Oliver's limp head in my hands, weeping and apologizing, wishing his eyes would at least close in rest. But they stared at something I couldn't see.

"I'm sorry," I whispered. I should have done more to save him. More than just watch him die.

Birdy moved cautiously into the kitchen, still keeping her distance. "Is he sleeping?"

I shook my head, my heart heavy. "No, Birdy. He isn't sleeping."

She gave a moaning sob. "He got sick and dropped the cup." She lifted a hand toward the window, where she must have been watching; she spied through Mr. Oliver's windows more than any others. "He got sick, so I came inside."

"*Poison*," Mr. Oliver had whispered with his final breath.

My gaze darted to the broken teacup and saucer, then up to the table. I saw two slices of toast on a plate, not yet bitten. And behind the plate, a bright blue tea tin—a unique container with scrolled, foreign lettering. Not ordinary tea. Did it make Mr. Oliver sick because it was unfamiliar? Mrs. Utley claimed to be allergic to all foreign foods.

Or had someone laced it with poison, knowing he would drink it in the morning?

Birdy released a keening wail. "I didn't mean to hurt him. I just touched him."

My attention shifted to her. "What do you mean, Birdy? How did you hurt him?"

"He couldn't move. He couldn't talk. So, I touched him, and he fell off the chair. He hit his head." She touched her forehead in the same place he was injured. "Did I kill him, Valtine?"

"No," I said. The head wound wasn't serious enough to have killed him. He'd gotten sick before falling off the chair. My gaze returned to the blue tea tin. Yesterday, Mr. Oliver had told me my mother was innocent, and now he lay dead. Did someone silence him?

*I fix this.*

A horrified sob rose in my throat. I pressed my hand against my mouth, looking down at Mr. Oliver's sprawled, lifeless form. Did Father do this because Mr. Oliver knew my mother was innocent? Did Father come here last night? Did he give Mr. Oliver a gift of poisoned tea?

I shook my head, tears leaking from my eyes. It must have been a heart attack or stroke.

"I didn't mean to hurt him!" Birdy wailed.

"You didn't hurt him. He fell when you touched him because he was already sick." I had to tell someone. I gave his chest a final, apologetic touch, then rose. "Stay with him, Birdy. You can sit in the other room, if you want. I'll return soon."

Outside, cold air hit my damp cheeks. I drew a weary breath, then ran toward town.

I wasn't sure who to tell—probably Sheriff Crane, but the jailhouse was on the far side of Feavers Crossing. So, when I saw an open door at Utley General Goods, I staggered through it.

Mrs. Utley stood at the counter with the beekeeper, counting jars of honey. "Not open," she declared.

"But . . . but Mr. Oliver." I drew an exhausted breath, sweat rolling down my temples. "Mr. Oliver is dead . . . in the rectory."

Mrs. Utley froze, her finger poised over the jars. "What do you mean, Mr. Oliver—" She couldn't say it. But her husband broke into quick action, darting out the door. "Are you telling fibs?" Mrs. Utley asked sharply.

"No," I said, inhaling a deep breath. "I'm sorry . . . no." As if it were somehow my fault. And part of me feared that it was.

Mrs. Utley shouted up the back staircase to her son Jack to pay the beekeeper, then hurried out the door, her ample hips swaying. And as soon as I'd caught my breath, I followed.

Word spread quickly. Two men on horseback trotted past me. Then the baker, Mr. Duncan, ran past, followed by his panting wife. The sheriff's black carriage rolled by. By the time I reached the church, a small group had gathered in the road between the church and the rectory, whispering and wondering. Weeping.

My own steps slowed as I neared the rectory. Suddenly, I felt out of place. But I had to tell Sheriff Crane what I knew, so I stepped through the door, crossed the quiet parlor, and entered the kitchen.

Poor Mr. Oliver still lay on the hard tile floor, just as I'd left him, with Sheriff Crane crouched beside him, his back to me. A young watchman stood nearby, a notebook in his hand. In the far corner, Mr. Utley watched with his usual long, mournful face, with Mrs. Utley beside him, sniffing. But her sorrow seemed mingled with morbid fascination, her eyes darting. By nightfall, half the town would have stopped by Utley General Goods to hear the story.

Sheriff Crane noticed me near the door. "Outside, Valentine. This is no sight for you."

"But . . . I've already seen it. I was here when he died."

The sheriff rose and turned. "You saw Mr. Oliver collapse?"

"No, he'd already fallen when I came in. I tried to help." Emotions tightened my throat. I kept my eyes on Sheriff Crane, avoiding the rector's vacant stare.

His eyebrows lifted. "You were here for breakfast? Was that a . . . regular thing?"

Mrs. Utley made an indignant sound.

My face warmed. "No, I only came because—" I halted, suddenly aware of how little I could say. If Father didn't do this, my careless words at this moment would cause a stain that would never wash away. Suspicion would haunt both of us for the rest of our lives.

"You look deep in thought, Valentine. I ask again, why were you here?"

"To . . . to talk about school. I was honored yesterday and wanted to talk to Mr. Oliver about it. But the door was open, so I came in and found him." I glanced around, suddenly realizing. "Where's Birdy?"

"Birdy?"

"She was here when he collapsed. She said he was drinking that tea." My gaze darted to the table, but the bright blue box with foreign writing was gone. My eyes skimmed the cluttered shelf on the wall. "Where's the tea tin? Did you move it?"

Sheriff Crane glanced at the young watchman, who shook his head.

"A blue box," I insisted. "It was there." I turned to inspect the wash table, then I moved to the cupboard and opened it. I searched the shelves and saw two ordinary brown tea tins, but nothing blue.

"Go home, Valentine. This has been upsetting."

"But it was here." I looked at the Utleys. Mr. Utley's coat pocket bulged. They'd probably arrived first and would recognize an expensive blend of tea when they saw it. But if they drank this tea, they might die. I had to warn them, but I knew it would sound mad. I licked my dry lips. "I think . . . I think Mr. Oliver's tea was poisoned. I think that's why he died."

Sheriff Crane glanced at the body, dubious. "He wasn't a young man. Probably a heart attack."

"That was his final word before he died—*poison*. And Birdy said he collapsed while drinking his tea. And now the tea tin is missing."

Sheriff Crane forced a polite smile. "Sounds like you've been reading too many novels, Valentine. I can't imagine why someone would want to harm the rector. Can you, Mr. Utley? Mrs. Utley?"

"Of course not," Mrs. Utley scoffed.

"Poison!" I insisted. "That's what he said—his dying word. He took great pains to tell me."

Mrs. Utley's eyes widened. "You said that half-wit was here. If someone served him bad tea, it was her—some poisonous plant she picked up in the woods."

I straightened, alarmed. "Not Birdy. She wouldn't."

"Perhaps by accident," Sheriff Crane mused.

"Or . . . on purpose," Mrs. Utley said with meaning, her eyebrows lifting.

"She would never!" I cried. "She adored Mr. Oliver!"

"Exactly," Mrs. Utley stated, quick to latch onto the more interesting story. "She was besotted. Everyone knows it. But he didn't feel the same way."

"Birdy would never hurt Mr. Oliver! She wouldn't hurt anyone!"

Sheriff Crane glanced at the table. "If the tea tin is missing, Birdy probably took it."

My heart sank, because I knew he was right— one of the pretty things she could never resist. I had to warn her not to drink it. And suddenly, it made me sick that we were standing over Mr. Oliver's body, arguing.

"I have to go," I said, backing up.

"Yes, this has been a shock for you," Sheriff Crane said. "I'll talk to Birdy and get to the bottom of it."

Which would only make matters worse. Birdy would apologize for hurting Mr. Oliver, which would sound like a confession. The poisoned tea would be found in her shack. And Mrs. Utley's malicious story would spread.

I left the rectory and made my way around the crowd in the road. I hurried across the graveyard and entered the woods, then broke into a run.

My thoughts turned as I ran along the trail, weaving around gnarled trunks, ducking under clawlike branches. If Birdy had the blue tea tin, I would take it and hide it, I decided, at least until I'd talked to Father and figured out what had happened. And I would convince Birdy to stop apologizing for hurting Mr. Oliver. I would make her understand.

But my heart thundered with dread, because Birdy never understood.

I turned down a narrow side path and a moment later came to a clearing with several makeshift racks for drying animal skins in front of a battered shack. I banged on the door. "Birdy? It's Valentine." I lifted the latch. "I'm coming inside."

The door wouldn't open fully, blocked by clutter. I gingerly stepped into the gloom, resisting the urge to cover my nose against the stench.

Birdy's hoarded stockpile filled the space, stacked in precarious piles, blocking the window light. I saw a cradle filled with mismatched china; a steamer trunk with a rusty birdcage on top; a pile of shoes in every style and size, no two the same; a collection of jewelry boxes; a tower of men's hats. I'd been here before, but the sight always appalled me. I'd once tried to help her clean it up—tried returning the stolen items— but she'd gotten so upset and angry, I'd given up.

I found her in the back corner, huddled on a filthy mattress, her knees pulled up. She sniffed loudly, wiping her nose on the back of her hand. "Mr. Oliver is dead."

"Yes," I said sadly. We both needed time to mourn, but not now. "Sheriff Crane is coming, and you can't tell him you hurt Mr. Oliver, or he'll think you killed him. Do you understand?"

Her face tightened in a scowl. "I don't want to talk to the sheriff." He'd locked her in jail a few times.

"Well, he's coming anyway." I glanced at the mess around the mattress. "Where is Mr. Oliver's tea tin? The blue box that was on the table."

Her scowl deepened. "His friend took it and said I can't have it."

"His friend?" My attention sharpened. "The Utleys?"

"No, not Utleys. His friend who saw me at the window. They got mad at me and ran away. Then I touched him and he fell over." Birdy touched her forehead where Mr. Oliver's head had been bleeding.

My heart beat faster. "Someone was there before I arrived?"

"They took the box. They said I'll hang by my neck."

They must have returned while I was gone. "Who was it, Birdy? Who took the pretty blue box?"

"His friend." She drew a long sniff. "They said I'll hang by my neck. I didn't mean to hurt him."

Someone had threatened her—not a true friend, or they would have stayed to help. And they'd come back for the poisoned tea. "Who, Birdy? Can you tell me their name?"

She shook her head, fresh tears spilling. "I don't know. I don't want to hang by my neck."

I fought for patience. "I won't let that happen. Just tell me—just tell me where they live in town." She didn't know many names, but she knew windows.

She started moaning, rocking back and forth on the mattress, and I panicked. When something upset Birdy, she either wouldn't stop talking about it, or she never talked about it again, pretending it hadn't happened.

I forced my voice to a soothing low. "Birdy, this is important. I need you to tell me what they looked like." But she only rocked harder—and my patience broke. I grabbed her wrist, my voice rising. "Just tell me—was it my father?"

She whimpered and jerked away, scooting back on the mattress, burying her face against her knees.

I groaned in frustration—more at myself than her. "I'm sorry, Birdy. I know this is hard. We both loved Mr. Oliver. But you must tell me who was there when he got sick. It's very important."

She tugged at her knitted cap and rocked.

*His friend.*

Father and Mr. Oliver were only passing acquaintances, but Birdy wouldn't know that. Or, it might have been the person who'd told Mr. Oliver that my mother was innocent. The secret witness—a friend who'd confided in him, then regretted it and silenced him.

But who would care enough after all these years? Only the real killer—who I feared was Father. No one else had been close to the gun that night.

Birdy held the answer. I would coax it from her eventually, but Sheriff Crane was about to arrive. She would apologize for hurting Mr. Oliver and end up in jail, so terrified of a rope around her neck, she'd never tell me anything. I had to get her away before the sheriff arrived. Then, once I'd gotten the truth from her, I would decide what to do with it.

"Birdy, you need to come home with me." She continued to rock on the mattress, her knees drawn up. I reached a cautious hand toward her. "Come on, it'll be nice at my house. You won't have to talk to the sheriff. And . . . I'll make gingerbread." The rocking stopped. "I'll make gingerbread and read you a story."

Slowly, I convinced her to leave the mattress, then the shack. She walked in front of me on the narrow footpath, her head bowed. But as soon as we reached the main trail, we heard men's voices in the distance, and she darted into the trees, disappearing. Which was just as well, for a moment later, Sheriff Crane and his young watchman came around the bend.

"She isn't there," I told them. "I was just at the shack, and she's gone."

"Perhaps we'll wait," Sheriff Crane said, continuing past, his eyes hard with suspicion. He'd been listening to Mrs. Utley. When he reached the shack, he would find Birdy's hoarded treasures and know most of it was stolen. He would haul it back to town, where towns-people would paw through it, searching for their missing things. There would be a cry for Birdy's arrest, fueled by Mrs. Utley's claims that Birdy had killed Mr. Oliver.

A handy way to get rid of someone who didn't fit in. Someone they didn't understand.

I hurried home, determined to stop that from happening.

# 8

Birdy wasn't in the kitchen when I entered through the back door. "Birdy?" I made my way toward the front of the house, glancing into the shadowy side rooms on either side of the grand foyer. "Birdy, are you here?"

Upstairs, a floorboard creaked. I started up the staircase—then stopped. She hadn't replied, which meant she wasn't yet ready to talk. She'd just seen Mr. Oliver die, then been threatened by his killer, then bullied by me. "I'll make gingerbread," I called up the staircase.

I got busy in the kitchen, poking at the fire to get the temperature just right. I'd already bought ginger for Christmas, and I had plenty of molasses. I pulled out the mixing bowl and flour bin.

As the gingerbread baked, filling the kitchen with spicy aroma, someone knocked on the back door, then Sam entered, and I saw in his worried eyes that he'd heard. "Val." He crossed the room and pulled me into his arms, his strength enfolding me.

For a moment, I remained stiff, then I allowed myself to sag against him.

As children, we used to touch every day and think nothing of it. But lately, we'd been more cautious. More aware of each other's warmth as we walked side by side, neither of us daring to cross a boundary that didn't used to exist. I knew that once Sam and I kissed, everything would change, and sometimes I didn't feel ready for that.

"I heard you found him," he said quietly.

I nodded against his chest, wondering if I dared tell him the full story. Sam didn't like Father, thinking him neglectful, and Father might be completely innocent.

Sam's strong arms rubbed gently around mine, and my bones started to melt. His chest always felt as solid as stone, yet moldable as clay. One of his hands slid behind my neck, and every part of me wanted to look up.

But today was not the day to cross that boundary. I gently separated myself.

"What did you hear?" I asked.

His gaze lingered on my lips. "That he was poisoned. That's what Mrs. Utley says, and Dr. Pritchard agrees. I don't know how he can tell, but that's what people are saying."

"Pritchard?" Nobody liked Dr. Pritchard, with his yellow teeth and stained bleeding bowl.

"He's the only doctor who'll look at the dead." Sam's eyes shifted. "They're saying Birdy did it."

Already the ugly story was spreading. "She didn't, Sam. He was murdered, but not by Birdy."

"She's not right in the head, Val."

"Someone else was there. She saw them, but whoever it was ran away, and she won't tell me who they are." I hesitated, then added, "She's upstairs."

Sam shook his head, frowning. "You can't get involved in this, Val. The last thing you need is another scandal for people to talk about. And she probably did it. She's strange, through and through. Remember those dead mice in the box?"

"She's a rat catcher. People pay her to do that."

"Not save them in a box. You can't ruin your reputation over the village idiot."

"Don't call her that!"

"You've spent years trying to teach her the alphabet—for what?"

"To teach her! Because she enjoys it! Have you seen her face when she remembers the letter *E*? She gets just as excited as anyone else when they accomplish something. I don't teach her because she's smart; I teach her because she needs to learn and grow, same as the rest of us. You think I should stop going to school because there are people who are smarter than I am? Because I don't always understand mathematics at first glance?"

Sam gave a dry laugh, looking away. He'd never understood why I bothered with Drake. He'd been happy to quit school at age twelve to shovel manure at a dairy. To Sam, shoveling manure was a lot more useful than Latin.

I turned my back, going to the fire to check the gingerbread. The flames were too high for baking. I grabbed the poker and stabbed at the log, and it collapsed into ash, filling me with satisfaction.

"She didn't do it," I snapped. "Someone else was there."

Sam didn't reply.

My temper collapsed as quickly as the log, despair taking its place. In the ashes, I saw Mr. Oliver's vacant stare and Birdy's tear-streaked face. I sank to the rocking chair next to the fire, my throat tight with the grief I'd been trying not to feel. I stared at the smoldering log. "She didn't do it, Sam. They'll hang her over this because she's not like everyone else. Because it's a way to get rid of her. But someone else poisoned him. She saw them."

Sam picked up the hearth stool and brought it close to my rocking chair, lowering himself. "If that's true, she just needs to tell Sheriff Crane, right?"

I looked up and found his face very near, full of concern. "Birdy won't talk to him. Or if she does, she'll say it all wrong and sound like she's confessing. She'll only talk to me." I swallowed. "But not if you're here, Sam. She's probably heard your voice."

His green eyes tightened. "You want me to leave?"

I saw his hurt, but nodded.

Sam stood, his large frame unfolding. "I don't know why you bother with her."

"Because she's like me," I said simply.

"How can you say that?"

"She lost everything as a child. Now, she's alone, just trying to survive. Never fitting in."

"You aren't alone, Valentine. You have me. But that never seems to be enough for you." Sam strode to the door and left.

When the gingerbread was done, I set it on the table to cool, then climbed the staircase. "Birdy?" She wasn't in my bedroom or my father's, which didn't surprise me; I knew which part of the house fascinated her.

I went to the curtain that hid the burned part of the hall, drew a breath, and pulled it back.

The air smelled thick with ash. Or maybe that was my imagination; the flames had been doused twenty years ago. Three doorways gaped, but the windows in those rooms had been boarded up, leaving a shadowed gloom. Dust motes floated like ghosts.

A heavy feeling settled over me as I peered down the dark hall to the charred door at the end.

I'd heard the morbid stories in town. My mother's twin brother, Daniel, had been my age when he'd fallen asleep at his desk and knocked a candle over. By the time someone had noticed the smoke, it had been too late; hungry flames had devoured everything inside—including Daniel. They'd found his body black and stiff, overcome as he'd tried to get out. According to Mrs. Utley, my mother had howled like the damned when she'd seen him . . . then remained silent for days.

I hadn't been beyond the curtain in years. I moved carefully, glancing through the doorway on the right to a storage room that had little damage. Then I came to my mother's childhood room on the left. I paused in the doorway.

Her bed had been hacked into black, jagged pieces to put out the fire, and the wall behind it had been reduced to charred timber. But the rest of the room looked untouched by flame, only browned by smoke and age, oddly frozen in time from when my mother was my age. A wardrobe door hung open, showing a row of limp dresses.

Birdy sat on the floor, leaning against the wall. She didn't look up when I entered, bent over something on her lap.

"The gingerbread is done." She didn't reply, so I slid to the ground next to her. "I'm sorry if I frightened you earlier. I just—"

I stared at the object she was holding: a dark metal box about the size of a book, its lid flipped open. It was filled with money. Gold and silver coins, and paper money tied with yellow string. I stared at it, dumbfounded. "Birdy, where did you get that?" She hadn't been carrying it when we left her shack.

She didn't reply, her head bowed.

"May I see?" I reached for the box, and she didn't resist when I took it. My fingers shuffled through the bills, trying to count, but my mind wouldn't settle and I lost track. Not a great fortune, at any rate, but more than I'd ever seen in one place. "Where did you get it, Birdy?" She didn't answer. I picked up a silver coin and held it toward her. "If you tell me, you can keep this."

She snatched the coin and stood, and I quickly followed, closing the box and bringing it with me. She passed the curtain in the hall and entered Father's room, pointing under the bed. I knelt and saw that two floorboards had been lifted, revealing a dark space below.

Leave it to Birdy to find hidden treasure in this house. She must have been hiding under the bed and noticed the loose boards. I wondered how long the money had been there—and why Father hadn't spent it when it was sorely needed.

I noticed an emblem on the box's lid. *Blackshaw Bank.* My heart beat faster. Father didn't have an account; he didn't trust banks and had little enough to put in one. I wondered fleetingly if he'd stolen the money, but I pushed that thought down. Someone must have given it to him. But why? And why not spend it when we needed it? Why hide it as if it were something shameful?

I decided to return the box to its hiding place for now. I reached under the bed and dropped it into the hole, then replaced the floorboards. I stood and straightened the bed.

Across the room, Birdy hummed quietly as she rolled her new silver coin across the top of Father's dresser.

"Leave the box in the floor, all right?" She gave no indication that she'd heard—which gave me little hope of learning anything soon. "You'll need to stay at my house for a while, Birdy. You can sleep in my room. If someone comes, hide in the burned room, behind the dresses in the wardrobe. If they find you, they'll put you in jail."

The coin stopped rolling. I hated to frighten her, but the threat was real.

As proven a few hours later when Sheriff Crane knocked on the front door. I gave Birdy a moment to scramble upstairs to her hiding place, then opened the front door a short distance. "I'm sorry, but I can't invite you in. My father isn't home."

Sheriff Crane wore a black cape and tall hat, the night dark behind him. "Have you seen Birdy? She hasn't returned to that hovel she lives in."

I shook my head, not wanting to say the lie aloud.

Sheriff Crane's gaze drifted over my shoulder to the staircase, then back to me. "Looks like Mr. Oliver was murdered, like you said, Valentine. I hope you won't make the mistake of getting involved."

"I'm already involved. He died right in front of me."

His eyes narrowed. "That woman is a troubled soul. We found cart-loads of stolen goods at her place."

"She doesn't understand personal property."

"An excellent reason to lock her up."

"Or people could help her," I snapped. "Collecting trinkets doesn't mean she killed Mr. Oliver."

"Then she has no reason to avoid my questions, does she?" He tipped his tall hat. "Please let me know if you see her. Good evening, Valentine."

I closed the door, then hurried to the window to watch as he walked away—his feet landing on the path where Nigel Blackshaw had bled and died.

# 9

---

I spent Sunday trying to coax Birdy into talking, without success. Any mention of Mr. Oliver sent her running to the burned room to hide in the wardrobe, rocking back and forth. Only the promise of favorite foods could coax her out, which kept me busy in the kitchen, cooking and cleaning up.

Then I made the mistake of trying to convince her to take a bath, which brought out her fear of drowning. I was relieved when she found mouse droppings in the cellar, which gave her something else to think about. She spent the remainder of Sunday repairing my old mousetraps, then baiting them and placing them throughout the house, even climbing the rickety ladder to the attic.

When I left the house on Monday morning, Birdy was still asleep, curled inside a pile of blankets on the floor next to my bed.

At school, no one seemed upset that the man who'd conducted their weekly devotionals was dead, only fascinated by the part I'd played. I saw their sly glances and heard their eager whispers.

*She was with him when he died.*

*She's friends with the mad lady who killed him.*

When they tired of Mr. Oliver's mysterious death, they began hushed retellings of my mother's infamous tale, no two versions the same. The most common story had always been that she'd killed Rowan's father because she owed him money. But Lucy Meriwether always included an illicit romance—my mother obsessed with Rowan's father, begging him to run away with her, then killing him when he'd refused. And some said she'd been insane and set the house on fire, even though the fire had happened years earlier, before I was born.

I'd heard all the stories before, never knowing which was true. And now, according to Mr. Oliver, none of them were. I was angry at myself for not seeking the truth earlier. But I'd been young when it happened and wanted to forget. I'd wanted *everyone* to forget.

But Sam was right: the new death dredged up the old.

Thankfully, it started snowing midmorning, drawing everyone's attention to the windows, and by the time school ended, Drake Academy was draped in billowing white. As the girls emerged from the schoolhouse, a pack of boys attacked with snowballs, sending everyone screaming. Some of the girls fought back at once; others ran for the safety of their dormitory. I avoided the battle, skirting around the edge, then walked behind the school stable and entered the woods—

And inhaled a cold, clean breath. I always loved the solitude of the woods, but never more than today. Snow powdered the trees like sugar, and my breath steamed in front of me. I slowed my steps, allowing myself a moment to enjoy the first snowfall of the year. In a week, I would loathe the icy slush, but right now, the world looked magical.

I heard the crunch of footsteps behind me and glanced over my shoulder, but I couldn't see anything through the tangle of trees.

Apprehension crawled up my spine. Whoever had killed Mr. Oliver knew that Birdy had seen them, which put her in danger. And everyone knew that I was her friend, which might put me in danger too. I quickened my steps, glancing back, but the footsteps quickened as well.

When the trail bent sharply, I stepped off the path and stood still behind a large tree, my heart racing. And, a moment later, Rowan Black-shaw walked by.

I drew a surprised breath. Rowan never walked in these woods; his house was the other way. But there was no mistaking those straight shoulders and that distinctive stride. He went five or six steps before realizing I'd disappeared, then stopped and swung around, searching—

And saw me.

He looked embarrassed for a heartbeat, then shrugged, stuffing his hands into his coat pockets. "You caught me," he admitted. "I was trying to catch up. I wanted to talk to you without other people around."

My heart stuttered into a faster beat. Rowan and I had known each other since grammar school but rarely spoke beyond asking each other's pardon in a crowded doorway. And here I stood, hiding behind a tree. I flushed, stepping back onto the trail.

"About what?" I asked.

He came closer, his gaze sliding down my blue cloak, then back to my face. Rowan studied everything with that keen attention, but it was always disconcerting when he directed it at me. As if he could see every part of me, down to my tattered shift.

*Contempt*, I reminded myself.

Only, in the feathery fall of snow, it didn't look like contempt. At the back of his eyes, I saw a piercing interest that made me want to hold perfectly still.

Rowan looked impeccable himself, as always. Charcoal-gray coat, perfectly tailored. Black boots shining against the snow. The only untidy thing about him was his dark hair. It always started the day perfectly combed but ended up like this, tousled and wavy. Which I liked. A weakness in his otherwise exquisite armor.

"I wanted to tell you I'm sorry about Mr. Oliver. It must have been hard, being there when it happened. I've never actually seen anyone—" He halted, not wanting to say it.

*I saw his father die.*

"Do you think the rumors are true?" Rowan asked. "That he was murdered?"

Was that why he'd followed me, to get the gossip firsthand like Miss Dibble in sewing class?

No, his blue eyes looked concerned. And it dawned on me that he'd endured the same gossip as I had today, his father's name whispered alongside my mother's. Which made me want to be honest. "I think his tea was poisoned. That was his dying word—*poison*."

"Maybe it was an accident. He just drank the wrong thing."

"No. Someone took the tea tin so it would look like a natural death. They didn't plan on me showing up. Or Birdy watching from the window. She saw someone but won't tell me who it was. She's too upset. She gets like that. She either can't stop talking about something or won't talk at all." I realized I was babbling myself and stopped, embarrassed.

But Rowan had listened carefully to every word. "So, you don't think Birdy did it?"

"No," I said flatly. "She never lies. She's not . . . clever that way."

"So, the sheriff has it wrong," he said, not doubting. "Mr. Oliver was murdered, but not by Birdy."

The tightness in my chest relaxed. "You believe me."

He shrugged. "You were there. And you know Birdy better than anyone. It's just hard to imagine why someone would want to kill Mr. Oliver. He was a nice man."

I wanted to tell Rowan the rest—that my mother might have been innocent. That someone else had murdered his father. That Mr. Oliver had been poisoned because he knew the truth. But it would sound mad.

Rowan's lips tilted. "You get that secretive look on your face I can never read. Like you're thinking some clever, mysterious thing. It makes me curious."

I gave a short laugh. "*Me?* You're the one who's impossible to read. I can never tell what you're thinking."

"Nothing mysterious. Just Euclidian geometry, lately. Or maybe magnetism. I'm a bit obsessed."

"Sounds mysterious to me."

"Congratulations on the award, by the way. I guess that means you'll be at the Honor Tea this year."

"I suppose so. I'm nervous," I admitted. I still had no idea what I would wear. Miss Dibble had brought in a couple of her old dresses for me to try on during sewing class, but they'd been too short.

Rowan shrugged. "It'll just be local people if this snow keeps up. No one will travel." He held out his hand to catch a snowflake. His hair was dotted with white, his cheeks ruddy from the cold. He wore a red knitted scarf that looked nice against his dark hair.

As I admired him, his mood seemed to sober. His blue eyes lifted to meet mine in a steady gaze. "I don't blame you for what your mother did, Valentine. I hope you know that. I've wanted to tell you that for a long time."

I drew a cold breath, not sure what to say.

*Never contempt, then.*

"Sometimes—" His voice dropped. "Sometimes I get the feeling you think less of yourself because of what she did. Or worry that other people think less of you. But I've never felt that way."

"I'm glad," I managed.

He turned his head to look into the bare winter trees. "I remember back in grammar school. The Fryes used to tease you about having messy hair, and I knew it was because you didn't have a mother, the same way I didn't have a father. That we shared that horrible event." A muscle in his jaw tightened and released. He turned to look back at me, his blue eyes intense. "I wanted to talk to you about it. But I just stood there, doing nothing while the Fryes chased you. I've always felt guilty about that. I should have stood up for you, Valentine. I should have been your friend."

I swallowed against a tight throat. "That was a long time ago."

"I hope we can be friends now."

"Of course," I said.

A sound made us turn, and I saw Sam striding toward us on the trail. My heart sank. Sam had never liked Rowan, calling him a privileged pup.

"Speaking of Fryes," Rowan muttered.

"Sam is different," I said under my breath.

But he looked like any other Frye as he stalked toward us, glowering, filling the trail with his impressive height and breadth. "Lose your horse, Blackshaw?" he called out as he neared. "It's back at the stable."

"Just out for a stroll in the snow," Rowan said evenly.

"Plenty of snow back there," Sam said. He stopped close to me, his large hand closing around mine.

Rowan's eyes lingered on our clasped hands, then lifted to my face. "I guess that's it, then. I'll see you at the Honor Tea, Valentine."

"Goodbye," I said faintly. I watched as Rowan strode back toward the school. He was as tall as Sam, but leaner, his coat perfectly cut for his broad shoulders and slim waist. His legs moved easily, almost gracefully.

"Arrogant ass," Sam muttered, watching him go.

I waited until Rowan had disappeared around the bend, then pulled my hand from Sam's. "I hate it when you act like that," I fumed.

"Like what?"

I didn't answer, but we both knew the answer: like a Frye. I folded my arms across my chest. "Aren't you supposed to be at work?"

"I saw him following you." Sam's gaze shifted from where Rowan had disappeared to me, his green eyes narrowing. "Did the two of you plan to meet out here?"

"Don't be stupid." I started for home.

But Sam came along. "What were the two of you talking about?"

I thought of all that had passed between Rowan and me, too personal to share. "The Honor Tea."

"That's all?"

I resisted the urge to glance back to where Rowan and I had just stood. "He wanted to say that he was sorry about Mr. Oliver. It's all anyone could talk about today."

"Oh." It was a reasonable answer, and Sam's bravado melted. "Don't be mad. I just saw him following you and wanted to make sure you were okay. I don't like the way he watches you."

I looked up, startled that Sam had noticed. Which meant Rowan's attention wasn't my imagination. "Well, I'm fine, as you can see."

"Is Birdy still at your house?"

"Yes, but I don't want to argue about that either."

"Neither do I." Sam took hold of my arm and gently pulled me to a stop. "I'm sorry for what I said about her, Valentine. If you say she didn't do it, I believe you."

"Thank you," I said, mollified.

And the argument was over. That's how things were with Sam and me. He had the Frye temper that flared hot but was easily doused. "Has she told you anything?" he asked.

"Nothing. If I mention Mr. Oliver, she starts rocking. I don't think she can accept that he's dead."

"It is hard to believe," Sam said. His green eyes shifted. "I don't suppose there's any gingerbread left?"

I gave a soft laugh. "If not, I'll make more. I have enough ginger."

"Then I'll be there as soon as I get off work." He took a few steps backward, still looking at me. "You should wear a bonnet like a proper young lady. You have snow in your hair."

I brushed at it, grinning. "So do you. And your nose is running!"

Sam sniffed and laughed as he turned away. I watched as he trotted down the trail—strong and steady and hardworking, with a heart as golden and soft as butter. Sam would do anything for me, and we both knew it.

# 10

I emerged from the woods behind the graveyard, my footsteps muffled by the snow. The headstones looked ghostly draped in white, bits of old stone peeking through. I walked between Angus Moore, who'd died in 1788, and Samuel Bagley, whose dates were missing—and a chill ran through me at the realization that Mr. Oliver would soon lie buried with them. That I would walk past his grave every day on my way to and from Drake.

I paused next to the forlorn-looking angel who guarded Mary Brinker—died age sixteen—and stared across the road. The rectory had already taken on the shadowed look of an abandoned building. As if the rooms Mr. Oliver had inhabited had died with him.

Someone had murdered him. Someone I most likely knew. Perhaps even Father.

Or the person who'd told Mr. Oliver that my mother was innocent.

My heart beat faster. Mr. Oliver had been known for the scribbled notes he wrote in an attempt to organize himself; they'd fallen out of his pockets and cluttered his desk. He may have jotted something down about this secret witness; he'd said it was recently. I glanced up and down the road, then quickly crossed to the rectory and slipped inside.

I stood still just inside the door, my pulse racing. The curtains were closed, the parlor dark and empty. All I could hear were my own nervous breaths.

I moved to the desk in the corner, trying to not think about the empty chair and cold hearth and the mantel clock that wasn't ticking because no one had wound it. I shuffled through papers—notes for sermons, mostly—and opened drawers. I found an appointment book with a few scrawled notations, but Mr. Oliver didn't seem to have used it much.

I heard men's voices on the road and froze, listening. But they moved on.

I searched the bookcase next, thumbing through books and opening trinket boxes. Then I hurried up the narrow staircase. But a thorough search of Mr. Oliver's bedroom revealed nothing either.

Except a letter from Mrs. Henny hidden in his sock drawer, dated two years earlier: her polite refusal of his hand in marriage. I was surprised. I hadn't known the rector felt that way about Mrs. Henny. Although, in hindsight, it seemed obvious. He'd often sat on her doorstep, reading aloud while she worked in her garden. But she'd rejected him. I refolded the letter and slid it into my cloak pocket, not wanting anyone to find it when they cleaned out his things. Not wanting Mrs. Henny to know that he'd cared enough to keep it.

I descended the staircase and forced myself to enter the kitchen. The blood on the floor had browned. I stared at it, a lump filling my throat. The only thing I could do for him now was find his killer. I opened the cupboards and searched every shelf, more carefully than I had the day he'd died.

The muffled voices reached me a moment before I heard the front door opening. I whirled around, but the only way out was through the parlor. I darted the other way, to the old storage room that Mr. Oliver had converted into an art studio. No window, I realized a moment too late. I quickly pushed the door shut behind me, but the old wood refused to close all the way, leaving a crack.

I stood perfectly still.

"I'm glad you came with me," Mrs. Henny's soft voice said in the other room. "I wouldn't have wanted to come alone."

"We'll just find the donation list and go," a stronger voice responded—Mrs. Blackshaw, Rowan's grandmother.

I closed my eyes, silently cursing myself for coming here. Mrs. Blackshaw was a trustee at Drake Academy, but more than that, I admired her. She was smart and outspoken and fought for what she believed in. An article she'd written had been printed in an abolitionist magazine. She'd spoken at an important women's convention in Seneca Falls. Mrs. Blackshaw was the last person I wanted to catch me snooping.

And she would tell Rowan.

"Is this where it happened?" another voice asked—Lucy's mother, Mrs. Meriwether.

"No, he was sitting at the table."

I heard the three women enter the kitchen and dared to peer through the sliver of opening.

Mrs. Meriwether's eyes widened at the sight of the dried blood on the floor. "Oh, my," she murmured.

Mrs. Blackshaw frowned at the stain, then looked away. At age sixty, she was still a striking woman, with a lean figure and dark hair barely touched by silver. Her gaze settled on a stack of dirty dishes in the sink. "Someone will need to clean out his things before the new rector arrives." I doubted she'd washed a dish herself in forty years—not since marrying George Blackshaw, an older gentleman who'd died a year later, leaving her an impressive fortune.

And one child, a son named Nigel, who'd been shot at age twenty-six.

"I'll do it," Mrs. Henny volunteered meekly. "I'll start tomorrow."

72

"No, wait until his sister arrives," Mrs. Blackshaw said. "She may want a few mementos."

"Of course," Mrs. Henny murmured.

"I'll host the funeral gathering," Mrs. Meriwether offered. She wore a vivid blue jacket that made the kitchen look shabby around her. But then, everything looked shabby around Lucy's mother.

"Something simple," Mrs. Blackshaw advised with a hint of a smile, since Mrs. Meriwether's parties tended to be extravagant.

"Oh, of course, just a cold buffet. And maybe a soup."

Mrs. Blackshaw's gaze shifted to the art studio door where I hid, and I leaned back, holding my breath. She kept her eyes on the door as she said, "The donation list won't be in here. You two go upstairs, and I'll search the parlor."

The other women left the room, their footsteps creaking on the stairs. But Mrs. Blackshaw didn't go to the parlor. She listened, her head cocked, then moved quickly to the door where I hid.

I spun, my eyes skimming the crowded space. An easel stood in the middle of the room, with a small table beyond it with a still life scene. A velvet drape had been nailed to the far wall as a backdrop. I hurried to the drape and slipped behind it, just as the door swung open.

I pressed my back against the wall, holding my breath. Through the fabric, I could see Mrs. Blackshaw's shadowy form as she entered. She walked to a stack of paintings leaning against a side wall and crouched in front of them. I tilted my head to the edge of the drape and dared to watch as she shuffled through the paintings with impatience, knocking a few over. She stood again, her back to me, her hands on her waist. Her attention settled on a second easel in the far corner, covered by a sheet. She went to it and yanked the sheet away—

And I stifled a gasp.

It was a painting of me.

And yet, not me. This girl was too beautiful to be me, her eyes looking somewhere over her shoulder, her lips slightly parted. Smooth skin with a hint of rosy flush. Honey-brown curls. Eyes that drew you in. Her face and shoulders filled the canvas, giving a feeling of intimacy. The painting was almost tender in its depiction. Done by Mr. Oliver—when? Recently, judging by my age. And it was still on an easel.

Something shifted inside me, uncomfortable. When had Mr. Oliver studied me so closely? He'd gotten the varied colors of my hair just right, lighter near my face.

I watched, fascinated, as Mrs. Blackshaw took the painting off the easel and carried it to a worktable. She grabbed a palette knife off the table and stabbed at the canvas, pulling the knife down in a vicious cut. She blinded my eyes. Severed my neck. Cut at my dress. The painting fell into mutilated strips, then she tugged at the remaining bits of canvas until she'd ripped them from the outer frame.

My heart hammered in my chest. I felt stabbed myself.

I'd always envied Rowan, wondering what it would be like to have such a grandmother. I'd watched from afar as Mrs. Blackshaw organized charity dances and collected books for orphaned children—even argued with men about politics.

But clearly, she loathed me.

She stopped abruptly, glancing at the door, then tossed the palette knife onto the worktable and the wooden frame into the corner. Ribbons of painted canvas littered the worktable and floor. She hastily gathered them and crammed them into a clay water pitcher, straightening as the other women entered.

I became rigid behind the drape, my pulse racing.

"His paintings." Mrs. Meriwether sighed. "He was never particularly good, I'm afraid."

"Oh," Mrs. Henny protested.

"His sister may want them," Mrs. Blackshaw said—with such composure I hardly believed what I'd just witnessed.

The women left the room, and I heard the front door open and close.

I went to the worktable and pulled the painted canvas from the clay pitcher. The strips were dry, so the pitcher must have been empty. I spread them across the worktable and assembled them like a puzzle—a jagged, freakish portrait. I stared at it, confused and touched that Mr. Oliver had painted me so beautifully. I'd never known him to paint people, only landscapes and still lifes.

I returned the strips to the clay pitcher and took it with me when I left.

Outside, the snow was still falling, the sun setting. I hugged the pitcher as I walked.

Mrs. Blackshaw had known of the painting's existence. She'd sent the other women upstairs so she could find it and destroy it. The truth of that panged me. What had I done, except suffer for her son's murder as surely as she had? I'd worked hard to overcome the shame of a crime I didn't commit.

To no avail, apparently.

I walked around the side of the house and entered through the back door, where I found the kitchen dark and cold. "Birdy?" I called. I tucked the clay pitcher into the back corner of a tall cupboard, then walked to the front of the house. "Birdy?"

The house felt deserted.

My panic rose as I trotted up the staircase. "Birdy? You don't need to hide; it's just Valentine!" I searched the bedrooms and burned part of the house, looking under beds and opening wardrobes. Then I went through the entire house again.

But Birdy was gone.

Sam arrived on his father's old farm horse and volunteered to ride to Birdy's shack. I wanted to go with him, but he told me to wait. "The snow is getting deep. I'll move faster alone." He was gone before I could argue.

I paced for more than an hour—aware that I was hungry, but unable to eat—and had just decided to go out on my own when the door banged open and Sam entered, brushing snow off his coat. "It's a regular blizzard out there."

He shut the door behind him, and my hopes collapsed. "She wasn't there?"

"No, and she hasn't been as far as I could tell. No tracks in the snow."

I groaned softly. "She must have been arrested. We have to go to the jailhouse." I reached for my cloak on the wall.

But Sam placed his gloved hand over mine. "There's no point," he said gently. "Not in this weather. Sheriff Crane isn't going to release her just because you show up, and she's warmer in jail than that shack of hers." He leaned closer, his voice low against my temple. "She'll be fine, Val. You can see her tomorrow after school."

What he said made sense. Outside, I could hear the storm howling. Reluctantly, I released my cloak.

The next morning, I detoured to Birdy's shack in the woods on my way to school, just in case. But when I entered, I found the room cold and deserted.

My heart clutched when I saw the barren space. Sheriff Crane had taken away most of Birdy's treasures, leaving only her mattress and blankets, and a few items necessary for survival. With the clutter gone, I could see the rough floorboards, caked in years of filth and rotting in places where the ceiling leaked. I felt a draft of icy air through the window.

"Oh, Birdy," I sighed. I should have invited her to live with me years ago. There was a housekeeper's room behind the kitchen that she could claim as her own. I would talk to Father when he returned.

If Birdy wasn't hanged first.

I longed to go to the jailhouse, but continued to school and forced myself to go through the motions of the day—reciting poetry and learning about Constantine the Great. At lunch, I couldn't bear the cheerful chatter of my classmates, so I ate quickly, then crossed the hall to the school library.

As I browsed the tall bookcases, I noticed a book on botany and pulled it out—then two others. I carried them to my favorite table under the window and flipped pages, my eyes skimming words and botanical drawings.

How much poison was needed to kill someone? Not much, I learned. And could it be easily hidden in tea? Yes, some poisons were tasteless.

"Interested in medicinal plants?" Mr. Smithfield asked, peering over my shoulder.

"Just browsing," I said, quickly shutting the book.

"Very sad about the rector," he said carefully, watching me through his spectacles. He'd caught me sneaking books under my coat my freshman year and had been suspicious of me ever since. "Poison is a quiet weapon. Preferred by women, they say."

"She didn't do it," I said, rising. One of the books lay open on the table, and I reached for it.

But Mr. Smithfield's hand got there first. "I'll put them away. You'd better hurry to class." He closed the book but kept one finger purposefully tucked between the pages, marking a description of poisonous monkshood.

As soon as school was over, I hurried through the frosty woods to Birdy's shack. But there were no new footprints in the snow and the interior looked unchanged from that morning. I decided to go home first, to make sure she wasn't there, then I would walk across town to the jailhouse.

As I emerged from the woods into the graveyard, I saw a crowd dressed in somber black drifting away from a gaping hole in the ground—and realized, with a drop in my chest, that I'd forgotten Mr. Oliver's funeral.

Rowan Blackshaw stood on the road, waiting as his grandmother stepped up into their carriage. As if sensing my presence, he turned and saw me across the graveyard, and for a moment our gazes held. Then he tipped his tall hat and stepped up into the carriage.

Through the window, his grandmother stared at me until the carriage pulled her away.

"Valentine," a man's voice said, and I turned to see Sheriff Crane approaching, wearing his black cloak and tall hat, his eyes glistening in the winter air. "I don't suppose you've seen Birdy? I went to her place twice today, but she doesn't seem to have been there."

My eyes widened. "I haven't seen her. I thought you must have arrested her."

He appraised me with shrewd eyes. "And I thought you must be hiding her."

Suddenly, I felt the icy bite of the wind. If Birdy didn't spend the night in jail, or my house, or her shack, where was she? "Excuse me, I have to go," I said. I turned and hurried toward home, hoping to find her sitting in front of the warm fire.

But when I entered, I found the hearth cold.

I ate dinner alone, as I had a thousand times before. But tonight, the house seemed to whisper and breathe around me. I saw the table's long stretch of emptiness and the vacant chairs. The stains and grooves in the wood, made by people who'd left a long time ago. I heard the scrape of my spoon against the bowl. The tick of the clock on the mantel.

I felt hollow with loneliness and worry. Had Birdy gotten lost in the storm? Or had Mr. Oliver's killer found her and silenced her?

I wished Father would return and answer my questions. He'd been gone four days. He'd warned me that this would be a long delivery, but I couldn't shake the feeling that his absence meant more than that. I thought of his veiled answers when I'd asked about my mother being innocent.

*I fix this.*

Did he kill Mr. Oliver because he knew the truth, then go into hiding until he could silence Birdy?

I didn't want to believe it.

Something creaked upstairs. I stood, my heart leaping. I'd searched the house for Birdy, but might have missed some hidden corner. I picked up the candlestick and made my way through the dark grand foyer, then up the groaning staircase. At the top, I paused, surrounded by my circle of wavering candlelight. "Birdy?" I called carefully. "Are you here?"

Something scraped softly on the other side of the hall curtain, in the burned part of the house.

A shiver of unease ran through me. The house felt deserted; and yet, I didn't feel alone. I pulled back the hall curtain and smelled dank, ashy air. I lifted my candle, but most of the hall remained hidden in black shadows.

The soft scraping sound came again, from my mother's childhood room. I approached slowly, my pulse racing, pausing in the doorway. Shadows danced in the flickering candlelight, across the charred bed and towering wardrobe.

And a memory rose: my mother sitting in the corner, quietly weeping, holding a small portrait of her brother, Daniel. I'd sat close to her, trying to comfort her, but she'd seemed unaware.

The scraping sound came again, and I saw that it was just one of the boards over the window shaking in the wind. I drew a shuddering breath.

No one was here, but I opened the wardrobe and pushed back the dresses, just in case. My hands lingered on the fine silk of an ivory gown, worn by my mother at my age. It had full sleeves and delicate tucks across the bodice. A wide ribbon at the waistline. I pulled it out and held it up against myself. The length seemed right.

Impossible to think of attending the Honor Tea with Birdy missing and Mr. Oliver dead. But a lovely gown like this shouldn't be left to rot, so I carried it back to my room.

# 11

---

The next few days melted together, full of exams at school and long hikes through the snowy woods, looking for Birdy. Sam kept trying to assure me that she was safe somewhere. But I saw in his eyes that he didn't believe it.

On Friday, my classmates chatted with excitement about going home for the Christmas holiday—all except Lucy Meriwether, who could talk of nothing except the Honor Tea, which had been moved to her house that evening, due to a broken window in the school dining hall.

I'd decided days earlier that I wouldn't attend. I wasn't in the mood for a party, and it didn't seem appropriate.

And yet, I'd cleaned and pressed my mother's ivory dress and practiced pinning up my hair. I'd even found a pair of gray velvet shoes with little buckles in my mother's old things that fit perfectly.

Classes ended, and I slipped past the tumult in front of the school: friends shouting farewell, carriages jockeying for position, Mr. Foley scolding one of the drivers. I spotted Sam in the distance, hoisting an enormous trunk onto a carriage.

As I walked behind the school stable, Rowan called my name, and

I turned to see him holding the reins of his horse. "Will I see you tonight?" he asked, and I could see in his smile that he hoped he would.

I only hesitated a moment. "Yes!" I called back. And, with a flutter of nerves, I realized I meant it.

The town looked eerily deserted as I walked to the Meriwethers' house, shops darkened for the night, lantern light glowing in upstairs windows. The snow glittered like diamonds beneath a full moon.

I shivered in my cloak, more from apprehension than cold. I wore warm boots and carried the gray velvet shoes in my pocket.

I was late because I hadn't been able to stop staring at myself in the mirror. Turning one way, then the other. Impressed by my own tiny waist. Admiring my hair pinned up in a crown of curls. Adjusting the gown's neckline—first worried that it showed too much of my pale shoulders, then wishing it showed more.

Above the butcher shop, the curtains were parted enough for me to see the Sweeneys gathered around the dinner table—including sixteen-year-old Emily Sweeney, who'd been smitten with Sam for years. She glowered every time I entered the butcher shop.

Two blocks later, I reached Lucy Meriwether's impressive house with its four white columns. Dark dinner jackets and pretty dresses fluttered inside the windows, and I could hear the lively murmur of party voices. I paused on the porch to remove my boots and pull on the gray shoes. My fingers shook as I did the tiny buckles, then I hid the boots behind one of the white columns.

I knocked, and the door was immediately opened by a servant who took my cloak and hung it in an alcove near the door. I smoothed the ivory skirt and tucked a stray curl into place, then took a cautious step into a large, square foyer with a chandelier overhead.

Mrs. Meriwether had remodeled the house last summer, talking of little else for months. The marble she'd ordered from Italy. The fabric from France. Mrs. Utley had whispered that the money came from Mrs. Meriwether's wealthy brother who'd died.

The headmaster, Mr. Foley, stood in the middle of the foyer, talking to a portly man who seemed more interested in the cake he was eating. Mr. Foley noticed me and halted midsentence, his eyebrows lifting as he took in my appearance. He almost looked impressed. Then he returned to talking to the portly man.

Beyond Mr. Foley, a group of younger students sat on a curving staircase, holding plates of food. I glanced into the dining room on my right and saw an opulent buffet on a long table. Ham and roast turkey. Gingered carrots. A platter of oysters. I saw a fancy white cake on a stand, plus smaller desserts below it. A handful of guests loaded plates with eager eyes.

Mrs. Meriwether swept past me into the dining room, leaving a trail of perfume. She looked beautiful, like usual, wearing a burgundy gown, her blond hair swept up in an elegant twist. She scanned the table and whispered to a maid, who scurried away. "You must try the mincemeat," she told Simon Greene's parents. "It's simply divine—the best thing my cook makes."

But I felt too nervous to eat. I moved back across the foyer, pausing in the arched opening to the drawing room.

A warm fire crackled in the fireplace, casting a golden glow. The large room had been decorated for Christmas, with green boughs on the mantel and a fir tree in the corner, draped with strings of popcorn and foil stars. Lucy had talked about the fir tree at school—inspired by Queen Victoria and Prince Albert. I could smell its piney fragrance.

Parents and trustees crowded the front of the room, closest to me. I recognized faces, even if I didn't know their names. Most of the women sat on sofas and chairs, while the men stood in small clusters around the edges, deep in conversation. The largest group surrounded

Governor Stiles, who listened carefully to what the woman beside him was saying—the only woman in the group.

Mrs. Blackshaw.

She looked elegant in deep purple, earrings sparkling against her dark, silver-edged hair. But she seemed unaware of her appearance, speaking with fervor to the governor, her hands moving. Maybe something to do with banking laws. Or the evils of slavery. Or her newest cause—women's rights.

My gaze shifted deeper into the room, where the students gathered, and my heart lifted at the sight of Rowan in the far corner, studying a painting on the wall. He bent at the waist to see it better, then straightened, his head tilting, seeming unaware of the party going on behind him.

He did the same thing at school: stared at the cornice over a doorway as students flowed around him; studied the portrait of the school's founder, Isaac Drake; stood outside Rochester Hall by himself, looking up at the roof. When Jack Utley had broken a newel on the staircase last year, Rowan had hovered over the carpenter as he'd worked, asking questions. Which was strange behavior for a seventeen-year-old, and yet somehow normal in Rowan Blackshaw.

Philly Henny approached him, and he turned, allowing me to admire his handsome profile. He was perfectly dressed, as usual, wearing a dark blue jacket and white neckcloth. He leaned closer to Philly to hear what she was saying and gave an easy laugh.

A knot tightened in my stomach.

I'd always thought Rowan would end up with Lucy Meriwether, with her successful father and sociable mother, but lately, he seemed more drawn to Philly. And I couldn't blame him. She'd grown into a beauty with a graceful demeanor and shy smile.

Tonight, she wore a peach-colored dress that looked nice against her porcelain skin and strawberry-blond hair. Mrs. Henny had little means, but Philly never lacked for anything—or lifted a finger, to my eye. But

Mrs. Henny was too in awe of her own daughter to expect any work of her. She'd pleaded with the Lord for twenty years before her precious Philomena arrived, and her husband's death soon after had only magnified the value of the blessing.

Philly shouldn't have been here, I realized; she wasn't an honor student. But she was Lucy's best friend, and this felt more like a Meriwether party than a school event.

Lucy leaned against the nearby piano, holding a wriggling black puppy, surrounded by three boys. Lucy wasn't as beautiful as her mother but carried herself with a confidence that drew attention, and her blue gown showed more bosom than most mothers would have allowed.

My gaze drifted back to Rowan—and I caught my breath.

He'd found me, his attentive eyes sliding down my ivory dress, then slowly rising again. He realized I was watching and looked a bit embarrassed, giving me a small smile.

I inhaled, knowing I should join him. But the thought of crossing the long room made my heart patter like a bird in a cage.

Lucy's little brother knocked into me as he ran past, and his mother grabbed his arm. "It is her puppy," Mrs. Meriwether told him in a harsh undertone. "I will not have the two of you fighting." But he broke free and ran toward Lucy.

Mrs. Meriwether sighed. Her eyes settled on me, then widened as they took in my pulled-up hair and ivory dress. "Why, Valentine! How lovely you look!"

"Thank you. It's a wonderful party." My eyes drifted back to Rowan, but he was no longer there. Instead, Lucy stood next to Philly, the two of them staring at me, whispering.

Mrs. Meriwether waved a graceful hand. "There's too much food, as usual. Have you been to the buffet yet?"

"No, but I—"

"Oh, you must! We'll be eating ham for weeks!" Mrs. Meriwether took my elbow and steered me into the dining room, rattling off the names of dishes as she handed me a plate. Then she spun back toward the drawing room.

I stared across the elegant spread, knowing I couldn't eat a bite.

"Josephine Blackshaw," a crisp, masculine voice said, and I looked up to see Lucy's father on the other side of the table—a handsome man with a short, dark beard—speaking to a man who had his back to me. "She'll monopolize the governor all evening, of course. No one else will get an opinion in edgewise."

The other man gave a low, gravelly chuckle—a tall man with iron-gray hair. And I realized it was Judge Stoker—the man who'd sentenced my mother to hang. "Is she still harping about that Declaration of Society?" he asked in a growling voice.

"Declaration of *Sentiments*," Mr. Meriwether corrected dryly. "I know it well from my wife."

"Careful," Judge Stoker warned. "She'll be demanding control of her trust, if you're not careful. You'll find yourself the proud owner of several dressmaking shops."

The two men laughed.

"This is a far cry from the usual stale cake and cold tea," Rowan's low voice murmured near my ear.

I looked up to find him only inches away. I drew a breath. "Oh. Hello."

"Hello," he said softly, the corner of his mouth sliding up. "I was starting to worry you wouldn't show up, but it was worth the wait. You look nice, Valentine." His gaze drifted over my bared shoulders.

I bit my lower lip. "Thank you. I'm a bit nervous, to be honest."

"Don't be. It's just school people."

"And the governor."

He shrugged. "My grandmother will keep him occupied." He nodded at my plate. "I interrupted you."

"Actually, you saved me. I don't think I can eat a thing."

"You have to eat something or Mrs. Meriwether will never invite you back." He scanned the table. "How about some cake?"

I glanced at the enormous white cake on the stand. Below it, I saw the simpler desserts. "I heard her say that the mincemeat is good."

"Mincemeat it is, then. I'll join you." Rowan slid a slice of pie onto my plate, then grabbed another plate for himself. "A fork for you. A fork for me. I never get anything like this at my house. My grandmother thinks sugar weakens a man's character."

At the mention of Mrs. Blackshaw, my gaze darted back across the table, where I found Judge Stoker watching me with a keen expression. He had a craggy face with a perpetual scowl and piercing eyes.

A shiver ran through me. *Did he think of my mother every time he saw me, the way I did when I saw him?*

Lucy's father downed his cup of tea and handed it to a servant. "We've done our duty, Ezra. Time for cards and a pipe. I'll find Barnes and Alders and meet you in the study." He exited the room.

But Judge Stoker's fierce gaze remained on me. I half expected him to say something, but he only nodded curtly before following his friend.

My heart drummed. Judge Stoker knew the facts about my mother's trial that I'd never bothered to learn. He might know something useful.

*He might know she was innocent.*

My thoughts raced. Maybe Judge Stoker was the person who'd confided in Mr. Oliver. Then, he'd worried the entire town would find out that he'd hanged an innocent woman, so he'd silenced him.

"One tiny bite," Rowan coaxed.

I obeyed, hardly tasting it.

"Tea or hot chocolate?" Rowan asked.

I swallowed. "Neither, honestly."

"Me neither. Let's join the others." Rowan took my plate and handed it to a passing servant.

I followed him into the drawing room, my mind still on Judge Stoker.

Rowan led me toward a circle that had formed in the center of the room, where Lucy, never shy of attention, sat on the Persian rug in her billowing blue dress, playing with the black puppy as the women on the surrounding sofas and chairs watched and laughed.

The puppy scampered toward the edge of the circle, and Rowan scooped it up. "Come here, you little fur ball."

"Princess," Lucy corrected tartly. Her blue eyes flickered from Rowan to me, then she stood and came toward us.

The puppy wriggled eagerly in Rowan's arms, making him laugh. "She's grown since your birthday, Lucy. I think you're spoiling her."

"As all Meriwether girls deserve," she said airily. Her gaze settled on me. "Hello, Valentine. What a lovely dress. I haven't seen sleeves like that in ages."

Her own sleeves were narrower, I noticed. My mother had worn this dress more than a decade ago. I decided to ignore the veiled insult. "It's nice of your family to host."

"Well, the Honor Tea is rather drab, to be honest, compared to my birthday party two weeks ago." Another subtle stab, since I hadn't been invited. Her voice rose, sweet and clear. "I'm so glad Mr. Foley allowed you to be an honor student, Valentine. After all that talk of cheating last year. When you got caught, I hoped you would mend your ways. And apparently you have—because here you are!" She smiled brightly.

I straightened, hardly believing what I'd just heard. I glanced around and found people watching. My face warmed. "You know I don't cheat," I seethed. "I work harder than anyone."

"Oh, Valentine," Lucy said kindly, tipping her head. "We all understood why you did it. It can't be easy, with your mother and all. But cheating isn't the answer. It was decent of Mr. Foley to forgive you."

"Stop it," Rowan ordered in a low voice, handing her the puppy.

Lucy's blue eyes moved to him, full of sincerity. "You never heard about it, Rowan, but all the girls knew. Like I said, we understood."

Philly and Jane Stiles stood behind Lucy, their eyes wide. They knew there hadn't been a cheating scandal, and yet said nothing.

My temper flared. "Does that make you feel better, Lucy? Smearing my name with lies so no one will know that I might actually be smarter than you? Me—of all people!"

Lucy's eyes tightened, but she kept her voice smooth. "Oh, Valentine, there's no need for rudeness."

I opened my mouth, but closed it again, seeing that arguing back had only drawn more attention. On the sofa, a woman whispered to the governor's wife. And across the room, Mrs. Blackshaw had turned, her face tightening at the sight of Rowan standing next to me.

I could think of nothing to do except turn and walk away, my spine rigid, my face flaming. Behind me, Rowan growled something at Lucy.

What a fool I'd been to come to Lucy Meriwether's house wearing an old-fashioned dress, thinking I would be welcomed. Lucy hated the way I outscored her on exams. Glowered when teachers praised my recitations over hers.

And she hadn't liked the sight of Rowan giving me attention.

I found my cloak in the alcove and left through the front door, pulling it on as I marched down the front path. It wasn't until I was two houses away that I felt cold slush on my feet and remembered the boots. I stopped and looked down, groaning in frustration. The beautiful velvet shoes were ruined.

"Valentine, don't go!" Rowan called, trotting to catch up. "No one believes her!"

I sighed, shaking my head. "I won't go back, but I left my boots on the front porch, behind a column."

"I'll get them." He ran toward the house and returned a moment later, wearing his coat and holding my boots.

I tried to switch shoes while standing and nearly fell over.

Rowan grabbed my waist to steady me, then knelt in front of me. "Here, let me do it." His palm slipped around my ankle. He removed one of the velvet shoes and gently slid my stockinged foot into a boot. Then he did the other. I nearly lost my balance and had to lean on his shoulder as he tied the laces. He stood, tucking a wet shoe into each of his coat pockets. "Come on, I'll walk you home."

"Go back to the party, Rowan. I'm fine."

He didn't reply, just started walking toward my end of town, buttoning his coat.

# 12

The night had deepened, the moon glowing silver. Our feet made side-by-side crunches in the snow.

"Lucy is just jealous," Rowan said.

I hugged my chest. "Yes, I have so much to envy."

"You're prettier than she is. You just walk into a room and every head turns."

A flutter ran through me. "Not for the right reasons."

"Sometimes the right reasons," he said quietly. He held my gaze a moment, then looked back at the path in front of us. "No one in that room believed her, Valentine. She's just . . . *Lucy*."

Mrs. Blackshaw had probably believed her.

"You should go back, Rowan. Your grandmother will wonder where you are."

But he kept walking, his hands in his pockets. "You're saving me. She expected me to spend the entire night trying to impress Governor Stiles so he'll help me get into a good law apprenticeship."

I glanced at him, surprised. "Law? What about the bank?"

"Mr. Pinchery runs that. She has bigger plans for me. Lawyer. Senator. Maybe president of the United States. I'll abolish slavery and give equal rights to women—all before I'm thirty, of course." He cast me a wry smile.

I remembered what Mr. Meriwether had said to Judge Stoker. "What is the Declaration of . . . something?"

Rowan's eyebrows lifted. "Declaration of Sentiments? It's a document demanding rights for women. A list of their grievances. My grandmother was one of its signers. Why do you ask?"

"I heard some men talking about it at the party."

Rowan gave a dry laugh. "Nothing good, I'm sure. Most people think it's absurd. Or ungodly."

Our arms brushed as we turned the corner onto a street lined with shops, and by some unspoken agreement, we both slowed our pace. "What sort of grievances?" I asked.

"I hardly know, to be honest. She holds a lot of meetings at our house."

"She thinks women should vote?"

"Nothing that extreme. She's mostly interested in property rights—women losing their money when they get married." He glanced at me and must have decided I was interested. "My grandmother was only twenty-three when my grandfather died, but she's never remarried because she would lose control of her money. That's the law. It would go to her husband—all her businesses and investments. She'd have no legal voice. And, if you know my grandmother, she likes having a voice. So, she never remarried and kept her money."

"That's horrible—not that she didn't remarry, but that she can't remarry without losing what's rightfully hers."

Rowan laughed. "Oh, no! I've converted you. You aren't going to start attending meetings at my house, are you?"

I smiled wryly. "I don't think your grandmother would welcome me."

He didn't dispute it.

We passed a hat shop, where the upstairs rooms glowed with candlelight and merry music skipped off a fiddle. I smelled something savory that made my stomach tighten. "I'm finally hungry," I admitted.

"Good. That means I don't make you nervous."

I glanced up, and we shared a quiet smile.

We turned another corner, and I saw Blackshaw Bank in the distance, its fancy windows darkened for the night.

"Your grandmother won't like that you've walked me home," I said.

"No," he admitted.

I kept my head bowed, watching as our feet landed in slow rhythm. "I know she hates me, Rowan, I just don't know why. I'm not the one who killed your father."

I felt his eyes settle on me. "It's not about you; it's your grandfather Silas Barron. You know about the two of them?"

I shook my head. Twice a year, I dusted my grandfather's enormous desk, but I knew little about him except that he'd raised my mother and her twin brother alone, then invested foolishly and lost his money. "He died before I was born."

"He jilted my grandmother at the altar. She never talks about it, but the cook told me. A month before the wedding, a new girl moved into town, and he decided he loved her instead. So, he just didn't show up. My grandmother was left standing there in her wedding dress, with a chapel full of guests. She was humiliated. That's why she hates the Barrons so much—even before your mother killed my father. And you're a Barron."

I frowned, remembering Mrs. Blackshaw's vicious cuts across my face. "She hates me because she was embarrassed forty years ago?"

"He broke her heart. A year later, she married my grandfather, but he was about sixty, so I don't think it was a love match." Rowan looked through the dark windows of the bank as we passed. "According to our cook, you look like your mother—who looked like *her* mother, the girl who stole him away. So, the old wound can't heal."

"I never knew any of this." Rowan knew things about my family that I didn't know.

We took a few strides in silence, then he asked in a low voice, "Did you know I was there the night my father died?"

I stopped walking, a chill running through me.

*The witness who talked to Mr. Oliver.*

Rowan stopped as well, turning, his face illuminated by silver moonlight. "I was in the carriage. My father told me to wait while he went up to the house."

My heart hammered in my chest. I hadn't noticed the Blackshaws' carriage, but it must have been there. Mr. Blackshaw wasn't the sort of man who walked around town. But my mind reeled at the thought of Rowan being a witness to that night. Because the witness had poisoned Mr. Oliver. Either that or my father had done it.

*Please, oh, please, don't let Rowan be the witness.*

"What did you see?" I asked carefully.

"Not much." Shadows darkened the masculine angles of his face. "It was late, and I must have fallen asleep. I think the gunshot woke me, but it's just a vague memory. I didn't even know my father was dead until the next day. I remember Sheriff Crane driving me home. Only he wasn't the sheriff back then, just a watchman. The next morning, my grandmother woke me and told me my father was dead. That an evil woman had shot him. There was a funeral . . . and life went on."

He looked away, his jaw tightening. "We never spoke of it again. My grandmother talks about how wonderful my father was—I hear plenty of that—but nothing about his death. So, I've never known why it happened." He looked back at me, his eyes glistening in the moonlight. "Do you know why your mother shot him, Valentine?"

I shook my head, feeling hollow. I was no longer sure that she'd shot him at all, but I hesitated to tell Rowan that. My thoughts felt scattered and confused. I wasn't sure how much to say. "Rowan . . . did you talk to Mr. Oliver about that night? About being there?"

"Mr. Oliver? No, why?" He seemed genuinely confused.

I spoke carefully, my heart thundering in my ribs. "Someone told Mr. Oliver that they were there that night and saw everything. If it wasn't you, do you know who it might have been?"

Rowan frowned, shaking his head. "Like I said, I was in the carriage asleep. I didn't see anything."

I sensed his honesty and wanted to be honest in return, as much as possible. But I'd never told these things to anyone, not even Sam. "I was there too, Rowan. In fact . . . I saw more than you. Their voices woke me, and I went outside. I saw them arguing."

"Arguing?" Rowan's interest sharpened. "What were they arguing about?"

"I don't know. I wish I did. They were both angry. Both crying. She was . . . holding the gun." I swallowed. "I'm not sure you want to hear all of this."

"I do," he said fiercely. He stepped closer, as hungry for details as I was.

I drew a breath. It felt good to talk about it—and yet, horrible too. "The gun fired, and your father fell backward on the path. I can't go near that spot now. I watched from my window as they carried him to a wagon, then they took my mother away. Three days later, she was hanged."

"But why did she do it?"

"I don't know. I've heard the stories."

He released a bitter breath. "Just rumors and lies. I want to know the real reason." His eyes settled on me, darkened by shadows. "I think we should always be honest with each other, Valentine. If you ever find out why she killed him, will you tell me? And I swear I'll do the same."

I hesitated, knowing I'd already been less than honest. I wanted to tell Rowan that she might have been innocent, but I didn't know enough. It might not even be true.

He continued in a low voice, "I can't help but wonder if he deserved it, somehow. It's like this gnawing question inside me. If you ever find the answer, you have to tell me, Valentine, even if it's hard to hear. I'd rather know."

"I will," I promised. And I meant it. I would speak to Father and learn the truth, and then I would tell Rowan everything. He deserved answers as much as I did.

He turned, and we started walking again. He kept his head bowed, his hands in his coat pockets. "I don't even remember him. My grandmother tells so many stories, I've lost my own memories. And her stories are too saintly to be true."

"I have the same problem," I admitted. "Only the stories I hear aren't so saintly."

We passed the Reverend Mr. Oliver's church—which was no longer his church—and soon came to my house. It looked even more haunted than usual, silhouetted against the night sky. I turned down the carriage drive that ran alongside the house.

But Rowan stopped, staring over the dark shrubs that divided the drive from the front yard. "Where did it happen?" he asked quietly.

I pointed to the walkway in the distance, leading to the front door. "Right there, where the path curves."

We continued along the drive, rounding the back corner of the house. At the kitchen door, I stopped and turned, suddenly cold and weary and glad to be home.

"Thank you for walking me, Rowan. I'm sorry you have to walk back alone."

"I don't mind." He turned away, but after a few steps, paused to look back. "So . . . you and Sam Frye. Are the two of you . . . ?"

I knew the answer was yes. But I wanted to say no. My stomach tightened with guilt. "I don't know," I admitted.

"You haven't promised yourself to him?"

"No."

His lips tilted in a slow smile as he turned away. "Good night, Valentine."

"Good night, Rowan." My eyes followed him until he'd disappeared around the corner.

# 13

The next morning, Sam came by the house to tell me he'd be gone for a few days, driving his mother to Middletown to see her ailing brother. "Pa won't drive her. He can't stand her brother. And she doesn't want Gil or Jep. Last time, they got drunk and beat up the neighbor. But I don't like leaving you here alone."

"My father will be home soon," I said, even though I was beginning to doubt it. He'd been gone eight days—longer than ever before—and it was getting harder to convince myself that he hadn't killed Mr. Oliver—and possibly Birdy—then run away, leaving me to fend for myself.

While Sam was gone, I sewed him a new vest for Christmas. I walked to town to buy dark green wool and buttons, then dug through my sewing drawer for an old pattern I'd used for Father. Sam was bigger, so I added inches to the length and width, trying to guess his measurements. I sewed for two days, then wrapped the vest in newspaper and tied it with red ribbon.

I also wrapped the scarf I'd knitted for Father a while back, wondering if he would ever open it.

Once a day, I walked to Birdy's shack, just in case. But she hadn't returned.

As I walked through the quiet, snowy woods, my thoughts inevitably settled on Rowan. I wasn't sure what his recent attention meant, but thinking about it filled me with a shivery sense of wonder. I remembered his slow smile of approval when he'd seen me across the Meriwethers' drawing room. The way his eyes had lingered on the neckline of the ivory dress. His strong hands grabbing my waist. Then, those same hands becoming gentle as he'd knelt and removed my shoes. I thought of our long walk through the dark streets, his low voice near my ear. I'd told him things I'd never told anyone.

Not even Sam.

I tried to stop myself from making too much of it. Rowan's attention was flattering but unlikely to last. He wanted to understand his father's death, but once those questions had been answered, his attention would drift. I thought of the way he'd bent his head close to Philly's at the Honor Tea. Half the girls at Drake imagined themselves in love with Rowan Blackshaw. He was headed for great things, like his grandmother planned, not a girl with a scandalous family.

And a missing father. Dark secrets still lurked below the surface of my life.

I wouldn't make a fool of myself over Rowan Blackshaw, just because he'd given me a few compliments.

And I wouldn't hurt Sam that way.

Sam was the surest, steadiest thing in my life. He knew me better than anyone. With Sam, I felt safe, not this quivering uncertainty. The next time Rowan asked if Sam and I were together, I would tell him the truth—that yes, of course Sam and I were together; we'd been together since we were ten years old, the two of us against the world.

I wouldn't hurt Sam over a foolish fling.

I bought a ham and Christmas pudding, like I always did; a bag of walnuts, because Sam liked them; and four oranges—one for each of us: Father, Sam, Birdy, and me. Then I chopped down a tiny fir tree and brought it into the kitchen, like the Meriwethers. I filled a bucket with water and set the tree in the corner, away from the fire.

Snow fell on Christmas Eve. I hummed Christmas hymns to fight off the loneliness as I strung popcorn on a thread and draped it around the tree. I cut snowflakes out of butcher paper and tucked them into the branches.

Around noon on Christmas Day, Sam rapped on the kitchen door and entered. I was so relieved, I jumped up and threw my arms around him. He laughed, nearly losing his balance, then his arms tightened around me.

"I guess you missed me," he murmured against my neck. "I should go away more often."

He admired my fir tree, then sat at the table to crack walnuts while I warmed the ham.

After we'd both eaten too much—especially pudding—I slid Sam's gift across the table. "Merry Christmas, Sam."

He unwrapped the newspaper, and his eyes widened when he saw the vest. He cast me a sly grin. "Guess you got tired of looking at that old rag of mine." He held up the vest and inspected it. "This is nice, Valentine. You're good at sewing."

I gave a short laugh. "It's huge! I'll have to take it in. Unless you plan on eating more pudding."

"Maybe later. Right now—wait here." He went out the door and returned a moment later with a bright red sled. "Merry Christmas, Valentine."

"Sam! You remembered the poem!" I jumped up to admire it. The paint was glossy red, with gold trim. "I didn't even think you were listening."

He grinned. "Just enough to get the idea. I was going to make it, but then Ma dragged me to Middletown. I saw this in a shop window. It's a lot better than anything I would have made."

"I hope it wasn't expensive."

He shrugged. "Plenty of fresh snow out there. You wanna go to Fletcher's Hill?"

"Yes—right now!" I ignored my blue cloak on the wall and hurried upstairs to get my old green coat.

Sam told me about his trip as we trudged through the snow to Fletcher's Hill. His uncle had lung fever and only a ten-year-old daughter to care for him. Mrs. Frye had wanted to stay longer—probably grateful for a break from her own life—but Sam had insisted on getting back for Christmas.

From the top of the hill, we could see all the way to the river and the bridge built by Jacob Feavers. The town looked small and tidy, the houses like toy blocks frosted with white.

The sled was too small for both of us, so I went first. Sam gave me a shove, and I went flying down the hill alone, screaming and laughing. Then I hiked to the top and Sam took a turn. While I waited for him to climb the hill, I built a stash of snowballs. But my first throw missed, and he quickly attacked with a stronger arm and truer aim. I ran, screaming, but Sam caught up in a few strides and lifted me easily, set me on the sled, and sent me flying downhill. I heard his howl of victory behind me.

Halfway up, I met Sam coming down, and we both agreed we were ready for a warm fire.

The sun was setting, the shadows lengthening. We walked slowly, our energy spent, Sam dragging the sled with one hand. He looked down at me with a lazy smile and held out his free hand. I smiled back as I took it, and his large glove closed around my mitten. He tugged me closer as we walked.

Neither of us spoke, the sled sliding on the snow behind us.

My heart beat faster, knowing what would happen when we reached my kitchen. Sam would build up the fire, then reach for me, pulling me into his arms for our first kiss. Today was the perfect day for it.

And yet, the knot in my stomach felt more like wariness than excitement.

At school, girls whispered about secret kisses, wondering if they dared, giggling when they did. A week later, they would despise that boy and have their eye on someone else.

But a kiss with Sam wouldn't be like that. A kiss with Sam would solidify years of trust and friendship. Laughter and tears. A kiss with Sam would be a confirmation of deeper feelings, assuring him that he could expect a future with me.

Once we'd kissed, I couldn't change my mind and break his heart.

Once we'd kissed, I would lose all other options.

A cold wind picked up as we walked, and my uncertainty rose with it. Suddenly, Sam's hand felt confining, not comforting. As we neared my house, I pulled free and bent to retie a shoelace that didn't need retying. When I straightened, I tucked both of my hands into my coat pockets.

Sam's gaze lingered on my pockets, his mood dropping with every step. "I don't understand," he finally said in a low rumble. "You always push me away."

I opened my mouth to deny it, but Sam deserved better than that. I just didn't know how to explain something that I didn't understand myself. "I don't feel ready, Sam. I just need more time. We're still so young."

"Not that young," he grumbled. "My parents were married at our age."

The Fryes were hardly a couple to admire. "I worry that once we change things—" The sled scraped on the ground behind us. "It'll be like riding that sled. Everything going too fast. Only moving one direction. Once we change things between us, we can never go back."

"I don't want to go back." He looked down at me. "You don't have to be scared, Val. I don't expect anything serious. Only a kiss. And that's not going to change anything, just make it better."

But my resolve was strengthening. "I'll graduate in a few months. After that, I can worry about other things."

He scowled. "So . . . I'm something to worry about?"

"That's not what I meant. But I have a lot on my mind lately. My school isn't easy, Sam."

"That's just an excuse. Going to school don't keep you from—"

"Doesn't," I corrected without thinking.

Sam gave a short laugh, walking faster.

I sighed, struggling to keep up. "I'm sorry." Sam hated it when I corrected his grammar. But it had made a difference; he spoke better than anyone in his family. "I just don't think we need to rush into things."

"Rush? You should hear my brothers talk. They think I'm a right fool, letting you lead me around on a leash. They kiss a different girl every week."

My own temper sparked. "If that's what you want, I'm sure Emily Sweeney would be happy to oblige."

"Maybe Emily Sweeney won't think she's too good for me!"

I gritted my teeth. "Whenever you're mad, you accuse me of that! But I've never said I was too good for you—never!"

"You don't need to say it; I see it in the way you look at me. I'm just a Frye and you're a Barron, living in that big house." The sled bounced on the ground behind him.

"My mother *hanged* for murder!"

He glowered. "Whenever I ask you what you're thinking, you say, 'Nothing,' like I'm too stupid to understand."

"Maybe I'm thinking about something I'd rather not talk about— like Mr. Oliver dying right in front of me! And Birdy gone missing! And now, my father didn't even come home for Christmas! He could be dead for all I know!"

"He isn't dead," Sam snapped. "He's probably with that widow on Grover Street."

I stopped short, drawing a cold breath.

Sam stopped a few strides ahead of me, his shoulders sagging.

"What are you talking about?" I asked tightly.

Slowly, he turned.

"What?" I demanded.

"Your father doesn't travel as much as you think he does, Val. He's got a woman across town. When he's not home, that's where he is."

I shook my head, frowning. "He drives a delivery wagon. He goes on long trips."

"Sometimes, yeah. But sometimes he's there. I've seen him entering her house on Grover—a yellow house with red shutters. She has a boy that he walks to grammar school. I think it started last summer."

I felt stunned. Father had started coming home later last summer, saying he wasn't hungry.

Because he'd already eaten with another family.

He'd never walked me to school. Not once.

My surprise sucked the air from our argument. Sam lifted a limp hand, trying to take back his words.

"I'm sorry, Val. I shouldn't have told you like that."

I shook my head, swallowing. If Father had been at this widow's house this whole time, maybe I'd imagined everything. Maybe my mother was guilty—and Mr. Oliver had died of a heart attack—and Birdy had gotten lost in a blizzard.

A dog barked at a distant house. I glanced at the horizon, where the sunset had deepened to purple. It was too late to walk to Grover Street now. But tomorrow, I would find Father and get answers. I started walking again.

Sam kept up, casting me an apologetic glance. "I didn't mean to tell you that way."

"I'm glad you did. I hate secrets. Don't ever keep secrets from me, Sam."

"I won't. And if you need more time about us, that's fine. I won't rush you."

I took a few more strides as my emotions settled, then met his gaze. "Thank you, Sam."

We walked along the carriage drive beside my house, then turned at the back corner.

I noticed the black horse first, its reins draped over a tree branch. Then I saw Rowan Blackshaw bent at the back doorstep, leaving a basket. He straightened and saw me, and his face relaxed with a smile. Then he noticed Sam. On the surface, the smile didn't change, but in his eyes, I saw the subtle shift from genuine pleasure to good manners. And, in that heartbeat, I understood Rowan.

"There you are," he said easily. "I was just leaving your shoes. I forgot to give them to you the other night."

Sam frowned, his gaze shifting from the basket to Rowan. "What night?" he asked warily.

My pulse raced, but I managed to keep my voice level. "The Honor Tea. I changed boots for walking home and left the shoes behind." It was a half lie, and I saw the flicker of understanding in Rowan's eyes. "Thank you, Rowan; it was good of you to bring them." The words sounded too polite after our long walk in the dark.

"I had the maid clean them up a bit." Rowan glanced down at the sled. "Looks like you two have been having fun."

"Sam gave it to me for Christmas."

Sam shot me a glowering look, as if I'd revealed something overly personal.

"Well, perfect weather for it," Rowan said smoothly. He wore a coat of fine black wool, with a gray scarf tucked into the lapels.

And suddenly, I was aware of my old green coat and wet curls, and Sam's tattered brown coat, handed down from two older brothers, the sleeves too short.

Rowan flashed a tight smile that didn't reach his eyes. "Well, I'd best get home. My great-aunt just arrived, and she and my grandmother can't go five minutes without arguing. Should make for a merry Christmas feast." He tightened his black leather gloves and moved to his horse.

"Thank you for bringing the shoes, Rowan. Merry Christmas."

"Merry Christmas, Valentine." He swung himself up into the saddle, suddenly towering over us. "And you, Sam." He kicked the horse and rode away.

Sam glared after him.

I picked up the basket and found the two gray shoes inside, brushed clean, and something wrapped in a white napkin. I opened the napkin and found a small mincemeat pie, just big enough for one.

Sam looked over my shoulder and gave a hard laugh. "Suddenly, it all makes sense." He let go of the sled and turned away.

"Sam," I called after him.

But he didn't look back.

# 14

---

I tossed throughout the night, my head full of Rowan leaving a basket on my doorstep. And Sam stalking away. And Father's secret life.

I awoke later than I'd hoped, dressed and ate quickly, then bundled myself and headed across town. I knew the general direction of Grover Street, in the low-lying river district—a part of town I usually avoided, where the buildings were shabby and smelled of rot. I wandered a bit and finally found a small, yellow house with red shutters. I knocked and waited, my breath steaming in front of me.

A boy of about eight with jam smeared above his lip opened the door, then darted back into the house. "Ma! Someone's here!"

A woman of about thirty years appeared a moment later, wiping her hands on a dishrag. She halted when she saw me, her expression darkening. "He's too cowardly to tell me himself? He sent you to do his dirty work?"

I blinked, startled. "No. I mean—he isn't here? He hasn't been home in more than a week, and I thought . . . I thought he might be here."

She frowned, suddenly less certain, then opened the door wider. "You might as well come in."

I entered a small, sparsely furnished room. The boy with the jam watched from the doorway, along with a younger boy. "Go play in your room," the woman told them, and they scampered away. She motioned me toward the only upholstered chair in the room and sat on a wooden chair herself. She was younger than I'd expected. Attractive, but not beautiful, with a scattering of freckles and a limp bun of brown hair. She studied me with obvious dislike. "Well, at least he finally told you about me."

"Actually . . . a friend told me. I'm sorry, but I don't even know your name."

Her scowl deepened. "Molly Gillis. He said he would tell you. I told him, don't bother coming back until you do. And when he didn't come back, I knew you disapproved. That you don't think I'm good enough."

"No, that isn't it at all. I wouldn't have disapproved. At least—I want him to be happy."

Her eyes shifted. "Then why didn't he come for Christmas? He said he wanted to marry me, and that's the last I saw of him."

I tried to hide my shock. Father had mentioned getting a woman to help me; I'd thought he meant a servant.

"I went to Hale Glass," Molly said. "But they said he hasn't shown up in two weeks. I thought he must have gotten a new job and didn't bother to tell me. I was going to walk to your place today and give him a piece of my mind."

"He isn't there either." I hesitated, unsure of how much to say. If Father wanted to marry Molly Gillis, he'd probably confided in her, which meant she might know something useful. "The last time I saw him, I told him something that upset him. He left the house, and I haven't seen him since."

"What did you tell him? Something about me?"

"No, about my mother. I told him . . . I told him that she might have been innocent."

Molly's eyebrows rose. "You knew? He thought you'd forgotten."

It took me a moment to fully understand what she'd said—then my heart leaped. *My mother was innocent.* Molly Gillis had just confirmed it. I struggled to hide my amazement, not wanting her to guess my own ignorance—not wanting her to become cautious.

"So . . . so my father told you what happened that night?"

Her expression softened a little. "You were only six. He never blamed you. He knew it was an accident."

A clammy chill spread through me.

"He blamed himself for not checking the gun before he set it down. It must have been cocked, ready to fire. Your fingers weren't big enough to pull the trigger on an old pistol like that. It was just a terrible accident. He didn't even know you were there until you picked it up."

My lungs stopped breathing. My heart stopped beating.

I closed my eyes.

*And saw a black pistol with a golden bird on its side, lying on the ground. Mama is crying, and I want to give it to her. I reach down, but it's heavier than I expect— and roars in my hand, sending a shocking jolt up my arm and a bullet the other way. Mr. Blackshaw stumbles, his eyes wide and startled . . . looking at me . . . looking at me because I'm holding the gun.*

I pressed my hands against my mouth to hold back a scream.

"You didn't know," Molly whispered.

I kept my eyes squeezed shut. Drew a breath through my clamped mouth.

Her voice rose to a wail. "I thought you knew! What you said—I thought you knew!"

I gave a jerky shake of my head. Lowered my hands and forced my eyes open.

Molly stared at me, horrified. "Joseph will be so angry. He didn't want you to know. He didn't want you to remember."

I swallowed and managed to find my voice. "I want to remember."

"He's so proud of you, going to that school. He thought it would ruin your life if you knew."

"What else did he tell you?" I asked hoarsely.

The dishrag twisted in Molly's hands. "He only talked about it once. He wanted you to forget."

"He thinks I'm still a child, but I need to understand what happened."

"He won't want me telling you."

"So—you're allowed to know, but not me?" My temper sparked. "*I'm the one who saw my mother hanging at the gallows! I deserve to know what happened!*"

Molly paled.

"Why did she confess? To protect me? They wouldn't have hanged a six-year-old! He should have stopped her!"

"He tried!" Molly cried. "She wouldn't listen to reason. That's how she was, he said, never listening to him. She didn't respect him as a husband."

It felt wrong, listening to Molly describe my mother that way. But I hungered for more. "What else did he say?"

"She was always moody. Melancholy for years, barely getting out of bed. Then, happy as a lark, saying she was divorcing him and marrying Nigel Blackshaw."

"*Divorcing* him?" I remembered my mother meeting Mr. Blackshaw in the woods. "Was that why he came to our house that night? They were running away together?"

Molly bit her lower lip, suddenly wary. "I shouldn't tell you these things. She was your mother."

"I barely remember her," I insisted, trying to hide my clawing need.

"Well, she was a troubled soul. Terribly spoiled and useless with chores." Molly warmed to the tale, suddenly eager to reveal the worst in Joseph's first wife. "She left iron marks on his shirts and burned everything she cooked. Bought expensive cuts of meat, then cried when he scolded her."

I felt a pang of sympathy for Isabella Barron, raised in affluence, then thrust into the role of humble housewife. "She didn't know how to do those things. Her father lost his money."

"Maybe so, but that doesn't excuse her behavior. The way she tricked him. Their marriage was doomed from the start." Molly's mouth tightened, holding something back.

I waited, hardly daring to breathe.

And she couldn't resist. "She only pretended to love him because she needed a husband. Joseph wasn't your real father. But you came early—big and healthy—and when he accused her, she admitted it."

The story hovered over me . . . then slowly settled, fitting too easily to be false. I bore no resemblance to my Italian father. And there were those moments when I saw the flicker of resentment in his eyes, before a kinder expression took hold. I'd thought it was because I looked like my mother. But maybe I also resembled someone else.

"Who was my real father?" I asked.

Molly shrugged, unconcerned with this detail. "I don't know. He couldn't have been decent, or he would have married her. Joseph thought Isabella was nice, because she offered to help him learn English. But she was just looking for an easy target—someone new to the country, eager to settle. She flirted and he fell for it. Then she made his life miserable."

My head throbbed. I didn't want to believe any of it, but it rang true to my memories. There'd never been laughter between them, only terse words.

"So . . . my father wanted her to hang? That's why he didn't tell anyone that she was innocent?"

"Of course not!" Molly cried, indignant. "Joseph told the sheriff everything, but Isabella just said he was lying to protect her. His English wasn't so good back then. He went to New York City to get his cousin, a lawyer, but when he got back, it was too late. Just three days, and they'd already hanged her."

"But afterward," I insisted. "He could have cleared her name."

"What was the point? He couldn't save her. He kept quiet for your sake, Valentine, so no one would know what you'd done—especially you."

Frustration knotted inside me. "But I'm the one who did it! He should have cleared her name!"

"You wish you'd grown up knowing that you did something like that—and everyone else knowing? You think they'd let you go to that fancy school if they knew you killed Nigel Blackshaw?"

My heart dropped, because of course they wouldn't—not with Mrs. Blackshaw on the board of trustees. I felt a tug of gratitude for Father. He'd kept my secret safe all these years—even from me, allowing me to grow up without the weight of that guilt.

*But someone knew.*

A chill ran through me. I looked at Molly. "Someone told Mr. Oliver that my mother was innocent. That's what upset Father the night he disappeared. He said he would fix it and left the house. Do you know where he might have gone? Do you know who knows the truth?"

Molly shook her head. "No one. He made me swear to keep quiet."

My gaze sharpened. "Did *you* tell Mr. Oliver?"

"I don't even know him, except by name. I'm a Methodist."

One of her sons started wailing in the other room, and Molly hurried away, returning a moment later with the younger boy on her hip. "I'm sorry, but there's a mess to clean up."

"Of course." I stood, my gaze settling on the tearful boy in her arms. When Father returned, there might be a wedding. I would have a stepmother and two new brothers. I wasn't sure how I felt about that.

"You'll let me know when he comes home?" Molly asked.

"I will," I promised. But I was beginning to wonder if he ever would.

I hadn't walked far before I started to cry. I bowed my head, unable to stop the flow of tears—or the torrent of thoughts.

My mother had confessed to a murder she didn't commit, knowing what lay ahead. She'd sacrificed herself to protect me.

*A pointless sacrifice.*

My sorrow sharpened into anger. They wouldn't have punished a child. She didn't protect me by confessing; she abandoned me. Left me motherless, in the care of a father who knew I wasn't his, in a town that would believe me the child of a murderer. What kind of mother did that?

A mother lost in melancholy.

Molly's stories had stirred up memories of quiet days when Mama had stayed in bed. My stomach rumbling as I'd foraged in the kitchen. Dirty dishes on the table. Laundry left on the line in the rain. Father's impatience as he'd ordered her to get up. But she'd only closed her eyes, blocking him out. They'd lived separate lives in the same house. Now, I understood the reason.

*I was the reason.*

After six years of bitter marriage, she'd planned to divorce him for Nigel Blackshaw—which explained Mr. Blackshaw coming to our house late at night, bringing his son in the carriage. Strange to think that Rowan and I would have grown up as brother and sister. But instead of running away, my mother had pointed a gun.

Why?

*You deceived me,* Mr. Blackshaw had accused.

*Yes,* she'd agreed. *And now I will kill you and not shed a tear of remorse.*

What had Mr. Blackshaw done to deserve such cold fury? Or had he done nothing and my mother was the villain, unhinged and irrational? Mr. Blackshaw had tried to calm her. *Give me the gun, Isabella, and we'll forget this ever happened. You'll think more clearly in the morning.* Father had eased the gun from her fingers and set it on the ground.

And I'd picked it up. I'd killed Mr. Blackshaw. I hugged my chest as I walked, looking down to hide my face.

Rowan sought a reason for his father's death, and I was that reason. *An accident. The gun was cocked. It would have gone off in anyone's hand.*

But it went off in mine. A sob welled in my throat. I thought of Father, enduring the same sly glances and rumors as I had for eleven years—tales of his murdering wife that he knew were false. He'd kept my dark secret.

*You say nothing, and I fix this.*

Where did he go that night? Did he poison Mr. Oliver for my sake, then flee town?

No, I didn't believe it. Not for so feeble a reason as my reputation. Maybe to avoid the hangman's noose, if he'd murdered Nigel Blackshaw. But Father never killed anyone. That was me.

*And someone knew.* Someone who'd kept my secret for eleven years. Then, in a moment of weakness, they'd confided in Mr. Oliver—who'd told me—and I'd told Father. And when Father scolded this person for their loose tongue, he'd disappeared and Mr. Oliver had died. Who would care that much about my secret?

Father knew who they were—if I could only find him.

*Joseph Deluca isn't my father.*

My heart emptied with that strange thought. With no other face to claim the title, it left me hollow. Joseph Deluca was the only father I'd ever known—and a better father than I'd ever acknowledged.

I would make it up to him. I would welcome Molly and her boys.

If he ever returned and gave me the chance.

I passed the church and entered the graveyard. The old headstones looked grimy and formidable against the pristine snow. I passed the dead who felt like friends—beloved daughter, Mary Frances, who'd died at age seven, buried next to her mother; Robert Grebe, 1811, with his towering stone obelisk—and continued to the back corner, near the woods. I stepped over the old rock wall that marked the end of hallowed ground and entered the small, neglected graveyard of criminals and heathens. Here, the headstones were small and roughly cut, their etchings worn away, the names forgotten.

Except one.

I sank in front of the gleaming marble headstone of Isabella Barron Deluca and rested my head against the cold stone. This was the first time I'd ever visited her grave. She'd sacrificed her life for me, and I'd turned my back on her. Even the good memories, I'd tainted with resentment.

And there *were* good memories: Mama laughing as I chased the chickens across the yard; sitting on her lap as I sewed my first stitches; Mama singing a silly song as we walked through the woods, our hands clasped.

A black carriage rattled to a stop on the road at the edge of the graveyard. I glanced up, wiping my eyes, my privacy stolen. I expected someone to emerge and visit a grave, but no one stirred.

And apprehension tingled up my spine. Inside, I could see the shadow of someone watching me. But the carriage was smaller than the Blackshaws', and I didn't recognize the driver.

Slowly, I rose. To get home, I must use the road, which meant walking near the carriage. I stepped over the old rock wall and crossed the church graveyard, angling toward the corner. But the carriage door opened, and a tall man with iron-gray hair emerged—and I recognized the scowling, chiseled face of Judge Stoker.

"Good afternoon, Valentine," he said in a low growl.

I remained a few steps away, my heart racing. "Good afternoon."

"I'm sorry to disturb you, but I saw you at your mother's grave and decided it was time we spoke."

"About what?" I asked warily. If Judge Stoker knew he'd hanged an innocent woman, he wouldn't want anyone to find out. He might care enough to poison someone.

"Nothing to be shouted in the street. Come, we'll speak in here." He patted the carriage door with a large hand.

I wavered, unsure. I had no reason to suspect Judge Stoker except my own wild imagination. He was a man of law. If anything, he could help me find the truth.

So, I summoned my courage and moved forward, stepping up into the dark, cramped space.

# 15

---

I'd never been inside a carriage, and it was smaller and darker than I'd imagined, the seat narrower. The carriage shook as Judge Stoker sat across from me.

"I was glad to see you at the Honor Tea," he said in his thick, gravelly voice. "Congratulations on your award."

He'd probably heard about Lucy's cheating accusations. "I deserved it. I work hard at my schoolwork."

His thick eyebrows rose. "I do not doubt it." He studied me in the shaft of light coming through the carriage window. "Tell me, Valentine, do they teach you about the scales of justice at that school of yours?"

The carriage was too small, the air too thick with tobacco.

"I don't think so."

"Well," he growled. "I have devoted my life to them. But that doesn't free me of their obligation. I must pay my requital to their stability, just like everyone else."

My heart beat heavily. I didn't understand his words.

"For more than a decade, I have watched over you, Valentine."

My thoughts shifted. "Watched . . . over me?"

"I knew you were worth salvaging, even when you were nothing but a dirty scamp of a girl with wild hair and muddy feet. I saw intelligence in you, and the strength of a survivor. So, I decided to help you. And, you have not disappointed me. Indeed, you have exceeded my every expectation."

The truth settled inside me like a cold stone. "You are my benefactor."

"Yes. As a trustee, I ensured your admittance at Drake four years ago, and I have paid your tuition. It has been, without question, the most worthwhile money I have ever spent."

I thought of the many times I'd seen Judge Stoker in town, always fierce and scowling, never indicating in any way that he noticed or cared about me. "Why?" I asked.

"Because I sentenced your mother to hang and knew it was a mistake as soon as it was too late to undo, and I have sought to redeem myself by paying your tuition."

Something slid inside me, like a wagon tilting toward a broken wheel. Judge Stoker knew that my mother was innocent. Which meant he was the person who'd told Mr. Oliver—and killed him. The thought should have terrified me, but I felt oddly still.

"You told Mr. Oliver," I said quietly.

Judge Stoker shifted, his knees scraping against mine. "The rector? What do you mean?" He sounded confused, not guilty.

And doubt rose. "Did you tell Mr. Oliver that my mother was innocent?"

"No. Why should I? What are you implying?" His eyes narrowed, his attention sharpening. "What do you know?"

My heart raced. *I must tread carefully.* "What do *you* know?" I countered.

"Nothing," he growled. "Just a gnawing feeling in my gut, but I've learned to trust my gut."

My nerves settled. Judge Stoker didn't witness the shooting. Or poison Mr. Oliver.

"Someday, Valentine, I shall meet my maker, and after all the good and bad I have done, I fear it is your mother who will bring about my eternal damnation. For I hanged her in haste, on the shallowest of evidence."

I knew very little about my mother's trial.

"Every judge makes mistakes. We seek justice amid a turbulent sea of lies and secrets. But I'm good at it—gifted, even. I have an instinct for knowing when someone is lying. But in your mother's case, I ignored those instincts. I sensed she was lying when she confessed. I pressed her with questions, but she would only repeat that one phrase—*I am guilty.* So, what could I do? The entire courtroom had heard, and Josephine Blackshaw would give me no rest. So, I sentenced your mother to hang. But I knew it was wrong—knew it with every judicial instinct within me, even as she walked up to the gallows and slid her neck through the noose.

"But it wasn't until a week later, when I saw a little girl with tangled curls roaming the streets alone, that my conscience reared its ugly head and I knew I should have demanded a more thorough investigation. Your mother pleaded guilty like a woman in a dream, and I should have waited for that dream to lift. But by the time I awoke myself, it was too late."

My mind raced. "So . . . you think she was innocent because of . . . instinct?"

"Years of experience," he corrected, watching me shrewdly. "Why? You have better evidence?"

Judge Stoker was my benefactor. I could trust him. With his influence, I had a better chance of finding Father and Birdy—and Mr. Oliver's killer.

"Valentine?" he growled.

"I was holding the gun." The words slid from my mouth before I knew they were there—and I drew a relieved breath. Father had carried the secret for eleven years, but it was too heavy for me. "My mother was innocent. Your instincts were right, Judge Stoker. She confessed to protect me. I was the one who killed Nigel Blackshaw."

"You?" He scowled, skeptical. "You were a tadpole."

"Old enough to pick up a gun off the ground. But I didn't mean to kill him; I remember that much. It was an accident."

His teeth gritted. "What madness made her confess? She didn't seriously think I would hang a child?"

I gave a weary shake of my head. "I don't know. She wasn't a happy woman. I only learned the truth an hour ago. All these years, I thought she was guilty. I've hated her for it. But I finally remembered. That's why you saw me at her grave."

Judge Stoker growled in fury, turning to look out the window, then back at me. He pointed an angry finger. "No one learns of this, you understand? You tell *no one*, Valentine!"

My heart beat faster. "Someone already knows. I think they killed Mr. Oliver."

"What are you talking about?"

I explained as best I could, with skips and halts, hardly making sense. I told him about Father leaving the house, and the blue tea tin, and Father disappearing.

Judge Stoker listened with a dubious frown, grunting when I'd finished. "You sound like Mrs. Utley with her colorful stories. No one murdered Mr. Oliver. He died of natural causes—as most of us shall in our own due time."

"But Dr. Pritchard—"

"Dr. Pritchard is a drunken fool who wouldn't know a poisoning if he was poisoned himself. He only called it that to please Mrs. Utley so she'll forgive his tick at the general store." His bushy eyebrows rose. "And I'd be careful about insisting it was murder, Valentine. If anyone murdered the rector over this matter, it was your father. No one else would care enough. He's the one who's covered up the truth all these years. And now, he's fled town."

"I don't think he would do that. He just asked someone to marry him."

"Well, Sheriff Crane will get to the bottom of it. Leave it in his hands."

"But then—" My thoughts turned. "I have to tell the sheriff that my mother was innocent. That's the only way he'll know what it's about."

"You tell no one!" Judge Stoker ordered, his expression darkening. "You hear me, Valentine? I haven't paid for your education at the most expensive school in the state to see your name dragged through the mud. I vouched for you with Governor Stiles, assuring him that his daughter wouldn't be tainted by association—and you will *not* prove me wrong!"

Gloomy disappointment filled me. Judge Stoker had no interest in finding Father or Mr. Oliver's killer, only protecting his investment.

"My mother sacrificed herself for me. I want people to know that she was innocent—that all their stories are lies."

"And destroy me in the process?" He glowered across the small carriage. "Is that what you want, Valentine—for me to be known forever as the judge who hanged an innocent woman? Because that will be my legacy, make no mistake. Is that the gratitude you show me for your education?"

"Of course not," I said, appalled. "I'm grateful for what you did—more than I can say. My education has meant everything to me. But how can I live with this—knowing what I did—never clearing her name?"

Judge Stoker grunted, unimpressed. "I see your sort every day, convinced by some prosecutor that confessing will save their souls. Well, all it does is land them in prison. Confessing won't change what you did, only ruin your life—and mine!"

The despair I'd been fighting since learning the truth from Molly washed over me. What Judge Stoker said made sense. And yet, it felt wrong.

He studied me with his shrewd eyes. "I saw you with the Blackshaw boy at the party. He seemed quite smitten. How do you think he'll feel if he finds out that you killed his father?"

I couldn't reply.

"And Mrs. Blackshaw," he continued. "If that woman catches a whiff of this, she'll show no mercy."

"She'll understand that it was an accident."

"Is that what you think?" Judge Stoker released a gruff breath. "You see her singing hymns in church. Well, I know the other side of that woman. She controls the money of this town with puppet strings. But her real wealth lies in secrets. She collects them like weapons."

His piercing eyes held me like a criminal in his courtroom.

"You have told me your secret, Valentine, and now I shall tell you mine. You want to know why your mother was hanged in such haste? Mrs. Blackshaw holds an incriminating document from the early days of my career, which leaves me at her mercy. She wanted her son's killer convicted and hanged without delay, so I complied. And that is the reason your mother received such a shoddy trial. Make no mistake, if Josephine Blackshaw finds out that you killed her son, she will destroy you."

My pulse throbbed in my temples. I felt weary and overwhelmed, unable to think, disheartened by everything I'd learned from both Molly and Judge Stoker.

His craggy face softened. "You're a lovely girl, with the world before you. Don't chain yourself to a mistake made a decade ago. You must never tell anyone, or it will ruin your life. Forgive yourself and forget. That is what your mother would want. That is how you honor her sacrifice—by leaving this carriage and never speaking of it again."

I swallowed the bitter lump in my throat. "All right," I said. "I won't tell anyone."

His fierce scowl returned. "Not a soul, Valentine. Not your best friend. Not your lover. Not your husband, someday. If you do, it will destroy both of us."

I nodded weakly.

"Shake my hand to seal our vow of silence." His large hand reached across the carriage.

And I shook it.

I spent the rest of the day digging through drawers, hope chests, and wardrobes, searching for some remembrance of my mother. Yearning to know her. To understand why she'd gone so willingly—so needlessly—to the gallows.

But there was little to find. It dismayed me, how thoroughly we'd erased her existence. Me, because of unfounded resentment. Father, for his own bitter reasons—although, I found a lace-trimmed nightcap at the bottom of one of his drawers, hinting that he hadn't wanted to forget everything.

In a cluttered desk drawer, in my grandfather's office, I found a letter signed by Isabella, written to her father when she lived in New York City. I read it hungrily, looking for clues. The penmanship was impatient, her mood exuberant, the words tumbling in long sentences. She mentioned two parties but seemed more interested in an opera she'd seen. She closed the letter with a complaint about her overly watchful guardian, Mrs. Maples.

I read the letter twice, trying to find something familiar in it. But the girl Isabella bore no resemblance to the pensive mother I'd known. I looked at the date and counted years. She'd been eighteen when she'd written it—a year before she'd become pregnant with me.

Who was my real father? A beau in the city, presumably.

I might never know.

As I put myself to bed, the wind picked up, whispering through the boarded windows in the burned part of the house. I pulled on thick socks and curled into a ball beneath my quilt, listening to the lonely scratch of a mouse in the wall, lost from its nest.

Finally, I drifted into sleep.

And dreamed of another lonely time.

*I am asleep, lying on the same mattress within the same room, small and curled . . .*

*When gray morning lures me awake.*

*The air feels thick with silence, and I know Mama hasn't returned.*

*It's been three days since the gun roared and Mr. Blackshaw fell and Mama walked to a carriage, looking back at my window. Three days without the sound of Mama humming or the gentle touch of her hand or the smell of good foods cooking.*

*And no sign of Father either.*

*My stomach clenches with hunger. Yesterday, I ate the last of the bread and finished the milk, then I'd stuck my finger in the jar of molasses and licked it clean. Today, I must be brave and light the stove. Then I can cook eggs. Then I can cook porridge.*

*I dress and wash my face, then attempt to brush my hair. But the bristles only skim the surface of my thick, matted curls. I look in the mirror and see large, frightened eyes surrounded by wild hair.*

*Downstairs, the front door creaks open—and my heart leaps because Mama is back. I drop the hairbrush and dart to the staircase, breathless with relief.*

*But I halt a few steps down, because it isn't Mama; it's Father. He rushes toward the kitchen, leaving the front door open behind him. I waver with hope on the staircase, waiting for Mama to follow.*

*But it's a man I don't know who enters. A man in a green scarf. He waits near the door—and I must make a sound, for his eyes turn upward and find me on the staircase. For a moment, our gazes hold.*

Then Father returns. "We must hurry," he says, rushing out the front door. The man in the green scarf hesitates, his eyes lingering on me, then he turns and follows Father. The door swings shut, sending in a swirl of damp air.

Too late, I realize I should have called out to Father, that I should have told him I'm alone and hungry and afraid of the whispers at night. I run down the staircase and press my face against cold glass. I see them hurrying toward town, hunched against a drizzling mist. I grab my coat off the hook and rush outside—

But stop short on the front stoop, drawing a cold breath.

Dark blood stains the walkway, melting in the rain . . . and I hear the roar of the gun—feel it in my bones and taste it in my mouth—and see Mr. Blackshaw's startled expression as he falls . . . and falls . . . his eyes on me . . . his black cloak billowing.

I hurry back inside and slam the door, my heart racing. But I have to catch Father, so I run down the hall and out the back door, around the side of the house to the road. I run toward town—past the Hennys' house and the graveyard and the Reverend Mr. Oliver's church—and finally see Father and the man in the green scarf ahead of me at the edge of town.

But the streets of Feavers Crossing are more crowded than usual, and Father disappears into a sea of muddy hems and boots. I dart around damp coats, looking up, searching faces beneath hats and bonnets. But none belong to Father.

Across the road, Blackshaw Bank watches the street with dark, unblinking eyes. Sometimes Mama meets Mr. Blackshaw inside. But when I cross the road and try the door, it won't open, and when I pound with my fist, no one comes.

My feet throb with cold, but townspeople shuffle past, everyone going the same direction. So, I wander with them, and finally, the flow stops and the people gather. But I can't see past them. I squirm my way between damp skirts and wet-smelling wool and finally reach the front.

And see what has drawn them.

Mama hangs by her neck from a rope, her head tilting and her eyes staring fixedly, her hands clasped behind her back. Her boots dangle motionlessly at the bottom of her best black dress. For a moment, I think she's crying. But it's only the rain. I watch as she slowly turns, trapped by the rope around her neck.

"Mama," I whisper, but she doesn't look at me.

"The daughter," a woman murmurs, and faces peer down, rain dripping off black hats and umbrellas.

A heavy hand lands on my shoulder, and I catch my breath. But it's only the Reverend Mr. Oliver, peering down with a worried frown.

"What does your father think, bringing you here?" He tries to turn me away.

But I resist, my gaze still on Mama. She looks oddly content, hanging by her neck, her eyes half-open, half-closed. As if she's awake and sleeping at the same time.

But I know she's dead, and my heart beats faster, as if it's beating for both of us.

The Reverend Mr. Oliver places a warm hand on each of my shoulders and bends low to look into my eyes. "It is a hard day for you, dear girl. But take comfort, for your mother confessed her sins. She is in God's hands now, and he knows all." Mr. Oliver straightens, removing his heavy hands from my shoulders, and I feel light enough to float. "Now, run home before you catch your death." He gives me a nudge that makes me stumble, but his large hand pulls me upright and steers me again toward home.

I run, bare feet slapping in the rain, cold breaths catching in my throat, wet skirt sticking to my legs. I run, trying to forget the sight of Mama hanging in the rain.

Trying to forget.

Trying to forget.

I awoke with a gasping cry, my cheeks damp with tears.

Because I'd finally remembered.

But now, I must forget again.

# 16

Sam stayed away after Christmas.

I was grateful. I needed time to ponder everything I'd learned, then store it away in a safe corner of my heart, where I wouldn't be tempted to talk about it. Or even think about it.

For a few days, I wallowed in misery. I spent hours in the rocking chair, staring at the fire. Then I bundled up and stood in front of my mother's marble headstone. I wandered aimlessly through the church graveyard, whispering names and missing Birdy.

From the shadows of the graveyard, I stared at the rectory across the road, wondering if Mr. Oliver had really been poisoned or just died of natural causes like Judge Stoker had said. His dying word had been hard to understand. Maybe Birdy had taken the blue tea tin and misunderstood my questions. She was hardly a reliable witness. And, as Judge Stoker had pointed out, no one would care enough about my mother's innocence to kill someone—except Father, and I just didn't believe he would do that, especially for something as insignificant as my reputation.

So, it must have been a heart attack after all.

Mr. Oliver's death was another weight I didn't need to carry.

After a few days, I tired of my own throbbing thoughts and picked up one of the books I'd snuck from the school library. I stayed up half the night and slept until noon.

Then I pulled out the keepsake box in the kitchen and reread every article and pamphlet I'd ever saved about Alvina Lunt. I especially liked the pamphlets she'd written herself; I could hear her fiery conviction in every word, demanding humane treatment of the simpleminded and insane. I spread out a map of New York City on the kitchen table and tried to guess which street she lived on. I wondered what state she would visit next and what cause she would champion. Last year, she'd written a pamphlet about prisons, saying they should have libraries for the inmates.

When I grew restless of that, I put myself to work. I started with the kitchen cupboards, wiping and reorganizing. Then I moved on to the rooms I rarely entered, sweeping and mopping and dusting. It felt good to move, sweat rolling down my temples. I wiped baseboards and beat drapes. I fixed the leaky window in the drawing room, as best I could.

When I realized Father had been gone three weeks, I faced the fact that he might never return. I counted the money I kept in a jar in the kitchen and determined that I had enough to feed myself for a couple of months, if I was careful. I would eat all the eggs I collected, not trade them for things I didn't really need. And I had flour and oats and beans in the cellar. Once I'd graduated, I could look for work. Maybe teach at the grammar school or watch children. I was a fairly good seamstress, thanks to Miss Dibble.

If things became truly desperate, I had the box of money under Father's bed. But that money felt tainted, hidden away as it was, so for now, I left it there.

Every time I passed Sam's red sled, I felt guilty for how we'd parted. Finally, with only a few days left in the school holiday, I summoned my courage and walked across town to the Fryes' farm.

The dogs barked before I rounded the bend, so when the log cabin came into view, Mr. Frye was already standing in the doorway. He filled the opening, as tall and well-muscled as Sam, but with an extra layer of fat. I'd seen what a punch from one of his enormous fists could do; Sam had outgrown them, but not Mrs. Frye and the younger boys. His shirt buttons gaped, exposing a soiled undershirt.

"Well, look who it is." He smirked. "Come to pay her respects. I thought you were supposed to bring food at a time like this."

I wasn't sure what he meant. I kept my distance, remaining back on the road. "Is Sam here?"

"He's in Middletown with the rest of them. I thought you come to see me, pretty girl, to comfort me in my time of grief." He laughed at my confusion. "My wife's no-good brother died. They're gone to the funeral. But you can come inside, if you want. Warm up before you start home again." He shifted, making room in the doorway.

I stepped back, unease running through me. "Please tell Sam I stopped by. And give your wife my condolences." I turned and hurried away, feeling his eyes on my back.

And a fleeting memory rose: *Mr. Frye at the rectory the day before Mr. Oliver died, angry because he'd been scolded for snooping in the art studio.*

School resumed in January.

I walked through the cold morning woods, missing my warm bed, but glad to return to a routine of classes and evening chores, with no time for deep thoughts.

"Back to school, I guess."

I looked up and stopped short. Rowan Blackshaw leaned against one of the large boulders that dotted this part of the woods.

My heart fluttered into a faster beat.

"Sorry," he laughed, straightening. "Didn't mean to scare you. I arrived early and thought I'd walk out to meet you." He came toward me, blowing into his hands for warmth. He looked relaxed, his stride easy, an old leather satchel slung across his chest.

But when he lowered his hands, I saw the same quivery awareness in his eyes that I felt.

I managed to move again. "I'm barely awake," I admitted, even though the sight of him had cured that.

He fell into step beside me. "I got back from Boston pretty late last night. I go every year after Christmas to visit my mother's family."

I didn't know much about Rowan's mother, except that she'd died giving birth to him. "Do you have a lot of family in Boston?"

He shrugged. "Two uncles, with the accompanying aunts and cousins. I always stay with my uncle George. I like him. He's one of those people who knows something about everything. But not in an arrogant way; he just reads a lot. I have four cousins at that house, plus three more a block away."

"I've always wanted cousins," I admitted. "Hannah Adams says they're better than brothers and sisters, not always underfoot."

Rowan laughed. "Maybe so. I wouldn't know." I felt his eyes on me as we walked. "One of my cousins reminds me of you. She's only ten, but she has really long, curly hair like yours. Well, not *exactly* like yours. I don't think anyone has hair like yours, Valentine."

I looked up with a scowl. "I'm not sure if I was just insulted or complimented."

"Oh, I think you know." He reached out and twirled one of my curls around his finger and gave it a tug. He released it with a soft laugh. "I've always wanted to do that."

Something warmed inside me.

Across a room, Rowan was attractive enough to draw attention. This close, he took my breath away. His lips were red from the cold, his eyes bright with interest.

*I killed his father.*

I looked back at the trail, my heart dropping. For a moment, I'd actually forgotten.

He walked closer than necessary, unaware of my tumbling thoughts. "What did you do over the holiday?" he asked.

*Learned the truth about myself. Visited my mother's grave. Cried myself to sleep.*

I'd promised to tell Rowan if I ever learned the truth, but now, I couldn't keep that promise. Even if I hadn't made a vow of silence with Judge Stoker, I wasn't sure I would have been brave enough to tell him what I'd done.

"I already know about the sledding," he added dryly.

I swallowed, unable to think of a witty comeback. "I scrubbed the house from top to bottom. Tell me more about Boston."

His voice lifted. "I saw Harvard. One of my cousins goes there. I've been planning on Yale—that's what my grandmother wants—but my uncle is trying to talk me into Harvard. He showed me some impressive papers written by a professor there." Rowan rambled on as we walked—about changing curriculums and progressive ideas—a welcome distraction from my own heavy thoughts.

"Sorry," he said as we emerged from the woods on the grounds of Drake Academy. "I've talked your ear off."

"I like hearing about Harvard. I'm jealous, to be honest. I wish girls could go to college."

Rowan glanced across at me. "I've heard there are some good schools for girls."

"Finishing schools. I already know how to manage a house and sit and stand. There's so much more that interests me." Across the grounds, I saw girls entering Rochester Hall, alongside the boys, and I remembered that there would be an assembly this morning to start the new term. "I'm grateful for Drake, at least. It just doesn't seem fair that the boys get to move on, but the girls are given no opportunity. As if we've been taught enough and don't need more. Or worse—are incapable of it."

Rowan grinned. "You sound like my grandmother. There are some women who want her to invest in a women's college, but when she looks at their finances, she says it doesn't make sense. She's torn between her heart and her head. And when it comes to money, my grandmother usually listens to her head. But she's always resented that she didn't get to attend a decent school. Not even Drake allowed girls back then. Even now, half the trustees would go back to all boys if she didn't constantly fight for it."

"Well, I, for one, appreciate her efforts," I said.

*She only had one child, and I killed him.*

"Rowan!" Jacob Macauley called, trotting toward us on the path. "How was Boston?"

And suddenly, I was aware of how strange it was for me to be walking on campus with Rowan Blackshaw. But Jacob didn't seem to notice, falling into step beside us.

"Did you see the medical school?" he asked.

"Only from a distance," Rowan told him. "But I think you made the right choice. It looked impressive."

I glanced at the side door of Rochester Hall, where Sam sometimes watched for me in the mornings. He must have returned from Middletown by now to work in the kitchen. But he wasn't there—which was a relief, since I was with Rowan.

On the front steps, we were joined by more senior boys, all of them talking at once. Simon Greene acknowledged me with a smile. "Morning, Valentine." Then, I was jostled through the doorway in the midst of them, with Rowan steadying me with a hand on my elbow. Once we were inside, he left with the other boys to hang up his coat on the right side of the wide hall, and I moved to the girls' side. I hung my cloak on a peg, then turned to see Rowan walking back to me.

He lowered his head close to mine. "Will you sit by me, Valentine?"

I looked at him in surprise. I always sat in the back corner with an empty chair beside me; everyone knew that.

His lazy smile teased. "If you refuse, I'll just follow you to the back corner. But it's always drafty back there, so I prefer the middle."

I bit my lower lip, fighting a smile. "All right, then. Middle it is."

We made our way toward the dining hall, followed by Simon and the other boys.

But my courage faltered when I saw Lucy Meriwether standing near the opening, surrounded by a cluster of senior girls. When she saw us, she straightened and stopped talking, and the other girls quieted.

I tried to summon some anger to give me courage, but all I could feel was churning nerves. I kept walking, staring straight ahead.

But Rowan took my arm and pulled me to a stop in front of Lucy. I looked up at him, alarmed, but his eyes were fixed on her.

"Good morning, Lucy," he said evenly.

My heart dropped. Behind us, Rowan's friends had stopped as well—and I suddenly wondered if this was all some sort of prank to amuse them. I stepped back, but Rowan's hand tightened on my arm, holding me in place.

Lucy lifted her chin. "Good morning, Rowan." Her blue eyes shifted to me. "Good morning, Valentine. What a pretty dress you're wearing. Is it new?"

She'd seen this dress a hundred times. My anger finally flared. This was all some hoax to make me look like a fool. I yanked my arm free of Rowan's grip.

"Valentine —" Lucy said quickly. "I just wanted to say how sorry I am about my little joke the other night. I didn't mean to offend you. I thought everyone would laugh. I mean, no one thinks you cheat. That's what makes it so funny." She glanced at the other girls, who murmured in agreement. "Anyway, I just wanted to say how sorry I am that my little joke fell flat, and I hope you can find it in your heart to forgive me." She forced a brittle smile, her eyes shifting to Rowan.

I saw his subtle nod of approval.

He'd forced her to say that.

Philly Henny leaned forward. "I thought that ivory dress you were wearing was beautiful, Valentine." Her smile seemed more genuine than Lucy's, but her eyes still darted to Rowan, seeking approval.

"I liked your hair pulled up," Jane Stiles said, her eyes wide and eager. "I wish I had hair like yours." Jane's own hair was thin and limp, always falling out of its ribbons.

Everyone waited, their eyes on me, but I wasn't sure how to respond. They'd been forced to say those kind things. But still, they'd said them.

"Thank you," I said uncertainly. I glanced at Rowan, suddenly seeking his approval as well.

He tipped his head toward the dining hall. "Come on, let's get our seats."

My heart pattered in confusion as he led me toward his usual row in the middle, followed by his friends. We sat next to each other, with Jacob Macauley on Rowan's other side, and Jane Stiles next to me.

Jane pressed her mouth against my ear. "We all thought what she said was horrible. I told my parents it was a pack of lies."

"Good morning, students," Mr. Foley said in his somber voice, and the room quieted. His gaze flickered across the rows of students—then shifted back to me, his eyebrows lifting at the sight of Valentine Deluca sitting among his most prominent students.

My chest rose and fell. I barely believed it myself.

For years, I'd tried to prove myself at this school, to no avail: I'd still been a scandal-ridden scholarship student wearing old dresses. A weed trying to look like it belonged in a flower garden. But somehow, now that I'd learned the worst of myself—so much worse than any of them imagined—they'd decided I belonged. Somehow, now that I felt least worthy, they'd accepted me.

At the piano, Simon Greene began the school anthem, and everyone sang. But I had a hard time finding enough breath for it. My lungs felt full.

Judge Stoker had been right. If I'd confessed, this miraculous morning would never have happened. Confessing would have started a new, thorny scandal that not even Rowan Blackshaw could have cut through. Entering the room with him would have only added to the shocked stares and whispers. I would have remained mired in the past forever.

I glanced up at Rowan's handsome face, only inches from mine. I smelled something masculine and musky on him—maybe the soap he used. He had a defined jawline above a silky blue neckcloth. Well-shaped lips. Dark eyelashes. Rowan Blackshaw was both beautiful and handsome. And sitting next to me.

He returned my gaze with a small, personal smile that let me know that he understood how much this moment meant to me. That it meant something to him too.

*He must never know. I will never tell him.*

*Never.*

The invocation was given by the new rector—a small, balding man named Mr. Newland with a surprisingly deep voice. We all murmured, "Amen."

As I lifted my head, I saw Sam watching from the corner doorway, wearing his soiled apron, his face heavy with hurt at the sight of me sitting next to Rowan. My heart tumbled. I would have preferred his temper. I forced a shallow smile, hoping he could see that this moment wasn't about Rowan. That I'd finally stepped free of my scandalous past and been accepted at Drake Academy. I silently begged him to understand that my life had just changed in some enormous, unexplainable, marvelous way.

And perhaps he did, because he turned and walked away.

# 17

I dressed with care the next morning, pulling back the front of my hair with a ribbon and putting on my favorite blue dress. Then I lamented the fact that I must cover the dress with my cloak.

I walked quickly across the snowy graveyard and entered the trail—then abruptly slowed my pace, worried I would reach the school before Rowan had a chance to stable his horse and walk out to meet me.

My heart turned over when I saw him leaning against the same boulder as the day before. He came toward me, making no attempt to hide his pleasure at seeing me. "My grandmother asked why I was leaving the house so early, so I told her I was helping Mr. Wells prepare for a chemistry experiment." He grinned, thinking it humorous.

But my spirits dropped.

And Rowan saw his error. "Sorry, I just meant . . . she wouldn't be happy about me meeting any girl in the woods."

I forced a weak smile. "It's all right. I know she doesn't like me."

"She would if she knew you. Just tell her that you think girls should go to college, and she'll put you in charge of some committee and work you to death."

I returned his smile, liking the idea of working on one of Mrs. Blackshaw's committees. Fighting for an important cause. Doing something that mattered. Maybe that was how I could redeem myself—in both her eyes and my own.

We talked about school as we walked: the terrible steak and kidney pie served at lunch the day before; our elderly English teacher, whose mind seemed to be slipping; Jack Utley's latest exploit—stealing Mr. Albright's coat and putting it on the statue of Isaac Drake.

Our voices finally faded, and we took a few steps in snowy quiet.

"Valentine," Rowan said in a cautious tone. "I've been trying to decide how to tell you something."

I looked up, my heart lurching, wondering if he'd learned the truth.

He avoided my gaze, frowning at the trail. "I was at the bank yesterday. I work there sometimes, after school, just to learn the ropes—enough to be a respectable owner. While I was there, the manager at Hale Glass came in. My family owns the company."

I was surprised. I hadn't known that Father worked for the Blackshaws. And I remembered what Judge Stoker had said about Josephine Blackshaw controlling the money in this town with puppet strings. When a business couldn't repay its loan, the bank probably took possession of it.

"The manager mentioned that he's looking for a new deliveryman, and I know that's your father's job. So . . . I asked him, and he said that your father hasn't shown up in a while." I felt Rowan's eyes on me. "I was just wondering if everything's all right. I don't want your father to lose his job."

My thoughts darted. I wasn't sure how much to say. I kept trying to convince myself that Mr. Oliver had died of natural causes, and Father's and Birdy's disappearances had nothing to do with the fact that I'd killed Nigel Blackshaw. But still, it all felt like a secret I shouldn't reveal.

"If you want me to speak up on his behalf, I'm happy to do it," Rowan said.

I looked up, touched by his offer. "I don't know where he is," I admitted. "He left home before Christmas, and I haven't seen him since."

Rowan's eyebrows rose. "Before Christmas? You mean . . . you've been at the house by yourself all that time?"

I shrugged. "I'm used to it. My father travels a lot for Hale. Only this time, it isn't for work, and I think something must have happened to him. Maybe thieves attacked him. Or there's that part of the road that overhangs the river. I'm wondering if he fell in and got swept away."

"Have you told Sheriff Crane?"

"Not yet." I'd avoided going to the sheriff, afraid he would ask probing questions that would make me say too much. I'd made a vow with Judge Stoker and intended to keep it, but the temptation to clear my mother's name was still there.

"I'll talk to the sheriff for you," Rowan offered. "I'll ride there after school. He might know something. Maybe he's found——" He caught himself before saying it.

*A body.*

"Thank you. I'd appreciate that. Will you ask him about Birdy too? I haven't seen her in a while."

"Birdy? I thought——" He glanced at me, frowning. "Sorry, I know you don't think she did it, but everyone says she killed Mr. Oliver and fled town."

"Well, they're wrong. Something happened to her." Again, I stopped before I said too much.

"Is there anything else I can do?" Rowan asked. "I want to help, if I can."

We were nearing the end of the woods. Through the trees, I could see the solid bricks of Rochester Hall. And suddenly, I knew what I needed from Rowan. But it wasn't an easy request. I stopped walking. "Actually . . . there is something."

Rowan turned, his face full of concern. "What is it?"

I bit my lower lip, not wanting to say it. But it needed to be said. "It's hard for Sam when he sees me with you."

Rowan's expression shifted, suddenly cautious.

I drew a breath. "I like walking with you, Rowan. Quite a bit, actually. But Sam often stands at the side door in the mornings, watching for me. He works long hours, and it's one of the few times we get to see each other. And . . . I just think it's best if he doesn't see us together."

"Ah." Rowan hadn't moved, but the distance between us suddenly felt greater. "From what you told me . . . I thought the two of you weren't . . ."

"We're not," I said, my face warming. "At least, not completely. But we've been friends for a long time, and I don't want to hurt him." I wasn't sure how to explain it. "Sam is important to me—and now, you're important to me too—and, I just don't know how to walk across campus with you without hurting him. So, I thought . . . maybe we shouldn't . . ." My voice faded. The words sounded like a rude dismissal after Rowan's thoughtfulness. "At least, not at school," I finished lamely.

He pulled on his mask of good manners. "I understand. I'll avoid you at school, if that's what you want."

"It isn't what I want—not really. But I do think it's best."

"Of course," he said politely.

I'd ruined everything. But I wouldn't take it back, if I could. In this, at least, I'd been honest with Rowan.

He tipped his head toward the school. "You can leave this way, like usual, and I'll go through the trees and come out on the road."

"I only meant at school, Rowan. You won't avoid me completely?"

He flashed a wry smile as he turned away. "You can't get rid of me that easily."

My eyes followed him into the trees, admiring the gentle sway of his back. His straight shoulders and slim waist. The leather strap of his satchel angled across the fashionable cut of his coat.

He turned to look back and caught me watching. "Oh, and I'll let you know if Sheriff Crane knows anything about your father." His lips tilted, suddenly playful. "Not at school, of course. Maybe I'll write a letter."

I laughed weakly as he disappeared into the trees.

For all my trouble, Sam wasn't standing at the side door, watching for me. One of the scullery maids wandered past and, when I asked, told me he'd been sent into town for supplies.

At least he wasn't avoiding me on purpose.

I made my way to the girls' schoolhouse, across campus.

Yesterday, as the story of Lucy's insult and apology had spread, she'd become quiet and sulky. But everyone else had suddenly become talkative, reaching out to me with friendly sympathy.

And today, that continued. In Latin, Jane Stiles insisted I sit in her study circle, saying my pronunciations were the best; in history, Tall Meg asked me how to spell *Constantinople*; and in my literature class, Hannah Adams leaned toward my desk to tell me she liked the poem I'd just read aloud. Even Philly cast me a nervous smile as we entered sewing class at the end of the day.

Everything had changed.

Or maybe I was the one who'd changed.

A year ago, Hannah Adams had accused me of being aloof—which was so ridiculous, I'd just rolled my eyes and turned away. But suddenly, I saw that sitting in the back corner of every class and never talking to anyone *was* aloof. I'd been so sure of their rejection, I'd rejected them first.

But now, I'd been given a chance to transform myself, and I intended to take it.

In sewing class, instead of sewing quietly by myself, I crossed the room and offered to help Hannah Adams mark the hem of the cotton dress she'd been sewing all year and had finally finished. She looked surprised, then smiled and handed me her pincushion, stepping up onto the hemming stool.

"I don't know where I could have put them," Miss Dibble muttered, shuffling through dress patterns on the cluttered table. Today, her scissors had been hidden by Tall Meg in the potted plant on the windowsill.

Hannah stifled a giggle, looking down at me as I marked her hem. And I grinned back, feeling like part of the joke for the first time.

That evening, as I washed up after dinner, Sam knocked and entered without waiting, like usual. I turned slowly, drying my hands on a dishrag, preparing myself for his jealousy and hurt feelings after seeing me with Rowan at the assembly.

But he wore a huge grin, looking like the eager, straw-haired boy I'd grown up with. He pulled out a chair at the table and plopped himself on it, spreading his arms wide. "I just hauled away my last pig carcass and hung up my apron. I'm done being a kitchen slave!"

I blinked. "What are you talking about?"

"I got a new job—a better job! And you'll never guess where."

An uneasy feeling slid into my stomach.

"Hale Glass! When I got home, Ma was all excited because the manager had sent a note saying I should come right away, that he heard I was a good worker. I got there just as he was leaving. One look, and he hired me. Said he needs someone strong to carry the heavy glass. I'm going to drive a delivery wagon, like your pa. It's almost *twice* the money."

My fingers curled around the dishrag. Within a few hours of our conversation, Rowan had solved the problem. I didn't know if I should be alarmed or impressed.

He was more like his grandmother than I'd known.

Sam lifted his hands, still grinning. "Happy for me?"

My emotions darted. Part of me was happy; Sam had a better job, and I'd no longer have to look over my shoulder every time I talked to Rowan. But another part of me resented the way he'd so easily manipulated Sam's life—and mine. I hoped Sam never found out who'd recommended him for the job.

"I'll miss you at Drake," I said, which was true. Finding Sam waiting in some hidden corner had always been the best part of the day.

His face sobered. "I know. But when I heard the money, I couldn't refuse. And it's better work. I won't have to carry stinky fish anymore. And I'll get to travel and see new places. I've never been much of anywhere." He paused, then added, "I'll be working with your pa, I guess." Sam had never liked my father much because of the way he neglected the house—and me.

"Actually . . ." I lowered myself to the chair across the table from him. "I think you're taking his job, Sam."

His expression turned wary. "What do you mean?"

"I told you at Christmas—he's gone. You said he was on Grover Street, but I went there, and Molly Gillis hasn't seen him either. She went to Hale Glass, and they said he hasn't been to work in weeks. So, if they're looking for a new deliveryman, that's why."

Sam frowned. "That doesn't make sense. Where did he go?"

I released a weary sigh. "I have no idea. He could be sick or hurt, or even dead. He's just . . . gone."

Sam sat straighter. "But that's terrible. What are you going to do?"

"What *can* I do, except keep going to school and hope he walks in the door? I counted my money, and I have enough for a while. I'll find work after I graduate."

"But—" Sam's gaze slid to the doorway that led to the rest of the house. "You can't live here by yourself, Val."

I gave a weak smile. "Haven't I always, more or less? I don't think my neighbors will even notice he's gone."

Sam considered that. He settled his hands on the tabletop, his fingers slowly drumming. "You could stay with us, I guess. Pa would be happy to kick out half my brothers." His green eyes flickered to mine. "But I don't think you want that."

"No," I murmured.

His fingers rubbed across the worn surface of the table. One finger paused on a dark knot in the wood and slowly circled it. "I could stay here, if you want. Sleep downstairs to protect you. Just until your pa gets back." His finger paused, awaiting my answer.

"I'll be fine," I said gently. "But thank you, Sam."

His hand closed into a fist, then opened wide, his fingers splayed. He frowned at the table. "Is something going on between you and Rowan Blackshaw?" he asked in a low voice.

My heart beat faster. I wanted to be honest but wasn't sure of the answer. "Maybe a little," I admitted. "We've become friends, lately."

A muscle in Sam's cheek tightened. "Is that why you won't kiss me? Because you're kissing him?"

"No, Sam, nothing like that. But . . . I do think it's one of the reasons I don't feel ready for it."

His eyes finally lifted to meet mine, tight with emotion. "Don't make a fool of me, Val. If you want me to go away, just say so, and I'll go away. But don't make a fool of me."

My throat swelled. I reached across the table and tucked my fingers around his. "I can't give you what you want right now, Sam, or make any promises, and I know it's not fair to make you wait. But I don't want you to go away. Please . . . don't abandon me now when I need you most."

His fingers tightened around mine. "I'll never abandon you, Val, you know that. But if you decide it's Blackshaw you want, you got to tell me. That's all I ask. Don't lie and keep secrets. You promise?"

I blinked back tears, knowing the promise itself was a lie. But I said it anyway. "I promise, Sam."

# 18

January snow hardened into February ice. Then February ice softened into March slush. Which hardened again in a frigid storm that buried Feavers Crossing in piles of deep snow, closing roads and felling trees.

It was the bitterest winter in memory.

And Father hadn't returned.

When Miss Dibble heard about Father's disappearance, she arranged for me to take in some sewing for her brother, who owned the nicest tailoring shop in town. A few times a week, I walked to Mr. Dibble's Fine Apparel to pick up a bundle and drop off the work I'd completed. Hems and buttons, mostly. Simple work for little money. But it was enough to keep my money jar from emptying.

At school, I snuck food into my pockets—rolls and apples and oranges—and sometimes Mrs. Henny crossed the road with chowder or stew, claiming she'd made more than she and Philly could eat.

Sam never arrived without a couple of potatoes or onions. He loved his new job at Hale Glass, talking eagerly about the places he visited and the men he worked with. I didn't see him as often, but when I did, it felt like old times, our laughter coming easily.

Sometimes a basket appeared on the back doorstep, and my pulse quickened as I pulled back the cloth to find a small ham or turkey.

Rowan continued to meet me in the woods in the mornings. I slowed my pace as soon as I saw him leaning against the boulder, forcing him to straighten and come toward me. Because I liked watching him walk—long legs and graceful stride. And I liked the old satchel he always carried, because he seemed to treasure it even though it looked out of place against his perfect attire.

Some days, we barely spoke as we walked, comfortable in silence. Other days, we talked over each other, debating some point of philosophy or whether soft bacon was better than crunchy. I told him about Alvina Lunt and her fight to help people who couldn't help themselves and how I hoped to meet her someday. And he told me about a group of French scientists who'd developed a new system of measurement. For days, he talked of little else, and I pretended to understand it all— the various units of mass and length and why it mattered if everyone called them the same thing.

I stole glances at him as he talked, mesmerized by his low voice and masculine profile, my gaze lingering on his mouth as he rattled off the names of German mathematicians with perfect pronunciation. He knew about art and politics and Egyptian artifacts. His favorite class was drafting.

"I don't even know what it is," I admitted. Girls didn't take it.

"Mechanical drawing. Engineering. You have to draw things out with precise calculations. It's both creative and mathematical, which I like." He cast me a sly smile. "I'm pretty good at it, actually. Better than most of my class."

Which didn't surprise me. Rowan paid attention to detail.

But he hated writing assignments, always leaving them to the last minute. One morning, he asked if he could come by my house after school to get help with a poem. "I know it's not proper without a chaperone, but I'm desperate."

I looked up, amused. "Is that why you just leave baskets and never stay to visit? Because of propriety?"

"I don't want to impose. Or presume."

I almost said something about Sam's frequent visits, but caught myself. "Come around to the back door and no one will know—or care. No one expects propriety of someone like me." I felt a twinge of guilt as I said it, like I always did at the thought of my mother's hanging.

The secret still lurked, but I was getting better at ignoring it.

Rowan looked pleased. "All right, I'll come today."

I hurried home after school to pull down the laundry I'd left drying in front of the fire. Then I swept the floor and quickly tidied up the clutter. He knocked, and my heart skittered with nervous excitement as I opened the door.

But Rowan seemed relaxed as he entered. "Prepare yourself for some appalling poetry," he warned as he sat at the table. He opened his satchel and pulled out a notebook.

"I can't promise to be much help," I said. "But I'm better at poetry than math equations."

But, as it turned out, Rowan didn't need much help, except for the occasional word suggestion. He became absorbed in the task, crossing off and starting again, muttering under his breath.

So, I pulled on my apron and got busy with the usual chores. I fetched water; tended the fire; peeled potatoes and sliced them, then put them in a pot. I caught Rowan watching me a few times as I worked, his head bent over his notebook but his eyes turned up.

"I like your kitchen, Valentine," he said as I hung the pot over the fire. "It's warm and smells good. And I like watching you cook. How did you learn how without . . . ?"

*A mother.*

I added a log, keeping my face to the warm fire. "I guess, like they say, necessity is the mother of invention. When you're hungry, you learn to cook."

"Didn't you have a housekeeper or nanny? At first, at least."

I returned to the table to clean up the potato peelings. "There was a woman with red hair for a while, but she didn't last long. I can't imagine my father paid her very well." I looked up with a wry smile. "Or maybe I drove her away. As I recall, I refused to speak to her and stayed in the woods all day."

Rowan gave a soft laugh. "That's the little girl I remember. I used to see you in town and envy you."

My eyebrows rose. "You expect me to believe that?"

"It's true. You'd be barefoot and on your own, and I'd be stuck in some tight suit, holding my grandmother's hand. I saw you in a tree once, and you looked completely wild and free, like you were born there."

"I was probably hiding from the Fryes."

Rowan watched as I scooped the potato peelings into a bucket. "My nanny read me this book about woodland fairies, and the illustration looked just like you. I showed it to my grandmother, and that's when she told me—" His voice faded.

My throat tightened.

*I killed his father.*

"You didn't deserve what happened to you," Rowan said quietly. "But you made the best of it."

*I did deserve it.*

"You've overcome a lot, Valentine."

*Please, stop.*

I went to the sink to wash up and compose myself, and when I returned to the table, Rowan was gathering his things. "I'd better go," he said. "Some mayor from a neighboring town is coming for dinner."

"Do you have a dinner party every night?"

"Feels that way. It's worse lately, now that she thinks I'm old enough to impress people." He stood, slinging his satchel over his shoulder.

"Would you mind if we did this again sometime? I mean . . . without pretending I have a poem to write?"

My eyes darted up, widening. "You mean to say you haven't been writing a poem all this time?"

He grinned. "Oh, I've been writing a poem. I just don't happen to need one this week. But I'm sure it'll come in handy at some point."

I threw a dishrag at him.

He laughed as he moved to the door. "See you in the morning."

"Enjoy your fancy dinner party," I said.

He paused, his hand on the latch. "To be honest, I'd rather eat potatoes with you." He lifted his blue eyes to meet mine.

And suddenly, I was falling through a clear sky, everything weightless inside me, my stomach swooping, my heart rising. And Rowan seemed to feel it too, holding my gaze, the two of us falling together in that endless sky. Falling . . . and falling.

"Good night, woodland fairy," he said softly. He left and the door closed.

I pressed a hand to my chest and sank to a chair. I drew a breath.

The sky did have an end. Someday, surely, Rowan would learn the truth. He might forgive me for killing his father, knowing it was an accident, but not for deceiving him.

And his grandmother.

When she learned what I'd done, she wouldn't stop until she'd driven us apart. How long could Rowan stand against that storm? He was a Blackshaw, heir to a banking legacy, with dinner parties and board meetings and political ambitions.

I was a killer.

Someday, I would shatter against that impenetrable ground. Hard stone and cold reality. Broken promises. Someday, I would reach the bottom of that billowing sky.

*Good night, woodland fairy.*

But with Rowan's voice echoing in my heart, I found it impossible to care.

◆

Rowan must have known the delivery schedule for Hale Glass, because he only visited my kitchen when Sam was out of town.

He sat at the table, bent over his notebook, stealing glances as I cooked. Or sometimes he read the newspaper aloud as I sewed buttons for Mr. Dibble.

He tried to help with my chores, but usually proved more hopeless than helpful—which amused both of us.

My rustic existence intrigued him. He asked questions as I made soap out of ashes and watched as I darned a sock. I purposefully waited to kill a chicken until he was there, showing off a little as I popped its neck and chopped off its head, then hung it to bleed. Rowan watched in fascination, then helped with the plucking, trying to not grimace.

For a while, he took charge of the fire, determined to help. But he added too many logs, wasting them. Or got lost in some book, letting it burn out. "Sorry," he apologized, jabbing at a smoking log with the poker.

"That wood is too green. Here, I know how to coax it."

Rowan watched, trying to learn, but after a few days went back to his newspapers and schoolwork.

At least, I assumed it was schoolwork. I'd never paid much attention. But one evening, I crept closer and saw that he was sketching. "That's Feavers Bridge," I said, surprised.

Rowan looked up, quickly covering the drawing—then he relaxed, tipping the notebook so I could see it. "No, it's Feavers Bridge as I would have built it. Better supports. Nicer to look at."

"It's amazing, Rowan. I didn't know you could draw like that. Is that what you're always doing over here?"

"Sometimes," he admitted. He turned the page, watching my face, and I saw a sketch of Drake Academy, viewed from down the road. On the next page, he'd drawn three doorways—so different from one another, they must have come from different buildings. In the bottom corner, he'd sketched a lazy dog, almost comical in style.

"Is that the Duncans' dog?"

"That's right."

I sat next to him and reached for the notebook, and after a moment's playful tugging, he let me have it. I turned to the next page and saw a sketch that confused me at first—squares and rectangles with math equations. He'd scribbled notes along the edge. *Widen hall. More windows?* A floor plan, I realized.

The next drawing showed the dining hall at Drake Academy, complete with students eating lunch. I smiled at Rowan's interpretation of Jack Utley; he'd gotten the expression just right.

"You're an artist, Rowan. How come I never knew that?"

"I'm good at hiding it."

"Why? You have real talent, nothing to be ashamed of."

"It's just for fun." He hesitated, then added, "I wanted to be an architect for a while. I was obsessed with it, reading all these books. I wrote letters to famous architects, trying to get an apprenticeship." He gave a soft laugh. "Most of them never wrote back."

I thought of all the times I'd caught Rowan studying things with those intense eyes of his—porticos and window casings and rooflines. He loved his drafting class. "You would be a wonderful architect."

"It was just an idea for a while. I've decided to go to Yale, then get an apprenticeship at a law firm and pass the bar. That's the most logical path for running for political office."

I turned the page and saw an impressive building I didn't recognize.

"I designed that one," he said, his head close to mine.

"It's amazing, Rowan. Are you sure you don't want to be an architect?"

He shrugged. "Like my grandmother says, it's legislation that changes the world, not pretty buildings."

Which might be true, but hearing Rowan say it made me sad for some reason. I turned the page and saw a sketch of an old man in rough clothes leaning on a shovel. The weariness in his eyes tugged at my heart. "That's our gardener, Wilcox," Rowan said.

"What do you enjoy more, drawing people or buildings?"

"Both, I guess. I used to nag my grandmother about going to Europe after graduation. I had this vision of roaming through ancient cities with a knapsack on my back. Sleeping in haystacks. Sketching castles and cathedrals. I thought I might meet some great artist and study under them for a while. Go to Amsterdam and Paris. No plan, just wandering where my feet took me."

I liked the image of Rowan roaming Europe with a knapsack on his back. "You couldn't convince her?"

He gave a short laugh. "I convinced her too well. She wanted to come. She arranged for us to stay with some woman she knows in London. She kept talking about the abolitionists she wanted me to meet and the meetings we would attend. And I realized our visions of Europe were very different. So, I told her I'd changed my mind."

"I think you should go, Rowan. Just take off by yourself and do it."

He flashed a wry smile. "Don't tempt me."

"Why not? You could go to Boston after graduation to visit your relatives, and just . . . get on a ship."

He took the sketchbook and closed it. "Drawing a bunch of old castles seems like a waste of time when I think about the things that really matter in this world. There are laws that need changing, and someone needs to change them."

It sounded like something Mrs. Blackshaw would say.

"Your grandmother can't expect you to change the world by yourself, Rowan."

"No, but I can get inside the places she can't go. She works day and night, writing letters and holding meetings, but the men in power don't listen or care. They only see a gnat that needs swatting."

I smiled dryly. "I doubt anyone sees your grandmother as a gnat."

"You'd be surprised. There are men who drive miles to put their money in another bank, just so they won't have to do business with a woman. They think it's against God's law." Rowan slid the sketchbook into his satchel. "So, yes, I think I would be a good architect. Maybe even a great one. But when I think about all the things I could do with my life, it doesn't seem very important."

"Does your life have to be important?"

"No—not my life, but the difference I could make." He cast me a cautious look. "I'm blessed, I know that, and I don't want to waste it. I've been born into privilege, but raised with progressive ideas. That puts me in a unique position to do some real good with my life. Oh, that reminds me." He shuffled through the newspaper on the table. "I found an article about Alvina Lunt."

I sat straighter. "What does it say?"

"She's helping a man in Boston get funding to build a school for people like Birdy. Here it is." Rowan slid the page toward me.

I eagerly scanned the article.

"Have you had any word of Birdy?" Rowan asked quietly.

My chest tightened. I'd tried to bury that heartache along with everything else. "No, nothing."

His eyes settled on me, softening. "I sketched her once. I'll see if I can find it and give it to you." He glanced at the clock on the mantel. "I'd better go."

"Another dinner party?" I teased.

"Reformers' meeting." His lips tilted as he stood. "I just can't remember what we're supposed to be reforming." At the door, he paused to look back. "Oh . . . and I'd rather you didn't tell anyone about my artwork, if you don't mind. Or about wanting to be an architect."

"You don't need to hide it, Rowan. Your work is good."

"Like I said, it was just a silly dream for a while."

After he left, I read the article about Alvina Lunt and tucked it away in my keepsake box.

# 19

Spring finally arrived, dripping during the day and freezing at night, creating icicles that crashed from roofs. Across the road, Mrs. Henny started working the muddy ground of her garden, and in town, farmers stood on street corners, debating the best week to plow.

My mood warmed with the weather.

Knowing about Rowan's art changed something between us, opening a door I hadn't even known was closed. He brought blueprints and spread them across my table, pointing out angles and calculations, trying to explain how a flat drawing represented a three-story building.

"I never knew it was so complicated," I admitted. "I thought you just laid out bricks. But it's like a dress pattern, isn't it? Someone has to imagine it first—someone with a mind like yours."

Rowan stopped hiding the fact that he was drawing all the time, and I tried to not mind the fact that he was always studying the imperfect details of my life. He sketched the sagging curtain at the window and chipped crockery on the shelf. He sat on the chopping block behind the house to draw the chickens.

"Don't move," he cautioned one evening as I stirred corn bread batter. I looked up to find his eyes rising and falling across the table, his pencil scratching. "I said . . . *don't . . . move*," he scolded. "Tilt your head back down. Just a little."

I obeyed, one hand frozen on the spoon, the other at the edge of the bowl. "How am I supposed to make corn bread if I can't move?"

"This won't take long."

I stood as still as I could, but suddenly, my entire body itched.

"Relax," he chided. "This is supposed to be a touching scene of domesticity, not Girl Facing Firing Squad."

"This batter will be ruined if I don't get it on the fire. It won't rise properly."

"The chickens didn't complain this much."

"Draw the chickens, then."

His lips tilted. "I've decided you're prettier."

"You flatter me."

"Hush, I'm drawing your mouth." His pencil scraped across the paper, his intense eyes rising and falling.

I held my breath, suddenly overly aware of my own mouth—and Rowan's focus on it. I wished he hadn't caught me with my lips slightly parted. I fought an urge to lick them.

"Breathe," he advised quietly.

My chest rose and fell.

"So, Valentine . . ." He kept his gaze on the sketchbook, his brow furrowed in concentration. "I was just wondering . . . if you've done much sledding lately."

My gaze darted across the room to where the red sled leaned against the wall.

All winter, I'd managed to keep Sam and Rowan in different corners of my life. When Sam was in town, he came for supper, filling my kitchen with his big grin and appetite. He seemed content, for now, preoccupied with his new job, no longer pressuring me as he had at Christmas.

And when Sam was out of town, Rowan came to visit.

I couldn't deny that my feelings for Rowan were more powerful, filling every inch of me. But sometimes, when our eyes met, the quiver in my belly felt more like fear than hope. I couldn't shake the feeling that he'd someday learn what I'd done—that his grandmother would learn—and it would all end in crashing heartache.

So, I selfishly clung to both of them, knowing I couldn't reject Sam, then expect him to pick up my shattered pieces when Rowan was gone.

"I guess your silence is my answer," Rowan said quietly, his pencil scraping. "No need to look so guilty. I just wondered if anything had changed."

*Yes. My heart has turned to brittle glass.*

"No, nothing has changed."

"Well, you can move now. Want to see my masterpiece?" He lowered his pencil and handed the sketchbook across the table.

I took it from him and caught my breath. With only a few hastily drawn lines, Rowan had captured my essence exactly—only lovelier. My long curls looked romantic, not unruly. My cheeks looked flushed from the fire, my hands graceful on the bowl and spoon. "Oh, Rowan, it *is* a masterpiece."

"Only because of the subject." He came around the table and stood behind me. "I didn't get your hair quite right." He reached around my waist and touched the drawing where my hair looked a bit smudged. "Hair is always the hardest, especially yours."

I tilted my head, making room for him at my shoulder, and he lingered there, his arm resting along my side, his chest warm against my back. "I love it," I murmured.

"Then, it's yours," he said softly, his breath brushing my neck.

I closed my eyes. If I moved at all, he would do the rest. I felt him wanting it, his lips poised above my skin, his heart only inches from mine. But my body swayed with uncertainty.

Even this close, I felt the lie between us.

Rowan moved away, leaving cold air behind. He found a paring knife on the table and carefully sliced the page from the book.

"I'll treasure it, Rowan." I avoided looking at him as I took the drawing.

He leaned back against the table. "I'll do a proper one, sometime, if you hold still long enough."

"No, I want this one." I couldn't take my eyes off it. The way my eyelashes brushed my cheek as I looked down. The shadowed fullness of my lips. "No one's ever drawn me before."

He didn't reply.

"Are you sure you want to be a politician, Rowan? I think this is what you're supposed to do with your life."

"What, draw pretty girls?"

"I'm serious. I think you should go to Europe, like you wanted."

"I want a lot of things," he said quietly. "I'm told some of them aren't very practical."

I ran my fingertip across the soft swirls of my hair in the drawing. "You can't abandon a dream just because someone tells you it's wrong."

"You mean —?" He waited for me to look up and meet his eyes. "You think I should listen to my heart, Valentine?"

I felt that familiar swooping sensation, everything rising inside me . . . then falling . . . and falling. I had to swallow before I could speak. "I hope you do, Rowan, when the time comes."

He smiled slowly, holding my gaze. "Don't worry, Valentine, I'm a very good listener."

The next morning, Rowan wore a mischievous grin as we met in the woods.

"What?" I demanded as he fell into step with me.

"Did you know that most of the flags in Feavers Crossing only have twenty-seven stars, but ought to have thirty?"

My eyebrows rose. "I didn't, actually."

"A sewing circle has been formed to make new ones, and they're meeting at the Hennys' house tonight at seven o'clock."

"I'm impressed by your interest in sewing circles."

"The thing is . . . my grandmother will be there." Rowan looked across at me, his smile sly. "So, I thought . . . you might want to cross the road to borrow a cup of flour. Maybe offer to help. I'm sure they could use an extra pair of hands."

My heart lifted. Rowan wanted me to sit and sew with his grandmother, so I could get to know her.

No, so she could get to know *me*—to see that I was more than just the descendent of the man who broke her heart and the woman who killed her son.

Rowan was fighting for us.

But the thought of sitting in a small parlor with Mrs. Blackshaw made me feel weak in the knees. "I don't know, Rowan. I'm not good at that sort of thing. It'll be a roomful of women I don't know."

"You know all of them. Mrs. Henny and Mrs. Meriwether and Mrs. Utley—and me. I'll be there the whole time."

I gave an incredulous laugh. "Sewing flags?"

"Helping Philly with algebra. She keeps asking me, so I'll offer to come tonight and drive my grandmother." His voice dropped with entreaty. "Please, Valentine, it's perfect. All you have to do is sew, and you're good at that. If she starts talking about one of her causes, you can offer to join the committee—if it interests you, of course."

I bit my lower lip, fighting a smile.

Because Rowan was right: it was perfect.

I changed my dress after dinner and turned in front the mirror, straightening my spine and squaring my shoulders. I leaned toward the mirror and pinched my cheeks.

The good posture was for Mrs. Blackshaw, the rosy cheeks for Rowan.

I felt like a jittery rabbit as I crossed the road. The sky had just darkened, taking spring's warmth with it. I walked past the Blackshaws' horse and carriage.

I'd decided to ask for apple cider, since I had plenty of flour in the cellar, and Mrs. Henny prided herself on the cider she made from her two apple trees. I drew a nervous breath, smoothed my dress, and knocked.

Mrs. Henny opened the door, looking even frailer than usual after a string of winter illnesses. I expected a warm greeting from her, at least, and was surprised to see a flicker of annoyance in her eyes.

And it dawned on me that Philly didn't care about mathematics.

Last fall, I'd overheard Mrs. Henny coaching Philly as they worked in the garden—how close to stand to a young man without being improper, how loudly to laugh at his jokes. Rowan Blackshaw would be a fine prize for the daughter of a timid widow who sold medicinal tinctures to get by. Tonight was Philly's opportunity to lean close as Rowan explained algebraic equations.

And I was an unwelcome distraction.

Mrs. Henny forced a smile. "Why, Valentine, what a surprise."

"I was hoping . . . I was wondering if I could borrow a little apple cider for a cake."

She hesitated, but there was only one civil response. She opened the door wider. "Of course. Come in."

I entered the hall, my heart racing. We passed a narrow staircase on the right, then came to the wide opening to the parlor. I paused to look in, forcing Mrs. Henny to stop as well.

Mrs. Blackshaw leaned over a table near the window, her back to me, smoothing a long stretch of red fabric. Her slim, regal build reminded me of Rowan. Her hair was as dark as his, but streaked with silver. "There's plenty of red," she said. "If we had more blue, we could make another flag."

"That's the last of the bolt," Mrs. Utley said briskly from the sofa, cutting stars from white fabric.

"I suppose I could cut up a blue dress," Mrs. Meriwether mused. She also sat on the sofa, lazily digging through a sewing basket.

"Don't be melodramatic, Alice," Mrs. Blackshaw chided with a hint of amusement. "These are flags, not war bandages."

Mrs. Henny leaned toward me to say in a hushed voice, "We're adding more stars."

The two women on the sofa looked up to see us in the doorway, their hands pausing in their work. But Mrs. Blackshaw remained busy at the table, her back to me.

My stomach quivered with nerves, but I forced myself to speak up. "What a noble cause! I would love to help, if I can. I like sewing."

The women on the sofa turned into statues, their eyes shifting to the window.

Mrs. Blackshaw turned slowly, her spine straightening, her eyes narrowing as they settled on me. She made no attempt to hide her dislike; everyone in this room knew she had reason for it.

My heart sank.

"Valentine!" Rowan called from the back of the hall, his voice ringing with false surprise. He came toward us, hiding a smile. He gently prodded me a step deeper into the parlor. "Do you see who's here, Grandmother? Valentine can help with the sewing."

No one was fooled—least of all Mrs. Blackshaw, whose lips curled in distaste. "How fortuitous that she happened to call at the appropriate hour."

Philly emerged from the kitchen, her lovely eyes widening when she saw me. "Valentine, what are you doing here?"

"Borrowing cider," Mrs. Henny said, looking uneasy.

"But she can help with the sewing," Rowan insisted.

"There's no need," Mrs. Blackshaw said coolly. "We have plenty of hands for the work, as you can see."

"Plenty," Mrs. Utley agreed tartly. Her eyes darted, relishing the scene. Tomorrow, everyone who entered Utley General Goods would hear about the Deluca girl trying to impose herself where she wasn't wanted—followed by a quick retelling of my mother's crime.

But Rowan still clung to hope. "Valentine can probably sew faster than any of you. She sews for Mr. Dibble."

Mrs. Blackshaw smirked. "Well, then, her talents are better spent there, where she can earn a little income. I hear that her father has been out of town. For quite a while, apparently."

Rowan's hope drained away. "Grandmother," he warned.

"Return to the kitchen, Rowan, and help Philomena with her school-work. Valentine will wait outside while Mrs. Henny gets the cider. And the rest of us can get back to work."

"Back to work," Mrs. Utley repeated curtly.

Rowan looked at me, his eyes full of apology.

"I'll wait out front," I said with as much dignity as I could muster. I turned and left the house.

Outside, I drew cold breath into my lungs. But my body burned with humiliation. I walked down the Hennys' front path and stopped at the road, folding my arms across my chest.

I'd been a fool to expect anything different.

Mrs. Henny scurried from the cottage, holding a jug. "Don't bother to repay it, of course. It's my gift."

"Thank you, Mrs. Henny." I took the cider—which I didn't need.

She placed a gentle hand on my arm. "I'll speak boldly, Valentine, since you don't have a mother to advise you." But her voice wasn't bold at all, barely more than a whisper. "I have seen Rowan visiting your house. You must realize, if word gets out, you'll be ruined. Those sorts of rumors might leave the boy unscathed, but never the girl."

My chest tightened. She was right, of course. "I'll bear that in mind."

She sighed. "Oh, Valentine, I fear you set your sights too high. A boy like Rowan likes to rebel a little at his age, to break the apron strings. But he'll be sensible when it comes time to make a serious alliance."

I swallowed, unsure if I agreed or disagreed.

"The Frye boy is clearly smitten. I think the two of you are very well suited." She patted my arm and returned to the house.

Even Mrs. Henny could see what I knew to be true.

I wandered home and wearily climbed the staircase. It was still early, but I felt silly wearing the dress I'd put on to impress Mrs. Blackshaw. I changed into my nightgown and climbed into the deep window well to stare into the dark night.

Across the road, the Hennys' door opened, and Rowan came out. I quickly blew out my candle and watched as he strode toward my house. He disappeared down the carriage drive, and a moment later, I heard his heavy knock on the kitchen door. But I remained where I was, hugging my chest. Mrs. Henny had been right about unchaperoned visits, especially when I was in my nightgown.

But mostly, I wanted him to feel as rejected as I did.

Rowan returned to the road, stopping in front of my house. I thought he might look up and see me at the window, but he stared at the dark walkway below, where his father had died.

Mrs. Blackshaw emerged from the Hennys' house, pulling a cloak over her shoulders. She walked to the carriage and realized he wasn't there. "Rowan?" she called sharply. She turned and saw him near my house and crossed the road.

I carefully opened the window a few inches, and cool air washed over me.

"Come away, Rowan. You're behaving like a lovesick puppy."

Rowan's voice bristled. "You dare to lecture *me* on behavior? I've never seen such rudeness. You should knock on her door right now and apologize."

Mrs. Blackshaw spoke with cool composure. "You're the one who put her in that situation, where you knew she wouldn't be welcomed."

"I expected civility! Five minutes, and you would have known that you're wrong about her."

"I am not wrong, Rowan."

"Of course not," he snapped. "You never are." He took a few angry steps away from her, then turned and came back. "I need you to try harder than that. She's important to me."

Mrs. Blackshaw shook her head. "I won't go through this again, Rowan. I watched your father fall into the same trap and didn't intervene, sure he would come to his senses. I have regretted it every day since, with every breath that I take. Hate me if you must, but I will tell you the truth, and someday you'll thank me."

He released a breath. "You have this twisted idea that she's like her mother, but she's nothing like her. Valentine didn't kill my father!"

My heart cowered with shame.

Mrs. Blackshaw's voice tightened. "Just two days ago, I saw that Frye boy leaving her house. I don't know what lies she's told you, but they're still thick as thieves. She's playing you for a fool."

She couldn't have aimed at a more vulnerable spot. Rowan looked away without replying, but I could imagine his roiling thoughts.

"You have a promising future, Rowan. A girl like that isn't for you. She carries a heavy scandal."

"*Scandal?* That happened a *decade* ago!"

"Your father died at this house," she snapped back. "You dishonor him by even standing here."

"It wasn't Valentine's fault! And it's wrong of you to judge her for something she didn't do!"

I pressed my fingers against my mouth. It warmed my heart to hear Rowan defend me with such passion. But he was wrong.

"That girl wants to ruin you, Rowan. She despises our family."

"Why would she? You don't even make sense!"

Mrs. Blackshaw answered in a strained voice. "There was animosity between her grandfather and me."

Rowan shifted, his feet scraping. "I know about the wedding that didn't happen. But that had nothing to do with Valentine."

"That girl learned to hate us from her mother, who learned it from her father. Isabella blamed our bank for her father's financial failures. She told me so to my face—screamed it at me, called me a thief—then sought revenge with the only power at her disposal. She led your poor father in circles for months, promised to run away with him, then killed him. And now, her daughter seeks the same with you."

Rowan gave a short laugh of disbelief. "You don't honestly think she's going to kill me?"

"She'll settle for breaking your heart—or forcing you to marry her—"

"Don't!" he seethed. "She isn't like that."

"I don't know what she's plotting in her devious heart, Rowan, but I know that deception runs in that family. She blames the Blackshaws for her family's fall from grace, just like her mother did, and she's set out to ruin you. You've told me yourself how clever she is."

"At schoolwork, not plotting revenge! Valentine doesn't blame us for her poverty!"

*Poverty.* Hearing that word from Rowan felt like a stab. When I was with him, it was easy to forget our different social standings. But maybe his view was clearer from the top.

"These are important years in building your career," Mrs. Blackshaw said with measured patience. "One false step, and your hopes are ruined."

"You mean *your* hopes." His voice turned heavy. "I'm not sure I want to spend the rest of my life trying to impress people, lobbying for votes and swapping favors."

She remained unruffled. "You're just angry. We won't talk about it now."

"Being angry is what gives me the courage to tell you." His voice strengthened. "I want to be an architect. That's what I've always wanted."

"I know," she said calmly. "And you'll have time for that, once you've established yourself. That's why I want you to meet with Senator Greely. He loves his music as much as you love your art. When I told him about you, he seemed very eager. With someone like him mentoring you, there's no telling how far you can go. How much good you can do."

Rowan groaned. "You never listen. I want . . . to be . . . an architect."

She raised her palms in surrender. "I understand. But first, let's talk to Senator Greely. We'll drive to Hartford tomorrow. I'll send a letter ahead so he's expecting us."

Rowan looked away.

She touched his arm. "I hate arguing with you, Rowan. Let's get a good night's sleep. Everything looks better in the morning."

He didn't reply, just followed her to the carriage. He helped her inside, then climbed up to the driver's seat and shook the reins. I watched as they disappeared into the dark.

My head felt heavy with all I'd heard. I didn't know how much of Mrs. Blackshaw's story was true—about my mother blaming Blackshaw Bank and plotting revenge.

Because I didn't know my own mother.

Because she'd died when I was six.

I sat there for a while, feeling the cool night air on my face, looking down from the window at the path where I'd killed Nigel Blackshaw.

# 20

The next morning, Rowan wasn't waiting for me in the woods. Which meant he'd given in to his grandmother and gone to Hartford. She would have him to herself for several days, filling his head with lies about me.

My mood darkened as I continued to school on my own.

In class, I avoided Philly, afraid she would mention the embarrassing scene at her house. She cast me a few curious glances, her brow furrowed. Then she whispered to Lucy, who whispered to Hannah, and all three of them turned to look at me.

I stayed in my back corner, bent over my schoolwork.

When I returned from school, I found a basket on the back doorstep. Rowan's baskets usually brought a swell of excitement. But today, the sight of it made me tighten with resentment.

*Poverty.* I could feed myself well enough without his charity.

I set the basket on the kitchen table without bothering to open the cloth. I built up the fire and tended the chickens, even mixed a cider cake and got it baking before I allowed myself to give the basket any attention. Finally, I pulled open the cloth.

And pressed a hand to my mouth.

It was a sketch of Birdy, set in a beautiful ivory frame. She sat in the graveyard, leaning against Ida's headstone, looking scrawny and unkempt, her lips quirked with some inner amusement. Rowan must have drawn it in the summer, because her hair was shorn.

Tears pricked my eyes. *What happened to her?* I didn't even know if she was alive or dead. Whatever had happened, I feared I'd caused it.

Beneath the ivory frame, I found a note from Rowan.

> *Please forgive me for last night. I've gone out*
> *of town for a few days. ~ Rowan*

I felt the tight confusion in those words. Like me, he didn't know how much of his grandmother's story to believe.

Did my grandfather really leave her standing alone in a wedding dress?

I went to his office, determined to find some clue as to who he'd been. I sat at his enormous desk and searched the drawers. I had done so before, but this time I pulled everything out and set it on the desktop: scrolled documents and loose papers; a magnifying glass; pens and dried ink bottles; a penknife with a mother-of-pearl handle, engraved with the initials *S. B.* I even found an old schoolhouse slate.

I unrolled a few of the documents and read dry business matters. Maybe someday I would read them more thoroughly to determine if Blackshaw Bank really had cheated the Barrons.

The loose papers were equally bland—except a small note signed by my mother's twin brother, Daniel. *If play practice goes late, I'll stay at Drake and sleep in the dorm.* Just a quick note, but saved because Daniel had died in the fire.

The day darkened into evening, and I lit the lantern on the desk.

A few books remained on the shelves, including the large family Bible. I thumbed through them, as I had before, but found nothing significant.

The bookcase ended with a tall cupboard built into the wall. I opened the cupboard and glanced inside, already knowing that the three shelves were empty. I started to close the door, but stopped, opening it wide again.

The tallest shelf, at eye level, was shallower than the others. I reached inside and pressed my hand against the back wall, but it felt solid. I formed a fist and rapped—and my heart leaped when I heard a hollow sound. I ran my fingers along the back edge and found it looser on the left side—a hairline gap. My fingers pulled and pushed and picked, but the back wall of the cupboard remained solidly connected.

A large wooden nailhead on the left side looked suspiciously out of place, but when I pushed it, nothing happened.

I withdrew my hand and studied it.

Then I reached back inside and pulled the wooden nail toward me— and it came easily, stopping a few inches out to become a knob. I turned it and heard a clicking sound as the back wall of the cupboard swung toward me like a door.

My pulse raced. A few items lay in the hidden space behind the shelf. I reached inside and carefully pulled them out.

Only four items: a slim red book; two letters; and a small, oval frame with the portrait of a young man.

The items throbbed with familiarity. I'd seen my mother looking at them—more than once. Which meant she hadn't hidden them from me; she'd hidden them from her husband.

I looked at the portrait first. The oval frame was no larger than my hand, with the young man's name painted across the bottom in tiny letters: Daniel. He looked about my age in the painting, but his likeness was so simply rendered, it was difficult to grasp what he'd really looked like; he might have been any teenaged boy.

I set the frame down and picked up the slim, red book. My mother had read it with reverence in front of the kitchen fire, slowly turning pages. I brushed dust off its cover and saw that it was a collection of poetry. I opened it and found an inscription:

FOR ISABELLA, MY VALENTINE.
ALL MY LOVE, RICHARD

*Valentine.* A warm shiver ran through me. The man who'd given this book to my mother must be my real father. Richard. I thought of the few Richards I knew in Feavers Crossing, but none of them were the right age to have courted my mother. She must have met him when she lived in New York City.

I turned a few pages, my eyes skimming poetry, and realized something had been tucked inside the back cover. I flipped to it and found two folded pieces of paper. I opened the smallest first, which was soft and worn.

*Come to the garden after they leave. I shall wait. ~ R*

A calm feeling slid through me. Richard had waited for my mother in a moonlit garden. They'd been in love.

I opened the second note, also softened by age.

*My darling, dearest Isabella,*
*In pride and foolishness, I failed us all.*
*Do not forgive me, for I shall not forgive myself.*
*They know not I knew thee,*
*Who knew thee too well.*
*Long, long shall I rue thee,*
*Too deeply to tell.*

It wasn't signed, but I recognized Richard's hand. He seemed a different person in this message, no longer the confident romantic, but wrenched by regret. I was vaguely familiar with the poem he quoted, recited by romantic girls at school.

Something had come between my mother and Richard. Perhaps others didn't approve, which was why they'd met in secret. *They know not I knew thee.* And Richard had misbehaved in some way. *In pride and foolishness, I failed us all.*

I recognized his penmanship on one of the two letters and opened it first. My breath caught when I saw his full name at the top: *Richard DeVries.* I whispered the name, but it wasn't familiar. A Dutch surname, I realized, which meant I was probably part Dutch.

*Dear Isabella,*

*I write to confess that I have not obeyed your orders to stay away. I traveled to Feavers Crossing just to glimpse her, hoping you would never know. But I was alarmed by the condition of the house and learned through careful inquiry that Joseph is out of work and you are in poor spirits. I long to assist in any way possible, as you must surely know. I do not wish to impose, only help. Joseph need not know.*

*I visited our park on her fifth birthday. Please write and tell me that I may meet her, and I will come at once with utmost discretion. If you refuse, I will respect your wishes and it will not change my desire to help—financially, or in any other way you deem appropriate.*

*Sincerely, Richard*

My heart stretched with a yearning that matched his own. He'd written this when I was five years old. I wanted to reach back through the years and catch him spying on me. I wanted to run to him—to know him as desperately as he wanted to know me.

Why didn't he marry my mother? Or did he ask, and she rejected him? *Do not forgive me, for I shall not forgive myself.* Was he the source of my mother's great unhappiness—the evil turning of Isabella Barron, as Mrs. Utley called it?

Well, I was no longer five years old. I would write to Richard DeVries and find the answers. I would arrange to meet him.

I held the remaining letter close to the lantern and saw that it was addressed to Isabella Barron in New York City—her maiden name, so she wasn't yet married. The paper had a crisp feel as I unfolded it, as if it hadn't been opened and closed a hundred times, like Richard's notes.

*Dearest Isabella,*

*Why do you not reply to my letters? I am desperate with waiting. Mother pressures me daily to marry Ruth, but I cannot do it until you tell me, unequivocally, that I have no hope with you. I know I am a fool. You have rejected me twice already, yet still I hope—and love. Please, Isabella, I beg, write at once and end my misery by either making me the happiest man on earth or allowing me to move on with Ruth.*

*Yours always,*
*Nigel*

I read it again, my breath held.

Nigel Blackshaw had been in love with my mother, but she rejected him twice. He'd written to her in the city, but she must have rejected him a third time, because he married Ruth Donnelly from Boston, who gave birth to Rowan.

I looked at the letter's date. It was written more than a year before my birth—before my mother knew she needed a husband. And by the time she did know, Nigel was married to Ruth Donnelly. So, she'd married Joseph Deluca.

Not Richard.

I went to the kitchen for fresh paper and ink, then returned to my grandfather's desk to write a letter to the father I didn't know. My sentences rambled, filled with the details of my life. I ripped it up and started again. Halfway through the second draft, I realized he might be married with other children and my existence was most likely a secret. I started a third time, using more caution with my words.

An hour and several drafts later, I kept it short, simply stating that we had a mutual friend and I hoped to meet him someday. My name would tell him the rest.

I addressed the letter to Richard DeVries, New York City, with no idea if he was alive or dead or would ever receive it.

The next day, Rowan wasn't waiting in the woods. Or the day after that.

At devotional, on Friday morning, I stood uncertainly at the back of the dining hall, wondering if I dared sit in the middle without him. I'd become friendly with Jane Stiles, but she was already sitting between Philly and Hannah. And Lucy Meriwether sat on the other side of Philly. So, I went to my old seat in the back corner, and it felt like home.

# 21

Sam came over on Saturday to help clean up the kitchen garden, yanking away old plants and winter debris.

"You should make it bigger," he said, standing in the middle of the weedy patch. "You need the food. I can take down that tree if you want." He waved a muddy glove at the back end of the garden.

"All right." I liked the idea.

"What about that one?" Sam asked, nodding toward the house.

I followed his gaze to the largest tree in the yard, but my mind was already tightening with resistance. The tree was too close to the house, and blackened by the fire, but my mother had told me stories about climbing it to go through Daniel's bedroom window. He'd hammered strips of wood onto the trunk, like a ladder, and insisted that all his friends enter his room that way during the summer, even my mother in her dresses. With Daniel, she'd said, everything had to be an adventure. She'd told me about the maps he'd pinned on his walls and his plans to explore the west. Dreams that never came true.

"No, leave it," I told Sam.

"Suit yourself." He picked up the heavy ax. "But mark my words, one of these days it's going to fall on the house."

He hacked at the smaller tree in the back of the garden, then dragged it away and started digging at the roots. "Ground's still cold," he said, sniffing. "Better wait a few weeks to seed." He wiped at his nose and ended up with a muddy mustache that made me laugh. "Oh, you think you look any better, Mistress of the Manor? You should see your forehead."

I immediately wiped at my forehead with a dirty hand, and Sam laughed. I threw the muddy weed I'd just pulled, and he tried to catch it, but slipped and fell. I howled in delight—then lost my own balance and landed in the soft mud.

We battled on, pulling weeds and throwing them, trying to not laugh so we didn't get mud in our mouths. Somehow, through the scuffle, the tree roots got hauled away and the ground cleared for seeding.

"You better grow some impressive-looking cabbages after all this," Sam said, pulling mud out of his straw-colored hair.

"I don't like cabbage," I said. "I'm going to grow peas and carrots—and strawberries. *Loads* of strawberries. I'm not going to eat anything but strawberries for a month."

"Better save some for the jam." Sam looked down at himself. "Ma's gonna have a fit when she sees me. She just pressed this shirt last night. Maybe I should jump in the creek on my way home."

"You'll die of pneumonia. It's freezing."

"No deadlier than Ma's temper."

Sam finally left for home, and I went inside for a much-needed bath of my own. I tracked mud up and down the staircase, fetching clothes, but I didn't care. I felt giddy from the day. I dragged the old tub in front of the fire and filled it with steaming water, then closed the curtains and undressed.

I slid into the warm water with a contented sigh.

I'd forgotten how easy it was to be with Sam. How good his arms looked with his sleeves rolled up. The sun-kissed warmth of his skin when he worked hard. He'd undone the top buttons of his shirt, and beads of sweat had slid down his collarbone. I'd nearly forgotten.

I closed my eyes and remembered.

*Sam.*

Strong and familiar. Earthy and real. Like pulling on a favorite pair of boots, already broken in. Soft, supple leather that molded perfectly. With Sam, I didn't have to try; I was good enough.

Rowan, on the other hand, was a new pair of shoes. Fashionable and well made, but not fully comfortable. Not yet anyway. The fit had started to soften, our lives molding together. But after the other night, I felt the pinch again.

I laughed at my own absurd notions.

When the water cooled, I stepped out and pulled on a clean chemise and dress, then I wrapped my knitted shawl around my shoulders and carried the stool outside to dry my hair. It was too cold for drying hair outside, the sun nearly gone, but I wanted to savor the day.

My cheeks felt tight with sunburn. Across the yard, the garden looked tidy and ready for planting. I smiled, knowing I would think of Sam with every sprout I tended and weed I pulled. Every strawberry I plucked and slid between my teeth.

I inspected my boots and decided to let the mud dry for a few days before brushing it away. They were old boots, only used for yard work.

Movement caught my eye, and I looked up to see a figure in the distance, disappearing around the back corner of my grandfather's old stable.

Mr. Frye, Sam's father.

I stood, alarm shooting through me. He had no reason to be on my property, especially sneaking around the stable. I quickly pulled on the muddy boots and grabbed the shovel Sam had been using, then hurried along the old carriage drive that led to the stable. I rarely walked this far past the house, and the drive was thick with weeds and saplings.

Apprehension filled me, and I slowed my steps, listening.

My grandfather used to breed award-winning horses, but now, the enormous stable looked as weather-beaten and haunted as the rest of the property. I walked cautiously around the side and saw footprints in the damp earth. I tightened my grip on the shovel, my eyes scanning the area—and I saw Mr. Frye in the distance, entering the woods on the far side of the pasture. He carried something large at his side but disappeared before I could discern what it was.

"Valentine?" Rowan's voice startled me, and I whirled to see him walking toward me. "What are you doing out here—with a shovel?" He looked amused, his eyes roaming from my wet hair to my muddy boots.

I hesitated, unease running through me. I didn't want to tell Rowan about Mr. Frye; that seemed disloyal to Sam. And thinking about Sam made me flush—as if Rowan could see the day the two of us had just spent together. The warm thoughts that had coursed through my mind as I'd soaked in the tub.

"Nothing," I stammered. "I just . . . I just needed to check on something. When did you get back?"

Rowan saw my discomfort, and his smile slipped. "A few hours ago. My grandmother asked me to bring a book to Mrs. Henny. I saw you from the road, and I thought . . . I thought you might need help." He motioned to the shovel.

"Oh. Thank you, but no. I was just preparing the garden."

Rowan glanced around for the garden that wasn't there, but back near the house. His gaze settled on the tattered building beside us. "This stable is rather large for a property this size."

"My grandfather used to breed horses."

"Ah."

*New shoes, not fully comfortable.*

"Did you have a nice trip?" I asked, my tone too polite.

And he answered with good manners. "The roads were good, which is always helpful."

A shiver ran through me, and I realized the sun was gone and my hair still wet. Rowan walked me back to the house and left without coming inside. And I was relieved, suddenly weary.

A few days with his grandmother had done its work.

The next morning, I spotted Mr. Frye on my property again, watching the house from the shadows of the stable. When I looked away for a moment, he disappeared, which didn't comfort me.

My skin crawled with warning.

I tried to occupy myself with sewing for Mr. Dibble, but I heard every creak of the house. Something scraped upstairs, and I leaped to my feet. Probably just a tree branch against a window, but I picked up my scissors and cautiously made my way toward the front of the house, glancing into shadowy side rooms, pausing every few steps to listen.

On the drawing room's dusty floor, I saw footprints. My heart thundered into a faster beat. I hadn't entered that room since my thorough cleaning at Christmas. But someone had—a man, judging by the size of the footprints. I turned and listened, but the house felt still.

Slowly, I made my way through the entire house, clutching my scissors, but I found nothing else unusual.

I locked the front door. The kitchen door didn't have a lock, so I barricaded it with a worktable—which wouldn't keep Mr. Frye out but would hopefully slow him enough for me to run out the front door. If I were upstairs, I would at least hear him entering.

I returned to my sewing in the kitchen, pausing at every sound.

Sam might show up soon, but I debated telling him. He no longer cowered from his father's mean temper, but fought back, and I didn't want to cause trouble between them. Sam had to live in that over-crowded log cabin. And for all I knew, Mr. Frye was working an odd job for one of my neighbors and using my property as a shortcut, and the footprints in the drawing room were Sam's.

The day stretched with nothing unusual happening, and I started to smile at my own overactive imagination. As evening approached, I went to the backyard to put the chickens away, laughing as I coaxed a stray. I closed the coop door and turned around.

And saw Mr. Frye walking away from the stable toward the woods behind my property. Like yesterday, he carried something.

My temper sparked. He hadn't come to hurt me; he was stealing. If I looked closely in the drawing room, I would probably find something missing. I hurried back inside for my knitted shawl, tossing it around my shoulders. I hesitated, then picked up a large knife.

The sun was almost gone, casting long shadows as I trotted past the stable and across the lumpy pasture. I entered the trees and was immediately cast into gloom.

The woods behind my house were old and tangled, with no trail, but Mr. Frye had trodden a faint footpath. Old snow still spotted the ground in places. I wound my way around gnarled trunks, breathing in the musky smell of damp dirt and bark. Now and then, I stopped to listen. Then I continued on, following Mr. Frye's faint trail, trotting a little to catch up.

I finally caught a glimpse of him in the distance—and saw that he was carrying two planks of old lumber. He stopped and cocked his head, and I panicked, ducking behind a thick tree, my heart thumping in my chest.

I tightened my grip on the knife, scolding myself for cowardice. I counted to ten, then forced myself to peek out.

Mr. Frye was gone.

I moved as quickly as I dared but after some distance hadn't caught up. I stopped to listen but couldn't hear anything except the usual woodland rustlings. Something moved, and I spun around—but no one was there.

"You're a sneaky little thing, aren't you?"

I spun, catching my breath, and saw Mr. Frye only four steps away, the boards he'd been carrying on the ground, his hands curled into large fists. I fought an instinct to flee; I hadn't come all this way to run away. Instead, I lifted the knife, feigning a courage I didn't feel. "What were you doing on my property?"

He sneered, amused. He had the same faint scattering of freckles as Sam, but his green eyes were cold and his smile mean. "That's a scary-looking knife, but if you try to use it, it'll be in your gut before you take your next breath."

My heart thumped.

"You look scared, pretty girl." He took a careful step toward me, his voice dropping in warning. "Well . . . you got cause to be scared, 'cause I know your secret. I'll bet Sam don't know, but I seen it with my own eyes."

My breath caught in my lungs. My thoughts raced, connecting the pieces.

Mr. Frye was the witness who saw me kill Nigel Blackshaw. Which meant he was the person who'd told Mr. Oliver—who'd killed Mr. Oliver. And now he stood in front of me with that knowing sneer.

My heart pounded against my ribs. We were far from anything, the woods thick around us. No one would hear me scream, and I wouldn't escape the trees before he caught me.

I stalled for time, stepping back. "I . . . I don't know what you mean."

"No use pretending, pretty girl. I know you're a killer."

My eyes darted to the trees. I couldn't run faster than Mr. Frye, but I could climb higher. "You're a twisted, wicked thing," he crooned as if he liked the idea. "More twisted than Sam knows, that's for sure. He thinks the sun rises and sets by you." He gave a smirking laugh. "But your secret's safe with me. You can rot in hell for all I care—and you will for what you done. I just got one request." He waved a hand at the boards on the ground. "I need lumber to fix up the barn, and you got more than you need. Seems like a fair trade to me."

My attention shifted. "You . . . you took those from the stable?"

"A few boards, and you don't hang for murder. I wouldn't turn it down, pretty girl. I'll even help you clean up the mess. You can't leave it like that, not with spring coming."

I tilted my head, trying to make sense of his words. "Leave . . . what?"

"Give me your word, and I'll start digging a hole. Otherwise, I'll make sure they're found. And you better decide fast, or I'm liable to start talking."

*Dig a hole.* A dark dread filled my chest, pushing its way up my throat. I opened my mouth, but no words came out.

"We have a deal?" Mr. Frye pressed.

I nodded numbly, having no idea what I promised.

And yet, fearing I did.

"I gotta say, I got a whole new respect, now I seen what you done." Mr. Frye bent to pick up the boards. "Sam don't know he's got a wild-cat by the tail." He laughed as he walked away.

I watched him disappear into the trees, my heart thumping, my hand damp around the knife. Then I broke into a run in the opposite direction, darting like a terrified deer, gasping and weaving.

It was fully dark by the time I emerged from the woods. A silver moon had risen. I stumbled across the weedy pasture, breathing hard, sweat rolling down my temples. I didn't stop until I'd reached the safety of my kitchen and slammed the door behind me. I lit a lantern with shaking fingers, trying to remember everything Mr. Frye had said— trying to believe he hadn't meant what I knew he'd meant.

Hard knuckles rapped on the back door, and my heart jumped. My gaze flew to the window, and I was relieved to find the curtains closed. The glow of the lantern was visible, but I didn't think Mr. Frye would barge in. I stood still, my pulse racing.

"Valentine?" Rowan's voice called.

I almost went to the door, but some instinct held me back—a dark suspicion that I didn't want Rowan with me when I went to the stable. I stood perfectly still, waiting for him to leave.

And he finally did, his footsteps crunching. I waited a few more minutes, then crept out the back door, into the night.

I followed the glow of my lantern across the yard, then along the rutted carriage drive to the old stable in the distance. Weeds clawed at my skirt. A lifetime ago, my mother had kept her own white horse in this stable, but I raised the lantern and saw warped carriage doors that hadn't opened in two decades.

I didn't see any missing boards—which meant Mr. Frye must have taken them from inside, where I wouldn't notice.

The carriage doors were too warped to open, so I walked around to the smaller door in the back. It opened with a stiff creak, and I stepped into a square, cobwebbed room. I lifted the lantern and saw a dusty cot. When I'd explored as a child, there'd been a small table and chairs as well, but those were now gone—probably stolen by Mr. Frye.

I walked to the door at the far end of the room and entered the long, main chamber. Horse stalls stretched down both sides, disappearing into darkness. I saw Mr. Frye's tracks on the dusty floor and evidence of his theft—missing stall walls. But I hadn't come here about stolen boards. If Mr. Frye had asked for the lumber, I would have given it to him, knowing Sam would benefit.

I took a few tentative steps, lifting the lantern, and saw two dark forms on the ground at the far end of the stable. Denial rose in my mind—as the smell rose in my throat, thick and rank. But not over-powering. The nights were still frigid.

But during the day, they'd started to melt.

I took a moment to steady myself, then moved forward, breathing through my mouth. I took slow, cautious steps until I was close enough to be sure.

Father lay on his back, staring upward, his eyes wide but seeing nothing. Icy and damp, both frozen and thawed. Both alive and dead. He wore his coat. His legs lay slightly bent, his arms flung to the sides, as if he'd collapsed and then frozen solid. He looked oddly beautiful, glistening in the lantern's glow.

He'd gone out that night and never returned. Never slept in his bed. He'd been here all winter. Dead and frozen.

Birdy lay on her stomach beside him. I couldn't see her face, but I would know that coat of patchwork hides anywhere. A dark gash split the back of her head, separating her thatch of short hair.

Horror rose in my throat. *Who did this? And why?*

*Why?*

A soft crunch behind me, and I turned to see Rowan a few steps away, staring at the bodies with wide, horrified eyes. His gaze lifted to mine. "Oh, Valentine," he breathed. "Explain this to me."

# 22

A moan slid through my lips. "I don't know. I just found them. I didn't know they were here."

Rowan stepped closer, studying the damp, glistening bodies with a combination of fascination and revulsion. "They've been here all along?"

"I think so. Yes. I never come out here. This is the first time I've come out here in years." Rowan's eyes darted to mine, catching the lie, because he'd seen me here just yesterday—holding a shovel, flushing with guilt. "Not inside," I insisted, my voice pleading. "I swear it. I would have told you, Rowan. I would have told you if I knew . . . if I knew my father—" My voice broke.

His tone softened. "What brought you out here tonight?"

The smell was starting to make me nauseous. I swallowed against it. "Mr. Frye. He's been stealing lumber. That's why I was out here yesterday." I lifted a weak hand in the direction of the missing stalls. "I saw him again—and he said he knew what I'd done. I thought he meant—" I caught myself.

Rowan's attention sharpened. "What?"

"It . . . it doesn't matter. He offered to dig a hole, and that's when I knew—I just knew—" A sob escaped.

Rowan finally came to me, wrapping an arm around my shoulders. He took the lantern from my hand and led me away from the melting corpses, out the back door of the building. I gulped clean air—gasped and swallowed and pushed myself away from Rowan—away from the building—breaking into a run. I didn't stop until I'd reached the yard.

Rowan finally caught up and pulled me against his chest, his arms enfolding me. I buried my face against him. "I didn't know they were there," I croaked.

"I know. I know you didn't." His arms rocked me back and forth as I wept. "I know, Valentine."

When I stopped crying, he handed me his handkerchief, then led me inside. I sat in the rocking chair while he crouched at the fire, building it up, his back to me. But he took longer than necessary, and I could see his taut wariness. I could almost see his mind turning.

The fire grew and the room warmed, but I couldn't stop shivering. I dried my eyes with shaky hands, sniffing back tears.

They were murdered in the stable. And Mr. Oliver didn't die of a heart attack. I couldn't think who would do this—or why—but I knew that Nigel Blackshaw's death lay at the heart of it all. I'd spent all winter refusing to look at it, but it hadn't gone anywhere, following me like a shadow.

Rowan brought the hearth stool and sat close to me. "Do you think Mr. Frye killed them?"

I sniffed. "No. He thought I did it."

"You?" He frowned at me. "That's mad. Why would you kill your own father?"

I stared into the fire, unable to meet his eyes or answer his question.

"Valentine?" Rowan prodded.

A log collapsed, sending sparks upward. My chest felt hollow. I tugged my knitted shawl tighter, trying to hold myself together.

Rowan's voice stretched with suspicion. "Is there something you're not telling me?"

My ribs crumpled, and I bowed my head. The secret was too heavy. It tumbled from my mouth. "I killed your father, Rowan. My mother didn't do it. She was innocent."

He didn't move or speak. All I could hear was the crackling of the fire.

I lifted my head and found his eyes narrowed on me, his head cocked as if listening for something.

*The truth.*

I drew a shallow breath. "My father took the gun from my mother and set it on the ground. And I picked it up. Not to shoot him. I didn't mean to kill him. But it must have been cocked, because it fired. It wasn't my mother who killed your father, Rowan; it was me. But it was an accident."

A muscle in Rowan's cheek tightened. "I don't understand. Your mother confessed."

I lifted a limp shoulder. "To protect me, I suppose. I can't ask her because she isn't here." I drew a shuddering breath. "Can you ever forgive me, Rowan?"

Firelight flickered across the handsome angles of his face. He looked strangely devoid of emotion. No anger or blaming. No hatred. "There's nothing to forgive," he said evenly. "It was an accident."

I released a slow breath. All these months of dreading this moment, for no reason.

His eyes shifted. "So . . . you've known all this time and never told me? That night I walked you home from the Honor Tea, when we promised to tell each other—"

"I didn't know. I only found out after."

"After." His voice tightened. "How long have you known, Valentine?"

I swallowed. "Since Christmas."

"Christmas." He looked stunned.

"I wanted to tell you, Rowan, I did. It's been unbearable. But I swore to someone that I wouldn't. I made a solemn promise."

"A promise?" His voice hardened. "You promised me something too, but this person obviously means more to you. Who is it—Sam?"

"No!" I cried, appalled. "Not Sam."

Rowan waited, his eyebrows raised, but my mouth opened and closed without words. I couldn't mention Judge Stoker.

He gave a bitter laugh and stood. "She's been right all along."

I rose to my feet. "It isn't like that, Rowan. She isn't right."

He walked toward the door. My heart dropped, thinking he was leaving, but he turned and strode back. "What about your father and Birdy? What happened to them?" His eyebrows arched. "Another accident?"

My own temper flared. "How can you think that?"

"Because you're hiding something," he snapped. "I knew it when I caught you by surprise yesterday and you wouldn't even look at me."

"Yesterday . . . yesterday I didn't even know they were there! I was following Mr. Frye!"

"Mr. Frye? What does he have to do with all of this?" Rowan's eyes narrowed. "Did he kill them? Are you protecting him for Sam's sake?"

"No! He just happened to find them when he was stealing lumber— and I wouldn't protect someone who killed my father!"

"Unless it was Sam," he said in a hard voice. His lips curled in a smirk. "That's it, isn't it? Sam killed them, and you're protecting him. The two of you have been waiting for the ground to thaw so you can bury the evidence. But Mr. Frye found them first, so you went out there with a shovel—"

"Are you mad?" I cried. "How can you believe any of that?"

He spoke through gritted teeth. "Because there are two dead people in your stable—clearly murdered. And I saw you out there yesterday with a shovel, looking guilty—not happy that I was back in town, but wishing I would go away. So, don't try to tell me that you don't know anything about it. No more lies and secrets, Valentine!"

I saw the hurt in his eyes, and my own anger collapsed. Father and Birdy were dead, and Rowan thought his grandmother was right about me. My legs trembled. I went to the rocking chair and sank to it.

Rowan remained where he was, his fists clenched at his sides. "Just tell me the truth, Valentine."

"I'll tell you everything," I agreed numbly.

Slowly, cautiously, he lowered himself to the hearth stool—as close as he'd been a moment ago, and yet much further away.

I swallowed against my tight throat. "Back in December, Mr. Oliver told me that my mother was innocent. But I didn't believe him. Because I didn't know." I lifted my eyes to Rowan. "When you walked me home from the Honor Tea, I had no idea."

I told him about my father's strange reaction when I'd asked him about it. How I went to the rectory the next morning, looking for answers, and found Mr. Oliver poisoned. I told him about the missing blue tea tin. And Molly Gillis.

"It was the day after Christmas when I learned that my mother hanged because of me."

Rowan's expression softened as he listened. When my voice grew hoarse, he fetched me a mug of water. As I drank, he put another log on the fire, then returned to the stool.

I clutched the empty mug in my lap. "I wanted to tell you, Rowan. But then you started walking me to school. And I sat in the middle of the room. I made friends, and I just . . . I just wanted to pretend it never happened. To become someone different." I dared to look at him. "I was afraid it would change how you felt about me."

Firelight danced in his blue eyes. "It was an accident," he said quietly. "I would have understood that."

"But . . . would your grandmother?"

He didn't reply.

"I kept telling myself that my father's and Birdy's disappearances had nothing to do with it. So I could escape the past. But now, I see how foolish I've been." My throat thickened. "Someone murdered them because of what I did that night. I don't understand why, but I caused it."

"You can't blame yourself for that." He frowned at the fire. "It just doesn't make sense. Who would do something like that?"

I looked up. "It wasn't Sam."

"I know," he said gently. "I'm sorry I accused you, Valentine. I was just angry and confused and . . . I'll admit, incredibly jealous."

"I never told Sam any of this. He doesn't know I killed your father."

Something seemed to relax inside Rowan. He drew a slow breath and leaned forward, his elbows on his knees, his head bowed. His shirt was rumpled, and I resisted the urge to smooth it across his back. I wondered what it would feel like to slide my hands across him, to feel warm skin and taut muscle beneath the fabric.

He spoke to the floor. "We need to tell Sheriff Crane, and he's going to suspect you, Valentine."

The warm feeling in my belly chilled.

He continued carefully, his head bent. "Everyone thinks Birdy killed Mr. Oliver. But she's dead in your stable, and people are going to remember that you were there when Mr. Oliver died. And your father is dead too." He straightened slowly. "You're connected to all three of them, Valentine. It just doesn't look good."

Mrs. Utley would start talking and the stories would grow, unbound by facts.

A new dread rose. "Rowan . . . your grandmother . . ."

"I know," he said heavily. "I'll convince her you're innocent." But I saw the impossibility of that in his eyes.

I swallowed. "Well. When the real killer is found, people will know it wasn't me. I'll tell Sheriff Crane that I killed your father, and then he'll understand what's behind it all and find the person who did this."

"I'm not sure that's a good idea, Valentine. Admitting that you killed someone will only make you look guiltier. And . . . if my grandmother finds out that you killed my father—" His head tilted with regret. "She'll be a voice against you, Valentine. And my grandmother has a very strong voice."

I remembered what Judge Stoker had said about Mrs. Blackshaw blackmailing him into a rushed trial for my mother. If I wasn't careful, I would end up on the gallows in three days myself. Fear shivered up my spine.

"We'll go to Sheriff Crane together," Rowan said. "I'll assure him that you had nothing to do with it. I'll tell him how surprised you were when we found them."

My thoughts shifted. "You can't be part of this, Rowan. All the gossip."

"You think I care about that? Not for a moment."

But I knew that he needed to care—if not for his sake, then mine. I remembered Mrs. Henny's warning about a girl without a chaperone. "It's dark outside, Rowan, and you're here at my house alone, just the two of us. It makes me look . . ."

Rowan looked away, unable to refute it.

My voice strengthened. "It's probably best if you stop coming to my house for a while. People will be watching me closely, and it will just give them one more thing to talk about. More stories to invent."

He stared into the snapping flames, his jaw tight. It was too warm this close to the fire, and a bead of sweat slid down his temple. "I'm not going to abandon you because of a few rumors, Valentine. You don't have to go through this alone."

Mrs. Blackshaw thought that I wanted to ruin Rowan's reputation over some financial matter that happened twenty years ago. True or not, the result of this scandal would be the same. Rowan would be dragged down into the mire of my life, his name added to the nasty stories and innuendo, our relationship turned into something sordid and wicked. No senator or governor would agree to mentor him then.

But I would never convince Rowan of that. Not for his sake, only mine.

I forced my voice to harden. "All winter, I should have been searching for my father and Birdy and finding a killer. You've distracted me, Rowan. It's been a lovely distraction, but now, I need you to stay away. You have to stop visiting the house and walking me to school. You don't help me by adding those rumors on top of everything else."

He scowled at the fire; I'd succeeded in wounding him—hopefully enough to protect him.

I rose to my feet. "You should leave first. I'll wait five minutes, then go to Sheriff Crane."

Rowan stood slowly. "I can at least walk with you. I'll leave before you knock."

"No." I resisted the temptation. "Someone might see us walking together in the dark."

He attempted a weak smile. "We've walked in the dark before."

"But that has to stop. I'm alone in the world now and have to be more careful. I'll need to find a job after graduation, and no one will hire a girl who walks with boys after dark."

"Valentine." Rowan waited for me to look up and meet his riveting blue eyes. "You're not alone in the world. But I'll stay away, if that's what you want."

*Those eyes.* They set me on fire and calmed me at the same time.

"It is," I said in a tight voice. "Please go, Rowan."

And he obeyed.

Sheriff Crane lived on the far side of town. The night was inky black, the road deserted. Flickering candlelight in the windows lit the way. A curtain fluttered, and I imagined eyes watching. A dog barked in the distance.

*Father and Birdy were dead.*

With every step, that truth settled a little deeper.

They'd been gone for months, so of course that possibility had occurred to me. But seeing them—

*Poor Birdy, with her head broken.*

*And Father.*

My throat tightened with grief. Who'd done that to them? I felt numb with the shock of it. Empty with the loneliness of it. Father hadn't been much of a parent, but I'd always known that he was there, just out of sight. At night, I'd heard his heavy movements in the house. I'd felt his heartbeat.

Now—

I had no brothers or sisters. No grandparents. No aunts or uncles or cousins. Only the name of a stranger in New York City who might never receive my letter.

Perhaps the Barrons were cursed. First, Daniel and the fire. Then, financial ruin. Then I killed Nigel Blackshaw and my mother hanged. And now, Father murdered. Would I be next—hanged though I was innocent, like my mother?

I wondered if Sheriff Crane would believe me when I said I'd just discovered their bodies tonight. Or if he would arrest me at once.

I wouldn't tell him about Mr. Frye, I decided. If Mr. Frye were questioned, he would tell the sheriff I'd done it, sneering the words with certainty. And if Mr. Frye were arrested for stealing lumber, Sam's family would suffer.

*Sam's family.*

Everyone had a family.

I reached Sheriff Crane's house and knocked. He opened the door, and I told him in a strange, flat voice that I'd found my father's and Birdy's bodies in the stable. He reacted at once, gathering his coat and gloves and telling his wife that he was going out. I watched as he hitched a horse to a buggy, then he helped me up, and we rode two blocks to the home of his young watchman, who was told to fetch Mr. Wilson's wagon and meet us at the old Barron place.

Sheriff Crane asked me questions on the dark ride back to my house, and I answered as honestly as I could. *No, I hadn't known my father and Birdy were dead—or in the stable. If I were to guess, they'd been there since December. Yes, I suspected foul play. Birdy had been hit in the head, but I wasn't sure about my father. No, I didn't know who'd done it.*

I didn't know much of anything.

I sat alone in my kitchen, listening as men's voices rose and tumbled outside. I heard footsteps and wagon wheels. The whinny of a horse. An hour ticked by, and my stomach rumbled, reminding me that I'd never eaten dinner. But I had no appetite. The young watchman came into the kitchen and asked if I knew who'd left men's footprints in the soft mud outside the stable, and I said no—lying to protect both Rowan and Mr. Frye.

"Oh, Valentine," Mrs. Henny said in her hushed voice, entering the room. "This is dreadful. So very shocking. I am so very, very sorry."

It was her kindness that broke me. I bowed my head and wept, and after a few awkward pats on my shoulder, she left. But she returned with chamomile tea. She struggled to heat water at the fire, muttering about my lack of stove, then handed me a steaming cup.

The tea soothed me, and I was grateful when Mrs. Henny brought a chair from the table and sat beside me. We didn't speak, but she made sympathetic sighs and hums, and I didn't feel so alone.

I finally heard the wagon leaving and knew Father and Birdy were gone, and then Sheriff Crane came into the kitchen, looking tired and irritable. "Birdy was hit in the head, like you said. But there's no sign of injury on your father. No wounds or blood. It all seemed rather peculiar until I remembered Mr. Oliver. Must be another poisoning." His shrewd eyes tightened on me. "Don't leave town, Valentine. It's late, but I'll be back with more questions."

Mrs. Henny gave a little mewl of protest. "You can't think Valentine had anything to do with it. Maybe . . . maybe Mr. Deluca drank himself into a stupor and froze to death. And . . . and Birdy tried to help him and hit her head."

It was a ridiculous story. For one thing, Father never drank in excess. But I appreciated her defending me.

# 23

In the days that followed, it became clear that Mrs. Henny was the only one who would defend me.

The murders were the most fascinating thing to have happened in Feavers Crossing in recent memory. I felt the gossip more than heard it. Conversations halted when I entered Utley General Goods or the Duncans' bakery. Mothers grabbed their children's hands and crossed the road. Even Mr. Dibble looked uneasy as I dropped off my sewing and picked up another bundle.

I understood their wariness. Two dead bodies had lain in my stable for months, not far from where I slept. People whispered about their current state, thawing and stinking. I saw their disgust as I passed, mingled with morbid interest.

There'd always been a whiff of scandal about me, and now the smell was rank.

At school, voices faded when I neared. A crowded staircase parted. Fragile friendships disappeared and teachers avoided looking at me. In a strange way, it almost made me feel powerful. When I coughed in class, Tall Meg jumped, and when I walked down the school staircase, a cluster of freshmen girls scattered like roaches.

Rowan distanced himself, as I'd asked—which surprised me somewhat. I'd expected him to find little ways to see me. To need a few scolding reminders. In the woods, I craned my neck, expecting to see him waiting near the boulders, pretending he just happened to be there. At night, I lingered in the kitchen, listening for his stealthy knock.

But it never came.

When I did catch glimpses of him on the school grounds, he stared stonily ahead. No tender smile of reassurance. No note pressed into my hand. I worried that I'd hurt him more than I'd intended when I'd told him to stay away. I tried to remember everything I'd said that night.

I wondered what hidden fears his grandmother was finding and prodding. What smoldering embers she'd managed to fan into flame.

If I could just talk to him, I knew I could reassure him. After lunch, I lingered in Rochester Hall after the other girls had left, watching as the boys clattered down the staircase for their own lunch hour. Rowan saw me. He smiled sadly, and I expected him to detour a few steps to talk to me. But he looked away and entered the dining hall.

The irony, of course, was that he was only doing as I'd asked.

At Friday morning devotional, he sat in the middle as usual, between Philly and Lucy. And I sat in the back corner, watching his back, craving some small indication that he knew I was there—that he knew I'd cried myself to sleep the night before, holding my father's shirt. But when Rowan finally glanced back, he found me watching and his eyes quickly darted away, filled with . . .

*Guilt*, I realized in surprise.

An uneasy feeling crept into my chest. Why should Rowan feel guilty? *I* was the one who'd coldly ordered him to stay away.

Absurdly, the more he avoided me, the more I sought him out. I finally found him alone near the school library, but when he saw me approaching, he stepped back, his face flaming with that same inexplicable guilt. "I'm sorry—I can't. She has eyes everywhere. I don't even dare write to you. Please, just know that I'm thinking about you." He turned and hurried up a back staircase.

I stood frozen, staring after him.

His grandmother had ordered him to stay away from me.

And he'd obeyed.

I reminded myself that it was what I wanted as well. That it was best for both of us. Rowan wouldn't avoid me forever, only until the real killer was found and I was no longer watched so closely.

Still, I felt abandoned.

That afternoon, as I left school, Sheriff Crane stood near a black carriage, beckoning me with a crook of his finger. I approached with reluctance, feeling the curious stares of my classmates on my back.

"Shall we speak inside?" he suggested, holding the carriage door open. "Bit more private."

I stepped up into the carriage, my heart hammering. It wasn't as nice as Judge Stoker's carriage, with sagging upholstery and a musty odor. Sheriff Crane sat across from me, his long legs brushing mine.

He didn't waste time on pleasantries. "Dr. Pritchard says that your father was poisoned like Mr. Oliver. Which certainly implies that the same person killed both of them."

"What about Birdy?" I asked.

"That blow to her head did the deed. Perhaps she just happened to be in the wrong place at the wrong time."

I'd already reached the same conclusion. I couldn't tell Sheriff Crane that this was about Nigel Blackshaw's death, but a few helpful nudges might point him in the right direction. "I think my father was murdered first. He left the house one night in December and didn't show up for work the next morning. The next day, Mr. Oliver died. But Birdy witnessed his death, and then stayed at my house for a few days before she disappeared. The killer must have lured her to the stable somehow. She was killed because she was a witness."

Sheriff Crane's eyebrows arched. "Stayed at your house? And yet, when I knocked on your door after Mr. Oliver's death, you assured me that you hadn't seen her."

My face warmed. "You were going to arrest her for murder, and I knew she was innocent—as now proven by her death."

His voice bit with annoyance. "Your lies don't help me find this killer, Valentine. Is there anything else you'd like to confess?"

I swallowed the real confession. "No. Did you ever find Mr. Oliver's missing tea tin?"

"No, but I doubt your father sat down to a cup of tea in that abandoned stable. For him, it was probably a swig of liquor." He watched me closely with his shrewd eyes. "It has occurred to me, Valentine, that the killer must have known both the rector and your father fairly well to have shared food and drink with them. Can you think of anyone like that?"

A shaft of afternoon sunlight came through the window, making the carriage too warm. "One of my neighbors, I suppose. The church isn't far from my house."

Sheriff Crane's eyebrows lifted. "Your father was friendly with your neighbors?"

"Well, no," I admitted.

"And Birdy? She was shy of strangers, which meant she must have known this person rather well to be led into the stable. Which means we're looking for someone who was close to all three of them. I made a list of people who match that description." Sheriff Crane didn't blink as he reached into his inner pocket and pulled out a slip of paper. "Would you like to know who I came up with, Valentine? Only one person." He turned the paper so I could see my name.

My pulse throbbed in my temples. "I didn't kill them. Why would I?"

"Why indeed?" The shaft of light hit Sheriff Crane's face, deepening the shadows below his cheekbones. "On the surface, you don't seem like the sort of girl who would murder someone. But then, I wouldn't have suspected it of your mother either. I grew up with Isabella." His lips quirked. "Even fancied her for a while. But she was far above my reach. Poor Nigel wasn't so lucky."

I shrank back against the carriage seat. No weapon could have stabbed deeper.

"Some are saying that murder must run in your veins. But I wonder if it isn't more of a learned behavior, handed down from mother to daughter." The sheriff held up a heavy book with a dark red cover. "Look familiar?"

I tilted my head to read the title—and drew a startled breath. It was a book on Greek and Roman mythology that I'd borrowed from the school library. "Where did you get that?"

"Your bedroom, late this morning."

Fury crawled up my spine, tangled with fear. "What were you doing in my bedroom?"

"Searching your house while you were in school. As you have already demonstrated, I can't trust you to tell me the truth." He flipped a few pages and held up an archaic sketch of a pagan god. "Looks like witchcraft to me. I've heard tales of it still existing in certain families."

I gave an incredulous laugh. *"Witchcraft?* Are you serious? That's *mythology!"* I could see that the word meant nothing to him. "Ancient religions and gods."

His eyebrows arched: I'd proved his point.

"Why would I kill my own father? And Mr. Oliver, who was kind to me? And Birdy, a close friend? I *loved* those people! My heart is broken that they're gone!"

Sheriff Crane studied me in the shaft of light coming through the carriage window. "I confess, that is the question that perplexes me. I just spoke to the headmaster, hoping for clarity, but he only assured me that you're an excellent student of good character."

I was surprised that Mr. Foley had spoken well of me. But then, he wouldn't want the scandal of a student hanged for murder. "May I go? Or are you going to arrest me for studying mythology?"

"Mind your tongue. I am on your side."

"Are you? You sound ready to burn me at the stake."

"If you didn't kill anyone, you have nothing to fear." His eyes didn't blink.

And my face warmed, because of course I had killed someone.

He leaned closer. "It may surprise you, Valentine, but I am the reason you aren't already behind bars. I used to see you in town with Birdy and was impressed by your kindness to her. So, I remain unconvinced. But people are screaming for justice, and you have drawn the ire of the wrong person."

*Mrs. Blackshaw.* "I didn't kill them, I swear."

Sheriff Crane's voice dropped to a warning purr. "Sometimes, the truth doesn't matter. Sometimes, you just have to be smarter than they are. Stay away from the graveyard; it makes you look like you're obsessed with death. Stay away from Mrs. Blackshaw's grandson. And for heaven's sake—no, for the sake of your own immortal soul—put a Bible on your nightstand, not this pagan *corruption!*" He held up the book, then slammed it onto the bench beside him. He looked away, releasing an impatient breath.

My heart pounded like a drum.

"I have a hard time believing you killed them, Valentine, but there are stronger voices than mine in this town. I cannot stop an angry mob. You understand?"

I couldn't speak.

He pushed the carriage door open. "You may go."

I stepped down. My legs felt shaky as I walked away. With every step, I felt his eyes on my back. He didn't want to believe I'd murdered anyone, but in the end, that might not matter.

I should have been looking for a killer all winter, not flirting with Rowan, not drawing the wrath of Mrs. Blackshaw.

I was glad to finally round the back corner of the school stable, putting me out of view.

But a few steps later, I halted, hearing voices inside. *Rowan's voice.* My heart leaped. Finally, a chance to talk to him—to tell him I was lonely and scared and couldn't stand the way he turned to stone every time we passed on campus. Ever since that night of sewing flags at the Hennys', something had been broken between us, and I felt a clawing need to set it right.

I peered around the stable door—then jerked back, catching my breath.

Slowly, I looked again.

Rowan stood near a far stall with Philly. He said something in a low voice, and she gave a pretty laugh. Then he entered the stall and led his horse out.

"They're always so tall up close," she said, looking nervous.

"Don't worry, he's gentler than he looks. Here, put your foot in the stirrup."

She lifted her foot, showing a long stretch of stockinged leg, then he grabbed her waist and helped her swing up into the saddle.

"My mother would be horrified. She thinks it's indecent, riding astride."

"Here." Rowan shook out Philly's skirt, covering her leg. "Now slide forward. Here I come." He swung himself up behind her, and she gave a little laugh as their bodies slid together. "You comfortable?" he asked, touching her waist.

"I'm not sure. It's so high." She wiggled into a better position, closer to Rowan. "Don't go too fast."

"I won't. I've got you." His arms reached around her waist to take the reins, then he gave the horse a gentle kick and they rode out of the stable toward town.

I sank into a crouch, suddenly light-headed and nauseous. I shut my eyes, trying to forget the image. Trying to forget Philly's pretty laugh and Rowan's gentle reassurances. *I've got you.*

When did this start? Or was it nothing new? Had he been stopping at her house before coming to mine? Flirting with her at school, then meeting me in the woods?

I didn't know. I couldn't think.

I felt foolish—and fooled.

Had I imagined the way Rowan watched me in my kitchen, his eyes warm with attraction? The way he walked closer than necessary in the woods, twirling my curls around his finger? Half the girls at Drake watched Rowan Blackshaw with dreamy-eyed infatuation. Was I just one of many?

I forced myself to stand and walk home, my chest crawling with uncertainty, my head throbbing with doubt. I rethought every moment Rowan and I had spent together. Every word we'd spoken. Every look we'd shared that might have meant something.

I had his drawing.

That night, I brought it into bed with me and studied it by the light of a single candle, unable to pull my eyes away. I saw the full softness of my lips. The gentle curve of my cheek. The beauty he'd imagined. This was how he'd seen me that day. I felt sure of it. Whatever feelings he'd put into this drawing had been real.

But temporary.

A few weeks ago, I'd found a baby bird on our walk to school and returned it to its nest, then insisted we watch for a while, making us late for school. As I'd watched the nest, Rowan had watched me.

"Maybe you really are a woodland fairy," he'd mused with a lazy smile. "Do you talk to the animals, Valentine, and tell them all your secrets? I want to know your secrets." The purr in his voice had sent my stomach floating into my throat.

But maybe Mrs. Henny was right. Maybe I'd been nothing but a rebellious fascination, not a serious alliance.

And now, I'd become too dangerous.

I couldn't forget the look on Rowan's face as he'd stared at the melting, rotting corpses in my stable. Not just abhorrence, but fear. *Oh, Valentine. Explain this to me.* For a moment, he'd actually wondered if I'd done it—or protected the true killer. Suddenly, his grandmother's twisted opinions had rung true. He'd enjoyed his winter flirtation with me, but seeing those bodies had slapped him awake, and he'd moved back to safer ground.

Back to his grandmother.

Back to Philly.

And I'd been foolish enough to push him out the door.

❦

Sam returned to town the next day. He came to me as soon as he heard, waiting for me in the woods after school. For one tumbling heartbeat, I thought it was Rowan walking toward me—then I recognized Sam's broader silhouette and had to swallow my disappointment.

But as soon as his strong arms enfolded me, my bones melted. "Oh, Sam," I breathed.

His embrace felt safe and familiar. Devoted. He smelled of homespun cotton and long summer days and years of fishing side by side, not needing to speak, just listening to the gurgle of the creek.

"It's going to be all right," he murmured against my hair. "I'm home now, and I'm not going anywhere."

I believed him and wept.

# 24

Sam became my rock, rarely leaving my side. He offered to bring a bed-roll and sleep in the kitchen, but I told him it wasn't necessary and people would talk.

Mostly, I didn't want Rowan to hear that Sam was leaving my house in the mornings—proof that his suspicions had been right. I wouldn't give him that satisfaction.

I tried to push Rowan from my mind. I'd wasted months lost in some spell, imagining the impossible, not appreciating the best thing in my life.

*Sam.*

He stood next to me as Birdy was laid to rest in the graveyard she'd loved, next to Ida Howe. Sam and I were the only people there—except the new rector, Mr. Newland, who hadn't even known Birdy. A wooden cross would mark the spot for now, but as soon as I could afford it, I intended to buy her a headstone to match Ida's.

The next day, Sam borrowed a wagon from Hale Glass and drove me to a neighboring town for Father's funeral; Feavers Crossing didn't have a Catholic church. We sat side by side in a vast, echoing chamber full of empty pews, while a priest I didn't know officiated over a ceremony I didn't understand.

I'd sent Molly Gillis a note about the funeral, but she didn't show up. Sam told me he'd seen another man walking her son to school. I tried not to judge her too harshly; she was a young widow with two boys to feed.

My mood settled as Sam and I rode home in the wagon along quiet country roads. Father's body now lay at rest, and the day was beautiful, full of spring. Green grass sprouted between piles of dirty snow. Sam allowed the horse to clop lazily, the reins loose in his hands.

As we neared my house, I asked Sam to stop at my mother's grave. I waited while he secured the horse, then he helped me down. We walked through the church graveyard and stepped over the old rock wall into unhallowed ground.

The white marble headstone glowed in the warm light of late afternoon. I slipped my hand into Sam's as we stood in front of it.

ISABELLA BARRON DELUCA
MAY SHE FIND REST

I felt calm as I read the inscription, my emotions already spent on Father.

I glanced around at the forlorn little graveyard of criminals and heathens and wondered how things could have gone so wrong. An argument late at night. The mistake of a six-year-old. A hasty trial and hanging—because that's what Mrs. Blackshaw had wanted.

"It's a fine headstone," Sam said quietly.

"Yes." My attention sharpened. Who'd paid for it? Not Father, who patched the worn soles of his shoes. Maybe the same person who'd given him a box of money that he couldn't bring himself to spend.

Mrs. Blackshaw could afford it. But why buy a headstone for the woman who'd murdered her son?

*Because she knew Isabella Barron Deluca didn't kill anyone.*

My heart beat faster. I thought back over everything I knew. I could picture Mrs. Blackshaw bringing tea to Mr. Oliver, but I couldn't picture her killing my father in an old stable half-hidden by weeds. She must have killed him somewhere else and paid a servant to move him. Wilky would do it, the old man who drove her carriage.

*No, Wilky was too feeble.*

*But Rowan was strong enough.*

My head revolted at the image. I pushed it away.

But it crept back.

Rowan claimed to have been asleep when I shot his father, but what if he saw everything? His grandmother wasn't there that night; she didn't know the truth; it was Rowan who'd known all these years. A sleepy six-year-old who didn't speak up and found out later that his silence had caused the wrong person to hang. For eleven years, he'd been tormented by guilt, knowing an injustice had been done.

Was that why I fascinated him—morbid curiosity in the girl who'd killed his father?

My pulse raced. I thought back to when I'd told him that I was holding the gun, trying to remember if he'd looked genuinely surprised or only pretended. I wasn't sure.

After eleven years, Rowan had finally confided in the Reverend Mr. Oliver—and immediately panicked, fearing people would find out that his silence had caused the hanging of an innocent woman.

He poisoned Mr. Oliver.

My heart beat heavily. I was making things up. And yet, it made sense.

I thought back to the night when I'd talked to Father about my mother's innocence. He must have gone to the Blackshaws' house because he knew Rowan was the only other witness. Rowan assured him that he would keep my secret . . . then followed Father home . . .

*No. No. No.*

Rowan wasn't like that. He was willing to give up his dream of being an architect so he could fight for noble causes.

I pressed my fingers against my temples. My head felt heavy, my stomach queasy.

"Let's get you home," Sam murmured.

We rode the short distance home in the wagon. Sam stopped in front of the carriage drive and helped me down. "Go inside. I'll return the wagon to Hale and walk back."

"Thank you, Sam."

The house felt empty without him. I made eggs—including enough for Sam, who ate four times what I did. I managed to eat a little, then sat near the fire, listening for him. I hadn't slept properly in days and felt shaky with exhaustion.

I awoke to Sam lifting me in his arms. I protested, but he murmured, "Go back to sleep," and it was a relief to sag against him. To be carried with so little effort. I felt the strength of his arms and gentle sway of his steps as he carried me up the staircase, and I was sorry when we reached my room. He carefully placed me on my bed, then turned to leave.

"Thank you," I murmured, sliding under the quilt.

Sam paused, then came back and sat at the edge of my bed. But he kept his hands on his lap; this wasn't an attempt at seduction. "I haven't wanted to ask," he said carefully. "But I haven't seen much of Rowan lately."

I shifted and sat up. Moonlight came through the window, illuminating half of Sam's face, casting the other half into shadow. "I think that's over," I said quietly.

He sat perfectly still, looking at the floor. "I worry about you living here alone, after what happened to your pa. I was going to ask you again about sleeping in the kitchen. But I know that isn't proper, and you worry about gossip. So, I thought—" His green eyes lifted to meet mine. "Maybe we should get married."

I bent my knees up to my chest, drawing a breath.

"I know you think we're too young, but it makes sense, now that your pa is gone." Sam kept his voice low, almost devoid of emotion. But in his eyes, I saw how he felt—how he'd always felt about me. "If we get married, I can live here properly. I'll fix up the house. Make it nice again. I can clear the pasture and plant crops this summer. I'll work at Hale and you can work for Mr. Dibble. You're a good seamstress. I know we're young, but we're both hard workers. And in a few years, when we're ready, we can start a family. We'll fill up this house the way it should be, the way it used to be, and you won't be so alone."

My heart thumped in a slow, steady beat.

Sam waited, his chest rising and falling. I saw his pulse throbbing in his throat. I saw his broad shoulders and strong arms. It would be a relief to lie in those arms at night, warm and protected. Sam's friendship had always been the one sure thing in my life. He loved me, I knew that, and expected little in return, waiting patiently for me to look up and see what stood in front of me—a straw-haired boy who'd grown into a man, without losing his scattered freckles and easy smile and green eyes that watched me with fierce devotion. My throat tightened.

"Oh, Sam."

I leaned forward and touched my lips to his in the kiss that should have happened a long time ago. A kiss that felt natural. I already knew the sun-warmed scent of his skin, and I wasn't surprised by the feel of his lips—masculine, but gentle. The kiss was tentative at first; neither of us had ever done this before. But our lips soon warmed and softened, our heads tilting into one another, his arms sliding around me.

Sam was the first to pull back, his hand moving to hold my face, his eyes searching mine, hardly daring to hope. My gaze fell to his lips. They hung slightly parted, moist from our kiss.

I pushed the quilt out of the way, and we moved together at the same time, our mouths finding each other again. My hand curved around his neck, and his arms pulled me closer—then closer still. My mouth opened, and the kiss deepened.

A year ago, Sam's younger brother Dan had jeered when he'd guessed we'd never kissed, bragging about his own conquests, until Sam had attacked him with embarrassed fury. But I knew Dan had never kissed a girl like this. I imagined few girls had ever felt so completely sheltered and adored in a boy's arms. And desired.

Finally, we stilled, holding each other close, our chests rising and falling.

"I love you, Valentine. I'm half-mad with it." His voice sounded raw against my cheek. "I've tried to not rush you, like you asked. But with your pa gone, I thought maybe . . ."

He fell quiet, waiting, his body still.

I loved him too. I must. I loved the way his arms felt around me and the vibration of his voice against my skin. But my throat tightened around the words.

He dipped his head so he could see my face in the moonlight. "Do you love me, Valentine?"

"I do. I love you, Sam." As I said it, I knew it was true.

His entire body seemed to settle. He closed his eyes and rested his forehead against mine, releasing a slow breath. "Say it again," he whispered.

"I love you, Sam."

His mouth slid over mine, more confident now, and my own lips responded, melting into his. But my mind felt busy, trying to catch up. His hand slid to my waist, tugging me closer, and I was suddenly aware of where we were, alone on my bed. I carefully extracted myself, and he let me go, grinning, keeping hold of one of my hands. "We'll be married soon, and I won't have to leave your room."

My own smile felt too thin, my body suddenly cautious. "It's all happening too fast, Sam. I need time to think before I promise anything. Before we're engaged."

He didn't seem concerned. "There's no rush. We love each other, and that's what matters. I can't believe I finally told you. You don't know how many times I've wanted to." He gave a little laugh, unable to stop smiling. "I'll let you sleep now." He stood and reluctantly let go of my hand, then bent low and kissed me again, his hands holding my face. "My future wife," he whispered, his thumb stroking my temple. And there was a part of me, low and deep, that didn't want him to go.

But another part of me felt tight with uncertainty. Was this what I wanted?

It had to be.

*Don't think about Rowan.*

His footsteps descended the staircase, light with relief. I lay back and closed my eyes, remembering the warmth of his mouth on mine, his large hand on my waist, drawing me closer. I imagined myself as Sam's wife. He would fix up the house, and we would live here together. Sleep in this room. It felt right. It felt solid and real, not some hopeless wisp of yearning.

And yet, some part of it also felt wrong.

I rolled onto my side so I could see the dresser drawer where I kept Rowan's sketch of me.

And when I awoke in the morning, I was still facing it.

# 25

---

It was hard to think straight with Sam always there, smiling and reaching for me. I kept reminding him that we weren't engaged, and he promised to not tell anyone otherwise, but I felt the pressure of his expectations.

I'd fallen into a fast-moving river and wasn't sure if I should swim to safety or let it carry me away.

I did love Sam and could picture our life together. He talked of roof shingles and new windows and installing a stove, then laughed at his big ideas.

"It all takes money, but we have time." He said his ma was warming up to the idea of me as a daughter-in-law.

"You weren't supposed to tell anyone," I chided.

"I couldn't help myself. I was so happy that night. She won't tell anyone."

"Sam . . ."

"I *know*," he droned, smiling. "We're not engaged . . . *yet.*"

I saw the trust in his eyes and felt the adoration in his kisses and wanted to feel the same way.

But it all felt shadowed by a lie.

I'd never told Sam that I was the one who'd killed Nigel Blackshaw, but I would have to tell him everything before he took sacred vows and joined his life with mine.

I felt haunted by death. At night, I saw their faces: Mr. Blackshaw with his startled eyes, falling backward; Mama sliding her head through a noose; Mr. Oliver, with his kind smile and wind-ruffled hair, gently telling me that my mother was innocent; Father, trying to fix my mistake, accepting a swig of tainted liquor on a cold night; and Birdy, coming to my house for protection, only to die in the stable.

Sam would be hurt that I hadn't trusted him with the truth, after I'd promised him that I wouldn't lie and keep secrets.

He never mentioned the rumors about me circulating through town, but I knew he must be hearing them. Sam deserved better than a wife suspected of murder.

But in my heart, I knew that wasn't the real reason I felt guilty every time we kissed.

Rowan.

I tried to push him out of my head, scolding myself for foolishness. There'd never been any real hope for us; our lives were too different, and his powerful grandmother despised me. I forced myself to remember his hands on Philly's waist as he'd helped her onto the horse. I even tried to convince myself he was the murderer.

But my heart never believed any of it. My heart remembered his eyes watching me as I peeled potatoes, as warm as any caress. His voice near my ear as we walked along the trail, low and teasing. His dark hair tumbling forward as he sketched at the table, lost in his own world—which somehow felt like my world too.

I missed him with a sharp pang. I couldn't shake the feeling that this was all some terrible misunderstanding. That all we needed was a moment alone. A moment to talk.

At night, I stared at his drawing of me, and tears slid down my cheeks. Foolish tears, because I had Sam, who loved me more than any girl deserved. Certainly, more than I deserved.

I told myself a thousand things.

But none of it stopped the longing.

◆

Sam reluctantly left town on a three-day trip for Hale Glass, and I was grateful for some time to myself. Sam hinted that he might buy a ring on his trip, and I wanted to accept him, but not with my heart so tangled.

And only Rowan could untangle it. I had three days before Sam got down on one knee, and since Rowan wouldn't come to me, I would go to him.

Friday night, I draped a dark shawl over my head and crept through town, slipping through the shadows; the sight of the Deluca girl on a dark night was enough to set off a wave of hysteria lately. A damp fog rolled in as I walked, which helped hide me.

The Blackshaws didn't live in the Meriwethers' new, fashionable neighborhood but on a narrow street lined by Feavers Crossings' oldest families. I had a vague plan to look through downstairs windows, hoping to find Rowan alone. I would tap on the window and draw him outside. Or I could knock on the kitchen door and convince a servant to fetch him without telling Mrs. Blackshaw. He'd mentioned the cook a few times, as if they were close.

There was also the possibility that Rowan would inform me, in a polite voice, that he'd enjoyed our friendship but was now too busy with the bank or some other responsibility. He would use his good manners, not mentioning Philly—or the fact that the entire town thought I'd murdered three people. He would avoid my gaze.

But I'd rather face that hard truth than wonder forever. Once I'd closed that part of my heart, I could move on with Sam.

I turned the corner and saw a carriage in front of the Blackshaws' house and a man and a woman approaching the door. I stepped back into the shadows and watched as they were ushered inside. Then another carriage arrived.

A dinner party, of course. I wavered, unsure what to do.

Then I crept around to the side of the house.

The parlor drapes were half-closed, but one by one, the guests passed in front of the opening: Mayor Banks and his new wife, who was much younger than he was; a wealthy businessman named Mr. Bloomfield and his wife; a fashionable young couple who'd recently returned from London.

Not a large party, then, and rather young for Mrs. Blackshaw, but all of them influential.

Rowan moved into view, and my chest tightened. He looked handsome, of course, but pale against his dark dinner jacket—and older, surrounded by grown men. They hovered near him, assessing the young man who would soon control most of the county's financing—laughing too hard at his jokes, as eager to impress as they were to assess.

Mrs. Blackshaw slid into view, elegant in dark blue. She watched Rowan with a look of smug satisfaction, then wandered closer and whispered something in his ear. He nodded and murmured back with no hint of defiance. No rebellion. Whatever the topic, they seemed in complete accord.

My stomach dropped in disappointment when Philly Henny and her mother arrived. They seemed an odd addition to such a prominent gathering, especially without the Meriwethers; Philly tended to be shy without Lucy. But dinner was announced, which meant no one else was expected, and Mrs. Blackshaw led the way through the doorway.

I moved to the next window to see into the elegant dining room. Mrs. Blackshaw sat at the head of the table, her back to me, and Rowan sat at the far end, with Philly next to him. I tucked myself into the shadow of a hedge, hidden from view, but still close enough to make out a few voices.

And it soon became clear why the Hennys had been included. More than once, Mrs. Blackshaw drew attention to the lovely girl sitting next to her grandson. *How pretty Philomena looked in that color. Did she enjoy gardening as much as her mother? She'd heard that Philomena's French was exceptional.* Philly flushed and gave simple answers—which somehow only made her look lovelier. And, as Mrs. Blackshaw's approval became obvious, Philly gained confidence, her smile relaxing. She wore dark green—a more sophisticated color than she usually wore—which looked nice against her strawberry-blond hair and luminous skin. She looked older. She looked beautiful.

And Rowan noticed, his gaze lingering. He murmured something near her shoulder that made her stifle a laugh.

Mrs. Henny watched her daughter's success with wide-eyed fascination. She looked like a gray mouse invited to dine at the palace. But no one paid her any attention; all eyes were on Philly.

This dinner party was a test, I realized, which explained the younger guests. Mrs. Blackshaw wanted to make sure that the daughter of a humble widow could stand up to the social rigors of the Blackshaw name.

And from what I could see, Philly was passing the test.

Disappointment tightened my throat like a bitter pill.

This was Rowan's life beyond my kitchen. Dinner parties with wealthy businessmen and politicians. Finance deals worth thousands of dollars. Servants in white gloves. The sparkle of crystal. The gleam of silver. I'd never been naive enough to imagine myself in this room, but I had been naive enough to believe Rowan preferred my humble kitchen to his life here. And maybe he'd believed it himself for a while, enthralled by his woodland fairy.

But here, I saw the truth—a truth Rowan had seen two weeks ago, staring at two decomposing bodies. He'd been the first to feel the slap of reality, but I'd finally caught up.

I gave myself a moment to mourn, watching them, my chest pulled by a heavy weight.

But tears didn't come, only numb acceptance. This was the only resolution that made sense. Rowan was never going to leave his life of prominence to join mine. And, in the last few weeks, it had become clear that I couldn't join his. I couldn't even blame him for his desertion. I felt no anger or resentment, only a sad sense of finality. Our friendship had been real, our attraction genuine. But it was over.

I'd reached the bottom of my billowing sky, and the landing was blessedly gentle.

My gaze drifted to Mrs. Blackshaw, who skillfully directed the conversation. Her questions of the other guests were probing but subtle. She doled out compliments with careful precision, not generosity. Her insults insinuated but were never obvious enough to draw offense. With just an arch of her eyebrow, she halted the mayor's wife in the middle of a sentence, easily steering the conversation back to her own topic.

No wonder she liked dinner parties; she was a master.

The suspicions I'd had about Mrs. Blackshaw at my mother's grave rose again.

She might have followed Nigel to our house that night to stop him from running away with a Barron. She saw me shoot him and had known that a child wouldn't be punished. But someone had to pay, so she'd manipulated Judge Stoker into a hasty trial and hanging. Eleven years later, she'd confided in Mr. Oliver.

I stared at her rigid spine and straight shoulders and believed her capable of murder.

At the moment, she was occupied with guests, her servants busy in the kitchen.

I moved quickly, before I lost my nerve, creeping back through the garden, around the back corner of the house—past the noisy kitchen, clattering with activity. I found another back door, glanced over my shoulder—

And slipped inside.

I stood in a dark hall, my pulse racing. In the distance, I heard the soft murmur of voices and clink of dishes. I'd never been inside the Blackshaws' house, but it was similar in layout to most of the older houses in Feavers Crossing. I stood still for several breaths, considering my own brash stupidity—then I took a few stealthy steps and entered what I guessed would be Mrs. Blackshaw's office.

Embers glowed in a small fireplace, casting enough light for me to see the hulking desk and chair. Muffled voices came through the wall, but no one would come in here for hours. I carefully closed the door and heavy drapes, then dared to light a candle.

I quickly searched the room, opening drawers and boxes and ledgers, carefully returning everything to the way I'd found them. I wasn't seeking anything specific. I wasn't even hopeful of finding anything; Mrs. Blackshaw wasn't the sort of woman who kept a diary full of confessions. But it was a place to start.

I discovered a secret compartment at the back of a desk drawer with two bank boxes like the one hidden in Father's bedroom floor. And when I opened them, I saw a similar amount of money—even the same yellow string tied around the bills.

A cold feeling crept through me. Why would Mrs. Blackshaw have given Father a box of money? Was it connected to my mother's hanging? Blood money that he didn't want to see, let alone spend?

I closed the bank boxes, trying to settle my racing thoughts for now. Below the boxes, I found a ledger filled with lists of names and dates, with jotted notes. I recognized some of the names. I turned the page and drew a quick breath when I saw Judge Stoker's name with two words beside it: *falsified evidence.*

This was Mrs. Blackshaw's list of secrets. Her weapons.

The papers stacked below the ledger were neatly organized with notes clipped to each document. I quickly thumbed through them and found Judge Stoker's name. I didn't read the attached paper, just rolled it up and slid it into my pocket; I didn't want to know his secret.

I finished searching through the documents, just to be sure—and drew a surprised breath when I saw a letter at the bottom, browned with age, signed by Silas Barron, my grandfather. I held it closer to the candle.

*Josephine,*

*There is no point in meeting again. You know my feelings. Continue with this sham of a wedding if you must. I will not show up.*

*Silas*

He sounded angry. Even back then, Mrs. Blackshaw had been a formidable opponent. For forty years, she'd kept my grandfather's rejection, justifying her hatred for the Barrons. I hesitated, then folded the letter and added it to my pocket. I didn't want a piece of my grandfather trapped in Mrs. Blackshaw's drawer of secrets.

I straightened, letting my eyes skim the room, but nothing else drew suspicion, and I didn't dare linger. I blew out the candle and crept out of the room, back toward the door.

But I paused at the base of the back staircase, glancing upward.

My heart beat faster. If I was discovered, I would end up in jail, accused of murder along with trespassing. But watching Rowan and Philly had pricked a nerve. He'd made his choice—and now I made mine. I glanced over my shoulder, then hurried up the narrow staircase, my breath held.

Unlike his grandmother, Rowan was the sort to leave evidence. Not a diary, maybe, but something.

Upstairs, I found the hall dark and deserted. I glanced into the first room and knew at once that it was Rowan's. I entered and carefully closed the door behind me, knowing I didn't have much time. I stood still, my heart racing, terrified by my own audacity. How would I explain my presence if I were found? There was no explanation.

But I didn't care. I felt reckless. I shut the curtains and lit the candle on his desk, then turned.

My chest tightened with endearment when I saw the disarray: stacks of books on the desk and floor; framed artwork crowding the walls; his own loose sketches everywhere—tacked on the walls, scattered across the desk, dropped on the floor. His old leather satchel hung from the bedpost.

I picked up a sketchbook and quickly thumbed through it. The dates on the pages were from last September and October. I saw a drawing of two cows in a pasture; a tall, angular house—his own, I realized; a rough sketch of Simon Greene at the piano. I'd seen these scenes a hundred times, but never the way Rowan drew them. As if he saw something in them that I didn't.

I started to shut the sketchbook, but a drawing at the back caught my attention. I turned to it—and released a little whimper of surprise. It was a drawing of me in the school library, reading. Rowan must have been watching and sketching from across the room.

I turned to the next page and my heart beat faster; it was another drawing of me—standing near a tree, staring fixedly in one direction. A few loose curls blew in a breeze. I didn't imagine myself this way—so lean and feminine, so content in solitude.

The next drawing showed only my head and shoulders, but it was so beautifully detailed, I half expected the girl to move. I doubted he'd drawn it in one sitting. He must have finished it at home, perhaps sitting in this room. At the bottom, he'd scrawled the date—last October. Before the Honor Tea.

My heart swelled.

There were five drawings hidden at the back of the book, all of me, all dated before the Honor Tea. None of Philly. None of Lucy. I found an older sketchbook with two more drawings of me at the back, dated from last spring.

For more than a year, Rowan had been drawing me. Studying the curve of my cheek. Sketching my lips with velvety softness. Shadowing the hollow of my throat with a moistened finger. Secrets held within a secret.

A lump of longing rose in my throat. *It didn't matter.* In the end, Rowan had chosen his grandmother and Philly.

One sketch drew me back to it—the one showing only my head and shoulders. Something about it thrummed with familiarity. The way I looked to the side, my lips slightly parted. The way my eyes—

I inhaled a sharp breath.

It was the painting slashed by Mrs. Blackshaw. Rowan was the artist, not Mr. Oliver. Now that I knew his work, it was obvious. He must have been taking art lessons from Mr. Oliver. When the rector died, Mrs. Blackshaw had panicked, afraid her grandson's infatuation with me would be discovered. She'd hunted for the painting and destroyed it.

A pan crashed downstairs—muffled and far away, but it jolted me back to the present. I closed the sketchbook, blew out the candle, and slipped from the room.

Judge Stoker's house wasn't far from the Blackshaws'. I knocked, and he answered himself, wearing a housecoat, looking annoyed by the interruption. When he saw that it was me, his thick eyebrows lifted.

"Valentine?"

I held out the document. "Thank you for my education."

His eyes scanned the paper, then darted up to my face. "How did you get this?"

"It's probably best if you don't know. Good night, Judge Stoker." I turned away.

When I got home, I added a log to the fire, then found Mr. Oliver's clay pitcher and poured the slashed painting onto the table. I assembled the pieces, my fingers trembling. Part of my shoulder was missing. Holes gaped where the knife had stabbed. But it was the same girl, the same artist. I touched the rich colors with my fingertips.

*Rowan.*

The girl looked monstrous. Her cheek scarred by a slash. One eye blinded. Her neck severed and pieced back together. But it was something to hold on to, a remembrance of what I'd almost had.

And what I would never have.

# 26

---

Sunday morning, I visited my mother's marble headstone and Birdy's wooden cross.

As I stood at Birdy's grave, I heard the closing hymn being sung inside the church and moved to watch from behind a large stone monolith as the congregation poured out.

Mrs. Utley was the first to emerge, already whispering in the ear of a friend. Her quiet husband followed, yawning. And then Mrs. Meriwether, beautiful like always—but looking a bit lonely; her husband only attended church on Easter and Christmas.

Lucy hurried past her mother, heading for the front corner of the churchyard where her friends usually gathered.

A sinking feeling ran through me when Rowan and Philly walked out together. Philly wore a pretty yellow dress with a straw bonnet, and Rowan looked perfectly tailored, as always, every hair in place. Mrs. Blackshaw emerged behind them, smartly dressed in pale gray. For a moment, the three of them stood on the doorstep together—a striking threesome. And people noticed—especially Lucy, scowling from across the churchyard. Mrs. Blackshaw paused to pull on her gloves, prolonging the moment.

My gaze slid back to Rowan—

And my heart stuttered. He was staring at me, his eyes unblinking, his expression heavy, and for several throbbing heartbeats, the two of us stood in that place we used to share. Connected without saying a word. Falling together.

Then his eyes shifted back to his grandmother. I followed his gaze to find her watching me—not with her usual loathing but something cooler and more assured. She waited for Rowan to prove his choice.

And he turned away from me to face Philly.

On Monday, I dragged my way through school, barely aware of my chattering classmates. I walked and breathed and read aloud in class like a wooden puppet. No heart or life, only obeying the pull of strings.

Ironically, with graduation only a few days away, my classmates had never been giddier. Lucy could talk of nothing except her upcoming trip to Paris; Hannah Adams was sure her childhood sweetheart would propose as soon as she got home; even Tall Meg became talkative, excited about moving to the city of Washington with her family.

But their eager chatter only made me feel more out of step. For me, graduation was an ending, not a beginning. No more escaping into ancient philosophy or the lineage of kings. No more wandering the library, touching book spines. Without school, my life would become—

*What?*

I sat in the back corner of the library after school, watching fat beads of rain slide down the window.

I would marry Sam, of course. Take up housekeeping while he

worked at Hale Glass. Wash his shirts and cook his favorite meals. Savor his kisses and sleep in his arms. The manager at Hale had already promised him a promotion in years to come. Sam would earn enough to provide for a wife and family. It would be a full life—a good life.

Shadowed by my past. Walking by my mother's grave nearly every day—a constant reminder.

The day after Sam had proposed, I'd asked him if he'd ever thought about living somewhere else, but he'd just laughed. "Why would we? This'll be the nicest property in the county, once we fix it up."

I would never go to New York City and meet Alvina Lunt. In my loftiest dreams, I'd imagined her so impressed by my passion, she'd asked me to stay and work with her. I'd written pamphlets and petitioned the government. In those dreams, I'd been brave and outspoken, like Mrs. Blackshaw. I didn't care so much about women's property rights, but it would have been nice to help people like Birdy.

Mr. Smithfield cleared his throat, and I looked up to find him standing near the library door. "It is nearly dark, Valentine, and my supper awaits."

"Oh, sorry, I lost track of time." I stood and pushed in my chair.

He scowled at me over his spectacles. "Tomorrow, I start my end-of-year inventory. I do hope you've managed to return all the books you've stolen over the years."

"Borrowed," I corrected. "And yes, every one of them." I cast a final look at the room I knew better than my own kitchen—the way the light moved across the floor, the musty smell of the books, even the click of Mr. Smithfield's dentures. I doubted I would ever have access to this many books again.

My footsteps echoed as I made my way through the quiet corridors to the front of the school. Classes had ended hours ago, and the aroma of dinner wafted from the kitchen. My stomach rumbled. Only dormitory students received dinner.

I was halfway across the front hall when a floorboard creaked, and

I turned to see the headmaster, Mr. Foley, standing in his office doorway, cast into silhouette by the lantern on his desk.

"A moment, if you please, Miss Deluca."

My eyebrows rose. Mr. Foley never spoke to me, and I couldn't imagine why he should start now, with only a few days left. The length of the main hall stretched between us, but neither of us moved to close the distance.

"Your time at Drake Academy is coming to an end, and we shall soon see no more of one another." Mr. Foley had three voices: the syrupy, aristocratic tone he used with the parents; the clipped, authoritative tone he used with the students and teachers; and the snide, sarcastic tone he used with the staff. And it was the snide sarcasm he used with me. "It is my duty to inform you, Miss Deluca, that you will be awarded the honor of valedictorian for the graduating girls."

I blinked, sure I'd misheard.

"Surprising, yes," he drawled. "But the scores have been tabulated and yours are, indeed, the highest. As valedictorian, you are expected to deliver a short oration at the commencement dinner on Friday. Parents and trustees will be in attendance. I trust you are up to the grandeur of the occasion."

In other words, would I embarrass him? A few months ago, I might have relished the opportunity to sit on the stand and give a speech, eager to fit in, but now, I saw no point in the charade. My classmates still whispered that I'd murdered my own father, and their parents had no doubt heard the rumors. "You needn't worry. I won't be attending."

"Your presence is not requested, Miss Deluca; it is required."

My stomach tightened. "No one will care. You can give my award to Jane Stiles."

"Nothing would give me greater pleasure, I assure you, but I'm afraid there is someone who cares if you are in attendance. Cares very much, in fact. You have surprising allies in high places, Miss Deluca."

*Judge Stoker.* I stifled a sigh. "You can tell my benefactor—"

"I am not your *messenger*, Miss Deluca. If you wish to express ingratitude, you must do so yourself. Your benefactor has invested sizably in your education and now requests this one thing in return—to see the results of that investment. Is that too much to ask? Too much to offer in return for an education at one of the finest schools in the country?"

I felt trapped. "No, sir."

"Then I will see you in the dining hall on Friday evening, seven o'clock, where you will sit on the dais next to Mr. Blackshaw and deliver a short oration."

My stomach lurched. Of course, Rowan would be the boys' valedictorian.

"Formal attire. I trust you have something appropriate?"

I nodded numbly; I would go through my mother's old dresses.

"Excellent." Mr. Foley entered his office, and the door snapped shut.

I left the school and walked through the woods, my mind twisting. Storm clouds brewed, but I had bigger concerns than getting caught in the rain.

*Valedictorian.* Not just one of three top students, but the very best. It was a flattering honor—and yet, absurd. How could I sit on the dais and give a speech—with Rowan beside me—while everyone whispered morbid rumors about the murders of my father and friends?

I couldn't.

And yet, I must or show ingratitude. Judge Stoker had given me Drake, and I would do this for him.

It was dark by the time I reached home, but when I turned the back corner of the house, the kitchen window glowed with light. I halted, my stomach tightening.

Sam had returned. My three days were up, and he was about to get down on one knee with a ring in his hand.

And I would accept him.

My heart beat heavily.

*I would accept him.*

But first, I would tell him everything—that I shot Mr. Blackshaw and sent my own mother to the gallows. That Father, Mr. Oliver, and Birdy had been murdered to hide my secret.

I opened the door and entered. Across the shadowed room, Sam sat in the rocking chair, asleep, his head on his chest. But my attention was stolen by the reassembled painting on the table. How would I explain it? What had Sam thought? I looked to his face to find out—

And uttered a little cry of surprise.

It wasn't Sam sleeping in the rocking chair. It was Rowan.

# 27

---

I took a tentative step closer.

Rowan sat in the rocking chair, his eyes closed, his long legs splayed in front of him, his arms relaxed.

*He'd finally come.* A whimper of relief rose in my chest.

I feasted on the sight of him, tall and lean and real, asleep in my kitchen, bathed in the flickering light of the fire. He'd removed his jacket and neckcloth, and his dark hair had gone wavy, the way I liked it. He looked unkempt—like the Rowan who used to sit in my kitchen, watching me with heavy-lidded attraction, not the Rowan who hosted glittering dinner parties with his grandmother.

I expected him to wake now that I was here, but he didn't stir. I cautiously took off my shawl and moved closer. His shoes shone in the dancing light of the fire—polished by a servant.

And my foolish hopes tumbled.

This didn't change anything. His presence here only prolonged the inevitable. He may have come to apologize—to say kind things that would make me feel better for a moment—but then he would return to his grandmother. And Philly.

This visit wasn't a kindness; it was a turn of the knife.

Annoyance prickled. He'd entered my house and made himself at home—taken a nap—as if nothing had changed. As if I were still his woodland fairy, willing to accept whatever small part of himself he would share.

I saw butcher's paper on the table and peeked inside to find bacon. A peace offering. I placed the bacon in a pan and set it over the fire.

It was the sizzling bacon that woke him.

He saw me crouched in front of the fire and quickly straightened, his eyes widening—as startled to find himself in my kitchen as I was. "Ah . . . sorry." He stumbled to his feet. "I must have fallen asleep."

I glanced at him, almost amused.

But I forced myself to be angry, turning back to the fire. "What are you doing here?" I prodded the bacon, and it popped in the pan.

"I . . . I brought that for you." As if that weren't obvious. His voice held a rasp from sleep.

"And you thought that entitled you to walk in and take a nap?"

"Sorry, I just . . . haven't been sleeping well . . . and this room—I feel at home here."

*Of all things for him to say.* A lump filled my throat, which I hid by pulling the pan off the fire and moving across the room to the worktable. I plucked the bacon out of the hot fat and set it on a plate, purposefully keeping my back to him, purposefully taking a long time. I cut a slice of bread—just one—then returned to the table and set the plate down hard, making the bacon bounce. I sat in front of it, facing the fire.

But my throat had a fist in it. I pushed the plate away.

"Why are you here, Rowan? I told you to stay away." As if I hadn't regretted those words a thousand times.

He stood between the table and the fire, as unsure of himself as I'd ever seen him. He swallowed, his throat rising and falling. "I came to explain."

"Explain what? I told you to stay away, and you stayed away. There's nothing to explain." But the tight anger in my voice said otherwise.

"I've missed you," he whispered.

A soft shudder rolled through me, but I fought it. "You haven't looked lonely."

His head tilted, his eyes sharpening. He released a ragged sigh. "You've seen me with Philly."

I refused to look at him but was acutely aware as he pulled out a chair and sat across from me.

"You look furious," he said.

I didn't want to be furious. I didn't want him to know how much it stung. "Maybe you shouldn't sit so close. I kill people, in case you haven't heard."

"Don't," he said softly.

My heart danced between emotions—and I went with anger. "No, *you* don't! You don't get to just walk in here, fall asleep in my home, and act as if you *belong* here—as if you didn't completely abandon me when I needed you most!"

"You told me—"

"I *know* what I told you, but that didn't mean—" My voice caught.

He looked shaken by my temper. "I can explain."

"Fine, then—explain."

He ran his fingers over his lips, suddenly hesitant.

"Go on," I insisted.

He drew a breath. "The day . . . the day after we found your father, my grandmother gave me two choices. Stop all association with you, or watch as you were convicted and hanged for murder."

His husky voice captivated me. I tried to fight it, but my eyes lifted, and he drew me in.

"She thinks you killed them, Valentine. She's sure of it. Someone told her they saw you entering the stable with Birdy, back in December."

I shook my head, panic rising. "That isn't true. I didn't—"

"Of course you didn't. It's the person who killed them trying to make you look guilty. It has to be. But she won't tell me who it is, and they've convinced her that you did it."

My thoughts darted. If Mrs. Blackshaw was the murderer, she'd invented this story to convince Rowan. But I wasn't sure how to tell him that—how to accuse his grandmother of murder with no evidence to back it up.

He continued in a low voice. "I told my grandmother that this person must be lying, that you would never hurt Birdy—or your father. But she thinks you've deceived me—that you want revenge over some financial deal with your grandfather. She thinks that's the reason your mother killed my father. Revenge."

"My mother didn't—"

"I know," he said gently, reaching across the table, but I pulled my hands back. "I'm just trying to explain what my grandmother thinks. Why she hates you so much. She thinks you're trying to lure me in and ruin my reputation. Maybe even kill me. I know—it's crazy, but that's what she thinks. That's what she tells me, over and over—that you're out to destroy the Blackshaws. She'll do anything to keep me away from you."

I gritted my teeth. "She's invented this stable witness."

Rowan shook his head. "I don't think so. I've seen her face when she talks about it. This person came to her for advice, not wanting to believe you'd do something so terrible. The problem is—my grandmother *does* believe it. For now, she's persuaded this person to keep quiet."

My eyes narrowed. "Why would she? A noose would be a convenient way to get rid of me."

Rowan released a dry breath. "Negotiating power, her specialty. Like I said, she's given me two choices. Stay away from you, and she'll tell this witness to remain quiet, or continue our relationship, and she'll tell them to go to Sheriff Crane."

I swallowed against a tight throat. "One witness. My word against theirs."

Rowan shook his head sadly. "It won't stop there. There are people who will lie for my grandmother—plenty of them. People who love her. People who are afraid of her. They'll say they saw you pouring poison down your father's throat, if that's what she wants. You will hang, Valentine."

A chill ran through me because I knew he was right.

"She also threatened to have you expelled from Drake. After four years, you would have nothing to show for it."

I gave a bitter laugh. "Which hardly matters if I'm dead. But she failed; I wasn't expelled—I'm valedictorian."

Rowan's face softened. "Because I took her deal. The only reason the trustees let you be valedictorian is because my grandmother convinced them. Because I made her promise to support it."

I remembered Mr. Foley's words. *You have surprising allies in high places, Miss Deluca.* "Do I even deserve the award?"

"You know you do. But it was only because my grandmother insisted on it that the other trustees agreed."

My mind sorted through all that he'd told me. "So . . . continue our relationship and I hang for murder. Or never speak to me again and I get to be valedictorian. Not a very equal bargain."

"You get to live," Rowan said simply.

"Ah, yes, there's that."

Rowan looked away, and I sensed there was more.

"What else?" I demanded.

"She's agreed to let me attend Harvard, and after that, study architecture instead of law. She's already written letters to arrange it— an apprenticeship with the best architect in the country, saving me a spot."

"Ah." I released a slow, surrendering breath, finally understanding. I couldn't even fault him.

"I wouldn't have agreed for that alone," he said heavily. "You know that."

"Do I? The career you've always dreamed of—or the girl who killed your father? Not an agonizing decision." I abruptly stood, scraping back my chair, unable to contain my frustration.

"Valentine." Rowan stood with me. "I've dreamed of more than architecture."

Maybe that was true, but it didn't matter. "You made your pact with the devil." Something else occurred to me. "Was Philly part of the deal?" His face stiffened, and I released a bitter breath. "Your side of the bargain looks richer by the minute. You get to train with the best architect in the country, I get to be valedictorian—"

"You get to live."

"—and you get Philly, the girl of your choosing."

"What? No." Rowan took a step around the table, shaking his head. "Philly was my grandmother's condition, not mine."

I stepped back. "Your grandmother would have chosen Lucy Meriwether."

"No, it's true. That was her final requirement. I have to propose right after graduation and marry her within a year. She even made me show my intentions right away, to prove I'll go through with it."

My chest tightened. "A year? Why so fast?"

"So I'm trapped, of course."

Mrs. Blackshaw had thought of everything—and Rowan had agreed to it. "You don't seem to mind this particular part of the bargain. I've seen you with Philly."

Rowan shook his head. He looked exhausted, shadows beneath his eyes. "I like Philly, but I'm not in love with her. The only reason I would ever marry Philly is to save your life."

"Don't!" I ordered, stepping back. "Don't blame this on me! I'm not the one who agreed to your grandmother's vile plan."

"Valentine . . ." Rowan stepped closer, his head tilting with entreaty, begging me to understand. "My grandmother wants me married within a year because she knows if I'm not, I'll run straight back to you."

I stepped back toward the wall, shaking my head, trying to resist the warmth that always filled my veins whenever Rowan was near. I lifted my hands, trying to force it down, trying to force myself to be angry. "You realize what she's done? She's threatened to *murder* me— that's basically what it would be! She'll have someone lie against me— and you agreed to her foul bargain—"

"No!" Rowan's own temper flared. "I went into it with my eyes wide open, fully aware! I thought about it for days—thought of every possibility—and only agreed when I was sure it was best for you, Valentine—for *you*, not me!"

"Oh, yes, I get to live! So very generous—"

"You get to *escape*! My final condition was that my grandmother buy your house. No one else would ever buy it, not with its history. You'd be trapped here forever. But my grandmother will pay a decent price for it—enough for you to start a new life. You can go to New York City and find Alvina Lunt, if that's what you want. Start fresh where nobody knows about your past."

I blinked, stunned. "Sell the house?"

"The property is valuable, and it's yours now. Have you thought of that?"

I shook my head. "I wouldn't. I couldn't."

"Of course you can. I'll make sure she pays more than it's worth."

"No." Mama had grown up in this house. Kneaded dough at that table. Bathed me in front of the fire, tapping my nose with a soapy finger.

"Valentine..." Rowan stepped closer, his tone softening. "I've barely slept, trying to think of a way to save you from the noose. And then it came to me—the answer. The only way you'll ever live a normal life—a *happy* life—is to get away from this town. And now my grandmother is forced to pay for it. You can go anywhere you want and build a new life."

My resolve melted when he looked at me that way. And I believed

233

him. He truly believed he'd accepted his grandmother's twisted bargain for my sake.

"You Blackshaws," I whispered, trying to feel some resentment that wasn't there. "Think you can manipulate the world and have anything you want."

"You're right," Rowan admitted, stepping closer. "I've been spoiled all my life. Handed everything I want."

I moved back, but hit the wall. And I was glad. I didn't want any more distance between us.

Rowan took the final, slow step that brought him close enough to touch. Close enough to feel his warmth and see the gleam of firelight in his eyes. "But in this . . ." He shook his head, his eyelids heavy. "In this, I'm not getting what I want." He reached up and touched my neck, his palm against my skin.

For several pulsing, tugging heartbeats we remained like that, his hand on my neck, both of us wondering if we dared do more.

He leaned closer and brushed his lips against mine. Just a touch, then he drew back.

I didn't move. I didn't breathe.

He kissed me again, a little longer, his lips full on mine, then pulled away.

I stood perfectly still, my heart thundering in my ears.

Then he kissed me again—and this time our mouths immediately molded to one another, warm and perfectly fitted, as if our lips had been made for this one purpose, for this tasting and breathing and exploring of one another. Our hands found places to settle—his fingers in my hair, my palm sliding up the curve of his neck, my other hand pulling at his waist. I heard his breathing, and my breathing, and our soft whimpers of surrender.

I leaned back, and the wall kept me upright.

"Run away with me," Rowan whispered against my mouth. "Tonight. That's all I want. That's what I want."

I kissed him long and deep, wanting the same.

"I have money," he murmured through our kisses. "We can do this, Valentine. We can escape tonight."

He kissed me until I thought I might faint, until it was only the tug of his lips and arms that kept me standing.

"Will you run away with me?" He kissed my temple, my cheek, my neck.

"Yes," I breathed.

"Do you mean it?"

"Yes. Yes."

Our lips finally stilled, and we clung to one another, our faces buried in each other's necks and shoulders, our hearts thumping in unison, my fingers curled around his shirt to keep him close, one of his hands holding the back of my head.

This was impossible.

Yet, happening.

Rowan pulled back to search my face, and the intensity of his gaze took my breath away. "Do you mean it, Valentine? You'll run away with me?"

"Yes," I said thickly. Hungrily.

"This isn't some mad impulse," he said. "It's what I've wanted all along. I only went along with my grandmother to protect you, until I could think this through."

I heard his words but had a hard time caring or understanding. I kissed his soft lips, my hand pulling him close, and it was a while before we separated enough to speak.

"Valentine, I've lain awake every night and came up with two plans of my own. One for you and one for me."

"One for you?" I murmured. His scent was intoxicating. I leaned my face into his neck and breathed.

"The first plan benefits me." He tilted his head so I could kiss his neck. "We escape together. I have some money saved. I thought maybe . . . the two of us . . ." He moaned and lowered his lips to mine, pushing me back against the wall.

We lingered there, our mouths separating for breath, then finding each other again.

Finally, I whispered, "You were saying?"

He smiled slowly, placing his hands on either side of my face. "I was saying . . . would you like to go to Europe, Valentine?"

My eyes widened.

He gave a low laugh. "Does that mean yes?"

"It means yes," I breathed.

"I was hoping you'd say that." He brushed his lips against mine. "But I do have two plans, if you'll recall. And the other plan benefits you, so you might want to hear it."

"Benefits me?" My head felt sluggish with his body this close, his breath on my skin.

"Where my grandmother buys your house and you escape on your own . . . and I take the apprenticeship."

I pulled back, frowning. "And marry Philly?"

He avoided my eyes. "My grandmother does seem rather set on that part of the bargain."

I gave an uneasy laugh. "You're not serious?"

Rowan's hands slid to my shoulders, his expression sobering. "If we run away, she'll have that witness tell Sheriff Crane that you entered the stable with Birdy. You'll be charged with murder and hunted down."

I stood still, trying to understand. "But . . . we'll be in Europe."

His thumb stroked my collarbone. "Forever? Is that what you want, Valentine?"

My heart drummed inside my chest. "I don't know," I admitted. My eyes rose to meet his. "But I want to be with you, Rowan."

His blue eyes flooded with emotion. "I want that too. But you have to be sure, Valentine. Because once we leave—once that witness speaks up—you can't change your mind. You'll spend the rest of your life on the run, looking over your shoulder."

"But . . . with you," I insisted, my heart racing.

"Yes, with me. But I've had two weeks to think this through and know it's what I want. You don't have that luxury. In a few days—the day after graduation—I'm supposed to propose to Philly. If I don't, you'll be arrested. But I won't propose to Philly if I don't intend to marry her. I saw what a broken engagement did to my grandmother. Which means we have to leave before then. And once we leave . . . we can never come back."

"Two plans," I said quietly, the romantic fog lifting. "One for me, one for you."

"We can sail to Europe and change our names and never return. Or . . . we can go our separate ways. You won't be accused of murder, and you'll have money from your house. A great deal of money; I'll make sure of that. You can go to New York City and start a new life. No murder charges. No looking over your shoulder."

"Without you," I murmured.

"Without me. But it's your best option, Valentine. I won't pretend otherwise."

The kitchen had turned dark and cold. I left Rowan's warmth to add a log to the fire. I prodded it into a blaze, then stood in front of it, hugging my chest, trying to think.

When I turned around, I found Rowan standing near the table, staring at the pieced-together painting.

"Where did you get this?" he asked.

"I saw your grandmother cutting it into pieces after Mr. Oliver died. I'd thought he'd painted it, so I saved it. I don't know why." I shrugged. "To remember him, I suppose."

"He didn't paint it."

"I know that now."

"You can burn it in honor of my grandmother." Rowan turned from the painting, reaching for my hand. He drew me to him, and it felt good to go there, to lean against his chest and feel his arms around me. To hear the low rumble of his voice. "I'm sorry I haven't been here for you these last few weeks. I know it's been hard. But I've never seen my grandmother in such a fury. I kept arguing with her, then realized I was only making it worse. So, I pretended to go along with it. I stayed away to protect you, Valentine. She watched me like a hawk, and I had to play my part."

I remembered the way Rowan had looked sitting next to Philly at that dinner party, surrounded by shimmering wealth. If he ran away with me, he would lose all of that. Harvard. His architectural apprenticeship. Ownership in Blackshaw Bank. Even his friends. His entire life, gone because of me.

"You're quiet," he said, his hands moving to my shoulders.

"You have a promising future, Rowan."

"With you, I hope." He dipped his head to look at me. "I know this seems sudden, but it isn't sudden for me. I've been in love with you for a long time, Valentine."

"But . . . is that enough?"

His expression turned wary.

And I knew that I should reassure him. That I should kiss him and lose myself in romantic madness and everything would be all right.

But suddenly, my head throbbed louder than my heart. I gently removed myself from his arms. "I need to think," I admitted, stepping back.

Rowan watched me, his eyes flickering with orange firelight. "It's a big decision. I want you to be as sure as I am."

"I just can't help wondering—"

In the window, I saw movement. I lifted my eyes—and gasped.

Sam was walking past the window . . . and glanced inside.

# 28

---

The door banged open and Sam strode in, as large and alive as I'd ever seen him, his expression livid. "So this is what you do when I'm away?"

Two truths immediately sharpened inside me.

First, the affection I felt for Sam was nothing in comparison to the intensity and complexity of emotions I felt for Rowan.

Second, if Sam guessed what had just happened in this room, he would attack Rowan with violent fury.

I had to lie.

"You're back!" I cried with false brightness, going to him, moving past Rowan—feeling Rowan's eyes on my back. I nearly embraced Sam out of habit, but his posture was so rigid, his temper so close, I settled for taking hold of his arms, which were damp. "Is it raining again?"

Sam's gaze shifted from me to Rowan, trying to understand what he'd interrupted. He must have seen Rowan's disheveled shirt and hair. My flushed cheeks. The heat in Rowan's eyes. He must have felt the nervous guilt pouring off me.

But he couldn't be sure. "Why is *he* here?"

"We were just—" My mind raced. "We're the valedictorians. We have to give speeches at commencement. Sit on the stand. We wanted to make sure our speeches weren't too similar. We both have to speak." I was babbling, my face burning.

Thunder rumbled in the distance.

Sam's head tilted, his eyes narrowing. "What does that mean—valedictorians?"

"I had the highest scores for the girls, added up over four years."

He lifted his chin toward Rowan. "And that privileged pup had the highest for the boys?"

Rowan sniffed with disdain. "At least I know the meaning of the word *valedictorian*."

Sam surged forward, but I grabbed his arm with all my strength, holding him back. I could feel the hatred snapping between them.

"Don't fight—*please!*" I looked to Rowan, tight annoyance crawling up my spine. Couldn't he see that I was trying to save him from a bloody face four days before graduation? "Rowan was just leaving—weren't you, Rowan?"

Rowan's eyes narrowed on me, and it was hard to believe he was the same person who'd stared at me with such tenderness a moment ago. He looked more like Mrs. Blackshaw's grandson than the person I loved. "I suppose I was . . . if that's what you want."

"It is," I said tersely, still gripping Sam's arm. "I think we've said all that needs saying tonight. We can talk more tomorrow."

"If there's anything left to say," Rowan said coolly. He grabbed his jacket off the rocking chair and strode toward the door.

I'd left his side the moment Sam walked in the door—after voicing hesitation about running away. That's all Rowan knew.

"Next time you have something to discuss with my fiancée, you'd best do it when I'm around!" Sam called after him. "It ain't proper, you visiting alone!"

My heart dropped.

Rowan's hand froze on the door latch. "So," he said carefully, keeping his back to us. "The two of you are engaged?"

"That's right."

"No, not . . . officially," I protested.

"She said yes, and I just bought a ring."

Sam had just blurted in anger what should have been a romantic surprise. And for some inexplicable reason, that made me furious at Rowan. Who was he to judge what I'd promised Sam in the last week? He'd made promises of his own.

"Just go," I ordered, biting back my temper. "I'll talk to you tomorrow."

"No need. I think we're finished." Rowan opened the door, and I saw the slash of silver rain before he stepped through. The door slammed shut.

"Arrogant ass," Sam seethed.

"I hate it when you act like that," I snapped, stepping away. "Like you're one of your wretched brothers and can't go five minutes without punching someone. You don't have to break into a jealous rage every time you see me talking to someone—"

"Only him! You said the two of you were finished. I don't ever want to see him in our house again."

"*Our* house?" I whirled on Sam, my emotions unleashed. "This isn't *our* house—it's *my* house—and I'll entertain whomever I like!"

"Is that right? Is that what you do when I'm gone? *Entertain* Rowan Blackshaw?"

"Sometimes!" I admitted. I turned to face the fire so Sam couldn't see my flaming face. He had good reason to be jealous—more than he knew. I shuddered to think what he would have seen if he'd arrived a few minutes earlier.

My chest rose and fell. I had to tell Sam the truth—that I didn't love him and couldn't marry him. But not tonight. Not with his temper so hot and Rowan only a few steps away and my head churning with confusion.

I pressed my hands against my warm cheeks. I loved Rowan, but I wasn't sure I wanted to spend the rest of my life in foreign countries, using a different name, always afraid someone would recognize me. I would never meet my real father. Or Alvina Lunt. And Rowan would lose even more.

Running away would end so many possibilities for both of us.

How had everything suddenly become so bitter and complicated?

"I bought you a ring," Sam said gruffly.

My heart sank. I shook my head, keeping my back to him. "I don't want it tonight. Not like this."

"Does that mean we're not engaged anymore? Because of one fight?"

I turned and found him holding a small, black box—and my chest hollowed out with regret. He'd been giddy since that first kiss. "Oh, Sam. We never were engaged. I told you that. I told you I needed more time."

"That's what you said, but that's not how you acted." His jaw tightened and released. Outside, thunder rumbled. "So, that's how it is, then? I ride for hours in the rain just to see you, and you don't want my ring? Fine, then. I'll keep it for someone else." He stuffed the box into his pocket.

"Sam . . ." But there was nothing I could say to fix this.

He gave a bitter laugh. "I've been a right fool."

"No—"

"My pa was right about you. He's had plenty to say since those bodies were found. Won't stop hounding me."

"Oh?" Annoyance prickled. I'd never told Sam about his father stealing lumber and finding the bodies first. "What has your father had to say?"

"That you're just like your ma."

"Your father didn't even know my mother!"

"He knows more than you think—more than *you* know. He used to see her in the woods with Nigel Blackshaw—a married woman!"

His cockiness infuriated me. "Your father is a thief! He ripped apart my stable in front of my poor father and Birdy, with no qualms or consideration! He offered to *bury* them for me, so no one would know!"

"Your ma tempted Nigel Blackshaw and then killed him! You can't deny that!"

"I do deny it! My mother never killed anyone!"

"Guess that means you're delusional too." Sam turned and strode toward the door. "I count myself lucky to escape while I can—*still breathing!*" He left, and the door slammed shut for the second time that night.

I quickly barricaded the door with the worktable. Then I slid to the floor, pulled up my knees, and sobbed.

The storm attacked with ferocity as I put myself to bed—wind screaming, rain battering, lightning flashing. Branches clawed at my bedroom window. I lay on my back, staring up at the dark ceiling, listening to the demons howling outside.

I touched my lips.

*Rowan loved me. He wanted to run away with me.*

It was a foolhardy plan for a hundred reasons, but living without Rowan—knowing he would marry Philly—was impossible.

So, I would do it. I would run to Europe with Rowan. My heart fluttered with both the thrill and terror of it. He'd left angry, but I would find him at school tomorrow and assure him that I loved him.

And Sam must be told the opposite.

*Oh, Sam.* He would know at once that Rowan was the cause. If he mentioned it to a friend at Hale Glass, word might get back to the company's owner, Mrs. Blackshaw, and she would know that Rowan wasn't keeping his end of the bargain. Her lying witness would go to Sheriff Crane, and I would be arrested before I had a chance to flee.

Which meant I couldn't tell Sam anything. I would have to disappear without saying goodbye, leaving my heart in a letter, giving Sam no chance to reply.

My thoughts sank deeper. After I'd run away, everyone would think I was guilty. That I'd killed three people I loved. Sheriff Crane would look no further, and the real killer would never face justice.

*The real killer.*

It had to be Mrs. Blackshaw. That's why she hated me so much: she knew I killed her son. She'd kept my secret so no one would know that she'd blackmailed Judge Stoker into hanging an innocent woman. But she'd confided in Mr. Oliver, and when Father scolded her, she'd killed him. And then Birdy, a witness. She'd even arranged a lying witness against me, hoping Rowan wouldn't keep his end of the bargain so she could finally see her son's killer punished.

Everything fit.

But right now, I didn't want to think about Mrs. Blackshaw. I touched my warm lips.

*Rowan loved me.*

Outside, lightning flashed and demons howled. But I closed my eyes and refused to listen.

# 29

The next day at school passed like a strange dream.

With only a few days left at Drake Academy, my senior classmates bounced with restless energy. Even the teachers were in celebratory moods, done with serious studies, chatting with the students about their own summer plans as they cleaned out desks and cupboards.

Word spread that I was the valedictorian, but with everyone's moods so bright, no one seemed to mind. The board of trustees had chosen me, and that seemed good enough for them. Jane Stiles leaned toward me in Latin class. "I told everyone you didn't kill them. And now they know I was right." As if the board of trustees had been my judge and jury and found me innocent—my case argued by Mrs. Blackshaw as part of her bargain with Rowan.

I needed to talk to Rowan and assure him that I loved him and wasn't engaged to Sam. I lingered in the main hall after lunch as the boys descended for their own lunch hour. My heart swelled when I saw Rowan on the staircase. He saw me, and I took a step forward, but he quickly looked away, his expression tightening as he disappeared into the dining hall.

*Because of his grandmother,* I reminded myself.

But I'd seen a harder emotion simmering at the back of his eyes and knew he was thinking of Sam and doubting how I felt about him.

In sewing class, Miss Dibble approached me with her whispery voice. "Oh, Valentine! Congratulations on being valedictorian. I'm so glad to know that all that nasty business is behind you." Like everyone else, she couldn't imagine that a valedictorian could have killed anyone.

"Thank you, Miss Dibble."

"You must allow me to help you dress. I used to do all my friends' hair when I was your age. In fact . . ." She glanced over her shoulder, then leaned closer. "I used to do your mother's hair, which was just like yours. You must come to my apartment one hour before commencement, above my brother's tailoring shop."

It was a kind offer, and I agreed.

School finally ended, and all the students made their way to the dining hall. Twice a year, Mr. Bonet and his fiddler visited Drake to teach ballroom etiquette and the newest dances from Europe. The girls lined up along one side of the room, and a larger group of boys lined up on the other. Mr. Bonet clapped his hands and ordered everyone to find a partner, and the more assertive boys surged forward to avoid dancing by themselves.

My eyes followed Rowan as he approached Philly.

"Valentine," Simon Greene said, extending his hand. "Would you do me the honor of dancing with me?"

"It would be my pleasure," I replied as we'd been taught. I placed my hand on Simon's arm, and he led me to one of the squares forming for the quadrille. I glanced over my shoulder and saw Rowan and Philly joining another square.

I usually enjoyed dancing, but today, Simon had to prompt me with subtle touches and tugs on my hand. Every time I turned, I saw Rowan and Philly moving in graceful unison. Their bodies turning. Their hands touching and releasing. Philly's eyes never left Rowan's face, and

I knew she and her mother would dissect every moment when she got home—every word Rowan had spoken, every place he'd touched her, every hint he may have offered. Philly stumbled, and Rowan saved her with an arm around her waist. She looked up at him with a breathless smile.

My heart tugged.

They made a beautiful couple. Philly was a sweet person when she wasn't with Lucy, and she would have made a good wife for Rowan. A proper wife for fancy dinner parties.

*But Rowan loved me.*

And would lose everything because of me.

I fought against the dark mood settling over me.

We needed to speak, but I wasn't sure how to arrange it. After dancing, I lingered near the school stable and finally saw Rowan striding toward the building. I made sure he'd seen me, then entered the woods.

I waited near the boulders, pacing, unsure if he would come. He finally appeared on the trail, but I could see that his mood was as dark and churning as my own. Before reaching me, he tilted his head toward the trees and walked into them, and, after a moment's surprise, I followed. I wound my way around dense underbrush and gnarled trunks, stepping over fallen logs.

"So . . . you're engaged to Sam," Rowan said over his shoulder. "You might have mentioned that. But I guess your mouth was busy."

Annoyance rose up my spine, but I pushed it down. I'd yearned to talk to him all day and wouldn't waste it on pettiness. I glanced back and saw that the trail had disappeared and we were buried in lush privacy. I stopped walking. "Rowan."

He turned to face me, but remained two strides away, his posture rigid.

"I'm not engaged to Sam. He asked me, but I told him I needed more time."

Doubt flickered in his eyes.

"I don't love Sam. I only went to him last night to protect you so he wouldn't know we'd been . . ." *Kissing* sounded too small a word for all that had passed between us. "Surely you know that? He would have beaten you senseless."

"You don't think I can handle myself against Sam Frye?"

"No. Not when he's in a jealous rage. And he had reason to be jealous; you know he did."

Rowan's lips twisted and released. "I spent all night wondering if after I left . . . if the two of you . . ."

My face warmed, because I had shared passionate kisses with Sam in nearly that same spot. "I refused to take his ring, if you must know. Which he didn't take very well. He left soon after you, furious."

"So . . ." Rowan drew a deep breath. "You're not engaged?"

"I'm not engaged." I moved closer, trying to smile. "There were days when I thought I would marry Sam. But last night . . ."

Rowan waited, his body taut.

"I love *you*, Rowan."

He released a groan and drew me into his arms, kissing me before I could catch my breath. A desperate kiss. A starving kiss, but so different from last night—Rowan's body too tight, my own too wary. Both of us fighting the doubts.

Our lips soon parted, but I kept my arms around his shoulders, holding him close, waiting for his body to relax and his breathing to slow. "I love you," I insisted, needing him to believe it. My lips brushed his cheek. "I love you." I kissed his lips like a feather, and when I pulled back, his mouth followed, desperate to believe.

I closed my eyes and believed with him for a while.

"You don't know the dark thoughts I've had," he whispered.

"For no reason."

My lips couldn't stop reaching for his. He smelled like his masculine soap and fine linen and wool. And Rowan's own intoxicating scent, which was easier to find near his neck. My lips kissed the skin in front of his ear, then lower. Then lower still. His neckcloth got in the way, so I slid my fingers inside the silk and loosened it.

"My grandmother says I have an artistic temperament."

"I like it." The neckcloth fell open, and my lips found the hollow of his throat.

Rowan bent his head and tugged my lips back to his. We kissed slowly, savoring.

"I was afraid I'd dreamed it," he breathed.

"This is a dream."

Finally, I gave a contented shudder and settled my cheek against his shoulder, his arms enfolding me. "I felt a little jealous myself," I admitted. "Watching you dance with Philly."

Rowan gave an apologetic laugh, his chest rumbling under my ear. "I couldn't even dance, I was so aware of you. I kept turning the wrong way. Everyone keeps asking what I'm doing after graduation, and I don't know what to say. All I can think about is you." He looked down, tucking a stray curl behind my ear. "So . . . does this mean you've decided to go to Europe with me?"

"Yes," I murmured. I closed my eyes, trying to close my doubts with them.

"This morning, I got us more time," Rowan said, his finger turning around a curl. "I convinced my grandmother to let me go to Boston to get my mother's wedding ring. My uncle has her things. I'll stay for two weeks to visit my relatives, then return and ask Philly to marry me."

Just hearing him say those words brought a tightness to my chest.

"At least . . . that's what I told her. I wanted the two weeks for you, Valentine, so you have time to think about it and be sure. Time to pack your things. I'll leave money so you can take the stagecoach to Boston. I'll book our passage on a ship, and by the time my grandmother realizes I'm not coming back, we'll be halfway across the Atlantic."

Running away from a crime I didn't commit, while the true killer— Mrs. Blackshaw—never faced justice.

The hand playing with my hair stilled.

"You're not worried about . . ." He hesitated. "I will marry you, just as soon as we're able. You know that? I won't expect us to . . . live as husband and wife until we've said our vows."

"I know."

He leaned back to see me better, his eyes questioning. "What's wrong?"

I carefully separated myself and stepped back, drawing a breath. "I think your grandmother murdered them, Rowan."

His eyebrows lifted.

I folded my arms and continued in a rush. "We know someone else was there when I shot your father. It must have been her. That's why she hates me so much."

He frowned, cocking his head. "No . . . I told you . . . your grandfather—"

"She blackmailed Judge Stoker into hanging my mother quickly. She told Mr. Oliver my mother was innocent—and my father got angry—and she killed him—"

"Stop!" Rowan ordered, raising his palms. "You're not making sense."

"But it *does* make sense! Don't you see? It's the only thing that *does* make sense! That's why she's made up this witness seeing me at the stable. She wants me to take the blame for what she did."

Rowan gave a strained laugh, stepping back. "You're serious? You're accusing my grandmother of murder? My *grandmother*?"

My tone stiffened. "She's capable of it. You've seen that yourself these last few weeks. She wants me to hang even though I'm innocent."

"Because she *believes* it! I told you—someone came to her—"

"No one came to her, Rowan! She invented that story to turn you against me!"

He gave a short laugh, turning away. He took a few aimless steps, then came back. His voice dropped, struggling to remain calm. "I know she can be manipulative, but in her own strange way, she's trying to save me. She *believes* you're the killer, Valentine. You should see her face when she talks about it. She becomes a different person. And she believes your mother killed my father. Just the name *Isabella Barron* sends her into her room for the rest of the day. And she *does* believe this person who says they saw you entering the stable with Birdy."

"There is no such person," I argued. "Because I never entered the stable until the night I found them."

"I know," Rowan said with measured patience. "It's the killer trying to throw suspicion on you."

The killer was his grandmother, but I could see that he didn't intend to believe it—not without evidence. "She wants me to hang for her crime, to keep us apart."

"Well, that isn't going to work, is it?" He drew me into his arms. "We'll go far away, where it's safe."

I tried to relax against him, but my thoughts thrummed. How could we be safe with murder charges hanging over me? We would have to hide for the rest of our lives, while Mrs. Blackshaw remained free, never facing justice. The deaths of the people I loved would never be answered.

Rowan's hand slid up the back of my neck, sending a delicious shiver down my spine. "I know this is sudden for you."

He would lose Harvard and an apprenticeship with a top architect. All his friends. Even his wealth.

"Are you sure this is what you want, Rowan?"

"Very sure. But you have to decide for yourself, Valentine. I'll be in Boston for two weeks, giving you time to think. I hope you'll join me. But if you don't . . ." His lips brushed my forehead. "I'll understand. I'll return to Feavers Crossing and arrange for my grandmother to buy your property. You can take the money and start a new life somewhere else, with no murder charges. Not haunted by the past."

*He would propose to Philly.*

Absurdly, that possibility terrified me more than the hangman's noose.

I looked up at him. "I'll come to Boston."

His blue eyes burned, and everything inside me rose. He lowered his mouth over mine and kissed me with a power that pulled the air from my lungs and weakened my knees. Only his arms kept me upright. "I love you," he whispered.

"I love you too." I just wasn't sure if it was enough.

# 30

I meandered home slowly, hugging my chest, trying to be happy. Trying to be sure that running away was the right thing to do.

But my head beat as loudly as my heart. In so many ways, running away felt wrong.

As I neared my house, I saw smoke curling from the chimney. I peeked through the window and saw Sam pacing in front of the fire, regretting his temper of the night before. Probably with a ring in his pocket.

I couldn't tell Sam the truth, but I wouldn't tell him a lie. I couldn't even tell him goodbye when I disappeared.

And I couldn't face him at this moment, with my heart so full and empty at the same time.

I turned and hurried away. When I reached the road, I broke into a run, lifting my skirt, overcome by a desperate, clawing need to escape.

To escape myself, not Sam.

I ran past the graveyard and church. Past a line of startled geese. Past houses that smelled of simmering dinners and loving families. My lungs begged for air, and sweat rolled down my temples.

But I couldn't stop.

When I was younger, I used to run in the woods, just to see how far I could go. I loved the feel of the solid earth beneath my feet, the rhythmic pulsing of my own heart, the power of my own legs. But I hadn't run this far in a long time. I turned down a narrow side road and slowed to a sustainable trot, my legs finding a steady rhythm. My feet pounded, and my heart thundered.

No thinking. Just panting. Just moving.

My thoughts fell behind, unable to keep up.

I turned down another lonely road, hardly aware of where I was going. I saw a wagon approaching and darted across a newly plowed field to avoid it. I reached an old apple orchard and continued through it, swerving around trees. When a footpath appeared, I took it, weaving my way through dense underbrush.

I stopped abruptly at the river, startled. I hadn't even realized I was running this way. But the sight of the rippling water calmed me. I placed my hands on my hips and drew a deep, strengthening breath. Then I turned and walked along the riverbank.

Gradually, my heartbeat slowed and my breathing returned to normal, and I allowed myself to think.

I'd been trying to run from my past all winter, but it had kept up, and it was time to stop running.

I couldn't go to Europe with Rowan. His grandmother had killed Father and Mr. Oliver and Birdy, and I couldn't run from her lies while she escaped justice. I had to stay and prove what she'd done.

Somehow.

I walked along the river, my thoughts swirling like the eddies along the bank. How could I possibly prove Mrs. Blackshaw's guilt? She was the most well-respected woman in Feavers Crossing. As Rowan had put it, it didn't matter if people loved her or feared her, the result was the same: she had their loyalty. She led an army of saints. What power could I possibly wield against her?

I stopped short, inhaling a breath. Because suddenly, I knew the answer. An answer so simple, I should have thought of it months ago. My heart lifted in amazement.

I would undo what Mrs. Blackshaw had done. She wanted the truth buried—so I would unbury it. I would tell the world that Isabella Barron Deluca was innocent and I'd killed Nigel Blackshaw.

My pulse raced. I stared out across the river, my eyes wide.

I wasn't sure why my mother's innocence mattered so much to Mrs. Blackshaw, but it did. I'd thought it was to hide the fact that she'd blackmailed Judge Stoker, but suddenly, that seemed too shallow a reason to murder three people. Judge Stoker was never going to reveal that secret.

There had to be something else.

On the surface, the river looked clean and bright, reflecting sunlight. But deeper, I saw murky silt—and I remembered the look in Father's eyes when I'd mentioned my mother's innocence. Something dark and secretive lurking along the bottom of that tragic night. After learning what I'd done, I'd assumed it was me. But Mrs. Blackshaw hadn't kept quiet for my sake.

She hid some other secret connected to her son's death. And my silence helped her.

The truth was my weapon. When I revealed what I'd done, whatever dark secret Mrs. Blackshaw was trying to keep buried would rise to the surface. She would crack, and I would force a wedge, and somehow I would prove that she was the killer.

My name would be cleared.

And Mama's.

I released a weak laugh. By admitting what I'd done, I would free myself.

I wouldn't run away to Europe. I would stay and face my past.

When I returned to the house, Sam was gone. But the next day, I came home from school to find a cluster of wildflowers on my doorstep, with a note.

IM GON TIL FRIDAY.

PLEASE THINK KINDLY OF ME.

IM SORRY PLEASE FORGIV ME. I LOVE YOU.

LOVE SAM

His broken, blocky penmanship brought a lump of affection to my throat. Sam had hated the strict confines of school, quitting at age twelve. But he was smarter than his penmanship implied. And wise beyond his years in ways that mattered: hard work and loyalty and loving with all his heart.

I was grateful for a few days to myself, to not have to dance around answers.

I had enough on my mind.

Judge Stoker wouldn't be happy when I revealed that he'd hanged an innocent woman. I decided to wait until after graduation so he could see me awarded as valedictorian before the world knew that I'd killed Nigel Blackshaw.

But the day after graduation, I would go to Sheriff Crane and tell him everything. Once he understood why Father and the others had been murdered, he would find the real killer—Mrs. Blackshaw.

Of course, he might also arrest me, thinking I'd killed once, so I must have killed again. But I was willing to take that risk.

No more hiding.

Rowan and I crossed paths a few times on campus and shared a private smile, but he was careful to avoid anything that might draw his grandmother's attention. In the evenings, I listened for the door, wondering if he would dare to sneak a visit. Part of me dreaded it, not wanting to tell him that I'd changed my mind about going to Europe. But he didn't come, and I used the time to work on my oration. I wrote and crossed off, trying to force everything else from my mind.

I went through my mother's old wardrobe and found a pale blue gown that I liked, but it wasn't quite fancy enough for commencement—and undoubtedly old-fashioned, as Lucy would notice. I brought it to school to ask Miss Dibble's advice, and with a little gasp of excitement, she insisted on making the alterations herself as a graduation gift. I stayed after school so she could pin and tuck, then she ordered me to leave it in her hands.

Friday evening finally arrived, and I knocked on Miss Dibble's door above her brother's tailoring shop.

"Valentine!" she gushed, ushering me inside. "I'm so excited! I've hardly eaten all day. I wish I could see you on the stand, but I'm not invited, of course, being only a sewing teacher. Follow me. I hope you like it. I hope it fits."

I gasped when I saw the pale blue gown spread across her bed. "Oh, Miss Dibble—it's beautiful!"

"Do you like it? I've altered the sleeves and neckline. Now undress; we haven't much time."

The icy blue fabric slid over my skin, silkier than anything I'd ever worn before, and when I looked in the mirror, I caught my breath. It was the prettiest dress I'd ever seen.

"The perfect fit," Miss Dibble breathed, adjusting the neckline. The bodice fit snugly, dropping to a point above a gathered skirt. "Now, sit at my dressing table and I'll see what I can do about that hair of yours."

I sat carefully, the skirt billowing around me.

"Your hair would be the envy of every girl in the school if you just tamed it properly. A little trim now and then. There is just far too much of it." Miss Dibble gathered my massive curls in her hands and twisted them up, arranging them one way, then another. She let them fall with a sigh. "I hardly know where to start." She picked up a hairbrush and began forcing it through. "Your speech is memorized, I trust?"

"Yes." I pulled my head forward against the tugs.

"Your mother was always good at recitation. But Daniel . . . well, Daniel was masterful. He excelled at all schoolwork." Her voice tightened, as it always did when she talked about my mother's twin brother. "He should have been valedictorian, of course, everyone knew that, but they gave it to Nigel Blackshaw."

"Because his mother was on the board of trustees," I guessed, not surprised. The brush caught on a tangle, and I winced.

"Partly, yes."

Something in her tone made me look up at the mirror. "What do you mean?"

Her lips twisted, holding back the answer.

My heart beat faster. Miss Dibble knew something about Nigel Blackshaw.

"Daniel was my uncle," I reminded her quietly.

Her eyes darted up to the mirror. "And he was a lovely boy," she said with feeling. "If they'd just given him that award, everything would have been different. He and I—"

I waited, hardly daring to breathe.

She lifted her chin. "Nigel cheated."

"Cheated at Drake?" I blinked, startled. Rowan was a good student, so I'd assumed his father was as well.

"He had that side to him. We all knew it." Miss Dibble returned to brushing. "He used to steal things when we were children. Just little things. Stick candy or a pocketknife. Daniel used to scold him, but they were still friends. Nigel was a fun playmate, and that's all that matters at that age."

"Daniel and Nigel Blackshaw were friends?"

"Oh, yes, they did everything together." Miss Dibble lowered the brush and dumped a box of hairpins on the dressing table. "Until their second year at Drake. They had a falling out and barely spoke after that. Isabella and I didn't know what it was about, but then Nigel was announced as valedictorian and Daniel told us everything. He was livid. He said Nigel had cheated his way through mathematics with the help of a teacher—and you'll never guess who."

I waited, my breath held.

"*Jethro Foley*," she said with hushed importance.

I frowned, unable to believe it. "Mr. Foley, the headmaster?"

Miss Dibble twisted my curls up. "He wasn't the headmaster back then, just a teacher. Nigel kept outscoring Daniel on exams, so Daniel snuck into Mr. Foley's office and figured it out. Mrs. Blackshaw was always bragging about her brilliant son, and Nigel couldn't bear to disappoint her, so he paid Mr. Foley to falsify his scores."

I wasn't surprised. And I suddenly wondered, "Does Rowan deserve to be valedictorian?"

"Oh, yes, he's much more studious than his father. They aren't at all the same." Miss Dibble slid a hairpin into place. "Daniel never told anyone about the cheating, out of loyalty, I suppose. But when Nigel was announced as valedictorian, well, Daniel was incensed. He was going to tell the headmaster, Mr. Gibbons, the next day. It would have been a *huge* scandal. Nigel would have been expelled a few days before graduation, and Mr. Foley would have been fired. And Mrs. Blackshaw—*well!* She would have been *mortified!* Her brilliant son, a cheat! She would have denied it, of course, and resigned from the board."

"But none of that happened."

"No." Miss Dibble's expression tightened. She took a moment to force a rebellious hairpin into place. "Daniel died that night, so he never got the chance to tell the headmaster."

I caught my breath—and saw the same suspicion in Miss Dibble's eyes. "Do you think the two things were connected—Nigel's cheating and the fire?"

She hesitated a heartbeat too long. "I don't see how. Daniel fell asleep at his desk. A maid saw him and shut the door. A while later, they saw the smoke. He must have knocked the candle over. They opened the door and the flames poured out."

But my mind imagined another possibility.

If Nigel knew that Daniel planned to tell the headmaster about the cheating, he would have wanted to stop him. Maybe he climbed the tree and went through Daniel's window, so no one saw him arrive. They argued, and when Nigel couldn't talk Daniel out of telling the headmaster, he panicked and silenced him—

*How?* Hands around the throat? A pillow against Daniel's face until his legs stopped thrashing?

He murdered his friend, then set the fire to hide the evidence and escaped through the window. No one even knew he'd been there.

My stomach roiled at the thought. I'd invented a horror story.

But it was entirely possible.

"Why didn't you and my mother tell anyone about the cheating?"

"We didn't have proof. And Daniel had just died. We were both in shock—utterly heartbroken." Miss Dibble pinched the heads off some small, white flowers and tucked them into my hair. "We heard that commencement was a somber affair. Nigel broke down in the middle of his oration and left the stand."

"But later," I insisted. "You could have told someone about Mr. Foley helping Nigel cheat."

Her face tightened. "I started teaching at the grammar school after I graduated—where Mrs. Blackshaw serves on the board. And a few years after that, I was hired at Drake, where Mr. Foley was the new headmaster. I am not a fool, Valentine—and neither are you." She met my eyes in the mirror. "I trust you will not repeat this." I didn't reply, and her lips tightened. "I should not have told you."

But she *had* told me, and my mind darted through the possibilities. "Do you think that's why my mother and Nigel Blackshaw were arguing the night he died? She found out that he'd murdered Daniel—"

"He didn't *murder* Daniel! I never said that! And it was a long time ago, Valentine. You only hurt yourself by dwelling on the past. To-night is about *you!*" She forced a bright lift into her voice. "And you'll be late if you don't hurry. Now, stand so I can get a look at you." I obeyed, and Miss Dibble's eyes widened. "Goodness, you look quite transformed!"

I saw my reflection and caught my breath. I hardly recognized my-self. Miss Dibble had somehow tamed my curls into a glorious halo, dotted with white flowers.

"Don't forget to smile," Miss Dibble advised. "You are far too seri-ous. But don't show your teeth. Boys may dance with bold girls, but they never marry them."

I ran my hands over the silky dress. I didn't have Philly's poised pret-tiness, but I did have my own sort of untamed beauty. Even my hair, so carefully pinned by Miss Dibble just a moment ago, looked as if the slightest breeze might set it free.

"Do you want to practice your speech?" she asked.

"No, I'll be late."

"Goodness, you must hurry. Grab the shawl." She hurried me down the stairs and walked two blocks with me, then called out well wishes until I'd disappeared around the corner.

# 31

The road to Drake was awash in evening glow. A carriage rolled past me—then another. But no more, which meant I was late. I quickened my steps, reciting my oration under my breath.

As I passed the Fryes' log cabin, Sam rose from a tree stump, tall and broad-shouldered, and my chest tightened. We hadn't spoken since he'd stormed out of my kitchen with a ring in his pocket.

"Hello, Sam."

"Good evening, Valentine." His tone was too formal, and I realized he was as finely dressed as I'd ever seen him, wearing a brown suit and green neckcloth, his hair still damp from its combing. He extended one arm. "May I escort you?"

"Oh, Sam." Affection washed over me, mingled with regret. "I would love it, but I didn't tell them I was bringing a guest. The dinner seats are assigned—"

"I know. I'll just walk you to the door."

I was already anxious about my speech, and there were so many things I needed to tell Sam. Painful things. But I wrapped my hand around his arm, and after a few stiff steps, we slid closer, and his near-ness comforted me.

I released a shuddering breath. "I'm nervous about my speech," I ad-mitted.

"You shouldn't be. You look beautiful, and I know you'll do a good job. I like your hair that way."

"Thank you. Miss Dibble did it." I gingerly touched it.

Sam looked down at himself. "Do you like my suit? I borrowed it from a friend at work. It's a little tight, but Ma says I got more grow-ing in me, so I shouldn't buy my own. Not until . . ." His voice faded.

Until he needed one for a wedding. My heart pulled. "You look fine, Sam." Beads of sweat dotted his brow. I'd been selfish and cruel to leave him wondering all week. I could trust him to keep quiet. I heaved a deep sigh of regret and released my arm from his. "I can't marry you, Sam."

His head bowed forward as he walked. "I know," he said heavily.

"I never wanted to hurt you."

His shoe brushed a pebble out of the way. "I just feel like a fool, that's all."

"No." My hand touched his arm, then fell back. "I'm the one who's been a fool. I've made so many mistakes. I shouldn't have let it go this far, with you buying a ring. But I honestly wasn't sure. I always thought it would be the two of us. Even when I sensed the truth, I didn't want to let you go."

His green eyes shifted down to me. "You don't have to," he said gruffly.

Tears stung my eyes. "I fell in love with Rowan. I don't know why."

Sam gave a bitter laugh. "I can think of a few thousand dollars why."

"It isn't about money. You know I don't care about that."

"Do I? I feel like I don't know anything right now—except that you lied when you said you loved me."

My mood tightened. "It wasn't a lie. You know I love you, Sam.

That's why this has been so confusing. But what I feel for Rowan is different, and you deserve a girl who feels that way about you."

He scowled at the road.

I bit my lower lip. "Sam . . . I know it's unfair to ask, but I need you to keep quiet about Rowan and me for a few weeks. It's important that his grandmother doesn't find out."

He released a breath of disbelief, his eyes narrowing on me. "He won't even tell his grandmother about you?"

"It's . . . complicated."

"Not that complicated, Val. He's ashamed of you. And as soon as he's bored, he'll move on to some other girl."

My temper flared. "It isn't like that between us."

"Believe that if you want, just don't expect me to be waiting around to take you back." He took a few angry steps, glowering at the road. "I haven't told you, but Emily Sweeney just happens to walk my way every morning on my way to work."

"I'm glad," I snapped. "I want you to be happy."

A carriage approached, and we shifted to the edge of the road, not talking for a while as it passed. Its wheels kicked up a trail of dust.

The sunset was deepening, the shadows lengthening.

Sam kicked another pebble out of the way. "I think you got your head in the clouds, Val. Maybe that fancy life looks good right now, but that's not how you are. You don't want to eat some fancy cake on china plates; you'd rather bake it yourself. And if you had to choose between eating dinner with a bunch of rich people with their noses in the air or Birdy, you'd choose Birdy every time."

I looked up at him, amazed that he knew me so well. But I could have described him just as easily.

But there was something Sam didn't know about me. "Sam, I need to tell you something."

I slowed our pace as I told him about meeting Molly and learning the truth about what I'd done. I explained how I'd tried to hide the secret all winter, but now knew that I had to speak out or the person who murdered my father and friends would never be found.

Sam listened carefully, then asked, "Why would your ma confess if she didn't do it?"

"I don't know for sure, but I want to clear her name. Tomorrow I'm going to tell Sheriff Crane what really happened."

Sam shrugged. "It was a long time ago. I think you should just forget about it."

I looked up at him, my heart warming. That was the Sam I knew—overcoming most of life's problems with an easy shrug and smile. A life with him would have been simple and straightforward, full of hard work and easy laughter, each day much the same as the one before. Rowan was more complicated, and my life with him would be more tangled. But that excited my heart and blood.

We'd reached Drake Academy. When I saw Rochester Hall, I stopped short, butterflies taking flight in my stomach. The ground-floor windows glowed with candlelight and finely dressed figures, and the terror I'd been forcing down all day tightened its fist.

Sam stopped beside me and said in a quiet voice, as if reading my mind, "Don't be nervous, Val. You're gonna give a great speech."

I turned to him, my throat swelling with a hundred unspoken words, but I only gave him three. "Thank you, Sam."

He turned away—then came back. He slid his large hand into my hair and kissed me one last time. His lips lingered, then he let go and walked away.

I watched until he'd disappeared around the bend.

Then I turned and entered Drake Academy for the last time.

I was late.

The early mingling in the entrance hall had ended, and the graduation guests were already flowing toward the dining room. Ahead of me, Lucy and Philly strode like princesses in their beautiful dresses, their mothers nearby; Judge Stoker walked with Mr. Meriwether, smirking at some shared joke; and Mrs. Utley scolded Jack, her mouth pressed against his ear.

I was the only student on my own.

I gasped when I saw the dining hall. The old tables had been covered by elegant white tablecloths, and everything glittered beneath tall candelabra. Even the guests sparkled, dressed in their finery.

No one seemed to notice me as I made my way up the right side of the room. At the far end, the low dais used for devotionals had been set up, with a long table in the center with three chairs facing the room. Rowan already sat on the left—handsome in formal attire, not looking at me with his grandmother in the room—and Mr. Foley sat in the center. Which meant the empty chair on the right belonged to me. I climbed the two steps to the dais, and Mr. Foley and Rowan stood as I approached.

Rowan's eyes slid down the pale blue dress, then returned to my face with a burning gaze of approval that made my heart rise.

"You are late," Mr. Foley hissed as he held out my chair.

"You wanted me at the opening social?" I asked quietly. "To meet all the parents?"

He didn't reply.

A blessing was offered by the Reverend Mr. Newland, and everyone's attention shifted to their food. It was the grandest meal I'd ever been served, but I could barely eat. I glanced at Rowan and found him watching me. His lips twitched in a small smile, then he looked back at his plate, no doubt aware of his grandmother watching.

*Mrs. Blackshaw.*

I looked up and found her at the trustees' table near the dais, watching me with steely disdain. I'd dreaded seeing her, but now that we faced one another, I felt unexpectedly calm. She looked thinner than

I recalled, her skin sallow against a black dress. We rarely stared this directly at one another, but tonight our gazes held and burned.

She'd murdered Father and Mr. Oliver and Birdy. Then she'd made her pact with Rowan, hoping he wouldn't keep his end of the bargain so she could see me hang for her crime. An end to the Barrons.

I wondered what sinister secret she was trying to hide. Something connected to her son's death and my mother's innocence. Something—

My thoughts lurched, remembering Miss Dibble's story.

My mother had pointed a gun with cold fury, her hands trembling, her eyes wild, screaming hate-filled words—because she'd known that Nigel Blackshaw had murdered her twin brother.

*Not revenge over some financial matter.*

My heart drummed in my chest. My eyes widened on Mrs. Blackshaw, suddenly seeing her clearly.

She knew the truth about her son. That was the sinister secret lurking at the bottom of the murders—the reason Mrs. Blackshaw cared so much about my mother's innocence. Anyone who saw me pick up the gun that night also heard my mother's fiery accusations against Nigel Blackshaw. Which meant—

My thoughts raced, gathering pieces.

Anyone who saw me pick up the gun also knew that Nigel Blackshaw murdered Daniel Barron.

*Who was there?*

*Father.* Paid off with a box of money, then murdered.

*Little Valentine.* An icy shiver ran through me. Mrs. Blackshaw hated me because I killed her son—and feared me because I was there when my mother screamed accusations. That's why she wanted me hanged.

*The secret witness*—the person who'd told Mr. Oliver. Was that Mrs. Blackshaw? Or someone else?

A dish crashed, jolting my attention back to the present, and Mrs. Blackshaw looked away.

I inhaled a breath.

There were still pieces to find, but I couldn't think about it now or I would never get through my oration. I took a sip from my goblet with a trembling hand.

Dinner finally ended, and Mr. Foley stood to give the same dry speech he gave at every school event, filled with platitudes about Drake Academy's charge to instill knowledge, virtue, and industry in the hearts of its students. But I heard very little, rehearsing lines in my head. And before I felt ready for it, Mr. Foley was introducing me as the valedictorian for the girls.

I stood to a brief smattering of applause and began my oration—more shakily than I would have liked, my voice too soft. My eyes didn't know where to land. I finally remembered to look for Judge Stoker and found him at the trustees' table—a scowling vulture with piercing eyes. Soon, I would break my promise to him, but tonight I could make him proud. I stood taller and my voice strengthened, and he offered a hard smile of approval.

Rowan stood next and delivered a perfectly memorized speech with a lively lift in his voice that held the audience riveted. His mood seemed jovial—because he thought I was going to Europe with him. Somehow, I needed to get him alone tonight and tell him that I wasn't going. That I wouldn't run away. That I intended to expose his grandmother.

Mr. Foley presented Rowan and me with our awards, then we were told to step down from the dais so our classmates could file up. Two chairs had been reserved for us near the trustees' table. We sat side by side, his leg touching my full skirt, our hands only inches apart, both of us rigidly aware of his grandmother not far behind.

I forced myself to watch as our classmates receive their diplomas. Jack Utley stumbled on the steps, then scurried toward Mr. Foley with squeaking shoes. Lucy's neckline was shockingly low. And Tall Meg looked even taller than usual with her hair pulled up, her long neck revealed.

Philly looked beautiful in cream-colored silk, but she seemed shaky with nerves as she waited her turn, casting furtive glances at Rowan.

"Now!" Mr. Foley announced. "If you would all please retire to the main hall, the dining tables will be cleared so we can begin the dancing portion of our evening!"

Chairs scraped back, and the room erupted in conversation.

I expected Rowan to leave me because of his grandmother, but he remained at my side. "I leave early tomorrow," he said in a low voice, keeping his gaze safely elsewhere. "I'll stop by your house on the way to leave some travel money. The Boston stagecoach leaves every other morning."

My stomach knotted. "I need to talk to you, Rowan. Tonight, if we can find a way."

His eyes darted to me. "Is everything—"

"Rowan Blackshaw! Well deserved!" A large hand landed on Rowan's shoulder, and we turned to see Governor Stiles. "Your grandmother tells me that you're planning to study law."

"Well, actually—"

"You're acquainted with my daughter Jane, of course. I know she'd be very pleased if you paid us a visit this summer. It's a bit of a ride, but you could stay for a few days. Visit my office. Meet a few people."

"Congratulations, Rowan!" Mr. Meriwether came up on his other side. "Hope you can make it for dinner before Lucy leaves for Paris."

"Rowan! Fine speech!"

As Rowan was surrounded, Judge Stoker took hold of my arm and drew me a few steps away. "Well done on your oration, Valentine," he growled near my ear. "And well done with your valuable gift the other evening. I only hope it didn't make you think less of me."

"I didn't read it."

His lips quirked in a relieved smile. "Well, then, we shall put it behind us, like that other matter. And now, if you'll allow me, I'd like to introduce you to a few of my fellow trustees." He steered me toward a large, ruddy-faced man. "Valentine, this is Mr. Tobin, owner of the largest dairy in the state."

Mr. Tobin inclined his head. "I enjoyed your speech, Miss Deluca."

"Thank you, sir." I glanced over my shoulder at Rowan, stifling my impatience.

"And here are Mr. and Mrs. Moffett." Judge Stoker led me down a line of introductions, and it wasn't until we neared the end that I realized he was leading me toward Mrs. Blackshaw. My spine stiffened. Surely he wasn't foolish enough to think we needed an introduction. But when I glanced at his chiseled face, I saw that he wasn't foolish at all; he was eager. I stepped back, but his fingers tightened around my arm, and I was forced before Mrs. Blackshaw like a criminal in his courtroom.

"Josephine," Judge Stoker greeted with smug satisfaction. "I believe you are acquainted with Miss Deluca."

The cloying sweetness of her perfume wafted over us. We were the same height, and for the second time that evening, I saw the flicker of fear in her eyes.

Which emboldened me. I knew her foul secret. "Good evening, Mrs. Blackshaw. You must be proud of Rowan."

She heard the presumption in my voice, and her chin lifted. "Indeed. I have reason to be proud of my grandson. He is a fine young man, deserving of his honor."

"As is Miss Deluca," Judge Stoker pointed out, enjoying this moment. "Valedictorian at one of the most demanding schools in the country. I think we can all agree now that Valentine is a disciplined student with a sharp intellect, deserving of a fine education."

Mrs. Blackshaw glowered, unwilling to agree to anything. And I realized this meeting had less to do with me than it did with them. Tonight marked the conclusion of a four-year war, and Judge Stoker was declaring victory. He hadn't wanted me at commencement so he could see me receive my award but so Mrs. Blackshaw would be forced to witness it.

"She even bested the governor's daughter," he crowed.

"I never doubted her intelligence, Ezra, only her worthiness. Her mother was clever, and look what became of her."

I looked over my shoulder and saw Rowan making his way toward the back of the dining hall, behind the dais. When he reached the door to the music room, he turned and glanced back at me, tilting his head with meaning, then he disappeared inside.

It was my chance to be alone with him, but my chest tightened, knowing the conversation that lay ahead.

I turned back to Judge Stoker and found him bickering with Mrs. Blackshaw about the new science laboratory. I'd fulfilled my obligation; he no longer even seemed aware of me. And Mrs. Blackshaw hadn't seemed to notice Rowan's departure.

I turned and made my way toward the back of the dining hall.

# 32

The music room was dark except for a golden shaft of light coming from the dining hall behind me. I paused to let my eyes adjust—

And my hand was taken by Rowan's, pulling me deeper into the dark room. His arm came around my waist, drawing me close. "Do you have any idea how beautiful you are?" he murmured, then his lips settled over mine. I tried to savor it, knowing it wouldn't happen again for a while. But my head felt busy and my body rigid.

Rowan lifted his head with a teasing smile. "You can relax now. Your speech is over."

"Sorry. I just have a lot on my mind."

"I know." His hands moved to my shoulders, gently caressing. "But everything is going to work out. Soon, we'll be far away."

*I needed to tell him.*

My heart tightened, wondering if I should also tell him what I'd guessed about his father—but no, not without a shred of evidence. He'd only get defensive, like he had about his grandmother. We would part angry. Or worse, he would believe me and not leave town.

He grinned, unaware. "So, tell me, Valentine . . . London or Paris?"

*Tell him.*

"Or maybe we'll just choose any ship with a name we like and see where it takes us." His fingers worked the tension from my shoulders. "I wish I could make a withdrawal at the bank, but they'd tell her. I have enough for a few months, while we get settled. Then I'll find work."

I frowned at him, confused. "I thought you wanted to study art."

He gave a soft laugh. "There'll be time for that. First, I need a job. I don't think you want to sleep in haystacks." He kissed my forehead lightly.

*A job.* Rowan knew Latin and advanced mathematics, but he'd never built a fence. Or learned a trade. If he was lucky, he'd find work as a bookkeeper—at a bank that he didn't own, hunched over a desk for ten hours a day. That wasn't his vision of Europe.

But then, I hadn't been in that vision.

"Rowan—"

"You'll meet my mother's family in Boston. I'll leave a letter with them to mail to my grandmother after we leave. They'll be happy to help us. They've never particularly liked my grandmother."

"Rowan . . . I have to tell you something."

His hands stilled on my shoulders, his expression suddenly wary. "What's wrong?"

I drew a breath. "I can't go to Europe."

He stared at me, not moving.

"I can't run away. Everyone will think I did it, and the real killer will go free."

His hands fell from my shoulders, his eyes narrowing. "You still think my grandmother did it."

"She killed three people and wants me to hang for it. I won't let that happen."

"Of course not," he said with impatience. "That's why we're leaving."

"Running away," I corrected. "Hiding for the rest of our lives. But

I won't hide anymore. I'm going to tell the truth about killing your father."

"Valentine—" he warned.

"I'm going to tell Sheriff Crane tomorrow."

"That will just convince him that you're guilty. You will hang, Valentine!"

"I don't think so," I said with more conviction than I felt. "Judge Stoker is my benefactor here at Drake. He already knows I killed your father, and he doesn't think I killed the others. He won't convict me. And Sheriff Crane . . . he asks hard questions, but I get the feeling that he doesn't think I did it. I'll tell him everything, and then he'll know enough to find the real killer."

Rowan released an annoyed breath. "It's not my grandmother. I wish you would believe me about that."

"Well, if it's someone else, we'll discover that. Either way, when the real killer is arrested, I'll no longer be at risk from this lying witness. We'll be free, Rowan. We won't have to spend the rest of our lives running and hiding. I'll send word to Boston and you can return to Feavers Crossing."

"You don't think I'm still going to Boston—that I'll leave you here to hang?"

"You have to," I insisted. "I need those two weeks. You have to keep pretending, or your grandmother will tell that lying witness to speak up. She has to think you went to Boston to get the ring."

Rowan took a few restless steps away, then turned back, his hands on his hips. "So I'm supposed to sit around playing chess with my cousin while you're getting my grandmother arrested for murder?"

I stiffened. "If she killed them, she deserves it."

"She *didn't* kill them! I keep telling you that!"

"Then I won't be able to prove it, will I?"

A muscle in his jaw clenched and released. "You said you wanted to run away with me. I don't understand why we can't just get on a ship like we planned and leave all this behind."

"Because I can't spend the rest of my life running and hiding from what I did!"

"You didn't *do* anything!"

"I killed your father, Rowan!"

The words hung between us, angry and horrifying and true.

Rowan sighed, his expression softening. "You know I don't care about that."

"But I do." I swallowed. "Someone killed my father and friends because of what I did. I have to find their killer, and I have to confess to killing your father and clear my mother's name. If I don't . . . if I don't, it will haunt me for the rest of my life. I can't run away from this, Rowan. It's *inside* me."

His expression turned wistful, acceptance settling over him. "I understand," he said quietly. He turned and walked to a row of music stands. He crossed his arms, his back to me, then said in a low voice, "You can't leave, but I can't stay."

My heart tugged.

He kept his back turned. "You don't know how it's been, these last few weeks, feeling her thumb on my life, pressing . . . and pressing. I've always known she was like that, but it just felt like loving concern." He turned slowly to face me. "Now, I don't even want her apprenticeship because I know it's just another move in her game. While I'm at Harvard, she'll find some way of twisting me back into becoming a lawyer. Before I know it, I'll be Senator Blackshaw, fighting for her causes. I want my own life, not hers."

I went to him and placed a hand on his cheek. "I know," I said gently. "That's why you need to go to Europe."

His eyes shifted to mine, suddenly hopeful. "You'll come?"

"That's your dream, Rowan, not mine. You need to roam through ancient castles and set up an easel in Paris, not work ten hours a day so I'll be comfortable."

He frowned, his head tilting. "What are you saying? You don't . . . want to be with me anymore? You've changed how you feel?"

"Never." My hand slid behind his neck. "When you're done exploring, you'll come back to me. And while you're away, I have some dreams of my own to follow."

"New York City and Alvina Lunt?"

"Partly. I also need to meet someone named Richard DeVries."

"Who is he?"

The whine of a violin being tuned wafted through the open door, reminding me that our time was short.

"I'll tell you sometime. Right now . . ." I pulled his head closer, and he came willingly. His kiss was familiar now, and I relaxed into it, savoring his touch and smell, knowing he would leave for Boston tomorrow and get on a ship, and I might not see him for years.

The first song started, and our kiss became hungrier, our breaths more desperate. Rowan's hands tightened on my back, unwilling to let go.

I was a fool to send him away. He would stay if I asked.

But Rowan needed to escape his past as much as I did. And he would thrive on his journey. Lounge in taverns with other young artists, rumpled and unshaven. Eat exotic foods. Sing foreign songs and dance to throbbing beats. In a year or two, he would return a different person—a lighter person, living his own life, not the one planned out for him.

And he would find me.

He rested his forehead against mine. "I'll come by in the morning on my way. I'll still leave you some money so you can go to New York."

"I have a little money of my own. I found a box under my father's bed."

"And I'll give you my uncle's address. Keep in touch with him so I can find you."

"All right," I whispered.

"Valentine—" He pulled his head back to look at me, his brow furrowed with concern. "If you can't find the killer in two weeks, you have to leave Feavers Crossing. Once my grandmother realizes I'm not coming back, she'll tell that witness to come forward. So you have to leave town before then. You promise me?"

"I promise." I forced a weak smile. "I don't want to hang."

Rowan bent for a final kiss, then separated himself. "I love you, Valentine." He turned and walked out of the music room.

I pressed my fingers to my lips, my heart beating heavily, trying to believe that I'd done the right thing. Music flowed from the dining hall, mingled with jovial voices and shuffling footsteps.

A figure moved into the doorway, silhouetted against the glow of the dining hall—a black figure in stiff silk. There was no mistaking that regal bearing. My heart jolted, and I stepped back, knocking over a music stand with a clatter.

Then I straightened and faced Mrs. Blackshaw.

# 33

We appraised one another from a distance in the shaft of light coming through the door.

On the surface, Mrs. Blackshaw looked like the impressive woman I'd once admired—the woman who organized church picnics and wrote fiery letters to newspapers about the inhumanity of slavery.

But in her eyes, I saw the cold gleam.

*She killed them.*

She came toward me, black silk rustling, and I smelled her perfume. "I will buy your house for more than it's worth, plus give you an additional sum. More money than you can imagine. But you must leave Feavers Crossing and never communicate with my grandson again."

My spine straightened. She thought I would choose money over Rowan. I wished I could tell her what I thought of her vile bargain, but I had to keep her fooled for two more weeks. "It's a tempting offer."

Her lip curled. "I thought it might interest you. I don't know what schemes you have planned in that pretty little head of yours, but Rowan has other plans now, and you've become an unwelcome distraction."

"You're the one with all the schemes, not me."

She stepped closer, her face darkening in the shadows. "Don't poke the bear, Valentine. One word from me, and you will hang. I know your foul secret."

My temper sparked. "And I know yours!"

She slapped my cheek, hard and unexpected, and I stumbled sideways.

But I quickly straightened, my cheek burning, and met her icy stare. I spat the truth with repugnance. "Your son murdered Daniel Barron!"

Her cheeks hollowed out.

"Oh, yes," I seethed. "I know all about that."

The blood seemed to drain from her face.

Warm victory blazed through me. "Did he tell you after it happened, hoping you could fix it—his all-powerful mother?" My mind flew, pulling at pieces. "I'm guessing it wasn't Nigel who paid Mr. Foley to cheat—it was you, wasn't it? You orchestrated the entire thing. That's why Foley was appointed headmaster a few years later. He helped your son cheat his way through Drake, and when Nigel murdered his best friend to keep it quiet, you dried his tears and hid his black secret."

Mrs. Blackshaw said nothing, her eyes wide and terrified, her chest rising and falling.

"But your son betrayed you, didn't he? After everything you'd done for him, he fell in love with Isabella Barron—the child of the man you despised. You must have been relieved when she rejected his marriage proposal and left town. Nigel dutifully married the girl you'd chosen for him, but she died giving birth to Rowan, and when Isabella returned to town with a husband and baby, Nigel went right back to his obsession."

"*She* was the one obsessed with *him!*" Mrs. Blackshaw spat. "She wanted his money! She wanted revenge for her father's financial stupidity!"

I shook my head. I remembered Nigel Blackshaw waiting for my mother in the woods. She'd avoided him at first, but over time, his persistence had won her over. She'd been so desperately lonely.

"She agreed to divorce my father and run away with Nigel, but you couldn't let that happen, could you? You came to our house to stop them." My thoughts darted. I hadn't seen her, so she must have come earlier. "You told my mother the one thing you knew would turn her against your son—that he'd murdered her twin brother." I remembered Mama's tearful fury, and it all fit. It wasn't something she'd known for a long time, but a new discovery. She'd been out of her mind with grief and rage because she'd just learned that the man she'd planned to run away with had murdered her beloved brother.

Mrs. Blackshaw's voice fell to a rasping hiss. "You can't prove anything."

But I felt powerful with certainty. "That's why she pointed a gun. That's why your son died—because you revealed his black secret!"

Mrs. Blackshaw's cheeks swelled with emotion, then hollowed out again, making her look like a corpse—a woman who died eleven years ago but continued to walk and breathe. A woman who blamed herself for her son's death.

But I felt no pity. "My father heard everything that night and knew the truth about Nigel, so you paid him to keep quiet. But he never spent your blood money. *You* were the one who couldn't keep your mouth shut! You told Mr. Oliver—then poisoned him because he knew too much! You *murdered* my father!"

She stood taller, suddenly defiant. "I had nothing to do with their deaths."

I didn't believe her. "My mother knew the truth, so you blackmailed Judge Stoker into hanging her quickly, even though you knew she was innocent."

"Innocent?" Mrs. Blackshaw gave a hard laugh, her strength returning. "Isabella Barron was a spoiled tramp of a girl, out for revenge. She tempted my son—and then shot him!"

"My mother didn't shoot anyone, as you well know! According to Mr. Oliver, you saw everything! *I* was the one holding the gun! We both know that, so let's not pretend!"

Mrs. Blackshaw's face turned to stone—all except her eyes, which flickered with confusion. Her chest rose and fell. "What are you talking about?"

"You were there! You saw me pick up the gun!"

She gave a jerky shake of her head, her face contorting with shock and bewilderment. Her voice dropped to a horrified whisper. "What are you saying? What did you do?"

The air seemed to leave my lungs. *She didn't know.* Rowan had been right. His grandmother didn't know I killed her son.

*But I'd just told her.*

Her eyes darted as she tried to make sense of it. "But . . . you were only a child. Why would you—? *Why would you do that?*"

I took a shaky step back, trying to swallow my panic. "It was an accident. I didn't mean for the gun to go off. I just picked it up and it fired."

"But . . . Isabella confessed." Mrs. Blackshaw shook her head, confused—then her gaze snapped to me. "To protect you! And you said nothing as she hanged—*your own mother!*" Her lips curled in disgust. "Did Mr. Oliver find out? Is that why you killed him?"

My heart jolted. The world had spun upside down. "No—that was *you!* You poisoned Mr. Oliver—you killed my father and Birdy!"

"Your *father!*" Her face twisted with revulsion. "You murdered your own father, then left him to rot for months—while you slept a few yards away. You are a vile, loathsome girl. But this time you won't get away with it. I will not rest until you are cold in the ground!"

My heart thundered in my chest. I'd been so sure it was her—and she was so sure it was me, like Rowan had said. "I didn't," I protested. "I didn't kill my father—or Mr. Oliver—or Birdy. I thought it was you—*I thought it was you!*"

But she didn't seem to hear. "And now you seek to destroy my grand-son. But no more! I will tell Rowan the truth tonight—that his pretty little sweetheart isn't as innocent as he imagines! *You killed his father!*"

I shook my head, still trying to believe Mrs. Blackshaw hadn't killed anyone. "Rowan . . . Rowan already knows. He doesn't care."

"You may have bewitched my grandson, but you cannot bewitch the entire world!" She pointed an angry finger at the door to the dining hall. "I will enter that room and tell everyone the truth—that their precious valedictorian is a *killer!*"

I swallowed against a dry throat, my heart racing. "I want them to know. I want to clear my mother's name. But I didn't kill my father—or Mr. Oliver—or Birdy. You must believe me!"

She leaned closer, snarling. "No more *lies!* I've known for *weeks*—since the night he was found! Someone came to me. They saw you entering the stable with Birdy back in December when she disappeared. They couldn't believe you would do something so horrible, so they came to me for advice. And for Rowan's sake, I convinced them to keep quiet—so he wouldn't get caught up in the scandal. I *protected* you! But no more! Before this night is over, you will be behind bars!"

Dread ran through me. I would never convince her.

But I still held one weapon.

"If your lying witness says a word, I will tell everyone about Nigel—that he murdered Daniel Barron and cheated at Drake. That you paid Mr. Foley and promoted him to headmaster. I will tell Judge Stoker, and he will believe me—you know he will! And then everyone will know the truth about the Blackshaws!" My heart raced.

Her eyes flickered with fear, but her voice remained icy and sure. "You think anyone will believe you—the girl who became a killer like her mother? Who killed her own father and now lies to protect her-self?"

"No," I admitted, my heart thundering in my chest. "But they will believe Rowan. I will tell him that his father murdered Daniel Barron, and *he* will tell the world. And they will believe him! He has no reason to smear his own family's name."

Mrs. Blackshaw drew a sharp breath, and I felt a spark of hope.

My own voice hardened. "Rowan doesn't know the truth about his father, but if your lying witness speaks out, I will tell him everything. That his father was a cheat and a murderer. That every time you listed his father's virtues—every time you made Rowan feel small in comparison—you knew the truth—that his father killed his friend and burned the body. Rowan will be disgusted—and furious—and tell the world *everything*! And they will *believe him!*"

Her voice fell to a furious hiss. "Rowan would never do that. He is a Blackshaw."

I lifted my chin, feigning an arrogance I didn't feel. "Rowan will do anything I ask of him. How did you put it? I have . . . *bewitched* him."

She came so quickly, my breath caught in my throat. She grabbed my arm and pushed her face close to mine, her teeth bared. "You foul . . . wicked . . . *horrid* girl! No better than your mother! No better than your grandfather—evil man with evil children, spawned by that tramp of a woman! You will hang for what you've done! And when you see your grandfather in hell, you can give him a message from me—"

Her voice choked to a stop. Tears glittered in her eyes.

"You can tell that wretched man that I was behind *everything*—every business deal that collapsed—every money rumor that was false— every finance scheme that failed! I *ruined* him! And when he died, I spat on his grave! And when you die, I will spit on yours—the last of the Barrons! You wicked, *murderous* girl!" Her black skirt swished and she strode away, back to the dining hall.

I inhaled a shaky breath, my heart pounding. For a moment, Mrs. Blackshaw had seemed possessed of madness. My knees shook, and I collapsed onto a chair. I pressed my hands to my mouth, horrified by all that had happened.

Would I be arrested tonight? Hanged in three days like my mother?

*No.* I still had some power. Mrs. Blackshaw didn't want Rowan to know that his father was a murderer. She thought he was going to Boston for a wedding ring, still trapped in her web.

But Rowan had broken free. I felt a surge of hope.

*Run, Rowan. Run far away.*

# 34

I tossed for most of the night, my thoughts churning, then woke to warm sunlight streaming through the window, the morning half gone, my nightgown damp with sweat. I sat up, groggy and blinking.

When I swallowed, my throat burned.

Across the room, the beautiful blue dress lay puddled on the floor, its hem soiled from my walk home through the dark woods. I would have to launder it today. I groaned at the prospect.

I felt wretched. I rubbed my stiff neck and found a stray hairpin and a couple of tiny white flowers. I pulled them out and added them to the pile on the nightstand.

Last night seemed like a dream. I'd told Sam the truth; given a speech; faced Mrs. Blackshaw and learned—finally—why my mother pointed a gun at Nigel Blackshaw.

And I'd sent Rowan away.

I gasped, realizing the late hour. I pulled my knitted shawl over my nightgown and hurried down the staircase in my bare feet, worried I'd missed him.

My heart dropped when I saw a large envelope on the table. I picked it up and saw a note scrawled on the outside in Rowan's hand. *I didn't want to wake you. Write to me every day for these two weeks, so I know all is well. My heart is full, but I will spare you my feeble attempts at romantic prose. Perhaps this will suffice.* He'd drawn a simple sketch of a young man on one knee, holding up flowers, more comical than romantic. I gave a weak laugh.

Inside the envelope was a significant amount of money—more than he should have left me when he needed it for his own travels. He'd included a slip of paper with his uncle's address. And another brief note: *The box contains a pistol that belonged to my father, and his father before him. I know you won't touch it, but you seek a killer, Valentine, and it comforts me to know that you have this should you need it.*

For the first time, I noticed a large wooden box on the table—a pistol case, wider than it was tall, finely crafted, with a ribbon of gold inlay around the edge. It looked old, with a rich patina. I hesitated, then turned the small key in front and lifted the lid.

And saw a large, black pistol with a golden bird on its side.

My ears throbbed, for I knew its frightful roar. I stared at it, both horrified and fascinated to learn that I'd killed Nigel Blackshaw with his own gun. How had it ended up in my mother's hands?

I closed the lid and stepped back, unable to take my eyes off the wooden box.

Rowan didn't know this was the gun that killed his father, or he wouldn't have brought it.

And he didn't know that his father murdered Daniel Barron.

I would leave him in ignorance, if I could; I knew the weight of a murdering parent. But we'd promised to tell each other if we ever learned why his father died, and this time, I would keep my word. I would have to tell him in a letter. But I could also write that he'd been right about his grandmother: she didn't kill anyone.

But someone had.

I rubbed my temples, realizing I was right back where I'd started, with no idea who'd murdered Father and Mr. Oliver and Birdy—or why they'd done it.

*The lying witness.*

I straightened with a startled breath. I'd thought Mrs. Blackshaw had just made up the story to convince Rowan that I was the killer. But last night, it became clear that someone did go to her with a story about me entering the stable with Birdy. And this lying witness was the killer.

*Mrs. Blackshaw knew their identity.*

I hurried up the staircase, my pulse racing. I dressed quickly, my hands shaking on the buttons. My body felt strangely warm and clammy, my throat sore. I was sick, I suspected, but it didn't matter. The answers were so close. I just had to convince Mrs. Blackshaw to tell me the name of this witness.

*Why would she?* She believed them, not me. She thought I was the killer.

I would go to Sheriff Crane instead, I quickly decided—tell him I shot Nigel Blackshaw, then tell him about this lying witness. He would convince Mrs. Blackshaw to reveal their name.

Or believe her and arrest me.

I descended the staircase, trying to not doubt, trying to ignore the trepidation tightening my stomach. This was the reason I hadn't left with Rowan—to admit what I'd done and clear my mother's name. And Mrs. Blackshaw knew the name of the killer.

I paused in the kitchen, my head dizzy, my stomach hollow. But I looked at the stale bread on the counter and knew I couldn't eat a bite.

Outside, a cool breeze hit the sweat on my forehead, sending a shiver through me. I walked around the house to the road.

Mrs. Henny straightened in her garden, holding a clump of weeds, smiling when she saw me. "I was hoping to see you today, Valentine. I wanted to tell you how much I enjoyed your speech. I don't know how you memorize so many words."

"I'm glad it's over," I admitted, walking closer.

Her expression softened. "I couldn't help but think how proud your mother would have been. You looked just like her up there. That's what I kept thinking."

I swallowed against my sore throat. Mrs. Henny was one of the few people who ever spoke kindly about my mother. They'd been friends, living across the road.

Her brow creased. "Are you feeling all right, Valentine? You look a bit pale."

"I think I'm sick," I admitted.

"Well, you must take willow bark. Come inside; I have some in the kitchen." She turned toward the house.

I hesitated, glancing down the road, then reluctantly followed her through the door.

"Philly is napping," Mrs. Henny said in a hushed voice, glancing up the narrow staircase. "Such an exciting night, but very late."

I followed her to the small kitchen at the back of the cottage and saw the source of the gently spiced aroma filling the air—a dozen small currant cakes arranged on a tray. Mrs. Henny was known for them.

"Just let me find it," she murmured, searching through the cupboard. Her fingers pushed bottles aside. She opened a tea tin and sniffed, then returned it to the shelf. My eyes roamed across the shelves, up to the top—

And I saw it.

A distinctive blue tea tin with scrolled lettering, half-hidden in the top corner.

I blinked, but it didn't change. It was the same box. The tea that poisoned Mr. Oliver and disappeared when I ran for help.

My heart leaped—then tumbled in horror. My mind spun, trying to understand the impossible. Trying to believe the unbelievable.

The jagged pieces slid into place.

Mrs. Henny lived across the road. She saw what happened the night

Nigel Blackshaw died. She saw me pick up the gun. She knew my mother was innocent.

Why didn't she defend my mother in court? I didn't know. I couldn't think.

Whatever the reason, she'd kept the secret for eleven years—until, in a moment of weakness, she'd confided in the Reverend Mr. Oliver— her friend, the man who wanted to marry her. And he told me. And I told Father—who immediately knew that the only other person who knew my mother was innocent was Mrs. Henny. He'd crossed the road and scolded her. *Tell the rector you made it up, before he tells someone else. Before the entire town finds out what Valentine did—before Valentine believes it!*

But Mrs. Henny took it one step further. She knew which plants were deadly. She went to the rectory and silenced Mr. Oliver.

Confusion swirled. Why would she care enough about my reputation to murder Mr. Oliver? It didn't make sense. I remembered his wide, terrified eyes, and fury rose up my spine.

"I don't see the willow bark," Mrs. Henny murmured, her back to me. "I must have given it to Mrs. Duncan. But you can use this." She turned, holding a jar of amber honey. "A spoonful, twice a day."

"You killed him," I said hoarsely.

Her eyes snapped up to my face, then quickly followed my gaze to the top shelf and the blue tea tin—and the jar of honey slid from her hand, shattering.

Hot anger pulsed through me. "You murdered Mr. Oliver!"

She stared at me, horrified.

"You served him poisoned tea—Birdy saw through the window— she called you his *friend!* Then you took the tea tin—you *saw* him lying there!" I remembered Mr. Oliver's slumped figure, and my temper flared. "He *knew* you'd poisoned him as he lay dying—the woman he wanted to *marry!*"

Mrs. Henny stepped back, trembling. Tears sprang to her eyes. "I . . . I had no choice. He shouldn't have told you. I spoke to him in confidence because I thought I was dying. But he was talking, and I knew he would ruin everything."

I shook my head, unable to imagine. "What . . . *what* could Mr. Oliver possibly ruin that would make you want to kill him?" My mind raced to make sense of it, as Mrs. Henny's eyes fluttered to the ceiling.

*And I knew the answer.* The only thing that could drive timid Mrs. Henny to murder. "Philly," I breathed. "What does Philly have to do with this?"

Mrs. Henny lifted her chin, and her voice steadied. "He was going to ruin her future."

Philly's future. I shook my head, not understanding.

And then I saw it all. I released a weak laugh. "Her future with Rowan."

"She . . . she is going to marry him. She is going to be an important lady."

My mind flew. "You heard them arguing that night. You heard Mrs. Blackshaw tell my mother that Nigel murdered Daniel. So you struck a deal with Mrs. Blackshaw. You agreed to keep quiet in return for—what? A wedding ring?"

"Philly is going to be a Blackshaw. A prominent lady—not scraping for every penny!"

This was the reason Mrs. Blackshaw insisted that Rowan marry Philly—she'd made another despicable bargain with Mrs. Henny. If Rowan didn't marry Philly, Mrs. Henny would tell the world that Nigel Blackshaw was a murderer.

Another horrible truth rose.

"You killed my father and Birdy!"

Mrs. Henny's eyes widened. "It was a mistake; I know that now. But Joseph frightened me—he was so angry. But he shouldn't have been. I never told Mr. Oliver it was you, Valentine, only that Isabella was innocent. But your father didn't want you to find out what you'd done. He was so proud that you went to Drake. He was afraid you'd be expelled if Mrs. Blackshaw found out."

Grief tightened my throat. I hadn't appreciated Father enough when I'd had the chance. "Why did you kill him?"

She shook her head, her eyes flooding with regret. "I shouldn't have. I know that now, but I panicked. He called me a stupid, lonely old widow who couldn't keep her mouth shut. He threatened to tell Mrs. Blackshaw that I was talking about Nigel. She would know I'd broken my promise. The money would stop."

"Money? What money?" Understanding fell. "She's been paying you for your silence."

"Your father was going to tell Mrs. Blackshaw that I hadn't been loyal to her. That's what she cares about most—loyalty. That's what she tells me every time she gives me money. I couldn't let her know I talked to Mr. Oliver. So, I told your father . . . I told him to go to the stable where Philly wouldn't hear us. He was coughing . . . and I brought him cough syrup."

"Laced with poison," I whispered. Father had taken a grateful swig.

It all made sense. She'd killed Father and Mr. Oliver because she didn't want Mrs. Blackshaw to know that she'd broken her vow of silence. Because she wanted money. Because she wanted Philly to marry a Blackshaw.

She continued in a strained voice. "I saw Birdy at your house. I knew she hadn't given me away yet, or I would have been arrested. But it was only a matter of time. You were at school, so I went inside and called up the stairs. I said you'd sent me to fetch her because your father had collapsed in the stable. It took some persuasion, but she finally came with me. I had a shovel ready. I told her to bend down to help him, and then I—" She stopped, swallowing.

Hit poor Birdy in the head.

Fury crawled up my throat, but more questions swirled, and

Mrs. Henny held all the answers, so I forced my voice to a calm low. "You were friends with my mother. Did she really set out to deceive Nigel Blackshaw in revenge?"

Mrs. Henny's brow furrowed. "Revenge? I don't know what you mean."

"She really did intend to run away with him?"

"Yes, but you mustn't believe the nasty rumors you've heard. Your mother wasn't unfaithful. But she was unhappy, so desperately unhappy. It started when her brother died. She was never the same after that. She went to the city for a while and came back married, with you. But things were never good between her and Joseph. I used to hear him yelling across the road. He never forgave her—" She stopped herself.

"I know he wasn't my real father." I stifled my temper, hoping to draw more information from her. "Do you know anything about my real father?"

"She only mentioned him once, and no details to speak of. But I could see that she loved him."

"Why didn't she marry him?"

Mrs. Henny shook her head. "I'm sorry. I don't know."

My head reeled with questions. I remembered Nigel Blackshaw's letter begging my mother to marry him, which she'd refused. "Why did she agree to run away with Nigel Blackshaw? She didn't love him."

"For you, Valentine. Things had become so bitter between her and Joseph, she thought it would be a better life. The four of you were supposed to leave that night. And I think Joseph was relieved. He just wanted it over. But Mrs. Blackshaw found out and wanted to stop them. She came to the house to convince Isabella. I was in my garden and heard everything."

I said, "She told my mother that Nigel killed Daniel."

"Not at first. She threatened to disinherit Nigel, but Isabella only laughed. She didn't care about the money. She accused Mrs. Blackshaw of hating the Barrons because she'd been jilted at the altar—and that's when Mrs. Blackshaw became enraged. She screamed that Silas Barron meant nothing to her, that Isabella was too stupid to see the truth—that Nigel murdered Daniel and started the fire. It was horrible. Isabella clawed at Mrs. Blackshaw. Joseph had to pull them apart. Then Mrs. Blackshaw panicked, knowing she'd said too much. She screamed that she'd made it up, but Isabella knew better. She collapsed, sobbing, and Joseph ordered Mrs. Blackshaw to leave."

*Poor Mama.* She'd seen her brother's black, stiffened body. She'd fled Feavers Crossing to escape the grief, only to receive letters from his killer begging her to marry him. And years later, Nigel Blackshaw still pursued her, until she'd agreed to run away with him to escape her bitter husband.

"Nigel arrived later, thinking they were still running away. Isabella looked mad with fury, screaming that she knew what he'd done. Nigel denied it at first, but then he broke down and cried. He said it was an accident, that some darkness had taken hold of him. They both seemed mad.

"Nigel finally went to the carriage, and I thought that was the end of it. But he came back with a gun. He warned Isabella and Joseph not to repeat his mother's lies. I was horrified. I didn't know what to do. But Isabella was clever. She pretended to forgive him and love him, and when he lowered the gun, she grabbed it and pointed it at him. But your father took the gun from her and set it on the ground . . ."

"And I picked it up," I said huskily.

"Oh, Valentine," Mrs. Henny breathed with whispery kindness. "It was an accident. We all knew that. I've always known that."

And yet, she'd stopped allowing Philly to play with me.

"Why did my mother take the blame? They wouldn't have hanged me."

"She wasn't herself. Hearing about Daniel's death broke something inside her. She thought she was doing something noble." Mrs. Henny seemed to hesitate, then said, "Once, in one of her dark spells, she asked me to watch over you if anything ever happened to her. I feared she would jump in the river. Then Nigel moved back to town and started visiting her—just friendly chats, but it lifted her spirits."

"My father must have been jealous. Was that why he didn't defend her in court? He wanted her to hang?"

"Goodness, no. He tried to stop her from confessing. He told the sheriff what happened, but his English was so hard to understand back then, and Isabella just said he was lying to protect her."

My gaze sharpened. "But *you* knew. You could have told Judge Stoker."

Tears sprang in Mrs. Henny's eyes. "I intended to. But Philly was sick, burning with fever. And then I came down with it. I could barely walk. By the time I made it to town, it was too late. It all happened so fast. I would have dragged myself to town if I'd known, I swear. She was my friend." A sob escaped her throat.

I felt numb. "Where did my father go? He left me alone for three days."

"To get his cousin, a lawyer. He thought he had time. But he returned a moment too late."

The man in the green scarf. I'd never heard of this cousin.

"When I heard she'd been hanged, I was heartbroken. I went to your father. I wanted to tell people the truth, but he convinced me to keep quiet for your sake. He didn't want Mrs. Blackshaw to know what you'd done."

So, I'd been wrong. Mrs. Blackshaw had never known. She'd given Father a box of money to keep quiet about Nigel, and she'd been paying Mrs. Henny for the same reason.

Only—

My thoughts shifted. Mrs. Henny had watched from her dark garden that night; Mrs. Blackshaw wouldn't have known she was there. My voice hardened. "You went to *her*. You've been blackmailing Mrs. Blackshaw."

Mrs. Henny stiffened, her voice dropping to a stubborn low. "I've been a widow for fifteen years. How else could I afford to keep my house and garden? Or send Philly to Drake Academy?"

Fury crawled up my throat. "And my father and Mr. Oliver and Birdy? Were they the price of Philly's fine education?"

Mrs. Henny seemed to shrink in front of me. "I shouldn't have done that. I know that now. I can't eat. I can't sleep. I am paying for my sins. But Philly—" Her voice caught. "Philly is going to become a great lady. Joseph threatened to tell Mrs. Blackshaw that I'd been disloyal." Her eyes widened like a terrified mouse. "She would have turned against us. She would have told Rowan to marry Lucy."

"*Lucy?* Rowan will marry whomever he likes! And *Philly*—" My stomach seethed with disgust. "Philly will never become the grand lady you imagine! Not when her mother is convicted of murder and hanged at the gallows! You want to know what Philly will become?" My voice shook. "People will whisper that she's just like her murdering mother— no matter how hard she tries! Children will taunt her and run away! Women holding babies will cross the road when they see her coming! She won't feel welcomed in polite society—she won't feel welcomed anywhere! Philly won't become a grand lady—*Philly will become me!*"

Mrs. Henny's face twisted with rage. She grabbed a kitchen knife off the table and lunged. I moved just in time, and she staggered past me, pulled by her own weight. She whirled, standing between me and the door, her eyes wild.

I stepped back, knocking over a chair.

"I almost poisoned you too," she hissed, clutching the knife. "The night you found your father. I wasn't sure how much you knew. How much you'd guessed. I was going to poison your tea. Not monkshood, but something slower."

My heart thundered in my chest. I moved carefully to the side, trying to draw her away from the door, but she matched my steps, turning with me.

"But I couldn't do it. You looked so fragile that night—like the little girl who used to play with Philly." Her voice broke on her daughter's name, but she shook the weakness away. Her eyes snapped with new temper. "You *stupid* girl! This is *all* your fault! Everyone would have thought Mr. Oliver died of a heart attack if you hadn't showed up."

I stepped to the side, and my shoe crunched on the broken jar of honey.

"I've seen the way you lure Rowan to your house," she seethed, stalking closer. "You think you can steal him from Philly!"

"Is that why you told Mrs. Blackshaw you saw me entering the stable with Birdy? So I would die at the gallows, no poison necessary?" My back hit the cupboard. I quickly turned and reached up, grabbing the blue tea tin off the top shelf. I turned to face her, clutching it to my chest. "I have the evidence now, Mrs. Henny, and soon everyone will know the truth—that my mother was innocent and *you* are a killer!"

She lunged with a furious screech. I darted to the side, but my shoe stumbled on the honey, and her knife sliced my upper arm. I cried out, jerking my arm away, and the knife skittered across the floor.

For a heartbeat, we both stared at it.

Then we dove at the same time, our bodies colliding.

Mrs. Henny reached it first, straightening with a triumphant cry. Terror shot through me. I was too close. She swung, and I grabbed her wrist, stopping the knife in front of my face. We struggled for control of it.

"Please—" I begged, gritting my teeth, pushing against her wrist. "You can't kill me in your kitchen. What will Philly think?"

"That you attacked me! That you confessed to killing everyone before you died!"

My heart dropped. No one would doubt it. With a desperate surge of strength, I shoved her arm. The knife jerked back against her forehead, and she stumbled back with a cry, blood flowing from a deep gash above her eyes. The knife clattered to the floor. Mrs. Henny swayed, looking startled, blinking against the stream of blood—then she snarled and reached for me. I gasped and pushed her with all my strength. She fell backward, her head hitting the stove with a loud crack, then she crumpled to the floor.

I saw the knife and snatched it up. I stood over her, breathing hard, ready for her next attack—almost longing for an excuse to fight.

But she lay still, looking small and frail, like the Mrs. Henny I knew, with gray hair and a faded dress. Only the ghoulish blood told the truth.

And her eyes staring at nothing.

The knife slid from my hand. "Mrs. Henny," I croaked. I dropped beside her. Her head tilted at a grotesque angle. I tried to straighten it, but it only flopped. I dropped it in horror, staggering to my feet.

My stomach roiled. I stared at my bloody hands.

Overhead, a floorboard creaked.

# 35

My eyes darted in panic. I saw the broken honey jar; the chair on its side; my slashed sleeve, now soaked in blood; the bloody knife on the floor. Mrs. Henny lay dead, another victim.

I was the one still breathing.

*No one would believe me.*

I saw the blue tea tin where I'd dropped it and snatched it up. I had my proof.

But it didn't prove anything. My chest tightened in dread. They would think the tea belonged to me—that I'd come to poison Mrs. Henny, but she guessed my intention and fought back.

The ceiling groaned. Philly couldn't find me here, standing over her dead mother. I moved from the kitchen, pausing to listen, glancing up the staircase, then I left through the front door, closing it quietly behind me.

I hurried across the street, my heart racing, wondering what I should do, where I should go. I needed to tell someone, but who would believe that timid Mrs. Henny was a killer? She might have admitted the truth under pressure, but there was no chance for that now.

I walked along the carriage drive, my thoughts darting. No one must know I'd been there when she died. But my head screamed in horror at the thought of another secret.

I turned the back corner of my house—and powerful hands grabbed my shoulders, shoving me up against the wall. I gasped and saw Mr. Frye's face only inches from mine.

"Now, you've gone and done it," he sneered.

For a heart-stopping moment, I thought he meant Mrs. Henny.

"My wife's crying, and Sam's yelling. Think you're too good for a Frye now that you got some fancy school award? Well, I seen those dead bodies in your stable. *You're* the one who's not good enough for my Sam!"

I blinked, forcing my thoughts from Mrs. Henny's dead stare to Sam's broken heart. My mouth opened and closed.

Mr. Frye released me with a scornful push. "You can't go back on a promise like that. You say you're going to marry him, and you're going to marry him if I have to drag you to the church myself."

I swallowed against the fire in my throat. His fury didn't make sense. "If you think I killed them, you should be glad I'm not marrying him."

He smirked. "Maybe so, but you're an orphan now, so I think it's worth the risk." He saw my confusion and laughed. "Seven of us stepping on each other in that poky little cabin, and you all alone on this grand estate."

I released a weary breath. Sam thought his mother was warming up to the idea of me as a daughter-in-law, but she was really just warming up to the idea of my property.

"You think I'd invite you to live here?"

"You got no choice. Family is family. If the log cabin were to . . . catch fire, say . . . we'd have nowhere else to go. I think my wife would look fine sitting in a proper parlor, serving tea to the church ladies. What do you think?"

I cringed at my narrow escape. "Sorry to disappoint you, but Sam and I aren't getting married."

"Oh, you'll marry him, all right; I'll make sure of that."

I stepped back, fear running through me. "You can't frighten me into making marriage vows."

"I don't know." He stepped closer, tall and broad, his fists curling. "I can be mighty frightening when I put my mind to it."

I turned to run, but he grabbed my arm—right over my wound. I gasped in pain, and Mr. Frye quickly released me, staring in surprise at the blood on his hand. His gaze darted up to my face, curious—

As Philly's scream rent the air.

I gave a gasping sob.

Mr. Frye's eyes narrowed with suspicion. "What'd you do now, pretty girl?"

Philly's cry turned to a guttural howl of anguish, and Mr. Frye hurried toward the road.

I reluctantly followed, stopping at the edge of the carriage drive to watch from the trees as Mr. Frye entered the Hennys' house. I waited, holding my breath, and they soon emerged. Philly wailed and tried to go back inside, but Mr. Frye kept her moving forward, his arm around her back. His gaze darted to me, tight with accusation, but he remained with Philly, guiding her down the road to the O'Donnells' house. I watched as Mrs. O'Donnell ushered Philly inside, then Mr. O'Donnell joined Mr. Frye, and the two of them hurried toward town—Mr. Frye casting a furtive glance back at me.

My body swayed. I hugged myself and felt damp blood on my arm. I looked down, surprised; I couldn't feel the pain. I knew I should walk to Sheriff Crane and explain what happened—before he believed Mr. Frye's version of the story. But I felt feverish, my legs shaky. I wavered with uncertainty, then returned to my kitchen.

As I set the blue tea tin on the table, I saw the wooden gun box, and a new wave of despair washed over me. I drank water, trying to soothe my sore throat, then sank to the rocking chair to wait for Sheriff Crane to come for me.

The only sound was the tick of the small clock on the mantel.

I would tell Sheriff Crane everything—about every death, including Daniel Barron's. I'd finally found all the answers, and there was some sense of victory in that.

But I might still hang for murder.

The sharp knock on the front door came sooner than I'd expected. I stood, waited for the room to stop spinning, then made my way to the front door and opened it.

Mrs. Blackshaw stood in front of me. I blinked, confused.

Her gaze darted to the blood on my arm, and she pushed her way inside, shutting the door behind her. "What happened to her?" she asked in a furious hiss.

She'd seen Mrs. Henny—and immediately come here, assuming I was to blame. "I'm . . . I'm waiting for Sheriff Crane," I said shakily.

"Oh, he'll be here soon enough, make no mistake. Now, quickly— tell me what happened so I can help you."

My foggy mind tried to keep up. "Help me?"

"I was on my way to make amends with you when I saw Mr. Frye and Mr. O'Donnell on the road, raving about Mrs. Henny being dead. I found her in the kitchen. Did you kill her?"

"No," I croaked. "At least—I didn't mean to. She attacked me with a knife. I pushed her. I didn't mean for her to die—I didn't *want* her to die! I need her to tell everyone the truth."

"And what truth is that?" Mrs. Blackshaw demanded.

I swallowed against my fiery throat. "She killed them—my father and Mr. Oliver and Birdy. She admitted it, then attacked me with a knife."

I expected scornful disbelief, but Mrs. Blackshaw didn't look surprised. "*Why* did she kill them? That's what I can't figure out."

*She already knew.* My mind swirled, trying to decide if that was helpful or just another secret to be used against me. I couldn't think. The house felt like an echoing tomb around us. Too warm. Too quiet.

Mrs. Blackshaw pressed a cool hand against my forehead and made a low sound in her throat. "You're burning up."

"Yes," I agreed limply.

"Sheriff Crane will be here soon, and he *cannot* know you were there when Mrs. Henny died. Do you understand, Valentine? Or you will surely hang."

I released a laughing breath. "That should please you."

Emotion flickered in her eyes. "I am not the devil you think I am. Now, quickly—you must change from this bloody dress, or it'll give you away."

I swayed uncertainly, and she took my uninjured arm and urged me up the staircase, walking alongside. I felt breathless when we reached the top, hardly believing Mrs. Blackshaw was inside my house.

"This illness suits our purposes," she said as we entered my room. "You are too ill to have been out. Take off that dress, and I will burn it." My fingers fumbled over the buttons, and she pushed my hands aside and did them herself. She helped me pull the dress over my head, then handed me my nightgown. "Put this on and get in bed."

"But—"

"You are not well, Valentine. Stay here. I will return."

I obeyed with relief, collapsing on the mattress, closing my eyes.

Mrs. Blackshaw returned with an armload of supplies. She arranged the items on the nightstand, then sat the edge of my bed and wiped my face with a damp cloth. She helped me sit up and pressed a cup to my lips. I drank cool water, then sank back.

She pushed up the sleeve of my nightdress and inspected my wound, frowning. "It doesn't look deep. I don't think it needs stitching."

Somewhere in my foggy mind, I knew this was wrong . . . that I shouldn't trust Mrs. Blackshaw. But her cool efficiency was reassuring. Even comforting. She dabbed tenderly at the cut on my arm, then wrapped a bandage around it with gentle fingers. This was the Mrs. Blackshaw who raised money for orphans and runaway slaves. She'd taken charge of the situation, and I was relieved to give it to her.

"Why are you being kind?" I asked hoarsely.

Her eyes met mine, then returned to the bandage she was wrapping. "We both spoke in temper last night. You were so convinced I was the killer, I realized it couldn't be you. Which meant Mrs. Henny lied when she told me she saw you entering the stable. Which led me to wonder if she killed them herself. Poison seems her style. And I know—better than most—that she is capable of dark deeds. I just couldn't figure out why she would do it. I was on my way to ask you when I saw Mr. O'Donnell and Mr. Frye." She knotted the bandage and looked up to meet my eyes with a grim expression. "Explain to me why a woman who can barely kill a spider murdered three people."

*Mrs. Blackshaw believed it.*

I released a shallow breath of amazement. I could have no stronger ally. "It started before Christmas."

I told her about Mrs. Henny confiding in Mr. Oliver and my father crossing the road to threaten her. "She didn't want you to know she'd been disloyal. She didn't want to lose your blackmail money . . . or your promise for Philly."

Mrs. Blackshaw's lips tightened. "I cannot pretend to be sorry she is dead. She has made my life a misery for over a decade, constantly reminding me of Nigel's mistake."

"Mistake?" I shifted up to my elbows. "He murdered my uncle!"

Her eyes tightened with impatience. "I am aware of what happened between my son and Daniel Barron—more than you. But it was twenty years ago, and they are both gone. Let them rest in peace."

"People should know the truth."

"Should they?" she snapped. "You think people should know that you shot Nigel and let your mother hang for it?"

"Yes." I sat straighter, leaning against the headboard. "That's exactly what I want—to clear my mother's name."

She gave a short laugh. "And that's why you've said nothing for more than a decade?"

"I didn't know—not until recently." It dawned on me that I'd never apologized. I swallowed against the fire in my throat. "I'm sorry I killed your son. I don't expect you to forgive me, but I want you to know how sorry I am."

She didn't reply at once, fighting some inner emotion. Her jaw clenched and released. Finally, she said, "I have my own regrets from that night. But that isn't why I came today. I came to make a deal with you, Valentine."

My stomach tightened. Another of Mrs. Blackshaw's twisted bargains. "I'm not interested."

"Do you love my grandson?"

The question caught me off guard. "Yes," I admitted. "Very much."

"Then you want what's best for him." Her eyebrows arched.

I felt the trap widening, but wasn't sure how to avoid it. "Of course."

"Then you will not tell him what his father did. Not ever."

I shook my head. "Rowan deserves to know. He's always wondered why his father died."

"You think it benefits him to know that his father did something . . . so horrible?"

I couldn't answer. My head throbbed. None of this seemed real—Mrs. Blackshaw sitting at the edge of my bed. Mrs. Henny dead on her kitchen floor.

"You think it benefits Rowan to be known forever as the child of a murderer? You know that life, Valentine. Would you wish it on him?" Her shrewd eyes held mine. "What do you think will happen to Blackshaw Bank after our name has been ripped apart by scandal? You think wealthy men will continue to hand their money over to the Blackshaws when we're known for murder and deceit?"

"Rowan doesn't plan on working at the bank," I said weakly.

"Blackshaw Bank will pay for Rowan to go to Harvard and his architectural apprenticeship. Would you steal that from him?"

I didn't respond. I wasn't sure. When Rowan returned from Europe, he might want those things.

Her silky voice washed over me. "At my core, I am a businesswoman, Valentine. I evaluate one asset over another. Last night, I sat up half the night evaluating the assets of my own life, and without question, Rowan is my greatest asset. My most valuable treasure. And I want him back. We've done nothing but quarrel for months. I've allowed an old wound to fester and affect my current happiness. Your grandfather used me poorly, but it was a long time ago, and it is time to move on. I want my grandson back."

I held my breath.

She continued in her smooth voice. "This morning, Rowan left to visit his mother's family, and I know he does not intend to come back."

My heart jolted in alarm.

Her lips tilted in a sad smile. "I see more than he thinks. Last night, he never even glanced at Philly, and then the two of you disappeared into that dark room. This morning, he packed his bags rather heavily for such a short visit. When I saw that he'd taken the sketch his mother drew of his father—well, I knew he wasn't coming home. I imagine the two of you plan to meet somewhere, then disappear where his evil grandmother can't find you."

I didn't respond, my chest tight with dread.

"Well, there's no need for that now. I am offering you my grandson, Valentine."

I didn't believe her. I forced my fevered mind to focus. "In return for what?"

"You must keep Nigel's secret."

"No," I said at once.

"Daniel Barron's death was a lifetime ago. Revealing what happened doesn't help anyone; it only hurts Rowan."

I considered that, my heart pounding heavily.

"You must also keep quiet about Mrs. Henny, of course. We can't explain why she murdered two people without revealing the blackmail . . . which leads to Nigel's mistake . . . which brings us right back to where we started—both of us wanting what's best for Rowan."

I shook my head, wanting to disagree, but unable to think past her logic. A bead of sweat slid down my temple.

She continued smoothly. "This also happens to be what's best for you, Valentine. No one will know you killed Mrs. Henny. No nasty murder charges. And, more importantly, now that my arrangement with Mrs. Henny has reached an end, I can allow Rowan to marry whomever he likes."

I wanted to believe her. With Mrs. Blackshaw's approval, Rowan wouldn't have to give up everything for me. He could still go to Europe, but return to both me and his grandmother. His friends. Even his wealth. But I knew there must be a trap inside the promise.

"You're just saying this now to keep me quiet. You think a girl like me brings too much scandal for a Blackshaw."

"Oh, gossip settles as quickly as it rises. Your school award helps. I'll talk about how impressed I was by your oration. How wrong I've been. I'll rebuild your reputation one tea party at a time. You'll be amazed by how quickly everyone agrees once they've seen us sitting together in church." She straightened my quilt. "Rowan's mentioned your interest in higher learning. I know of an excellent girls' seminary not far from Harvard, with a curriculum that rivals the boys'. I could write a few letters on your behalf. Pay your tuition and arrange for housing."

I swallowed against my sore throat. My entire being yearned for what she offered—to be accepted into Rowan's life so he didn't need to abandon it. To attend a good school near him.

"Of course," Mrs. Blackshaw added carefully, "I must insist you keep quiet about your mother's innocence as well. We can't have people talking about you shooting Rowan's father, just as I'm trying to rebuild your reputation. It would undermine everything."

My fragile hopes tumbled. I shook my head. "I have to clear my mother's name."

Her tone softened. "She is gone, Valentine. Your sacrifice won't save her, only mar your own future. Learn from my mistake. There's no reward in holding on to old wounds, only a bitter heart." She took my hand in hers. "You impressed me last night, Valentine—not only with your speech but by standing up to me. I think the two of us could get along quite well together, once we set our minds to it."

My head throbbed. Her price was silence. I would be trapped forever inside my wall of secrets.

*But . . . was that so terrible if the reward was Rowan?*

"I'll let you rest. You'll think more clearly once the fever has broken. In the meantime, I'll keep Sheriff Crane away. Oh, and I'll send a message to Rowan at his uncle's house, letting him know you've taken ill. I'm sure he'll rush home."

I didn't protest. Because I wanted him home.

Because I wanted the dream Mrs. Blackshaw had just given me.

# 36

My body burns with fever, drenched in sweat. My nightgown clings to me. I kick the quilt away . . . then shiver and claw for it again, my teeth chattering. Mama wipes my brow and helps me drink cool water.

Only, it isn't Mama. It's Mrs. Blackshaw.

She fades away.

I dream of Mrs. Henny's wild fury . . . and Father's frozen corpse . . . and Birdy. I hear Mr. Oliver's last gurgling word. Poison. I dream of Mr. Blackshaw falling backward, his black cloak billowing, his startled eyes looking at me . . . looking at me.

I hear Mama laughing as the two of us pull weeds in the garden. "Look, Valentine, a fat carrot."

"Valentine . . ." A gentle hand shakes my shoulder, and I blink myself awake. Mrs. Blackshaw bends over me. "Can you stand? Just for a moment." Behind her, I see a maid and manservant in uniforms.

Mrs. Blackshaw helps me stand as my mattress is taken away and a new, fat mattress with clean ticking put in its place. The maid spreads clean linens over it, and I'm allowed to lie down. My head lands on a downy pillow. A soft blanket is pulled up to my waist. "Thank you," I whisper. I've never known such comfort.

Dr. Wellington comes and examines me with kind eyes and gentle hands, murmuring instructions to Mrs. Blackshaw. Thick, brown medicine is spooned into my mouth.

I sleep and do not dream.

I awake to a single candle burning. Mrs. Blackshaw sleeps in an armchair near my bed—the chair from Father's room.

He wasn't my father.

I slide into darkness.

I hear Father's voice and force my eyes open . . . but it's Sheriff Crane standing at the foot of my bed, murmuring with Mrs. Blackshaw. He looks concerned. My entire body aches. Every joint, every bone, even my skin.

I close my eyes.

"Can you manage a little broth?" Mrs. Blackshaw asks the next time I wake. Orange sunset comes through the window. Another day gone. The second or third? She spoons broth into my mouth, rich and flavorful, then helps me change into a clean nightgown—too white to be mine. She washes my face and brushes my long curls and braids them.

This is what it feels like to have a mother.

"Your fever has lessened," she says gently. "You just need to rest."

"Rowan?" I ask hoarsely. If she hasn't written to him, he will board a ship and disappear.

"Shh, you'll see him soon. Take this medicine."

I swallow a bitter spoonful and cough. She wipes my mouth, then helps me lie down. The bed holds me like a mother's embrace. I am not alone. I am not afraid.

I sigh with contentment and sleep.

# 37

My mind awoke all at once, my eyes snapping open to murky daylight. I closed my eyes and burrowed into the downy mattress, trying to return to oblivion.

But my mind felt fully alert. I finally gave in and sat up, groaning at the stiffness. I tilted my neck to loosen it—and saw Father's empty armchair. I sat still, listening, and sensed that I was alone in the house.

I saw Dr. Wellington's brown bottle of medicine and knew that it had helped me sleep. *For how long?* Three days at least, maybe four. Mrs. Blackshaw had left a pitcher of water and cup on the nightstand. I tried to pour, but my hand shook so badly, I drank straight from the pitcher in thirsty gulps.

I rose slowly, testing my strength. I found my knitted shawl and wrapped it around my shoulders, then padded to the staircase. I descended carefully, clutching the handrail.

When I reached the kitchen, I swayed and blinked. The room looked gloomy, darkened by heavy clouds outside. Through the window, I saw a drizzling mist.

I considered starting a fire but doubted I would be downstairs long enough to enjoy it.

The wooden gun box and envelope of money were gone. In their place, someone had left a basket of food: a wheel of cheese, a cluster of strawberries, a fluffy loaf of bread. I saw a folded note with my name written on it, tucked behind the bread. I stared at it, blinking slowly . . . then recognized the handwriting. I whimpered in relief and hurried to it.

*Dear Valentine,*

*I am distressed by your illness, but my grandmother assures me you are on the mend. She is quite protective, not allowing me to wake you.*

*I would rather tell you in person, but you must know at once—Mr. Frye has been arrested. He murdered your father, Mr. Oliver, and Birdy—and now, poor Mrs. Henny. He will be hanged later today, and this ordeal will be over. Mrs. Henny's death has shaken my grandmother and softened her heart toward you—as you see by her kind nursing. I will tell you all when I see you next, but I have never felt so free. The killer has been found, and people know it is not you, Valentine.*

*Love, Rowan*

I groaned, leaning both hands on the table to steady myself.

Suddenly, the web was visible, no longer hidden behind gentle touches and beautiful promises.

Mrs. Blackshaw had kept me drugged and sleeping while Mr. Frye was arrested and tried for murder. She knew he had nothing to do with the deaths, but he made a convenient scapegoat. He'd been in the house and probably tracked blood on his shoes. No one would doubt his guilt; Sam's father was known for his violent temper. All Mrs. Blackshaw had to do was keep me sleeping until it was too late. Once I woke up, I wouldn't dare admit that I was the one who'd pushed Mrs. Henny into the stove.

Frightened into silence—again.

And beholden to Mrs. Blackshaw to keep my secret—forever.

I glanced at the rainy window, my head swimming. Sam's father was a bully of a man, but he didn't deserve to hang for murders he didn't commit.

I had to stop it.

I half ran, half crawled up the staircase. I yanked off the pretty nightgown that didn't belong to me and pulled on one of my own plain dresses. My fingers shook as I did the buttons. I sat on the downy mattress and pulled on my shoes, resisting my body's need to lie down.

*This time, I must get there in time.*

I stumbled down the staircase and out the front door. Cold rain hit my face. My feet trampled over the ground where Mr. Blackshaw had bled and died. I pushed through the broken gate with a hand as white as a corpse.

I ran.

Past the silent houses of my neighbors. Past the graveyard with its weeping headstones. Past the rectory and stone church. My foot landed in a puddle, and I nearly fell, but I drew a sobbing breath and ran on. Every stride was an effort. Every heartbeat a pounding drum. My dress clung to my legs, soaking wet. My face throbbed with cold. I should have worn a coat, but it was too late for that.

*Too late.*

*Too late.*

Did Sam's father already dangle from a rope, his eyes staring fixedly? Did tears of rain already slide down his slack cheeks?

The streets of Feavers Crossing seemed eerily deserted. I ran past the Duncans' bakery. Past Utley General Goods. I staggered to a stop to catch my breath—and saw Blackshaw Bank with its dark, unblinking windows. I growled in fury and ran again.

As I neared the jailhouse, I saw townspeople on their way to the hanging. I darted around them, my shoes splashing. The crowd thickened in front of me, then became a wall. I stopped, struggling to breathe, craning my neck to see past the dark coats. In the distance, I saw the wooden gallows.

*Mama.*

I groaned and pushed my way through wet wool. A black umbrella blocked my view. "Let me through," I pleaded. I stood on tiptoe, my heart racing—and saw Mr. Frye on the platform, a rope around his neck—but standing, not dangling. Breathing, not dead. I sobbed in relief. The new rector, Mr. Newland, stood beside him, reading scripture in his deep voice.

"He didn't do it!" I cried, but my voice came out smaller than I intended. I squeezed my way between dark coats. "Please," I begged. I pushed myself through—and stumbled forward at the front, falling to the wet paving stones in front of the gallows. My exhausted body longed to stay there, but I forced myself to my hands and knees . . . heaved a breath . . . and climbed to my feet.

I inhaled and forced the air from my lungs. "Mr. Frye is innocent!"

Mr. Newland's prayer halted. Mr. Frye stared at me with wide eyes, his head in the noose, his hands bound behind him. In the crowd, voices murmured.

I steadied myself, then raised my voice. "Mr. Frye didn't kill Mrs. Henny! He wasn't even there! It was me—I pushed her—to defend myself!"

Mr. Frye gave a triumphant cry. "I told you! It was her, just like I said!"

"She killed them!" Sam's mother shrieked from the far end of the gallows. She looked even smaller and more browbeaten than usual, dressed in black for her husband's hanging. Her six large sons stirred around her like angry bees—including Sam, who looked shocked to see me.

Sheriff Crane grasped my arm. "Valentine, what are you doing here? This is no sight for you."

I turned to him, relieved; Sheriff Crane had the power to stop this. "Mrs. Henny was the killer, not Mr. Frye. She poisoned them—and killed Birdy. Mr. Frye didn't do it."

"You're mad with fever. Go home." He prodded me toward the crowd.

I jerked my arm away, frantic. "You must listen to me! Mr. Frye didn't do it! *I'm* the one who pushed Mrs. Henny!"

Sheriff Crane squeezed my arm, dropping his voice in low warning. "*Go home*, Valentine, before this gets out of hand. You don't know what you're saying."

He didn't believe me. I swayed, light-headed. I was too late—*again*. The world tilted, and I closed my eyes to keep from falling.

"Valentine!" Rowan called.

I opened my eyes, whimpering in relief when I saw him hurrying toward me from the jailhouse door. Above him, Mrs. Blackshaw stood horrified at a second-floor window, her hands pressed against the glass. She shook her head, desperate to stop me.

But I'd woken up.

Rowan pulled me into his arms, nearly knocking me over, then quickly pulled back. "You're soaked. You should be home in bed."

"Mrs. Henny did it," I told him in a hoarse croak.

His brow creased. "You're confused. It was Mr. Frye. Come on, I'll take you home. You shouldn't be out in this rain." He took my arm.

"Proceed!" Sheriff Crane called to the executioner.

I looked up, horrified, yanking myself away from Rowan. "You can't do this! Mr. Frye is innocent!"

"It was her!" Mr. Frye cried, panicking. He fought against the rope that bound his wrists—trying to not pull against the rope around his neck. "I saw the blood on her! I didn't do it!"

"Hang them both!" a man shouted.

I whirled to face the crowd. "You must listen to me! Mr. Frye didn't kill anyone! It was Mrs. Henny! She killed my father and Mr. Oliver—

she poisoned them because of Nigel!" I drew a breath and forced my quavering voice to rise. "Nigel Blackshaw murdered Daniel Barron! Mrs. Henny has been blackmailing Mrs. Blackshaw—because she knew—"

"*Lies!*" Mrs. Blackshaw shrieked from the jailhouse doorway, her eyes wide and terrified.

I looked at her—and something hardened inside me. She'd kept me drugged for days so she could control my secret. But now, I controlled hers. I straightened and faced the crowd. "Nigel Blackshaw murdered my uncle, Daniel Barron—and Mrs. Blackshaw knew it! She's been paying Mrs. Henny to keep quiet!"

"She's lying!" Mrs. Blackshaw screeched. Her eyes darted across the damp faces in front of us. "She lies to protect herself! She's a killer—just like her mother!"

"My *mother* . . ." I drew on my last bit of strength, shouting it for everyone to hear. "My mother was *innocent!* She never killed *anyone!* I am the one who shot Nigel Blackshaw! It was *my* fault! She confessed to protect *me!*"

The crowd erupted in noise and movement. On the platform, Mr. Frye shouted in furious panic, fighting against his ropes. The Frye boys swarmed toward their father on the platform—all except Sam, who stared at me. Mrs. Blackshaw screamed in fury. Rowan tugged on my arm. Sheriff Crane pulled my other arm, shouting something I couldn't understand.

A shiver ran through me. My legs trembled and weakened . . . then crumpled like paper. I fell a long distance . . . slowly . . . through a bleary sky. I landed on wet paving stones, staring up at the rain.

*I'd done it.*

The rain washed over me.

# 38

---

Sheriff Crane's young watchman lifted me into his arms and carried me into the jailhouse. Rowan tried to follow, but Sheriff Crane slammed the door and slid the bolt—and the chaos outside was instantly muffled.

"Take her to the back cell," Sheriff Crane said curtly.

"Mr. Frye didn't—" I croaked.

"I heard you!" Sheriff Crane snapped. "Half the town heard you. The hanging will wait until we sort this out." He left through the door, returning to the gallows. I heard Rowan's angry voice briefly, then the door banged shut.

I was carried down a hall and through a door, into a dimly lit room. The young watchman placed me on a cot, then left, and I heard a bolt slide into place.

I forced my weary body to sit up. My wet dress clung to me, and my teeth chattered. The room was small and foul smelling, lit only by the small, barred window in the door. I sat on a thin mattress, stained by countless criminals in the past. The only other furniture was a small table.

In the distance, I heard Mr. Frye being brought inside, cursing and complaining. A door slammed, and his voice faded.

*I'd arrived in time.*

I inhaled a shuddering breath.

Men's voices rose in the hall, arguing. Footsteps tapped, and keys jangled in the lock. I blinked in surprise when Judge Stoker entered, his craggy face twisted in a furious scowl, followed by Mr. Meriwether in an impeccable black suit. Sheriff Crane was the last to enter, arguing about proper procedure—but he stopped short at the sight of me shivering on the cot. "Everyone, out. She needs dry clothes before anything else."

Judge Stoker looked annoyed, but withdrew, pausing in the doorway to point an angry finger. "You broke your word to me, Valentine!"

I nodded numbly in admission, my teeth chattering too much for speech.

The young watchman brought me a dress and blanket and bowl of soup, then left, sliding the bolt. I changed into the brown dress—which swam on me—and managed to drink a little of the cold barley soup. Then I curled back on the cot to wait, leaning against the wall, the scratchy blanket draped over me.

My shivering slid away, and my thoughts settled. I'd shouted the truth about Rowan's father to a crowd before telling him privately. He must have been shocked to hear the truth—or thought me crazed with fever. Perhaps even furious that I'd destroyed his family name.

But I didn't regret a word of it. I was locked in a jail cell, but I'd never felt freer.

The three men returned, bringing two rickety chairs. Judge Stoker and Mr. Meriwether sat, while Sheriff Crane remained near the door, frowning.

"Well, Valentine," Judge Stoker said in his low, scraping voice, glowering at me. "Thanks to you, I shall be known forever as the judge who sentenced not one but two innocent people to hang."

"I'm sorry, but I had to stop it. I couldn't let it happen again."

He grunted. "You've certainly stirred up a hornet's nest. I've asked Mr. Meriwether here to represent your interests, so you must listen to him and not answer my questions if he advises against it."

Lucy's father inclined his head. He looked out of place in my gloomy cell, with his perfectly trimmed beard and well-tailored suit.

Judge Stoker continued. "I saw everything from the courthouse window, but couldn't hear, and no one seems clear on what you said, exactly." He cast an annoyed glance at Sheriff Crane. "So, please, tell me what that madness was about."

"Mrs. Henny murdered them. It was her all along." I swallowed, realizing I'd begun at the wrong place. "It started long ago, with Nigel Blackshaw."

I told them about Nigel cheating with the help of Mr. Foley, then murdering Daniel and starting the fire. How Mrs. Blackshaw had told my mother the truth in a desperate attempt to keep her away from her son. How Nigel had pointed the gun first, but my mother had fooled him and taken it. When I got to the part where I picked up the gun, my voice faltered.

Judge Stoker waved an impatient hand. "Get to the part about Mrs. Henny. I find it impossible to believe."

My throat felt raw, but I told them about Mrs. Henny overhearing everything that night and blackmailing Mrs. Blackshaw. "She did it for Philly, so Philly could have fine things and go to Drake. She thought Philly would marry Rowan and become a Blackshaw. But she told Mr. Oliver when she thought she was dying—and he told me. My father was furious and threatened Mrs. Henny. He said he would tell Mrs. Blackshaw that she'd broken her vow of silence. She panicked and killed both of them—for Philly's sake."

None of them looked doubtful. Mrs. Henny's adoration for her daughter was no secret.

I looked at Sheriff Crane, who stood near the door. "I saw the blue tea tin in her kitchen. That's when I knew. I tried to leave with it, but she attacked me with a knife. I pushed her away, and she hit the stove. I didn't mean for her to die. I didn't *want* her to die! She was the only one who could prove my innocence."

Sheriff Crane looked at the other men. "When I searched Mrs. Henny's house, I found a ledger in her room with lists of payments and scribbled notes, going back for years. I wasn't sure what it meant until now." He nodded his head toward me. "I think Valentine must be right about the blackmail."

I drew a relieved breath.

"Philly has been staying at our house," Mr. Meriwether said uneasily.

"She had nothing to do with it," I said.

"She's going to live with her uncle in Albany, next week, when Lucy and my wife leave for Paris. I'll encourage her to leave sooner, before the gossip spreads."

*Poor Philly.*

Judge Stoker made a low grumbling sound in his throat. "So, what does Mr. Frye have to do with any of this?"

"Nothing," I said. "He's a brute, but he didn't kill those people." I wondered what Sam had been going through these last few days as his father was tried and convicted of murder.

Judge Stoker grunted. "I thought we were finally rid of him. That man is hardly innocent."

"Unlike Valentine," Mr. Meriwether stated crisply. "I think we can all agree she only fought Mrs. Henny to defend herself. She is guilty of no crime that I can see. She must be released."

I looked up, startled.

"By all means," Judge Stoker agreed, standing.

But Sheriff Crane looked hesitant. "She won't be safe at home. I'm about to release Mr. Frye. He and his boys will drink in celebration, then be on the warpath. They still think Valentine is the killer."

"Valentine will stay with me," Judge Stoker stated.

I just wanted to go home—and see Rowan. But I had the feeling Sheriff Crane was right. "Very well," I agreed.

We left the cell and made our way down the gloomy hall. Judge Stoker opened the outer door but hesitated on the threshold. Outside, heavy rain still poured. The gallows were now empty, the crowd gone.

"Valentine, my carriage is at the courthouse. We'll have to run for it."

"Wait," I said.

The three men turned.

"Judge Stoker, you said no one is clear on what I said out there. But I want people to be clear. I want them to know that my mother was innocent."

"Word will get around," he grumbled.

"No. False rumors will get around." My gaze shifted to Mr. Meriwether. "Please go home and tell your wife everything I told you—about Nigel Blackshaw killing Daniel Barron and Mrs. Henny killing the others. But mostly, about my mother being innocent. Tell her to go to the Utleys' store for a little shopping. Right away, even in the rain."

Mr. Meriwether's eyebrows rose. "Shopping?"

"If Mrs. Utley is going to start spreading the story, she might as well get it right."

Judge Stoker gave a short burst of laughter.

Mr. Meriwether's lips twitched. "I am quick to obey, Miss Deluca. Good day." He opened his umbrella and stepped out into the rain.

# 39

I slept deeply in Judge Stoker's guest room and awoke to his housekeeper delivering breakfast on a tray.

"The judge says you're to remain in bed all day, and if I see a touch of fever, I'm to summon the doctor."

"I'm feeling better," I assured her. And I was. I felt like a princess eating in bed—bacon and strawberries and toast with jam. Bright sunlight came through the window.

The rain was over.

After the housekeeper took the tray away, I washed at the basin in the corner of the room. The soap was perfectly formed and smelled like flowers, and the hairbrush had a silver handle.

I returned to bed, and the housekeeper entered a short time later, looking hesitant. "There's a woman here to see you. Says you don't know her, but you might recognize her surname." She glanced at a white card. "Miss Martha DeVries."

*DeVries.* I jolted upright in bed, my heart beating faster. "I'd like to see her."

I waited, barely breathing, as the woman was ushered up the stair-case. She remained near the door until the housekeeper had left, then cautiously approached my bed. "Forgive me for disturbing you." She was a sensible-looking woman of about thirty-five years, finely dressed, but not overly fashionable. "I've been to your house several times, but the woman who answered wouldn't allow me inside. Then I heard you were here."

"I've been unwell," I said faintly.

"Yes, and I don't wish to intrude, but I've been rather anxious—" She stopped abruptly with a sigh. "I apologize. I haven't even introduced myself. I'm Martha DeVries. You wrote a letter to my brother, Rich-ard. It sat in his law firm for a while, until someone finally thought to bring it to me."

A tingle of unease ran through me. "He hasn't seen the letter him-self?" I asked.

Her expression softened. "I'm sorry, but my brother died of cholera nearly a decade ago. I didn't think you were aware of him, or I would have gotten in touch."

*A decade.* Not long after my mother's death. I leaned back against the headboard, my lungs hollowing with a grief that seemed foolish since I'd never even met him. But now, I never would.

"May I?" Miss DeVries motioned toward a chair near my bed, and I nodded. She sat, and for a moment we just studied one another. She had intelligent brown eyes and light brown hair that had probably been blond in her youth.

*She was my aunt.*

"You have your mother's hair," she observed.

"You knew her in New York City?"

"I met her a few times. We didn't exactly run in the same circles. Isabella was a society girl, and my brother and I were . . . well, poor."

I liked her direct way of saying things. "How did they meet?"

"Richard was always ambitious. Most of the boys in our neighborhood grew up to be sailors or soldiers, but he got a job as an errand boy at a law firm. He practically slept at that place, running documents up and down the stairs. Eventually, he talked his way into a clerkship. He used to go out in the evenings with the other young clerks, and that's how he met Isabella." Her sensible mouth quirked in a smile. "Love at first sight, according to Richard. Of course, her guardian didn't approve of an impoverished clerk, but I imagine that just made it more exciting. They met in secret and behaved rather . . . well, recklessly, I'm afraid."

"Why didn't they get married?" I asked.

"They argued. I'm not sure why. They both had fiery temperaments. This was before they knew of your existence. I think the intensity of the relationship frightened Richard. He still had a long road ahead of him, building his career. He was young and needed time." She flashed a rueful smile. "Unfortunately, your mother didn't have that time."

"She was expecting me."

"She came to our apartment one evening—something she'd never done before—and I told her that Richard had just sailed to London to help with some legal case. The news seemed to devastate her. He'd left without saying goodbye, which must have seemed like a final rejection. When he returned from London, she was married to our cousin, Joseph."

My eyes widened. "Your cousin?"

"He stayed with us when he first came to America. Our mother was half-Italian. Richard introduced him to Isabella, and she offered to help him learn English. The two of them used to walk in the park, and, well, I imagine Joseph fell in love. Your mother had that quality about her." Martha DeVries flashed a wry smile. "Richard inherited all the charm in our family. I'm a spinster."

I liked her candor.

"It was around this time that Isabella's father died, and she found out she wasn't an heiress after all, but buried in debt. Her society friends turned their backs. Overnight, she became a penniless woman expecting a baby—utter ruin. So, when Joseph proposed . . . well, she had few other options."

"When did my father—Joseph—learn the truth?"

"You arrived three months early, large and healthy. We all guessed the truth. The three of them had a terrible row. Richard was heartbroken, of course. He truly loved your mother. I have no doubt their quarrel would have ended in marriage eventually, with or without you. It was just . . . an unfortunate turn of events."

*Poor Mama.*

"Richard tried to know you, but Joseph wouldn't allow him near you. And then you moved to Feavers Crossing, and he never saw you again."

"He came twice," I said quietly. "Once, when I was five. I found a letter. And again on the day my mother died."

"Joseph came for him because he was a lawyer—a rather successful one by then. But they arrived too late. Richard wanted to tell the judge that a grave injustice had been done, but Joseph said he wanted you to forget what you'd done. All Richard could do was buy the headstone."

*My mother's beautiful marble.*

Martha DeVries continued in a more delicate tone. "I was sorry to hear about Joseph's death. I didn't know. I came at once when I received your letter, hoping to meet with both of you. But when I arrived . . . well, I heard the news."

About Father's body lying frozen in the stable. Rumors that I'd killed him. My face warmed. "It's a complicated story," I admitted.

"From what I hear, you were something of a hero yesterday."

I gave a startled laugh. "Hero?"

"It's all anyone can talk about. The way you saved an innocent man from hanging. Finding your father's killer."

For once, Mrs. Utley's stories were in my favor.

"Well, I don't wish to tire you. I'll leave for now and return later, if that's all right." Martha DeVries stood but lingered near the bed. "To be honest, I've been rather nervous about this meeting, Valentine. I wasn't sure what to expect, but you're a lovely girl. The innkeeper told me about your award at Drake Academy. You must have inherited Richard's intellect."

"I wish I knew more about him."

"And I should love to tell you everything." She drew a breath and spoke with sudden fervor. "It was my brother's dearest wish to know you, Valentine. He never had any other children. He was married for a few years, but Rachel died shortly before he did, and I have no other family. So, I was thinking it would be quite nice if we could be friends. In fact, I was wondering—" Spots of color appeared on her cheeks. "I was wondering if you might like to come stay with me in New York City for a while, so we can get to know one another."

I sat straighter, amazed. "I'd like that. Very much, in fact."

"Would you?" Her face brightened. "I'm so glad. I have Richard's town house, with plenty of room for both of us. It gets a bit lonely, to be honest. And there's plenty to do in the city. Museums and plays, if you like that sort of thing. I do get invited to a few parties."

"That sounds wonderful." I hardly believed what I was hearing. "I don't suppose you know a woman named Alvina Lunt?"

Her brow creased. "I don't think so."

"That's all right. I'll find her."

"You could travel back with me tomorrow, if it's not too soon. I know you've been ill—"

"I'm much better," I assured her. "Well enough to travel."

Her face brightened in a smile. "Excellent. That's perfect, then, isn't it?"

"Perfect," I agreed, smiling back.

And a rightness seemed to settle over both of us.

# 40

Judge Stoker came home for lunch and asked about my mysterious visitor, and I told him everything, including the fact that Richard DeVries was my real father. He listened intently and seemed pleased that I was leaving for New York City.

"This is just what you need, Valentine. I'd like to meet her."

He got his wish when Martha DeVries returned that evening. I heard them talking downstairs, then she came up to my room, carrying two boxes tied with string.

"He's a frightful old thing, isn't he?" she whispered as she came near my bed, which made me laugh. "I hope you don't mind, but I've taken the liberty of buying you a few travel things. It gave me something to do with my day." From one box, she pulled a pretty dress and matching jacket; from the other, a bonnet with long ribbons.

"They're lovely," I said, gingerly touching the fabric. The dress looked like something Lucy Meriwether would wear.

"Your visit is just what I need, Valentine. I haven't been this excited in ages." She moved to the wardrobe to hang up the clothes. "We'll leave at noon tomorrow, if that suits you. We can stop by your house on the way to get your things. And I imagine you have a few farewells to make."

"A few," I admitted.

I could probably find Rowan at the Blackshaws' house. But Sam would be more of a challenge. I didn't dare go near the Fryes' farm on my own. I could ask Judge Stoker to escort me in his carriage, but that wasn't how I wanted to say goodbye to Sam.

I decided to write a letter. After Martha left, I sat at the desk in the corner, my pen poised, my mind turning over eloquent phrases, trying to find the perfect words to tell Sam that I was leaving town. How much he meant to me. How sorry I was for hurting him and how much I hoped for his future happiness.

In the end, I kept it brief, knowing Sam didn't care about eloquent words. I cried a little as I signed it: *Your friend, Valentine.*

I awoke early to find Judge Stoker's house quiet around me. I washed up and put on the new dress and jacket, leaving the bonnet on the bed for now.

I needed to see Rowan privately, not with Martha DeVries hovering. And I wanted to say goodbye to my home without her eyeing its shabbiness with distaste. I left a note on the bed saying I would return soon, then slipped downstairs and out the front door.

It felt good to breathe fresh air after days in bed. I walked slowly, savoring every sight and sound, knowing it might be the last time I walked these streets for a long time.

Or ever.

I didn't know what my future held, but I knew it wasn't Feavers Crossing. I'd finally stepped away from my past, and I was eager to keep going.

My heart beat faster as I neared the Blackshaws' house. I knocked and waited, prepared to face Mrs. Blackshaw if she answered. But it was a young maid who opened the door, her eyes widening at the sight of me.

"Is Rowan home?" I asked.

She shook her head. "Gone. Said he isn't coming back."

My heart tumbled. "Are you sure?"

"Left yesterday." She hesitated, then leaned closer to tell me in a lower voice, "They had a fight about you, then he packed his bags and marched out. Mrs. Blackshaw is beside herself." The maid stopped abruptly, glancing over her shoulder. She cast me a final worried look, then shut the door.

I walked toward my own end of town, my thoughts reeling.

Rowan hadn't bothered to say goodbye—which meant he must be angry about the things I'd shouted at the gallows. And who could blame him? I'd cleared my mother's name, but destroyed his father's. He probably thought I'd known about it for months and kept it from him, like my mother's innocence.

I would write to him at his uncle's address and explain.

But there would be no final goodbye.

I entered the graveyard and wandered past every grave, whispering the names I knew so well, my fingers trailing over stone pillars and tilted crosses. I paused at Mr. Oliver's new, clean headstone, then made my way to Birdy and Ida Howe. Lastly, I entered the neglected burial ground of heathens and criminals. I smiled at the sight of my mother's marble headstone rising above the weeds, purchased by the man she'd loved, still gleaming despite years of neglect. I touched the smooth marble and found it warm from the sun. I whispered goodbye, then turned away, knowing I would most likely never return.

As I neared my house, it looked larger and darker than I'd remembered—and more haunted. Not a happy home in many ways. And yet, I'd been happy here. I glanced at the Hennys' quiet cottage and felt a pang of sympathy for Philly.

In the backyard, I saw the coop and decided I would stop at the O'Donnells' on my way back to town and ask them to take the chickens, adding them to their own coop.

I entered the house and found the air thick and stale, as if I'd left years ago, not a few days. I smelled overripe strawberries and saw mold on the bread. On the mantel, a spider had already spun a straggling web.

I climbed the staircase, my hand sliding along the banister, and felt light-headed by the time I reached the top. I pulled back the curtain in the hall and walked through the burned rooms as far as it was safe. Bright slivers of sunlight leaked through the boarded windows, washing away the dark feeling that had always inhabited these rooms.

In my bedroom, I filled a travel bag with my best clothes and most prized possessions: my mother's red book with its love notes; the small, oval portrait of Daniel; a wooden bird Sam had whittled for me, years ago; Rowan's sketch of Birdy in the ivory frame; and his sketch of me mixing corn bread.

I stopped in Father's room to retrieve the metal box from under his bed. I didn't want Mrs. Blackshaw's blood money, but I would find a way to put it to good use. I added it to my travel bag and descended the staircase.

In the kitchen, I added my keepsake box, hardly believing that I might soon meet Alvina Lunt, then I turned in a slow circle, trying to decide if there was anything else I should take.

Someone knocked on the back door, and I wondered if Martha DeVries had come to fetch me. The idea chafed. I would have to get used to someone watching over me.

But when I opened the door, Rowan stood in front of me, more rugged and unkempt than I'd ever seen him. I uttered a cry and threw my arms around him. He laughed and steadied himself, then his arms tightened around me.

We held one another, connecting the broken pieces.

"I thought you left town," I murmured against his neck.

"I've been at Simon's house. Mrs. Greene washed my clothes, so I had to borrow from Mr. Greene. How do I look?"

I looked down. The clothes were too wide and short and not remotely fashionable. I laughed. "Never better." My lips found his briefly, then I pulled him inside.

"You're a hard girl to find," he teased. "I thought you were in jail, but that boy who works there wouldn't let me inside. Then I heard you were at Judge Stoker's house, but his housekeeper wouldn't let me inside either—said you were in no fit state to entertain *gentleman suitors*."

"Are you my gentleman suitor, Rowan?" I took his hand and drew him to the rocking chair. As he sat, he kept hold of my hand, pulling me down onto his lap. I nestled myself into a comfortable position with my legs draped over his.

We lingered over a kiss, my hands curled around his neck, then I sighed and sat straighter. "You're distracting me. I have important things to tell you."

Rowan leaned back against the rocking chair, looking content. "Very well, tell me something important."

"I'm sorry I told everyone about your father, Rowan. I didn't intend for that to happen."

"I know." His mood sobered. "My grandmother and I argued when we got home. She admitted what my father did, but still made excuses for him. She kept telling me how wonderful he was. Then she started arguing about you, and I packed my bags and left for Simon's."

I hesitated to tell him more but didn't want any more secrets between us. "She knew Mr. Frye was innocent but kept me drugged so I couldn't defend him. She almost had me convinced to never tell anyone that Mrs. Henny was the killer."

Rowan gave a dry laugh. "What did she promise you? With her, there's always a promise."

I hesitated. "Something rather tempting, actually."

"Oh?" His eyebrows lifted.

I pulled my lower lip between my teeth.

His expression turned sly. "I hope it didn't involve me, because . . . I should warn you . . . my heart is already taken."

"Is that so?"

"Completely." He wrapped both of his hands around curls and gently pulled my head closer. "But I could probably be persuaded."

I did my best to persuade him for a while, but the ticking of the clock on the mantel eventually made its way through the haze. "*Important things,*" I whispered.

"In a moment."

I slid my fingers between our lips and drew back. "Rowan, I'm leaving for New York City today."

He leaned back, suddenly attentive.

"I told you I wanted to meet someone named Richard DeVries. Well, he was my real father." I told Rowan the details, ending with Martha's invitation. "I'm terrified, and excited. And, now that I'm here with you, I don't want to leave. But I know it's the right thing to do."

Rowan didn't reply at once, looking a bit confused, his blue eyes searching mine. "I thought . . . I thought you might come to Europe with me, now that everything else is settled."

I forced myself to hold his gaze, my heart beating faster. I could still feel the warmth of his lips on mine. His hand on my waist. His heart beating only inches from mine. Being with Rowan was what I wanted.

But it wasn't the only thing I wanted. "I love you, Rowan, but I'm going to take a different road for a while. And you have your own journey to make. Someday, I hope our roads will—" I halted, my eyes fixing on his with a fierce shake of my head. "No—I *know* our roads will bring us back together."

"Yes," he agreed quietly. A muscle in his jaw tightened. "We'll stay in touch through my uncle in Boston."

"You have to write and tell me everything," I said. "Every interesting thing you see and person you meet. I know you don't like writing school papers—"

He laughed softly. "I think writing love letters might be a bit more fun. Especially if I get a few in return."

"Dozens of them. Hundreds of them. When will you sail?"

He pondered the question, his brow furrowed. "Not right away. I'm angry at my grandmother, but her life has just fallen apart, and I don't want to leave until I know she'll be all right. I stopped by the bank yesterday, and Mr. Pinchery is in a panic. Investors are already withdrawing their money." He gave a rueful shrug. "I'll still go to Europe, just not right away."

A lock of dark hair had fallen across his forehead, and I gently pushed it back. "Well . . . I do rather like the idea of being on the same continent as you."

He smiled slowly. "Blackshaw Bank has a few investments in New York City. I'm probably overdue for a visit."

"That doesn't sound like much fun—visiting investments."

"Oh, I'm sure I can find other amusements." His hand slid behind my neck, drawing me closer.

Every kiss was different. And the same. And perfect.

But it was time to go. I reluctantly stood, sighing as my gaze scanned the kitchen. "I'm leaving at noon, but I still have so much to do to close up the house. I need to throw out the food and give the chickens to the O'Donnells. There's grain in the cellar."

"I'll take care of it," Rowan said as he stood. "In fact, if you don't mind, I'll stay here for a few days. It's a little crowded at the Greenes', but I'm not ready to go home yet."

"It's not quite what you're used to. There's a family of mice that runs through the walls at night."

He grinned. "It'll prepare me for haystacks." He picked up my heavy travel bag and turned toward the back door, but I took his hand and pulled him toward the front instead.

His eyebrows rose. "Front door?"

"No more ghosts," I told him with a smile. I led him past the quiet, shadowed rooms. When I felt ready for it, I would sell the house and a new family would move in, filling it with voices and laughter.

I opened the front door.

But my feet hesitated at the edge. Out of habit, I looked for the spot where Mr. Blackshaw had died—the patch of gravel walkway that had haunted my nightmares for so many years. But one bit of gravel looked much like the next, and I was no longer sure if he fell there . . . or there.

I lifted my face and breathed fresh morning air. Green grass and spring blossoms and dappled sunlight. And possibility.

"What's wrong?" Rowan asked, standing close behind me.

I smiled. "Not a thing." I stepped out of the house and down the gravel walkway. When I reached the road, I turned and took Rowan's hand so we could walk together.

And we did not look back.

THE END

# Acknowledgments

---

Heartfelt thanks to my smart, funny, fierce literary agent, Barbara Poelle. Life changer. Just life changer. Just hearing her voice makes everything seem possible. Thank you to my wise, insightful editor, Amy Stapp, who shined a light in the fog so I could see the true story, then gave me the time I needed to develop it. We slid into that deadline together. I'm grateful for everyone at Tor Teen who shepherded my precious *Girl at the Grave* into publication.

Thank you, Aubrey Hartman. A first draft friend is a true friend. You were the first person to meet Valentine. Thanks also to Melanie Jacobson, Brittany Larsen, Tiffany Odekirk, and Jen White for moral support and sharp-eyed critiques. Also, Swapna, Donna, Kari, Connie, and Carol for helping me rediscover writing, years ago. Beth Udall, for listening. Rona Hawkins, for shared talent at a moment's notice. Hugs all around for my beloved lunch friends—you know who you are— for years of laughter and sage advice and occasional sharing of tears.

I owe so much to my parents, who had seven children in ten years and nurtured creativity. Our house was filled with reading, writing, sewing, drawing, painting, hammering, planting, dreadful piano playing, healthy food, spiritual wisdom, and deep conversations late into the night.

My siblings are my best friends and supporters: Carol, Barbara, Steve, LaRee, Robin, Teri, Janet. (I have to put my name in there because that's the way the chant goes.) Also grateful for Bobbylee, Annie, Gay, Marguerite, and the rest. Special thanks to Tom; it's on my bulletin board.

Love and gratitude for my husband, Mark, who gets me. And I get him. And that's priceless. Also, four children who have been way too easy to raise. Well, except Kelsi. Having a child with disabilities brings unique challenges, but also blessings. Her sweet smile keeps me company while I write all day.